A BOY
called
M.O.U.S.E.

A BOY
called
M.O.U.S.E.

Penny Dolan

Illustrated by Peter Bailey

BLOOMSBURY

LONDON NEW DELHI NEW YORK SYDNEY

Bloomsbury Publishing, London, New Delhi, New York and Sydney

First published in Great Britain in September 2010 by Bloomsbury Publishing Plc
50 Bedford Square, London, WC1B 3DP

This paperback edition published in August 2011

Text copyright © Penny Dolan 2010
Illustrations copyright © Peter Bailey 2010

The moral rights of the author and illustrator have been asserted

A CIP catalogue record for this book is available from the British Library

ISBN 978 1 4088 0137 6

MIX
Paper from
responsible sources
FSC® C020471
FSC
www.fsc.org

Typeset by Dorchester Typesetting Group Ltd
Printed and bound by CPI Group (UK) Ltd., Croydon, CR0 4YY

3 5 7 9 10 8 6 4 2

www.bloomsbury.com

This book is dedicated to Michael James Dolan,
and to all who work behind the scenes, wherever they are

Contents

Dramatis Personae..x

Prologue 1

PART ONE

Gone!...5

A Game Begins 13

PART TWO

1. Mouse, Dreaming 23
2. Roseberry Farm 25
3. A Search Begins...28
4. A Stranger Arrives 31
5. An Education Is Arranged...39
6. A Carriage Arrives...45
7. Mouse's Game...53
8. The Closed Mouth...57
9. A Useful Talent...61
10. Friends and Enemies...68
11. More and Less 74
12. A Change of Face...80
13. A High Point...86
14. Meanwhile, Revenge...93
15. Passing Time 97
16. Debts and Doubts...100
17. A Ladleful of Trouble..104
18. An Agreement...112
19. Hidden Words...114
20. Strange Fruit 117
21. Silence Breaks 126
22. The Last Course 128

PART THREE

23.	Home	137
24.	A Change of Plan	151
25.	Punchman	154
26.	The City	166
27.	Biter Bit	175
28.	A Place of Great Cleanliness	177
29.	Beneath the Cupboard	185
30.	New Faces	187
31.	Following On	198
32.	Behind the Scenes	200
33.	Idle Words	212
34.	Time Passing	215
35.	A Different Laughter	222
36.	Caught in the Act	224
37.	Elsewhere, a Cart Stops	228
38.	Himself	230
39.	Meanwhile, on a Small Island	235
40.	Cloaks and Daggers	238
41.	A Small Visitor	243
42.	Found and Lost	245
43.	Some Words of Direction	254
44.	A Request	258
45.	Down by the Docks	267
46.	The Emporium	270
47.	A Cunning Plan	276
48.	Scrope Alone	282
49.	Kitty Caught	286
50.	Homecoming	291
51.	Clutching at Hairs	293
52.	Question Time	299
53.	Finders Weepers	302
54.	Pause for Thought	312

55. A Step into the Dream 315
56. Shouting Out..321
57. Doubled Trouble..323
58. The Prodigal's Return 333
59. Flying High 336
60. Words Indeed..346
61. Painted Faces...348
62. Exit Stage Left 351
63. Disappearing Act...354
64. Adnam's Lair 358
65. Post Haste..361
66. On the Scent..363
67. Mistaken Identity 366
68. Morning Tea 369
69. A Trick of the Light...373
70. A Kettle on the Boil 377
71. Adnam the Great..379
72. Different Places 384
73. A View from the Stalls 389
74. Dreams in Midwinter...392
75. A Prime Position 395
76. A Gift from the Gods 396
77. A Firm Hand 398
78. A Sense of Direction..400
79. After the Fall...404
80. Eggs and Tea..408
81. One Last Look 415
82. Mirror, Mirror, on the Wall 419
83. Making Up...431
84. The Last Act 433
85. The Long Path...437
86. Mouse, Dreaming 448

Author's Notes and Acknowledgements.........................451

Dramatis Personae

A BOY CALLED MOUSE

Proudly Presents – In Order of Appearance:

MOUSE

Our Hero, A Boy Unafraid of Heights

HANNY

A Kind and Resourceful Nursery Maid

SCROPE

A Man Misguided by Debt and Envy

OLD EPSILON

A Firm Paternalist and Sulker

MR BUTTON

A Person Who Makes Use of Secrets

ISAAC

A Kindly Son of the Soil

BULLOUGHBY

Unwilling Headmaster and Frequent Snuff-Taker

MADAM CLAUDINE

Originator of an Interesting Educational System

NIDDLE AND PYEBERRY

A Pair of Cheering Chums

GRINDLE
Definitely Bulloughby's Son

JARVEY
A Man of Great Education and Unfortunate Debts

SHANKBONE
A Kitchen Cook, Much Misunderstood

WAYLAND
A Mysterious Tramping Man

CHARLIE PUNCHMAN
Good Sort and Puppet-Master, and
His Amazing Dog TOBY

KITTY
Our Heroine, Whom We Find in Difficult Circumstances

FLORA AND DORA
Her Small But Insistent Sisters

AUNT INDIGO AND AUNT VIOLET
Two Strong-Minded Seamstresses and Washerwomen

NICK TICK
A Minute But Clever Clockmaker

SMUDGE
Doorkeeper and Nasty Piece of Work

MISS TILDY

Dancing Teacher of Great Neatness

HUGO ADNAM

A Person For Whom the Theatre Is Everything

PETER

Adnam's Dresser

VANYA

The Power Behind the Albion

BELLINA LANDER

A Woman Who Shows That Beauty Is Not Everything

MR SPANGLE

Owner of a Renowned Emporium

CAPTAIN MARRINER

A Naval Gentleman, With Ship

ALBERT AND ADELINE

A Pair of Passionate Botanists

SERGEANT TRUDGEWELL

A Stalwart and Cheery Officer of the Law

PLUS ASSORTED COACHMEN, NEEDLEWOMEN, ACTORS, STAGEHANDS, STREET CRIERS, WEARY CONSTABLES, FAIRY HORSES AND MONKEYS.

PROLOGUE

'Once upon a time there was a boy,
and they called him
Mouse . . .'

That is how my story began
when I told it to myself
in the long darkness.

Of course,
it wasn't the whole story,
but back then
I knew nothing,
almost nothing at all.

PART ONE

GONE!

The fourth-floor window was wide open, and there, on the sill, stood a very young boy. Little Mouse laughed and reached his arms out towards the birds in the tree-tops and the clouds blowing across the sky, as if he longed to be flying with them.

Hanny, the nursery maid, saw all this. She also saw Uncle Scrope with one hand raised behind the small boy's back, waiting. One strong hand, one quick push, and what then?

Hanny rushed forward. With a quick sweep of her arm, she gathered the child back into her apron and lifted him down to the floor.

Scrope blinked. The strange light in his pale eyes died away, as if some wild urge had been halted. He slipped his hand – the one that had been poised behind Mouse's back – casually back into his own pocket.

'Oh,' Scrope drawled, 'it's you. The nursery maid.' He stared at the gravel path far below. 'Long way down, isn't it?'

'Yes, sir. It is,' Hanny replied, trying to calm the fear in her heart. 'I'll take Mouse safely back to the nursery now, sir. I was surprised to find him gone.'

'Good girl. Children do wander so, I hear.' Scrope did not even look at Hanny. 'And get someone to close this window properly. It seems to have become unlatched.'

By the time Hanny reached the nursery, she was shaking all over. She pointed towards the supper tray.

'Eat, please, Mouse.'

The boy peeped up at Hanny out of the corner of his eye. He studied her round, pleasant face and her rosy cheeks. Then, smiling mischievously, he carefully picked up a triangle of buttered bread in his fingers and popped it in his mouth. Then he opened wide to show he was doing what she had asked.

'Oh, Mouse!' Hanny said sadly, while she smiled at the boy, at his soft tufty hair, his bright brown eyes and his slightly sticking-out ears. 'Mouse, what am I going to do about you?'

Only when Mouse was safely in his cot did Hanny dare to think about what she had witnessed. A child like Mouse could fall down a flight of steep marble stairs, or topple from a balcony, or drop from a window so, so quickly. A child like Mouse could slip and trip and crash to his doom so, so easily. A man like Scrope would find

6

it very, very useful if such an accident happened to happen.

Nurse Hanny had seen the secret self hidden within the unremarkable Uncle Scrope. She knew he was someone who lived two lives.

Here, in the grand mansion that was Epton Towers, Scrope lived quietly. He seemed content. Obedient to his elderly father's commands, Scrope acted the perfect aide, attending to the family papers and letters and ever at his side. Scrope's voice, when he spoke, was as soft as feathers.

Yet Hanny had caught sight of Scrope returning from trips to the city, with his pocketbook full of winnings and his eyes as bright as those of a hawk seizing its prey. She had seen Scrope come skulking home when the cards had turned and brought him bad chance. At such times, his eyes brooded malevolently on young Mouse.

Why? Simple. Scrope was the second son of old Epsilon. Mouse, too young to know about such differences, was the first son of the first son – and the one who stood between Scrope and his family's fortune.

Hanny shivered again, remembering that wide-open window. One push, one shove, and Mouse would be no more. Other dangers were waiting too. Hadn't Scrope enquired very, very eagerly about when Mouse could be set on a saddle and taught to ride?

Hanny fretted. The worry would not go away. If Mouse, her young charge, was to grow from baby to boy, she had to do something, say something, and soon.

*

Hanny tried to do the right thing. On Sunday, when the bell rang for Mouse to make his weekly visit to Grandfather Epsilon, Hanny tucked her yellow curls into her nursemaid's cap, put on a fresh starched apron and dressed Mouse in his best clothes.

Then, as the clock struck four – no earlier, no later – they went downstairs, entered the vast drawing room and waited silently, as instructed, near the terrible tiger-skin rug.

Mouse stared back into the glass tiger-eyes, and snarled silently back at the sharp tiger-teeth. He did not like seeing the tiger. He did not like seeing the old man either. Grandfather Epsilon, nodding within his huge claw-footed armchair, reminded Mouse of the ancient tortoise in his alphabet book. Mouse was glad Hanny did not bring him to this room very often.

Many years before, Epsilon had energy. He had built and bought and schemed and toiled until he possessed – at last – the grandeur of Epton Towers, whereupon he had stuffed it with riches. He had all he wanted, despite the early death of his unfortunate wife, until the day that Albert, his eldest son, his beloved heir, disobeyed him. From that moment, Epsilon's heart had turned cold as iron and his head had become a hive of bitter thoughts.

Though the nursery nurse and the boy waited on the rug, Epsilon barely saw them. He sat, letting his mind churn continually on Albert's folly. A useless expedition!

How could Adeline, Albert's young wife, have urged his son to go adventuring, to disobey Epsilon's orders? How could they have sailed away, leaving him, the father, all alone in Epton Towers? After all he had done for them. Why had they not stayed to do their duty? Ungrateful heir! Ungrateful pair!

Epsilon's eyes narrowed. How he would punish them! How he would punish the one they had to leave behind! If Albert was not here to speak to his own child, why should he, Epsilon, do so? Not one word, not one breath, would he bestow . . .

What, what? A voice had interrupted his tangle of complaints. Someone was talking to him. That young nurse in her drab grey dress was pleading with him, begging him to pay some kind of attention to Albert's toddling infant. Silly woman! It could not be done.

Epsilon rapped his ivory-headed cane on the floor. No, no, no! No requests. Go away! Go away! Go away to the nursery, and bother me no more! The cane spoke clearly of Epsilon's displeasure.

Mouse's lip quivered in alarm, but then the boy turned and ran out quite happily, with Hanny following. There, at the end of the corridor, was the grand marble staircase, ready for his infant ascent. Up those chilly heights crawled Mouse, climbing higher and higher, eager to touch the topmost step of all.

Alone once more, Grandfather Epsilon sniffed with bleak satisfaction. 'When Albert returns, he will be sorry for what he has done,' he muttered, aching for his moment of cold triumph.

*

Rarely did Epsilon look beyond his nose. Rarely did he ponder on his second son, Scrope, sitting at a desk scribbling away. That feeble creature would always do what he was told.

No wonder Scrope's long face was pale as the parchment on which he copied his father's papers. *Scritch-scratch* went Scrope's dutiful quill, so humbly, so bitterly. Scrope knew he would never be his father's favourite, never compare well against the absent Albert. Epsilon had made this clear to Scrope almost every day of his life.

Quietly, Scrope brooded on this and on other hurts. He brooded on Albert's only son too, the one who was Adeline's child and would one day be heir to Epton Towers. He brooded, and he dreamed.

Back in the nursery, while Mouse picked the currants out of his cake, eating them one at a time and counting each bite, Hanny was in despair. How could old Epsilon be so deaf to her warnings?

Around midnight, as Hanny stitched at another small nightshirt, thoughts started stitching themselves together in her mind.

Mouse's grandfather didn't want him. Mouse's uncle wanted him even less. Mouse's grandfather didn't want him . . . Mouse's uncle . . .

An idea popped into her head. At once Hanny knew the idea might be wrong. How could she even have thought of such a thing? But she had, and now she could not unthink it. Slowly, as the dark hours of the night passed, Hanny stitched the pieces of her plan together.

*

There had been, Hanny remembered, a much earlier plan, a departure day when all was ready for the expedition. It was the same morning that Hanny discovered the baby burning with fever in his crib, too ill to be moved. Hanny's mistress, Adeline, was torn apart with anguish. How could her baby face the dangers of such a long voyage?

What had Adeline said at that moment? What had she decided? Hanny almost spoke the words aloud.

'I have to go with Albert, Hanny. I promise to send word as soon as I can, but, until then, take good care of my child for me. Keep Mouse safe, please, Hanny. Keep him safe and well!'

Safe and well. Safe and well! Those had been Adeline's exact words. Now Hanny had to make her choice too, and she would do what she must do. Hanny would keep Mouse safe, no matter the cost.

So, when first light came, Hanny lifted Mouse from his nursery bed. She wrapped him warmly and tied him tightly to her back with a shawl, like a country child. His little legs dangled in their button boots.

'Shh, Mousekin!' said Hanny. 'I'm taking you where we will be wanted and where you will be safe.' Even, she thought, if this might not be exactly the end of the problem. 'Go back to sleep, child.'

The small boy tucked his thumb back in his mouth and closed his eyes.

Hanny slipped out of the nursery, stepped down the long back stairs and, as dawn warmed the sky, was off and away with her burden.

Hanny knew nobody would notice that she and Mouse had gone, not for a while, because she attended to all the child's cooking and laundry. For a time, life at Epton Towers would carry on as normal.

Nevertheless, she left things in some kind of order, ready for when people came looking.

'*Dear Sirs,*' she had written, on the notepaper that lay on the side cupboard, '*Please excuse this hurried departure. The cough Mouse suffered from last month may be returning. He needs some country air most urgently. So I am taking him somewhere where he will grow strong and happy and healthy, and all will be well.*

Yours sincerely,
Nurse Hanny.'

She left no forwarding address.

In fact, as Hanny hurried along, she felt sure she was making life easier for everyone. Who but she cared about the boy anyway? Certainly, by the time a cart, trundling early along the high road, stopped to offer her and the child a lift, Hanny's heart was much lighter. All would be well!

Oh dear, oh dear! The young Nurse Hanny did not know quite enough about Uncle Scrope; nor did she know who else would act in the life of a boy called Mouse.

A GAME BEGINS

However, Uncle Scrope was not thinking about Mouse. He too needed to escape from Epton Towers. He wanted to be away from that place, to be himself again, not just a pawn moving to the commands of his critical father. Uncle Scrope was off to the city.

Around late afternoon a hansom cab delivered Scrope to the elegant warmth of the Golden Cockatoo Club, where he had a fine dinner followed by several satisfactory hours at the gaming tables. This – the familiar touch of cards and dice – was what he had longed for, even when the bets proved expensive.

Scrope's wagers floated along on the rumours of Epsilon's wealth. Often he was tempted into playing dangerously, but what harm was there in that? Often he won, didn't he?

Scrope had practised concealing his passion from his

father, and this made him clever at hiding his intentions during games. At each close of play, as Scrope gathered up his winnings and downed another goblet of wine, he felt well and truly comforted.

Scrope woke late, groaning. His eyes stayed shut, but the noise of traffic beyond the windows told him he was still in his rooms in the city. Then a sudden polite cough informed him he was not alone. Scrope opened one eye.

Mr Button was there. Scrope's stomach knotted in panic. He did not remember giving Button any key, and he could not immediately recall how much ready money he already owed Button. Then the success of last night's games broke into his memory, making Scrope smile lazily at such foolish anxieties.

'Good day, sir!' said Mr Button. He was perched on a wooden chair, with a pot of coffee on the table at his side.

Mr Button was a small man. He wore a tight black suit and tight black boots. His hair shone glossily on his head. His cheeks were as rosy as an apple in a fairy tale. Button poured a second cup of coffee for himself, then filled Scrope's delicate china cup.

'Are we ready to check our accounts yet? It is well past one o'clock.'

Sliding his chair a fraction closer to Scrope, Mr Button opened a discreet leather-bound notebook. His hard, round eyes scanned page after page, his pencil pecking down the columns of numbers.

Scrope adjusted his nightshirt awkwardly and struggled to sit up against the plump pillows. As he sipped at the strong coffee, he grew less groggy.

Mr Button was most efficient. He checked through the persons who still owed Scrope – and therefore Button – money. He extracted several scribbled IOUs from Scrope's discarded garments, then he smoothed out the sheets, circling amounts and adding on percentages very precisely.

One by one, Button entered the names from last night's games into his little black book, with details of each promise to pay and all addresses. He liked to know where people lived.

Button knew every name in his book. In fact, he had visited many so he could get to know them even better. Alas! Some people did not, or could not, pay their debts. When the time was right, Button made life uncomfortable for such persons.

Scrope, sipping his coffee comfortably, ignored such small facts. Did not Button, at least, treat him as someone who was owed respect? Did not Button, at least, understand the excitement of the cards? Scrope chose to be well content.

Who or what was Mr Button? Button was far more than a servant, for no servant could be trusted with such matters. No servant could have helped Scrope out six months before, when his luck hit a sticky patch, none except a man as wise and clever as Button.

Mr Button, Scrope believed, was a treasure. Was Button a friend? No. Their lives did not mix, except at times like this. Furthermore, Mr Button was definitely not a gentleman. Amiably and a little disdainfully,

Scrope pointed Button to the decanter of brandy set among the collars and studs on his dressing table.

Button shook his head. 'Not now, sir. Not for me. I live simply.'

As Scrope shrugged, and stirred brandy into his own coffee, an almost malicious smile licked across the little man's lips. 'Tell me, sir, is the dear son and heir well?'

Scrope's cup rattled violently on the saucer. Mouse? Mouse! Scrope's easiness vanished, and, not for the first time, he felt unsure about Button. He shook his head sulkily, grumpily. He did not want to think about Albert and Adeline's child today. Time enough for that when he was back by old Epsilon's side, back in that dreary world. Drat the wretched brat!

Fortunately for the Golden Cockatoo, Scrope recovered his humour in time for a good evening's play.

So several days passed, and Hanny's bold deed was still undetected.

Also undetected was the storm that crashed across a vast and distant ocean. It churned waves into mountains of salt water, whipped sea foam into white avalanches and destroyed any shipping in its path. The raging tempest ripped down sails, snapped masts like matchsticks and threw the broken vessels into the open maw of an unseeing ocean.

Scrope returned to his dutiful self at Epton Towers, to his seat at the long dining table and to face his father for another silent meal.

Once the tedious hour was over, Scrope hurried to

his own chamber. He flung himself into his favourite armchair, picked up his newspaper, and flicked through the pages.

Before he reached the racing news, he stopped. As he stared at the print, his face began to glow. There, right in front of his eyes, were the words that Scrope, in his heart of hearts, had longed to behold.

THE IMPERIAL INDIES INSURANCE COMPANY LTD.

TODAY OUR OFFICE RECEIVED THE SAD NEWS OF THE LOSS OF *THE TROPICANA*, GONE DOWN IN A FIERCE STORM FIFTEEN MILES WEST OF THE FLORA MAJORA ISLES.

THE CAPTAIN, OFFICERS, ALL HANDS & PASSENGERS ARE BELIEVED TO HAVE PERISHED WITH THIS UNHAPPY VESSEL.

MAY GOD HAVE MERCY ON THEIR SOULS.

ALL CLAIMANTS SHOULD CONTACT OUR MAIN OFFICE.

Scrope read, and read again. The good ship *Tropicana* was lost and was no more! Lost and gone, his spoilt eccentric brother Albert! Gone too Albert's wife, the beautiful Adeline!

Ah, dearest Adeline . . . Something glistened unexpectedly in Scrope's eye and ran down his cheek. He wiped it away briskly, blinking hard. That woman chose Albert instead of him, did she not, and without a single word of explanation. Ha!

Scrope went back to the paper, a smile tickling the edges of his mouth as he read the announcement aloud, his finger moving under the words, just to be very sure. Joy! He, Scrope, was at last rewarded! The two silly fools were lost, lost for the sake of unknown plants in a godforsaken land. So much for the Glory of Travel and the Power of Science!

Scrope gazed gratefully at the pots of lush tropical ferns on stands and shelves that decorated his room and almost every corner in the huge house.

He glanced thankfully through the windowpanes to where Albert's folly, the great glasshouse full of flame-bright flowers and exotic plants, dominated the lawns. Plant-hunting in remote places was such a dangerous passion, and for that Scrope was well and truly grateful. Cards were so much safer!

Scrope folded the newspaper so that his father would not miss seeing the announcement. His heart brimmed with happiness. He had won. He, Scrope, was the surviving son, the lucky one, and only the toddling Mouse stood in his way.

Only Mouse? Scrope paused in his stride. His brow

18

furrowed. Mouse? When had he last seen his wretched nephew? Scrope never enjoyed seeing the child, because it hurt him twice over to see Adeline's features alive in that small eager face, but when exactly had Hanny last brought the boy downstairs? When *had* he last seen Mouse?

Scrope counted the days. Perhaps his luck had tripled while he was away in the city? Maybe the child had gone down with measles, or scarlet fever, or worse?

Now, with the terrible news of the shipwreck, Scrope felt an urgent need to keep close watch on such a precious heir. Surely dear little Mouse deserved a visit from his loving uncle?

Humming slightly, Scrope started to climb the long staircases all the way to the nursery.

Within the hour, Scrope, biting his lip, penned an urgent message to his trusted familiar, Mr Button.

'*I must see you at once. It is about the boy they call Mouse . . .*'

PART TWO

Mouse, Dreaming

I move, and the rough sacks scratch my cheek. A family of cats, thin and hungry, slip down from the curve of my covers and away. They are not pets. They are angry and hungry, and they sleep against me for warmth.

Do I mind? Not at all, for the nights down in the depths of the school are so, so cold, and the kitchen fire falls to a sullen glow. As the cats slink away, their eyes shine, for they are off to scavenge the corridors of Murkstone Hall.

I am lying wide awake now, because the dream came again. It was not the happy bright dream that woke up in my head so recently, full of flowers and fruit. I do not understand where that came from, nor why it was in my mind. No, tonight was the bad dream. I understand the bad dream very well, because it is the story of how I was first brought to this place.

I reach out my arm, and stretch my fingers against the pale grey square of the scullery window. There is enough light for me to see my hand, grimed with cinders, stinking of onions and dishwater. That is how things are down here. Nobody can keep clean in this kitchen – not me, not Shankbone, not a single dish or kettle or spoon. Nobody cares that the dirt gathers here, certainly not Master Bulloughby.

The hand I see at the start of my dream is almost clean. It smells of hay and horses and the open air. It is a small child's hand. It is my hand as it was when I was taken away from the sweet life of Ma's farm. It is the hand I had when I trusted everyone, before the bad time began.

Weariness swirls round me and drags my eyes closed, and I know the bad dream is waiting to haunt me again, waiting just beyond my first memory . . .

ROSEBERRY FARM

I never thought I would leave Roseberry Farm, or Ma Foster's laughing, round, rosy-cheeked face, or big Isaac's slow smile. Ma looked after me and big Isaac, and I never saw fear in her eyes until the day a certain man arrived and called her by another name.

Big Isaac was my very first hero. His blue eyes peered shyly through the sun-bleached hair that fell across his forehead, and his wide shoulders almost brushed the timbers as he stooped to enter a door. Isaac seemed as strong as the huge horses he loved and, like them, was peaceful and content and unsure of strangers.

Isaac had lived at Roseberry Farm all his life. As a young man he did not ask for more until the day he took his cart to market and saw Ma waiting by the stone cross in her neat cotton dress and with her yellow curls

25

escaping from her straw bonnet. But Ma was already on her way to work for a grand lady at a grand house, so she could not come to Isaac or Roseberry Farm that day. Then, when she did come, some six years later, Ma brought me with her. Isaac was glad to see us both, and the church bells rang out for him and Ma.

Sometimes other children visited Roseberry Farm, but they were just little babies. Some had golden hair, some had dark and some were in-between. They came and they went, but I remained.

I got used to the babies squawking and sucking and squealing in their cradles. I tiptoed past when they were asleep. When they were awake I made funny faces for them and did silly tricks and head-over-heeled until they laughed. When the babies grew bigger they toddled after the chicks and hid from the milk-cows and were mostly happy till they went away again.

Only twice did Ma have to send babies to be angels. When the vicar took the two small boxes to his church-yard Ma cried, because she cared for her babies very much, as much as Isaac cared for his horses.

Even so, I always knew that I was Ma's best boy, and that she and Isaac loved me. Wasn't I the one Isaac wove his straw animals for?

'Where do the babies come from, Ma?' I asked one day.

'From here, there, everywhere,' she told me, laughing. 'I am minding them for their mothers.' Then she hugged me hard and said, 'But you, Mouse, are my own special child.'

'Are you my mother then?' I asked, because I was getting old enough to think about such things.

'Come and have some honey cake, Mouse,' she said, so I did.

A SEARCH BEGINS

Scrope handed Hanny's note across to Button.

'She's taken the brat somewhere where he can grow happy and healthy,' Scrope scoffed, trying to ignore the incident of Mouse and the windowsill. Had that scared her into action? 'How can we be sure the boy is safe, Button?' he said, but even he heard his own words ring false. He tried again. 'How can we discover where the child is?'

Button locked his soft pink fingers patiently together into a fleshy steeple. 'Calm yourself, sir. It will be best if you let me deal with this. Does old Epsilon know?'

Scrope shook his head. 'Not yet. It is so soon after the loss of Albert.' The shipwreck had shaken the old man badly.

Button came to the rescue with an amazingly good suggestion. 'A word of advice? Pretend it was *your* plan,

Scrope. Tell Epsilon that *you* arranged this holiday. Tell him *you* were concerned that the sight of the boy might cause him distress, especially while the house is still in mourning. It will give us the time to work out exactly what to do.'

Such cleverness made Scrope beam enthusiastically.

'Do not worry, sir,' added Button, his smile wide as a frog's gape. 'I'll spy those runaways out soon enough.'

Button was a man who played his own games, and the small boy was a valuable piece. In Button's line of work people were not allowed to disappear, especially if they owed money. Certainly if a person had carried away the heir to a fortune, they had to be found.

Epsilon had given orders that Albert's wing of the house was not to be disturbed, but Button quietly ignored this request. His slender pick-locks slipped open the door to Adeline's room and unlocked her writing desk and her inlaid rosewood boxes.

Button rustled through all the watercolour sketches, botanical dictionaries, journals and correspondence from learned friends and professors. He found what he wanted in a tiny drawer below the scented wedding greetings and love letters from Albert: Hanny's neatly folded letter.

Written some years before, it was Hanny's humble reply to Adeline, accepting the post as Adeline's own maid. There, at the top of the sheet, in a tidy girlish script, was the name of Hanny's home village.

Button tucked the letter inside his small black book. He had not spent time studying the family's accounts, properties and maps without reason. That tiny village would be found on Adeline's lands, and there, or somewhere quite nearby, was where Hanny would have run with the boy.

His search would not take long, and in any case he had plenty of time. The good-hearted Hanny would not do any harm to such a precious infant. Button stowed his notebook back in his pocket with an air of contentment.

And Scrope, though he did not know it, had slipped even further into Button's debt.

CHAPTER 4

A STRANGER ARRIVES

One hot summer evening, when Isaac was off harvesting in the far fields, a horseman came to Roseberry Farm.

'Hanny?' I heard him say, as Ma opened the door. I was tucked up in bed, so I did not see his face. Not then.

Ma gave a short sharp cry, like an animal recognising a hunter. I remember this, because it was the season when crows and rooks circled the wheat fields watching for runaway creatures, especially on moonlit nights.

Hanny? Hanny? Who was this Hanny, and what were they talking about? I peered through a crack in the wood, but all I saw was the shadow of a small man in a big coat.

'If he chose, he could have you strung up . . .' he hissed. 'Or transported for life.'

'I left a note explaining,' Ma whispered.

'Did you? The old one never saw it. He told him he'd sent the child to breathe good country air.' Ma murmured a question. 'You were easy to find, silly girl. I read your mistress's letters. Did you know the ship was lost?'

'Adeline?' Ma asked, and I heard quiet weeping. 'You searched through her things?' she said at last.

'I am not a gentleman,' said the voice, 'and I am not a good and loyal servant either. I am someone who finds things out for myself. Nobody will make sure that I am "nicely safe from harm",' he sneered. 'Nor you either, if this theft was widely known.' There was a rustle of cloth as Ma sank down into Isaac's chair.

'Now, Hanny. There's good news too. You can keep the brat —' I heard Ma gasp — 'until we want him back, but he must never . . .' I heard more mutterings, and Ma making something that sounded like a promise. Then the stranger strode out of the door and was gone.

There was a rumble in the distance, so I clambered out of my bed, because I did not like thunder and because the visitor had made Ma sad.

She hugged me so tightly. 'Oh, Mouse! You can stay.'

I heard her heart's fast beating and I patted her hand because she had tears in her eyes.

You might be old enough to understand what was going on, but I did not, not then. I had important things to worry about, like playing with the sheepdog's puppies next morning, and whether the hard green apples had turned golden and sweet. All the while, the big bad dream was gathering, dark as a summer storm.

After the stranger's visit, Isaac started to teach me to rough and tumble and fight, but always as friends. How glad I've been of his lessons!

Sometimes, in play, he threw me up into the air, so that the trees and sky seemed close enough to touch. Then, as I fell thrillingly down, he would catch me in his strong hands, and I knew he would never let me fall. I begged for this game over and over. However high Isaac threw me, I was never ever afraid. But that was not all.

Though I did my tasks around the yard and house, I spent hours in the stables alongside Isaac, helping him groom his two huge horses, each one as gentle as their master.

The horses lowered their heavy heads, and snuffled close to my face when I called their names. Their big brown eyes watched me when I patted the warm smooth hair on their long whiskered noses. I loved their whinnying breaths and the way they flicked the flies from their ears, and how they pounded their hoofs eagerly at the rustle of the fresh fodder.

Their legs were sturdy as the trunks of trees, with long tendrils of hair falling softly over their giant hoofs, but Isaac taught me to be wary of that strength.

'A single kick from one of those feet can strike a man's life from his body, boy,' he warned. 'Don't you do nothing to provoke those horses.'

The horses knew me as the small boy who struggled to bring them nets of sweet hay or small handfuls of oats. Then, one lazy afternoon, Isaac lifted me off my feet.

'Up you go, my boy,' he said, and set me there, high on a horse's back. I was not at all afraid of falling. Isaac's weather-brown grip tugged at the bridle and he led my mount out into the yard. 'Come on!'

My fingers reached into the horse's flowing mane, searching for the thin braids Isaac plaited there as a charm against bad luck. I held them tight. There I sat like a little king, high above my world. With my legs stretched across that broad back, I swayed with the stride of the horse, imagining myself to be a story-time hero riding a trusted steed to victory. Such long sunny summer days!

Of course, our life was not always like that. We had bad, hard times too at Roseberry Farm. There were weeks when winter gripped its icy fist, and the milk froze, and beasts grew thin – as thin as I am now maybe – and we slept huddled together in all our garments while the last log smouldered in the grate. There were months when the rains fell, and the bridges broke, and the yard was flooded, and sullen puddles seeped across the floor.

I could tell you about those hard seasons, but now I am remembering the good times. Like that last glowing log, I need these thoughts to warm me as long as they can.

When there was no work to help with, I played in the barn. My noisy games sent the cats out into the yard and the pigeons swooping off on the summer air. Even the rats dug deeper into their dens when I went whooping through the piles of hay.

I swung on ropes, jumped on bales of straw and slid over heaped-up sacks. I climbed up and down the ladders and made hideaways in the hay stored high up in the roof of the barn.

34

It was about this time that I made another discovery, something about myself, but back then I hardly realised how important this would become.

One morning, while I was playing about in one of the haylofts, I saw a small brown mouse. Like many mice before, it poked a tiny head from the hay and then darted out across the floor. However, this mouse did not run down the wooden ladder as most did, falling and tumbling safely from rung to rung until it had reached the ground.

No, this clever mouse ran straight across the loft floor and out along the great oak beam that stretched from one side of the barn over to the other. Its tiny pink feet pattered earnestly along the huge beam, high above the threshing floor. I watched, astonished, as it went busily across. At last, the creature reached the floor of the loft opposite and disappeared among the bales of hay.

'Mouse?' I murmured, excited, for that was the name they called me. 'Mouse!'

I had never imagined anything crossing from one side of the barn to the other in that way. If an ordinary mouse could manage it, I thought, surely someone called Mouse could cross along that high beam too. So I set out to do just that.

I moved one foot, then another, balancing very, very carefully, high above the cart and the hay rakes and the pitchforks. The air below swam with hay dust, but I edged forward, bit by bit, further and further.

Just as I reached the midway point, Isaac shambled in. I giggled, and he looked up and saw me there,

balanced on that oak beam high above his reach.

Isaac paused, like a strangely surprised statue. Then he smiled at me. 'You be going well there, my boy. Don't you go rushing just cos I'm here. Take your time, Mouse.' That was all he said.

Soon I had reached the other side. I clambered down, proud of my adventure.

'Once is enough, boy,' said Isaac as he hugged me. 'Understand?' He was trying to put me off my new trick.

His words did not work. I became bolder. Whether Isaac was there or not, I would balance my way across the wide oak beam, if only to see the golden sunlight make a patchwork on the floor far below me.

All was well until the day Ma came into the barn and saw me high above her head. It was the only time I saw her in a raging fury.

'What do you think you are doing with him?' she shouted at Isaac.

I stopped halfway across and grew anxious. I started to wobble. 'Ma?' I squeaked, my voice high and nervous.

At once Ma was beaming widely too, as if she felt just like Isaac after all. 'Keep going, Mouse. Get to the end, my pet,' she urged. 'Clever boy.'

'You be a brave old boy, little Mouse,' Isaac said. 'Go careful like. Look ahead.'

So, one proud step at a time, I crossed that beam, and I didn't look down, because I knew their eyes were watching, admiring my bravery.

When I got back to the floor, Ma snatched me up

and hugged me. Her cheeks were wet. 'Whatever would I tell them, Isaac?' she said.

Isaac hung his head. 'It was what the child needed to do,' he said. 'He hasn't come to any hurt.'

Ma sighed. 'You must take more care of him, Isaac. One day they will come asking.'

'Asking what?' I said, my head still full of my own cleverness.

'Asking if you are a good boy, pet,' she answered.

That night I heard Ma and Isaac talking, but did not understand what they were saying.

'Yes, my love, I wish he could stay here for ever too,' Ma said, 'but who knows what they will want. Maybe . . .'

But then I fell asleep.

From then on, Isaac would not let me climb too high or too hard, especially if Ma was around in the yard, but he had a tough task of it. This climbing up things had got into my soul, and I was always scampering off up trees, or on top of the hay carts, wanting to be Isaac and Ma's brave boy and the king of the castle.

Stop! Enough! I want to pause in this story now. I want to hold on to that picture for a moment. Roseberry Farm! Thoughts of that place shine in the cold of this night's kitchen. In my mind, Isaac is smiling and Ma is smiling. They had good, happy smiles. But the smile on the face of the man who came to Roseberry Farm was as full of poison as an adder's bite.

CHAPTER 5

AN EDUCATION IS ARRANGED

Scrope sprawled on his sofa, one arm flung wearily above his head and his long face sunken into sullen folds. The five years that had passed had not been kind to him.

Scrope had hoped that once Mouse was out of the house, old Epsilon would forget the boy for ever. After all, he had ignored the child well enough before. However, lately the old man had started murmuring the child's name in his sleep, muttering it over and over.

Had Epsilon ever murmured Scrope's name? No! No matter what Scrope did to appear dutiful, Epsilon showed him less regard than before. Scrope squirmed uncomfortably and got restlessly to his feet. How would things stand if Epsilon knew how bad his debts had become, or how much Scrope was in need of some ready funds?

'Button?' Scrope said.

'Sir?' The small man fingered the edge of his note-book, all attention and reassuring smiles.

'Any news on that boy?'

'Only that all is well. He thrives.'

Farmyards seemed to be safer places than Scrope had imagined. 'Maybe it is time to find somewhere . . . somewhere . . . somewhere a little less healthy?' he asked at last.

'A place where a child might be toughened up a little?' Button suggested, amusement glinting in his eyes.

Scrope bit his lip. 'Just so.'

'A school? A distant school? A discreet school? By chance, I know of such a place.'

Scrope imagined Epsilon's guineas wasting away needlessly. 'Won't an education cost?' he asked quickly. It was hard to avoid reminding Button about his own particular debts. 'Especially,' he added 'if it is a board-ing establishment.'

'I have a small interest in this school,' said Button. 'It is a kind of charitable enterprise, run by an old acquaintance. See here?' Opening his notebook, Button underlined a name. 'Remember a time when this fellow haunted the Golden Cockatoo?'

'A most unlucky player?' Scrope was swiftly amused.

'Unlucky? Who can say? He is certainly someone fonder of cards than of children. All the same, he did not refuse when I asked him to be headmaster of Murkstone Hall. Cost? Very little. The school is run on economical lines.'

'Economical?'

'Extremely economical. The boys live a very simple life.' Button gave his most helpful smile, and then, because he liked to keep all dealings with Murkstone Hall in his own hands, he added, 'Do you want me to approach the school? There is no need for you to be troubled by such matters.'

How could Scrope refuse? 'I must speak to Epsilon first,' he said, but they both knew a choice had already been made.

That evening Scrope leaned over the back of his father's armchair. He had to speak quickly before the clouds of melancholy returned.

'Father, I have been thinking. The woman has had the boy long enough. He needs somewhere better for his schooling than a farmyard. May I arrange his education?'

For a second Epsilon's hooded eyes oozed with self-pity, then he raised his wrinkled hand dismissively. 'As ever, Scrope,' the old man croaked, 'just do whatever is best. Go!'

That was it. That was all. He had been sent away as if he was a servant. Scrope strode to his own room in a torrent of anger. Why had his brother Albert been so loved, and he not? He despised himself for caring about such matters.

'*Do whatever is best.*' If Scrope was bolder, he would definitely not do his best. He would do his worst. He would do more than merely dream of that child's destruction. His hands curled into fists and his knuckle-bones whitened.

Then he thought of the little boy's face, and murmured a name. Oh, Adeline!

Scrope cannot forget that haughty girl, now plunged down to her doom in the ocean, her child left behind her. If he had truly loved her, or if she had loved him, or even if she had ever asked him, he would have cared for the boy, or so he told himself.

So thank heaven – or another place – for Button's steady determination.

'I shall do what must be done, Father,' Scrope promised softly. 'Trust me.'

The scheme was settled.

'What will the boy be told?' asked Scrope.

'Nothing,' Button pulled on a pair of neat travelling gloves, 'just as he has been told nothing about where he comes from. I made Hanny – that silly woman! – promise she would say not a word.' He smiled, but it did not reach his eyes. 'The boy called Mouse lives in utter ignorance.'

In a distant county hail fell, rattling like bad dice against the cracked window glass of Murkstone Hall. The wind forced smoke back down the chimney, so that it filled the private parlour where Headmaster Bulloughby was reading a letter.

It brought him no pleasure and suddenly he scrunched the paper into a ball.

'Button,' he groaned, pushing back his thick orange wig and revealing a scalp marbled with strands of greasy hair. He scratched his head furiously and then slid the wig back into position. 'Wretched Mr Button!'

Despair settled across his blotched features. Taking a small rectangular box from his desk, he sprinkled a large pinch of snuff on one stained cuff, raised the cuff to his nostrils and inhaled the dark dust – as if the chimney smoke was not enough – then, bleary eyes swivelling upwards, sneezed and spluttered explosively.

These small detonations at an end, he unfolded the letter and reread the contents.

'*Friend Bulloughby . . .*'

Friend? He knew only too well what it was to be a friend of Button's. He cursed the debts that kept him in Button's grip, the mistakes that had brought him and his nearest and dearest to this thankless situation. He cursed too the pitiful amount that the boy would bring him, arranged as such sums were by the smiling Mr Button.

Bulloughby followed the message to its end: '. . . *I will bring the boy to you myself.*'

He let the letter fall to the threadbare carpet and kicked at one of the table legs.

'A dead weight! A useless brat! A wretched burden! What's the point of edication if it ain't to make a profit for some?' said Bulloughby mournfully. 'The boys I do get something for are enough trouble, and there's almost nothing for my pains with this one!' He nuzzled at his musky cuff, sneezed again and stared bleakly into the fire. 'Life's cards are stacked against me right enough.'

Life was always against Bulloughby. It had tricked him in those gaming houses, and tricked him into being tied to Mr Button and stuck in this establishment so horribly infested with brats. Lately he had felt he would never be free of Button's hold.

And now Button was about to deliver a farthing brat, a child that brought no profit at all. Bulloughby did not even care enough to wonder who the child was.

Far away, Button rubbed his palms together contentedly, thinking of the difference between the rich music of the fees that jingled into his money chest and the few coins needed to drop on Bulloughby's table. Farthings for a fool and guineas for a genius!

A CARRIAGE ARRIVES

Roseberry Farm was at the end of a long lane, away from the busy highways. Sometimes a shuttered coach came, bringing or taking one of Ma's small babies, but the passers-by were mostly local folk.

Each summer the old men, all whiskers and wrinkles, wandered over from nearby farms. They leaned on our gate, sucking on grass stalks. Each winter big Isaac trudged through the snow to visit their small cottages, carrying gifts of food or fodder for their beasts.

Spring and autumn were the seasons when the dealers came, wanting to buy livestock or grain, and the hagglers and pedlars arrived with wagons or packs laden with goods. Ma bought what was needed.

'Too many lives get troubled and torn by lack of money, young Mouse,' she told me, 'and some by too much of it as well.'

*

Every now and again, a tall wayfaring man would stop and make his camp close by Roseberry Farm. I liked to see his lean figure arrive, his hair and beard blowing about him, for he was as tattered and worn by the wind as any scarey-crow or vagabond minstrel.

While Ma found him food, or some old clothes of Isaac's, the tramp sat by the horse trough playing tunes on his penny whistle. I sat beside him and sang along, and then I'd show him how well I could walk on my hands. The tramp said little back to me, but his eyes were bright and kind.

Ma would bring out a full supper bowl and then shoo me away so the man could eat in peace. 'Thank you kindly, ma'am,' he'd say.

I envied that tramp, with his long coats and his cloak. He slept among our hay bales that night and was off and away on his travels the next morning, as if he was always following some mysterious trail of his own making. Once the tramp was gone, all he left behind him was a patch of flattened straw, and the tunes haunting my mind.

Then one day – a day I will never forget – the dreadful carriage came. It clattered into the yard and waited like a large lacquered stag beetle. My mouth hung open at the sight of the two black horses, their coats shining glossily in the sun.

Then the door swung open and a small man dropped down. His cheeks were as rosy red as Snow White's apple, and his eyes were hard and round and bright.

Standing there in his tight black suit, amidst the muddle and roughness of the farmyard, the man looked as if he had been polished all over.

As Ma opened the door, her face went pale as watered milk.

'Isaac! Isaac!' she cried, her arms held rigid against her sides, though I knew by her face she wanted to run over and grab hold of me. The man only smiled more brightly.

Ma bobbed a quick curtsy. 'Come in, sir,' she said, and led the man into the farmhouse. She gave one long, long look at me as I stood in the yard. Then she closed the door.

So I went back to floating straws in the horse trough and wondering if I could sneak away to a very good climbing tree I'd found at the end of the meadow.

I have often wondered why I didn't run in and find out what the visitor wanted, but I didn't. Now I would go. I would watch and listen. I'd listen to every gasp and cough and whisper and word that passed between the man and Ma. I'd write things down, if I could, so I knew what happened. But back then, and barely six, nothing bad had happened to me, not anything that I knew about.

Besides, the only alphabet I knew was the letters Ma made me scratch into the hearth dust each morning. The only words I'd read were the names carved above the horses' stalls, or some verses in Isaac's Bible. I traced carelessly over the odd unknown words I found on the farm bills and on any scraps of paper that blew along the lanes, slowly saying what words I could. But back then I did not know the power of words.

After a while the farm door opened again. Isaac came towards me, and something was clearly wrong, because he walked as if he was hurting inside. Taking me by the hand, he led me into the comfy gloom of the farmhouse.

I scuffed my feet across the rag rug by the fire, fidgeting because I wanted to get back to the horse trough, not to meet the beetle-coated stranger, despite his smart carriage.

'This man is Mr Button,' Isaac said, 'and he has come for an important purpose. You must listen to him, Mouse.'

I pouted, and glanced at the table to see if there was anything good to eat, but it was empty except for a letter. The scrawled ink curled across the page. I moved closer, trying to study the strangely inked patterns. The signed name was like a splattered spider.

'Do you like what you see? You could learn to write like this, child,' said Mr Button. A fat finger stabbed at the letter.

'No, thank you, sir,' I said, for Ma had taught me to be a polite child. 'But you can leave us a bottle of ink and some paper, if you please, sir.'

Ma took a deep, deep breath. Then she began to speak, but her mouth was not like her kindly, everyday mouth. She seemed to be holding another set of words inside, the words she really wanted to speak, words full of sadness.

What Ma said was this: 'Mr Button has come to tell

us that it is time for you to go to school, Mouse.'

'Well, I don't want to, thank you!' Even then, I knew school was not a good idea.

Isaac shook his head, and his blue eyes flooded with tears. 'You must, my boy,' he said. 'This gentleman has come to take you away.'

I stared hard then at the hateful letter, and at the words that had tangled themselves up into a scribble of loops and tails. The man picked the letter up, reading it so crisply that the words were sharp as tacks. I heard only fragments, but the words were not like farm talk.

'*No wish to see him . . . Nevertheless, a fitting education . . . A suitable place has now been chosen.*'

Though the words made no sense to me, they did to Ma. She was overawed by whatever the letter told her.

At that moment I promised myself that I would never again let any unknown writing have power over me. Babyish words scratched in cold ashes had no power against ink and paper.

Ma was fighting back tears too. 'Please, sir, we've had no warning. Can't you come back in a month?' she said. 'Let us have a little more time together, please.'

'You have had the child long enough. I must take him now.'

Isaac gave one loud sob.

'Let me have a word with the boy alone,' Ma said, 'for pity's sake, Mr Button.'

'A moment. That is all. Hurry.'

Ma took me through to the back room, where there was the wooden bed I had slept in for as long as I could remember. Then came a shock, a surprise. From under the bed Ma tugged out a sturdy trunk. It was full of garments: shirts and socks, and two sets of breeches and waistcoats and jackets.

'These may be a little big for you, Mouse, because I did not think the request would come so soon. But you will grow into them,' she told me.

I touched the clothes and felt a growing sickness. Ma had made every item with her own hands. She had sat there, stitching garments with the best cloth she could buy. She had sat there knitting, not telling me what she was using her best wool to make. Ma had known this day would come, and she had said not a word. She knew, and I did not. It made my head spin, but I would not cry.

'It will be good for you to go, Mouse,' Ma said, smiling bleakly. 'You have so many things to learn! Such a life to lead!' She wiped my face with a cloth, and I had to put on my new clothes.

Then, when I was finally ready, Ma reached inside her own treasure box, where she kept a curl from every baby she had looked after. She found a folded muslin cloth embroidered with fine white thread. As she unwrapped the fabric, a long silver chain slipped out.

'For you.'

As I lifted the delicate chain in my sunburned farmboy hand, suddenly some kind of sturdy silver medal hung dangling there, grand enough to ornament a gentleman's watch chain.

The medal fell into my open palm, and there, on one side, was a finely engraved mouse, with small round ears and bright eyes and whiskers. On the other side were five curling letters. I read the word they made. This was easy to do, for they spelled my name: M.O.U.S.E.

Quickly, Ma put the medal round my neck and tucked it well down inside my new shirt. She buttoned the collar so firmly that I squirmed.

'My mouse?' I whispered, delighted.

'Yes, and remember, my own Mouse,' she said, in a trembling voice, 'that this is yours, and it is more than precious. You must keep it safe, in case of . . .'

'Case of what, Ma?'

'In case anything happens to me.' Seeing my face crumple, she added, 'But nothing will, pet, nothing will.'

Ma hugged me tightly and pushed a new nose-wiper into my pocket. Though I felt rather grand in my new clothes, my heart was full of alarm.

Then, just as she was about to take me through to the button man, Ma hesitated. She had a look in her eye I had never seen before.

'You must keep your medal hidden, Mouse. You must! I have taught you to be honest and truthful, but now you must keep your mouth tight shut if anyone asks about it. Anyone. Do you understand?'

The fierceness in her voice was like the wind blowing against the door in winter, so I said I did, though it was all very puzzling, and we returned to where the stranger waited.

Isaac lifted me up so high that my head touched the ceiling. It was a sort of farewell. Though his strong hands were around me, they could not protect me from Mr Button. Isaac's eyes were sad, and I knew he was only pretending to play.

'Holidays. There will be holidays. You will come back then, boy,' he said. 'We will have fun together then.'

I got into the hard, glossy carriage. Mr Button clicked his teeth impatiently. The driver cracked his whip, the horses pulled, the wheels turned, and off I went. There was no sign of holiday in the man's hard eyes, and my happy life was ended. Neither Ma nor Isaac could do anything to stop it all happening.

Perhaps it was seeing the two of them so powerless that made me decide that, from then on, I must take care of myself.

MOUSE'S GAME

The waving was over. Roseberry Farm was moving further into the past. The coach blinds flapped to and fro, snipping up the disappearing landscape.

Ma and Isaac had spoken of holidays, but Mr Button had not. Maybe he would not know where to send me, or how to send me back. How would I get home?

I would have to help myself, like the little red hen in the tale Ma often told me. Sitting at a certain angle in the carriage, I could just eye-spy the places we passed. I would have to remember each one, but I was very good at remembering.

This was not because I was clever, but because each winter, when the ice and snow made it too cold to go outside, Ma played a special game. She spread all kinds of objects on the table and covered them over with a clean apron. Once she was ready, she called me to her and slowly drew back the cloth. I had to remember as many things as I could.

'Look, Mousey, look hard!' she'd say. 'Say the names to yourself.'

Then, all at once, she pulled that cover over again. I had to tell her each thing I could. At first I only remembered five. Then I got more – ten, twelve, eighteen, twenty-one. I chanted the names under my breath like a secret nursery rhyme, and got very good at remembering what I'd seen. Sometimes Ma took an object away, and I had to say what was missing. I grew very good at that game.

So, trapped in the carriage with bright shiny Button, I hoped that Ma's eye-spy game might save me. As the blind flipped and flapped, I studied all the buildings and churches and taverns that the coach passed. I watched where the coach halted, or where it turned at crossroads. I stared at unusual sights: a twisty spire, a white horse carved on the hill, a new-built railway bridge and the narrow dark glass of the canals, and gave them all their own funny names.

I studied the tavern signs where the coach waited while Button went inside, having locked the carriage. He returned smelling of roasted meat and puddings, with one hard bit of biscuit for me. Though some sights were lost when I dozed, and some when it was dark, I tried to believe that one day those images, strung out like beads on my memory, would help me.

This peeping work gave me some comfort. Surely I would remember at least one sight, even if it was only a water well beside the road, or the tower of a tumbledown castle, or an ancient market cross that I could ask about? And something was better than nothing, when you had left your home behind.

I want to remember all these sights. I want to remember all my happy times. Some people only want to hear the worst.

What was the worst? One name sticks in my throat. One name floats like a dead rat on the grey soup of my childish dream. One name appears in my story all too soon.

Mr Button and his carriage travelled far, far from any town, the horses cantering so fast there was not a moment to jump down or escape. The track crossed an open heath and entered a scrawny wood, where the boughs of tangled trees cast webs of shadow across Button's cruelly smiling face.

Then we passed through iron gates, and the trees parted, revealing a vast bleak house wrapped in mildewed ivy. Sadness seemed to drip from those leaves, sliding down the coach windows like grimy tears.

I was not yet seven, and knew very little, but even so I was sure that this was not the kind of place that Ma Foster thought she was sending me to. I had arrived at Murkstone Hall, my dreadful new home.

Button dragged me inside to a place where boys whirled loudly and angrily around me. Some shrieked from the staircase, some yelled, none stopped, and all were much bigger, much wilder than I was. I saw that I would not be a king here, and that there was no Isaac around to catch me if I fell.

Button yanked me into some kind of waiting room. Horsehair grew from the cracks in a dusty sofa and lay in coils on the grimy rug.

He glanced at me as if I was dirt on his polished boots. 'Well, boy! Now you are delivered,' he snapped, 'but you haven't heard the last of me, or the one who sent you here.'

'Who sent me here?' I asked him. It could not be Isaac or Ma. I'd realised that much.

Button scoffed. 'That's for me to know and for you *not* to find out. Sit!' He pointed to the one hard wooden chair and strode through to an inner parlour.

'Bulloughby!' he called, and I did not know whether this was a threat or a greeting.

THE CLOSED MOUTH

Waiting on that hard chair, I remembered what Ma had told me about my new treasure.

'Keep your mouth shut tight . . . Keep it safe.'

More swiftly than my fingers had ever worked before, I unclasped Ma's silver chain, slipped that mouse medal off it and popped the disc into my mouth. I poked it with my tongue so it lodged against my cheek, like a fat sugar drop being saved for later. The silver tasted cold and metallic, but I was keeping my secret safe.

I closed my lips tightly, knowing I must not swallow my medal, because that could be the death of me. I fastened the chain around my neck just in time.

Button reappeared, with that smile on his face that was no smile at all, and then he was gone.

*

'Come!' roared a voice, and I went into the dreadful parlour to meet the man who would turn my life into a nightmare.

Headmaster Bulloughby whisked a bamboo switch rhythmically against the carved leg of his desk. His cravat was stained with snuff, and a half-supped tankard stood before him. His hairy ears supported an orange wig, and his nose was almost purple.

At first I smiled, for he looked comical, like a character from a puppet play I'd seen on the village green.

Bulloughby let the switch fall on the rug and beckoned me over. I trotted amiably to his desk, trying to be pleasant. As soon as I got within reach, he grabbed me by my collar, twisted it, and thrust a letter against my face, rubbing it against my cheek. His eyes bulged wildly.

'See what it says, boy? *He* sent you to me. *He* says I have to keep you here until *he* decides what to do with you.'

I squirmed. My own eyes were popping, and I was too afraid of spitting out my medal to gasp for air. Bulloughby laughed bitterly, as if this was the usual way to welcome children.

'You don't even know why you were sent here, do you?' Bulloughby pulled me so tightly towards him that I saw the spittle threads hanging from his yellow teeth. 'What do they call you, boy?'

'Mouse,' I squawked.

'Mouse? Mouse? Vermin, more like, not worth a farthing!' He jabbed his finger at my forehead. 'I did not want you here. I did not ask for you. I did not send for you, or request your company in any way at all. Remember that! You, young Vermin, is nothing but the payment of a debt!'

An open ledger lay on his table, with the names of boys listed down each page, and each name marked *For Return* or *Not Return*. I could not spot my name there yet, but I saw thick ink scratched right across some lines. The never, ever returnable.

Busily, Bulloughby examined my pockets. He dragged out the clean handkerchief Ma gave me. 'Barely more than a rag you've got here,' he sneered. 'Not fine at all.' Then he studied my jacket and breeches, the clothes that Ma had made so carefully for me. 'You're not much more than a pauper, are you?'

It was as Bulloughby twisted my collar that he caught the glint of the silver chain. He tugged hard enough to burst my shirt open, and snatched so quick and slick that I thought of Isaac's tales of the pickpockets in the market crowds.

In a moment my silver chain was within a drawer in his desk, among watches and signet rings and trinkets that must have belonged to the other boys he had so personally welcomed into his care. Any precious guineas, crowns or sovereigns would end up in his safe-keeping too.

Then Bulloughby flung me from him. 'Off you go, Vermin. Turn left. Down the corridor. Round the corner. Pair of doors. Knock. That's it.' He loomed over me, and even his wig trembled with his rage. 'If I spot you anywhere from now on, boy, you'll feel it, so take care! Out!'

I staggered to my feet and hurried off. The taste of blood was in my mouth, but the silver medal was safe within my cheek. It was a tiny triumph: I had kept the one important thing that belonged to me. Turning the corner, I spat my medal out and wiped it dry on my sleeve. I slipped it down inside the ankle of my boot, wiggling my leg about until the disc lay inside my sock, securely under the sole of my foot.

'I kept it safe, Ma,' I said to myself, though I knew she could not hear, and walked slowly towards the two doors. I knocked.

A USEFUL TALENT

'In!' An awkward crop-haired boy hauled me into the classroom. Across the back of his ragged jacket was chalked the letter M.

I gazed at him, puzzled. 'Please, what –'

'Monitor!' he gasped, and raced back to the few inches of splintered wood that was his place on one of the benches.

Rows of long desks rose like steps up to the ceiling, filled with more faces than I had seen in my life. Small boys were squashed tightly at the front, and bigger boys crammed together at the back. They gave a shout of delight, as if they had just seen something amusing.

'New Boy, New Boy!' they called, banging hard on the desks and shouting. 'New Boy, New Boy!'

I looked around for this amusing person, and then saw that *I* was the New Boy, so there and then I decided to do something friendly and entertaining in reply.

I balanced, first on one hand and then on the other, then walked with my face just a breath above the grimy floorboards, and heard cheers. Adding in a somersault or two, proud of my greatly amusing skills, I then gave at least one cartwheel.

The boys smothered their laughter and clutched at their jiggling cheeks. Yes, it was me, full of fun and cheer. The boy Mouse had arrived!

Then, even though my world was upside down, something much less amusing came into view. Raised high up on one wall was a panelled desk, far higher than Ma's wardrobe. It was carved deeply as a church pulpit, and inside that desk was a dusty grey woman.

Still upside down, I paused, transfixed by this ancient fledgling in her wooden nest. Her hair was scrunched back tightly into a wispy bun, her nose was curved like a beak, and her bony hands darted about, rearranging the trails of her musty gown. All at once her head shot forward and she stared at me through thick metal-rimmed glasses.

So I stopped parading about on my hands, aware I might have done a very wrong thing. As slowly and politely as I could, I turned myself the right way up again and stood there before her.

Her voice, when it came, was pinched and bitter. 'I am Madam Claudine. Your name, new boy?'

'Mouse!' I tried to smile, but the class burst into another roar of laughter.

'Mouse! Mouse!' they shouted.

She rapped on her pulpit with hard nails, and all fell silent. 'Boy, I repeat – what is your name?'

'Mouse.'

'Mouse?' Her eyes narrowed. She was not amused.

'That's what I'm called. Honest,' I said. 'I'd tell you another name if I had one, Madam Claudine.'

She sensed that if these questions went on any longer, things would get worse. Two or three boys were already squeaking and calling out, 'Cheese, cheese!'

Rustling about, she dipped a quill into a gigantic inkwell. A note, still dribbling ink, floated down to me. 'For the Headmaster,' she ordered, with an oddly sneering smile.

I trotted down the corridor again and offered the note at the dreadful parlour.

'I told you never –' came the roar.

'Madam Claudine –' I began.

Bulloughby snatched the sheet, slamming the door shut. A moment later the door opened and the note was thrust back at me.

As I trotted back, I struggled to read her copperplate question. '*What is this boy's family name?*'

Bulloughby's reply was scratched across the paper. '*He no longer has one.*'

'Who am I then?' I wondered, confused.

Then I set off, stamping my answer with each step as I went back to that classroom.

'I am Mouse, that's who. I am Mouse no matter what. There's Ma, and Isaac, and there's me, a boy called Mouse. So there.'

They would not make me into a nothing here. They would not.

I handed over the note.

'Mouse you must be then,' sniffed Madam Claudine, writing it down on her own register of names. 'Stupid name. Over there! Now!'

The boys on the front bench shuffled along, as I squashed into a few inches at the end. There were so many of us that I had to cling on to the desk to keep my place. My boots dangled in the air.

'And now to work!' she ordered, 'Keep together!'

A chorus of voices filled the room, and only gradually did I understand what they were chanting.

'Twelve times twelve is one hundred and forty-four.

'Thirteen times twelve is one hundred and fifty-six.

'Fourteen times twelve is one hundred and sixty-eight.

'Fifteen times twelve is a hundred and *Niddle*.'

Niddle? Niddle? What? Someone had spoken the word 'Niddle' in my left ear. Though the boy next to me faced Madam Claudine, he winked one eye cheekily in my direction.

'Mouse!' I whispered back.

'Know that, silly,' Niddle said, grinning quickly, then returning to the noise.

'Seventeen times twelve is two hundred and four.

'Eighteen times twelve is two hundred and sixteen . . .'

On they went, on to the twenty times table, and then returning to the beginning, repeating and repeating. I kept up where I could.

Suddenly, as I was almost falling asleep, Madam Claudine rapped on her desk twice and the chant changed.

'A is for Armadillo.

'B is for Buffalo.

'C is for Camel . . .'

And that, or so it seemed, was to be the style of my schooling.

Madam Claudine believed in nothing but long lists of tables, words, phrases and definitions. Anything that could be listed – any creature, place or object – was listed. Hidden like codes within the rhythm of the chants, the boys kept secret conversations moving around the class.

How did this woman keep us in order? Around the room were hung texts she believed to be inspiring.

'Regard the Exhortations!' she cried. 'Clutch them to your hearts. Recite!'

'In Murkstone Hall, We Will Become More Worthy!

'In Murkstone Hall, We Will Become More Obedient!

'In Murkstone Hall, We Will Know Our Place!

'In Murkstone Hall, We Will Recite To Our Utmost Ability!'

And on and on and on, with the words screwing themselves into dried dust on our tongues.

Madam Claudine had one other more practical method. Each day she chose one of the bigger boys.

'Today's Monitor!' she declared.

The chosen one climbed the steps to her desk to receive a large M in chalk upon his back. For that day the Monitor's job was to walk up and down the aisles, wielding something rather like a long feather duster capable of giving a punishing blow to any boy not doing as Madam Claudine required.

Looking back, I see Madam Claudine was crafty. Choosing a Monitor daily meant that nobody whacked anyone else too severely, for he would surely be hurt in return. Nobody became over-powerful, and so Madam Claudine's own authority was never challenged.

However, any Monitor who Madame Claudine felt was too kind or gentle soon found himself sent swiftly to Mr Bulloughby's office, and he was in no way kind or gentle in return.

So, was it Bulloughby? Was he the bad dream, the bad time?

Certainly Bulloughby made the hours stand still in this horror of a place. Bulloughby made the nightmare begin. He sat in his stuffed study like a bloated toad, taking no care of any child within those walls, Returnable or Non-Returnable. But worse was to come.

On my first day, after the chanting had gone on for several hours, Madam Claudine gave a loud squawk.

'Monitor! Kitchen!'

The Monitor scurried away, returning with a cloth-covered basket. Madam Claudine seized it and sat munching away at whatever was hidden inside.

Still droning, we watched her claw-like hands move

the food piece by piece to her mouth while our own hunger groaned in our stomachs.

When the bell rang, I hurried along behind Niddle. We entered a large draughty room, filled with long tables and mean rough benches, where vast vats rose up from the hidden depths of the kitchen.

Here I discovered – maybe I should have guessed? – that Murkstone meals were bowls of cold grey gruel or a grimy broth laced with vegetable peelings, and pieces of coarse bread. Everything tasted the same, but foul though the food was, there was never enough.

Later on, I would learn about that dark, hidden kitchen, but on that first day, as soon as my meal ended, I raced out with the others into the grounds. I did not know that this was where a gang of the biggest boys gathered. Among them sat Bulloughby's son Grindle, cracking his knuckles, the King Rat of Murkstone Hall.

FRIENDS AND ENEMIES

We charged outside. Ma and Isaac had taught me always to be hopeful, so, as I breathed in the clean fresh air, my spirits lifted.

Niddle and I and some of the youngest boys raced around, partly to keep ourselves warm. The harsh wind snapped at our ears and hands and whipped away our cries and shouts.

Pyeberry, a boy with a frizz of dark curls, found a rough lump of wood, scarred with knots, and flung it down on the ground.

'Kick it, Pyeberry, kick it!' we called.

Pyeberry grinned at me, then kicked it in my direction, and we all charged after the misshapen thing as if it was a ball.

Of course, the lump would not roll straight, but bounced off in odd directions. Eyes fixed, I ran headlong after our wooden ball and found it trapped under the toe of a steel-rimmed boot. I beamed eagerly up at whoever had so helpfully stopped our toy rolling further. Then I backed away.

Two red-rimmed eyes glared at me. A pasty white face moved closer to mine, the mouth set in a twisted line of hate. Bristly hair stood like a rough brush from the scalp. As the other boys stepped back, I was left in a wide space, almost alone. Just me, and the boy called Grindle Bulloughby.

'Hello.' It seemed the only thing to say. 'Can we have our ball back?'

Grindle chuckled and slowly shook his head. 'No. Only if you can get it, Vermin.'

He picked up the lump of wood, all bashed and cracked from our game, and held it out tantalisingly.

As I reached forward, he smirked, and whirled the wood as hard as he could right across the yard so it bounced on the roof, rolled down the slates and lodged behind an old chimney on the side of Murkstone Hall. Grindle strutted off, satisfied that he had spoilt our game and that the ball was out of reach.

Not my reach though.

Without a thought, I ran over and shinned up the thick ivy that grew on that wall. Soon I was high above the other boys, though somehow it didn't feel much higher than that beam in Isaac's barn. Up I went. I grabbed the lost ball, shoved it inside my jacket and scrambled down.

Only when I reached the ground did the web of silence break and the yard fill with whoops and cheers. I turned, beaming, to find that Grindle's face was afire.

'You trying to mock me?' he spat, shoving me so hard I fell down. 'You'll be so very sorry, Vermin, you and your friends.' He turned away and stamped into the school.

From then on, Grindle was my foe. There was one saving piece of good fortune: the biggest boys spent their days in a so-called study of their own. Grindle was not kept in Madam Claudine's tender care, and for that I was very glad.

How I remember that first night at Murkstone Hall! All round the walls of a cold dormitory, beds were raised like sets of shelves, five high.

There was no sign of the trunk full of Ma's clean clothes for me. There were no trunks or chests or cupboards at all in that bare room, just a gaggle of children shivering in whatever they had once arrived in, though now their clothes were torn and worn, and what was left of collars and cuffs was rimed with dirt.

The boys clambered up into their beds in their day clothes, dragging blankets with them and bundling jackets to make pillows.

I too snatched a threadbare blanket from a heap by the door, then found each boy curled up within his narrow bunk. Where should I go?

'Take Ollie's place,' Niddle called, in an odd, strained voice. 'Top bunk, third row along.'

'Doesn't Ollie need it?' I asked, looking around. The chattering fell away.

'Not now.' Niddle pointed awkwardly to Ollie's

empty bunk. It was just below the ceiling. 'Ollie started sleepwalking.'

I clambered up, for there was no other space to take. 'Sorry, Ollie,' I said silently, and hoped his spirit was peaceful.

There I crouched, just below the crumbling grey plaster. The single candle flame sank within its tallow stub, inviting the darkness.

In those flickering shadows I took off both my boots and tugged one bootlace free. The lace, as I gnawed it, tasted of mud and long journeys. I chewed until it snapped to make two short laces for my boot-tops the next morning. I pulled out the long second lace and, under cover, felt inside Ma's knitted sock for my hidden secret.

Carefully, imperceptibly, I threaded my small silver mouse medal on to it. I did not tie the lace around my neck, because then it might be seen. Under the thin blanket, I wriggled about until I had tied the lace across my chest and shoulder. My metal namesake wedged uncomfortably against my side, but I was glad to feel it there.

The darkness did not hide the many other shufflings and scratchings, nor the chattering of teeth.

Then, after a while, Pyeberry piped up with a gleeful chant. 'Sleep tight till the morning light –'

'And we don't care if the bedbugs bite. *Amen!*' the boys chanted in joyful reply.

As I dropped into sleep, my brain echoed with this odd night-time prayer. It was not one that Ma or Isaac had taught me.

*

In the blink of an eye, or so it seemed, morning arrived. All round the dormitory, tousled boys dropped down from their bunks like spiderlings.

I stayed curled up for a moment, hiding my eyes, but the stink of the blanket brought back the knowledge that this was my true, real life. Ma and Isaac and the farm were the dream now.

'Mouse,' called Niddle. 'Come on! Be quick!'

I dropped down to the floor too, tucking in my shirt and pulling on my jacket. As I put on my boots and tied the shortened laces, the door opened and in came three big boys. One carried a bucket, one a large cloth, and the third was Grindle.

'Faces!' shouted Grindle, eyes glinting with joy, as the smaller boys lined up. Then he stood back, arms folded, to watch.

First the foul cloth was plunged into the dirty water, then rubbed all wet and dripping across our faces, one by one. Anyone who tried to back away got the sodden cloth for twice as long. I waited at the very end of the line.

So far Grindle had let his friends do the work. But as soon as he saw me he laughed maliciously. 'My turn now,' he said.

Taking the bucket, he poured a puddle of water across the stone floor, then handed me the cloth.

'Wipe it up, Vermin,' he ordered, chuckling. '*Please.*'

I felt something bad coming, but all I could do was wipe and wring the cloth back into the bucket again and again, until the floor was almost clean.

'Thank you,' said Grindle. Grimly he swirled the cloth around in the bucket. 'Now it's your turn for the wash, Vermin!'

He lifted the dripping cloth, one of his friends seized me, and Grindle forced the filthy rag into my face, into my eyes and ears. As I cried out, he pushed the cloth into my mouth, squeezing it so that the foul water ran down my throat, and I could not help swallowing.

'That's better,' Grindle said, releasing me at last. 'And don't you dare puke!' Somewhere, a bell started ringing. 'Breakfast,' he remarked, as they swept out of the door. 'Hope you find it tasty, Vermin.'

The boys, in their own damp clothes, went quietly down the stairs towards the sound of the bell. Niddle and Pyeberry kept close to me, whispering sympathetically, but my head was so full of shame and rage that I did not take in a word they said.

MORE AND LESS

We trudged into the echoing chill of the dining hall. This time I studied my surroundings more warily. Where was Grindle?

Always cold, the fireplace held grey ash and pigeon droppings. The unwashed floorboards were marked by the trails of small rodents who cleared away our crumbs by night. Sparrows darted through the gaps in the windows and perched on the ancient pulley hanging from the ceiling, waiting to spy any crumb or scrap. I saw, around the huge mechanism, rusted chains that trailed down into the deep shaft below. We waited, and waited, and our hunger grew.

Then, with a shout, Bulloughby leaned over and shouted down into the depths. 'Kitchen? You there? Now!'

A weary groan came in answer. Four bigger boys

started hauling on the creaking chains, and up rose a kind of ridged tray bearing a gigantic pan. Bubbles spat and popped across its surface and congealed around the huge ladle. The four boys dragged the slopping vat across to the floor.

Down went the tray again. When it rose, I could not believe what I saw: a generous bowl heaped high with sugared bread-and-milk, and a jug of golden cream. Bulloughby glared at Grindle, who sprang up and hurried, almost meekly, over to his father.

Carefully, our headmaster withdrew a china dish from one of his pockets. It was gold-edged and patterned with rosebuds. He spooned the soft white bread into the pretty dish, then poured the jug of thick cream over it. Every mouth ached with the longing to taste that cream.

A blob fell on Grindle's thumb, but when he went to lick it off, Bulloughby smacked his son's ear. 'Don't you dare, wretch. Take it to Madam Claudine, and don't spill a drop. Tell her there is more if she wants it.'

As Grindle passed me, I saw that the hard pride had gone from his face, and his eyes were small and sad. He scurried anxiously from the hall, delivering the strangely dainty dish to the ancient Madam Claudine in her own chamber.

Another haul, and this time the shelf brought a platter heaped high with hot chops, potatoes and onions. While gruel was being ladled on to our plates, Bulloughby dug his fork and knife into his dish and gnawed away at the chops.

By the time my dish of gruel came, it was slobberycold, but I ate up all the same, trying not to recall the golden honey of Roseberry Farm.

The days went on, and time went on. Each morning we chanted facts and figures for Madam Claudine. Each noon we shivered in the yard, though the days got slowly warmer. If anyone could have placed that school in a windier, colder place, it would have been at the top of a mountain.

Each night we slept until Grindle woke us with his cloth and bucket, and I soon saw that he had other victims besides me.

At times I caught Bulloughby watching me, as if he bore me a special grudge or I reminded him of something he did not want to think about. Then he'd snarl some curse at me. I tried hard to keep out of his way.

Each Friday Madam Claudine chose two Monitors to give out pottery inkwells, twisted dip-pens and thin, porous paper. As the last sheet of paper was given out, Madam Claudine unclasped a big book and started to read aloud. Whether the pot of ink was as thick as glue or as thin as drain-water, we had to take down her rapidly dictated words as best we could.

First we wrote down the middle of the paper, and then we turned it upside down and wrote in the spaces between the lines. After that we turned the sheet on its sides and wrote around and around the edge of the paper, turning it as we went. Madam Claudine did not think well of any boy who ran out of paper.

'Smaller,' she cried, rapping her knuckles on her

desk, 'smaller. Only gentlemen can write their words with flourishes.' Sometimes she pointed to a trembling penman and uttered a fearsome cry: 'You, boy, are an absolute blot, an utter waste of ink.'

Any such blot of a boy was forced to scribe to and fro across a cracked slate, his sleeves frosting with chalk-dust under the torrent of words.

Sometimes Madam Claudine would surprise us by screaming out a sudden calculation. Add! She called long lists of numbers, which we had to follow in our heads, trying to be first with the total. At other times we took one long number from another, with lots of carryings, or worked out something through long long divisions.

'I hate this so much,' grumbled Niddle, 'My head is full up, right to the top.'

'Just concentrate,' said Pyeberry, his dark eyes bright and happy because he had reached the total already. 'Madam, Madam Claudine!'

Madam Claudine never looked pleased when he answered. She always chose another boy to answer, but Pyeberry did not care.

'Numbers are like a beautiful pattern,' he explained. 'They always work out. They are never sad or bad or mad, unless someone makes them so. Numbers are never cruel or mean. Numbers are like a magical language.'

Niddle and I glanced at each other, puzzled. That was not how we felt, not with Madam Claudine's glare frizzling our brains.

One afternoon, as our bored voices croaked in our throats, Headmaster Bulloughby himself came into the classroom, holding a glass jar. He handed it up to Madam Claudine, bowing his head very slightly, almost like a child.

Madam Claudine paused a moment too long, as if she was enjoying his wait, then snatched the jar from his grasp. A beautiful peacock butterfly fluttered feebly inside. She sniffed, and put the jar on her desk without any comment.

As Bulloughby turned to leave, she snapped out a question to the class. 'Signing of Magna Carta?'

I saw Bulloughby flinch, as if he was in fear, as if he did not know the answer either.

'Twelve hundred and fifteen, Anno Domini,' sang out Pyeberry, unable to stop himself. I never knew where he had acquired his knowledge, and he never said anything about his past life.

This time Madam Claudine responded with a cunning smile. 'Very good, Pyeberry. What an excellent thinker you are, child.'

Bulloughby gave Pyeberry a glance more threatening than a thundercloud, promising to get him for being the cleverest boy, for knowing the right answer.

As Bulloughby slammed the door behind him, Madam Claudine looked most satisfied, like an owl that has swallowed a chick. It was only then that I thought about Bulloughby and Madam Claudine, and wondered about them, stuck in that wretched place.

Maybe I started to wonder because week by weary week, month by dismal month, I was getting a little older and wiser. But not quite wise enough, as I soon found out.

A CHANGE OF FACE

Some people imagine bad times are all excitement. They are not. We dared not hope for any change, as it might bring something worse. Change came all the same.

One morning we filed into class. Madam Claudine sat, as ever, within her high panelled desk, but her eyes stayed closed. We stood and waited. And sat and waited. And waited, while Madam Claudine coughed in her sleep, but did not move. Questions fluttered round the room, growing louder and louder, and still she did not wake.

One of the big boys climbed up on the bench, and triumphantly on to the desk, then froze. Madam Claudine inhaled violently, then slumped forward and lay lolling across the pulpit. One arm swayed slightly, but nothing more.

At once every boy followed his example. We rose up and stamped and danced about, and sang out rude words to the lists Madam Claudine had imposed on us for so long.

As we reached full riot, Bulloughby entered, twitching his switch. Instantly we dropped into our seats, silent.

'If any of you so much as blink, you'll feel more regret than you can imagine,' he snarled, slowly approaching Madam Claudine's perch.

'M . . . M . . . Madam?' he called up. She sighed and spluttered, but did not wake. He tried again. 'Er, Madam Claudine?'

He tugged at the desk, and her basket tumbled down. Out spilled fragments of gnawed chicken bones and the rosebud bowl. He mounted the steps, moving hesitantly towards her. As he disturbed her fusty shawls, several empty bottles rolled out and shattered across the floor. Strong medicinal fumes rose in the air.

Awkwardly, Bulloughby lifted her down until she rested in his two arms. That was when we knew that though Madam Claudine might be alive, she could no longer trouble us.

Bulloughby fixed the class with a malevolent stare. 'Outside!' he ordered. 'Do not come in until you are told, boys.'

'The snow. . . ?' someone bolder than I said.

'Go!' he ordered.

I was the last one out. As the door slammed, I heard a desperate cry.

'Mother!'

Then a far more awful sound: Headmaster Bulloughby was weeping in huge, awful, painful sobs. I scurried out into the yard, thinking of my own lovely Ma, who was far, far away.

As for Madam Claudine, a narrow carriage took her away, a grim-faced woman at her side, and we never saw her again.

However, on that day we wandered round the yard, faces pinched and blue, trying to keep warm. Boys huddled in groups or sheltered in doorways, taking turns to face the wind.

An old oak grew in the empty field beyond the yard, so Niddle and Pyeberry and I made for that trunk. We climbed inside the hollow bole, taking some younger boys with us. Clustered there like squirrels within a drey, we shivered together for warmth. Evening came. The oak swayed with the wind and creaked and sang.

Pyeberry hummed along with the sound, trying to stop the younger ones grizzling.

'Don't like that noise much,' Niddle muttered.

'It's what trees do,' I said, thinking of the trees around Roseberry Farm. 'It's a good noise. Keep still, and listen.'

It was dark when we heard a bell ringing. We entered the stony silence of Murkstone Hall and crept to the dormitory without anything in our bellies.

The next morning, at breakfast, Grindle was not asked to take the pretty rosebud bowl anywhere, and Bulloughby's face was grimmer than ever.

*

With Madam Claudine gone, more changes came. Button brought Headmaster Bulloughby a new teacher.

Mr Jarvey had seen trouble. His left leg dragged slightly, and the pearly line of an old scar marked one cheek, but he did not crouch in Madam Claudine's carved nest, ready to prey on the class. Jarvey was a man who stood level with his pupils. He spoke to us face to face.

It was not exactly a miracle, but it felt like it, though we knew he had not come to save us. The bitter cough that racked Jarvey's chest meant that he was at Murkstone Hall because no other place would have him. We guessed, from Bulloughby's passing sneers, that Jarvey was paid only a pittance, and Grindle spoke openly about the debtor's prison.

We did not care, for our Jarvey had a mischievous light in his eye, and a twisted, rebellious expression, even on the bad days when he used the back of a chair to help him stand upright.

'Good morning,' he began, giving a gently cynical smile. 'I am here with you in this happy place, and I am most interested in everything you clever pupils have so far learned. Please, do instruct me in this matter, boys,' he said, eyes twinkling.

'A is for Armadillo, B is for Buffalo . . .' Right away we started our usual chanting. Jarvey stared at us, his eyes widening as if he could not believe what he was hearing. We went on and on, desperate to show him all that Madam Claudine had taught us.

'Stop!' he shouted, raising a hand. 'Stop, stop, stop!'

We stopped, the room still echoing with our noise.

Jarvey's eyebrows were raised almost high enough to hide under his hair. 'Boys, is this it? Is this all? Do you never read, write, listen to entire stories?' While we shrugged, he paced about, perplexed. 'Do you measure, weigh, puzzle?' he tried. 'Paint? Draw? Make?'

'This is what we do, sir,' said Niddle, and we all started up again.

'Twelve times twelve . . .' Our chanting resounded.

Jarvey slapped his hands over his ears. 'Enough. Stop, stop!' he yelled. 'Quiet, please! Quiet!'

When there was silence once more, Jarvey gave a deep and mighty sigh. 'Then it is high time that you boys knew rather more.'

From that day, Jarvey started to give us a proper education. He talked about inventions and discoveries, globes and lands and languages and all sorts of new and wondrous things. He took down Madam Claudine's Exhortations. Instead, with his voice, he unwrapped a host of heroes and villains and myths and legends and spread them before us.

Such fine stories, such stunning adventures, such words! Each night these tales wound themselves around in my head, and each morning they sprang up like pictures in my imagination.

It was as if all the windows had been cleaned – though they had not, of course – and we could now see a world outside, away from the drudgery of Murkstone Hall. Not everyone thought that things were better, for now we had to use our brains, and ask and answer real questions, but I did and Pyeberry did, and probably Niddle did too.

It was strange. We had almost forgotten there could be bright times. Does everyone meet someone like our Jarvey, someone who makes the world a better place, who makes the dull days exciting? Someone who changes lists of facts into living ideas? I hope so.

Headmaster Bulloughby made good use of Button's gift. As Murkstone Hall had been given this new teacher, every boy had to go to Jarvey's lessons. Though our room was cramped before, now we were packed tighter than the creatures within old Noah's ark.

The youngest boys squatted on the floor, at the front. My friends and I, now we were older, squashed into the middle benches. Finally Grindle's gang joined us, glowering from the back rows, flicking pellets at our heads, sticking us with pen nibs and reminding us that they were the secret lords of the class.

Most of these fellows had lived in freedom before, learning little except how to play cards and race red-eyed rats. At first they lounged about, trying to ignore Jarvey but without success.

Jarvey advanced upon them, demanding they think, asking them to learn. Whatever had befallen him before, Jarvey had been to places, had done things, knew things. Gradually these boys could not help being interested, for his tales stood against the everlasting grimness of Murkstone Hall. In some ways, it was an easy contest for Jarvey.

Still Grindle did not want to listen. He shrank down,

afraid of more than Jarvey's twisted smile and thin cough. He was afraid of his own ignorance. Each day he sat, scratching his name on the desks with a pocket-knife, looking for trouble, looking for a way of making up for his missing card games and his lost idleness. And he found it.

CHAPTER 13

A HIGH POINT

I was climbing around in the branches of the old oak tree when I saw Grindle waiting below. The moment I reached the ground, he clamped his hand on my shoulder.

'Right, Vermin, I've got a good idea,' he said, squeezing tighter. 'A very good idea.'

I tried to get free, sure that this would not be a good idea for me, but Grindle pointed up at Murkstone Hall itself and the dark forbidding stonework.

His finger traced where a narrow ledge ran across the side of the building, almost parallel with the upper windows. A curtain of thick ivy grew up one side, and some half-dead creeper had tangled itself around the opposite corner.

'See that ledge up there? I bet a measly scrap of vermin like you could climb from one side to the other.'

I shook my head. 'Don't 'spect I can,' I muttered.

He squeezed even tighter. 'I said, I bet you can climb along that ledge, Vermin.'

'What if I don't, Grindle?' I asked.

'Well, if you do, I win several bets, and that will be most useful to me, won't it? Clinkety-clink and all that. Not everybody wants to be as piss-poor as you, young Vermin.' Rubbing his palms together gleefully, Grindle added, 'And if you don't, or won't, your friend Niddle will get more than a gift from me.' He clenched his fist and grinned, his yellow teeth bared. 'Understand?'

I should have told on him, as anyone should do who meets a Grindle. I should have run and told Jarvey, because Jarvey was someone who would listen, but life's not exactly simple. Some days Jarvey was stretched out in his room, coughing and sleeping, and then we were left to run wild. It was on such a day that Grindle made his request.

'Tomorrow afternoon, right?' Grindle told me. I agreed, because I had no choice.

The boys gathered in the yard to watch.

'Don't do it, Mouse,' begged Niddle, tugging at my sleeve. 'It's not safe, you know. You don't have to do this for Grindle.'

'I do, Niddle. Now don't worry.'

I rubbed my palms dry on my breeches, then grabbed hold of the gnarled stems of ivy. The first part of the ascent was easy, although the branches shifted and sagged and smaller stems pulled away, releasing showers of grit from the wall.

Up I went, higher and higher, the boys cheering as I reached the top. Then it was time to cross the side of the building.

Were Grindle's palms sweating like mine? I wondered. Coins clinked and Grindle's voice rumbled somewhere down below.

I paused, rubbed my hands one at a time against my jacket again. Then I stretched myself thin, and edged my way out across the ledge. Moss had smeared the stone with damp dripping patches. My face and clothes were soon green with slime.

Carefully, carefully. My palms squelched across bird-painted sills, and my fingernails tore on the rough stone ridges. Rooks swooped down from their nests in the nearby trees and swirled around the building as if they thought I might suddenly fly.

'Come on, you rooks! Get him! Peck out his eyes!' yelled Grindle, suddenly more amused by this thought than by winning his bet.

Halfway along, a lead waterspout stuck out from the roof, crowned with a curling fern that dripped thick tears of watery mould on to the wall. This was a section that needed some careful footwork.

'For Niddle,' I muttered grimly, up where nobody could hear me. 'For Niddle.'

Slowly, hand over hand, foot after foot, I clambered across the side of the house, grasping at the guttering, and grabbed, at last, at the thickened stems of the creeper. Down I went, though sharp pointed twigs hid under the crumpled leaves, and dropped the last foot to the ground.

Such cheers! Such triumph! Satisfied, Grindle palmed his winnings. I was just glad that my dare was over.

I did not realise that this was only the beginning of Grindle's entertainment. Over the next months, whenever he felt more than usually bored, he sent me scrambling up the walls of Murkstone Hall. In between, he amused himself by thinking up ways of making the route of the climb a little harder and longer.

I could have protested. After that first time I could have spoken to Jarvey, but – I admit it – I had my own secret. Though I was terrified each time, once I had reached a certain point high on the wall of Murkstone Hall, a strange emotion filled me, a feeling that was nothing to do with Grindle's bullying. Once I had begun climbing, going higher and higher, all my life suddenly seemed calm. When I hung there, clutching at the stems, or edging along with my nose close to the crumbling stone, I reached a magical space. Up there, I forgot Bulloughby and Button and how much I was missing Ma and Isaac. All I held in my mind was my next step, my next handhold. Grindle didn't know that his threats became almost a pleasure to me. Up there, I was as free as I could be. I was proudly me, myself, and for that short while I could imagine I was escaping everything that weighed me down.

Did my secret joy stop me thinking ahead? I am sure someone else would have seen what was coming, but I did not.

*

A day came when I could not do the climb. I was shivering in my bunk, spitting and coughing. I felt unable to stand or stagger across the room, let alone climb anywhere. All the same, Grindle's familiar request arrived, delivered by my friend Pyeberry.

'Tell Grindle I'm not coming,' I groaned, curling up under my blanket, and drifting off into the swirling fever that thickened my brain.

'Mouse?' Pyeberry's voice came from a long way off.

'Go! Tell Grindle that I just don't care,' I sobbed, and dropped into an aching sleep.

I must have been dreaming about my climb, for I imagined I was reaching for cobwebbed ivy and crumbling ledges and worn sills. I woke with a start and clutched at the bedpost, afraid that I might fall to the ground.

But I was not balanced on the ledge, even though I could hear the boys cheering as usual, hear the urgent rhythm of their calls.

'Go, go! Higher, higher!' they chanted.

Groggily, as I turned over, I wondered who was climbing, if it wasn't me. An awful thought clanged in my echoing head, and I heard the name they shouted.

'Pyeberry! Pyeberry!' the boys called.

'Stupid, stupid!' I whimpered, and dropped to the floor. Trailing my blanket behind me, I struggled desperately across the room, toppled down the stairs, and made my way out into the yard.

The bright light burned into my aching eyes, but I saw a shadow moving across the wall of Murkstone

Hall. It was Pyeberry, climbing my climb. He had reached the very critical place, where the ledge was worn and could only bear weight for a moment. I was small and light, nothing but a Mouse, but my amiable friend was not so slight.

Pyeberry hesitated, then tried to reach out for safety, but I saw he had misjudged the stretch, and the timing. He missed, did my friend Pyeberry. Like a shot bird, he plunged down, down, to the clump of bushes below, and bounced on the ground.

The boys rushed forward. Pyeberry's face was blue-grey, his eyelids fluttering and his fingers twitching. I pushed through, wrapping my blanket around him and shouting his name. Niddle was holding the others back, telling them to give Pyeberry some air.

Somehow I stumbled back indoors. My fists thundered on Jarvey's door until he appeared, his own cheeks blotched with scarlet, and I told him what had happened.

Jarvey placed a hand on Pyeberry's forehead, gazing at him intently. 'He must be kept warm,' he said, covering Pyeberry with his own jacket, 'and don't try to move him yet.'

Coughing, Jarvey loped to Bulloughby's study, leaving every door wide open. Jarvey's reasonable, insistent voice rose against our headmaster's reluctant growl. Then, with a roar, Bulloughby stormed out to see the fallen boy. Angrily, he ordered some older pupils to carry Pyeberry inside the school. Jarvey went with them.

'The rest of you – wait here!' Bulloughby ordered, his eyes blazing.

It was dusk before we were let back inside. For the next three days we waited for Pyeberry to return to us, but he did not.

'There's news,' Jarvey told Niddle and me at last. 'Your young friend Pyeberry's been sent home.'

So Pyeberry was a Returnable, though to what we did not know. I suspected that Jarvey had something to do with this choice, and I hoped that Pyeberry was now happy. Poor Niddle grew anxious and quiet, as if he feared he might be next in Grindle's line of victims.

Not long after Pyeberry had gone, Grindle started up again. He shoved me across the yard.

'Up, up, up!' he shouted, his gang stamping their feet as my hands clutched at the ivy. Then, when I was almost at the top, the uproar stopped. There was silence, except for the cawing of the crows. Had I gone suddenly deaf?

Bulloughby was holding Grindle tight by the nose. 'Enough!' he yelled. 'Down, Vermin, down now. There is to be no more of this clambering, do you hear? Don't hang there blinking like a fool, boy. Get down!'

Why had Mr Bulloughby come to my aid? Why, despite everything, did he choose to take some care of me? Was I wanted for someone or for some purpose?

Back then I didn't know the answers and I didn't care, because from that day on the climbing task was at an end.

CHAPTER 14

MEANWHILE, REVENGE

Scrope gnawed away at his fingernails, but many other things gnawed away at him these days. Time had not eased his mind.

Always he nursed the knowledge that Adeline – the dear, drowned soul – had chosen his brother, Albert. Always he nursed the knowledge that if he, Scrope, had been the first son, Adeline might have chosen him instead.

Always there was – Scrope shook his head fretfully – the knowledge of that child, Mouse. Though the wretched boy was far away, Scrope had no peace. At night, dreams snatched at him, dreams of a half-seen face, and he woke unable to tell whether it was his lost Adeline or that boy – her son – he had seen.

Moreover, Scrope could feel his own good fortune failing, and he found it hard to fix his attention on the cards. His spinning golden guinea had fallen and revealed itself as a dented copper penny. Mr Button had, as ever, been helpful about extending his loans, but Scrope had seen a greedier glint in that man's eyes.

Maybe, thought Scrope, if the matter of the Epsilon inheritance was clearer, Lady Fortune might smile on him more sweetly. Perhaps this was the right time to get a new will signed. Helpful lawyers could be found later. It was certainly worth a try.

Scrope chose a pleasant, mellow afternoon, when the sun shone like gold through the drawing-room windows, and the scent of full-blown roses wafted in from the gardens.

'Father?'

Scrope slid the prepared document on to the table, in front of the old man. The names of Albert and Adeline had disappeared. Now it was the boy's name that stood at the top of the list, though Scrope's own name nudged neatly up against it. Scrope, the heir-almost-in-waiting.

With pen, inkwell and sealing wax to hand, Scrope tried to sound both caring and kind.

'Father, if you would add your name . . .' His long finger pointed to the space left for the old man's signature. 'I can add names of witnesses later. It will be no trouble.'

'Pah!' With unusual energy, old Epsilon pushed the document away as if it was nothing. He dragged a faded newspaper clipping from his waistcoat pocket and waved it in Scrope's face, shouting furiously.

'*LOST!*' he screeched. 'Can you not read, Scrope?

The ship is missing. Albert is *LOST!*'

'Father, it has been more than three years since –'

'Do you not understand? They are merely LOST! They are NOT YET FOUND!' He tore the unsigned will in half and threw it back at Scrope. 'Leave me, you foolish man!'

Scrope's hopes shrivelled away. Though he had stayed where his father wanted him and did what he was asked – almost – even after all this time Epsilon treated him as if he was nothing. Bile surged up in his throat. Unfair, unfair.

The moment Scrope entered his own room, he thrust the tattered pieces into the fire. As the parchment blazed, he paced up and down, up and down, raging at everything: at Albert, Adeline, Epsilon, the boy. He was trapped by each and every one of them.

As he strode past a small table, he knocked it so hard that it toppled. A bowl of dried flower heads spilled across the carpet, filling the room with the soft nursery scent of lavender.

Hah! Nursery! Scrope grimaced. If that nursery maid had not interfered all those years ago, things would have worked out. This was all her fault.

Now, while he was suffering here, that silly Hanny lived on at the farm, as happy as the day was long. She did not even have to worry about looking after the wretched child, for the boy had been taken away from her. Curse her, curse her! So unfair!

In fact, Scrope determined, it was about time that things should be made fairer, a lot fairer. That bold

Hanny should be punished for what she had done. She should get what she deserved. She should know what bad luck was like. She would!

Suddenly Scrope felt he had a grasp on things again. He would summon Mr Button and ask him to send some of his special friends to Roseberry Farm. Scrope wanted Hanny to know how angry he was, to make sure Hanny knew how it felt to suffer one's plans being spoiled.

Hah! His friend Mr Button was not one to resist that sort of a challenge. Scrope folded his hands across his waistcoat, and savoured a moment of satisfaction.

By the end of the week, Friend Button had sent four of his men to visit Roseberry Farm. A job worth doing was a job worth doing well.

PASSING TIME

I grew. The clothes Ma had made me fell away to rags. How many other boys had worn the garments that dressed me, I did not know, nor who else had worn the broken shoes on my filthy feet.

Seasons passed, and passed again, and three or four years had disappeared. Boys arrived, boys went, but Niddle and I were still among those at Murkstone Hall.

Bulloughby was watching me more and more, his eyes full of a deep resentment, as if I was to blame for something. Often, in the darkest corridors, I glanced over my shoulder to be sure I knew what was behind me.

Murkstone Hall had patches of happiness too. Every Sunday, if Jarvey was well, he read out lines from the Bible, and long poems about King Arthur and Odysseus and Hercules and other heroes. Those words had far more music and enchantment than Madam Claudine's dreary fragments of facts.

Sometimes we learned scenes from plays and spoke the lines aloud.

'Declaim, boys, but don't let your tongue trip you up. Speak slowly and clearly!' Jarvey said, trying not to wheeze. 'A strong voice is a great benefit, and will serve its owner well. Now, let me hear those lines again.'

When the weather was bad, or if Jarvey was too ill, Niddle and I learned what we could for ourselves. We went to the library on the second floor, where mildewed stacks of books were strewn around like miniature mountain ranges. We discovered stories and legends, though often pages were so glued and furrowed by damp that we had to imagine the missing scenes, or act out fights and adventures without knowing which hero became the victor, or whether the monstrous dragon had perished after all.

When we played out those stories, in that gloomy library, I sometimes wondered who exactly was real and who was not. Was Merlin real, or Arthur, or were they just an ancient dream? Was I real, or was I just a forgotten story? Was my happy life with Ma no more than a tale I'd dreamed up?

I decided that my stories should be true, because I needed to believe in them more than I needed to believe in Murkstone Hall. In my stories, I could climb and fly and swoop and dive. No one could stop me, or lay money on me, or judge me. In every tale and telling, I could escape and become free of all that held me down.

*

One afternoon, when the weather was particularly foul, Jarvey sent me with a pile of books to his study. Rain had come pouring through the ceiling of the main corridor, leaving the floor awash, so I took the route that passed by the entrance of the school, which was too close to Bulloughby's parlour for my liking.

With a gush of wind and water, Mr Button entered the school. Rain ran from the brim of his hat and his umbrella left a trail of puddles as he strode towards our dear headmaster's door.

Nothing ventured, nothing gained, I thought, and peered around the piled volumes.

'Mr Button?' I tried to sound calm, though my knees shook. 'Is there any news from Roseberry Farm? Any news of my Ma, sir?'

Button's eyes gleamed as if he was laughing, and at me. His rosy cheeks bobbed in some silent amusement, making the raindrops jump on the tip of his nose.

'Aha! Of course! It's dear little Mouse. How you've grown! Well, boy, I swear there is no news for you from Roseberry Farm, not any news at all! Your Ma sends you no message, boy. That is how life goes, I fear.' Briskly Button entered the parlour. I glimpsed Bulloughby's face as he shrank back from his visitor.

I felt uneasy, as if something had happened that I should know about.

DEBTS AND DOUBTS

'What is the matter?' Button said, gazing around the Headmaster's parlour.

Bulloughby leaned forward, clenching and unclenching his fingers. 'This is how it is, Button. This Mouse boy. This Vermin. He grows, he eats, he needs learning.'

Button nodded slowly. 'So?'

Bulloughby grew more insistent. 'But I get almost nothing for my troubles. Is so little still sent for the child?'

Button pursed up his plump mouth, seeming neither pleased nor displeased, though he was calculating his next action. Had he pushed Bulloughby a little too far? He needed to soothe his disgruntled partner.

'I will mention it,' Button began hastily, 'the very next time I visit Epton – ah!' he broke off, a little rattled to have revealed so much. He recovered his composure, and continued smoothly, 'The very next time I visit that grand house.'

'Grand house?' echoed Bulloughby, who had heard the illustrious name.

'Yes.' Button beamed as brightly as he could. He even patted Bulloughby's hand. 'No need to bother yourself. Trust me.'

Once Button had gone, Bulloughby thought as hard as his head could bear. At last he set off for a room he rarely visited. Struggling up dismal flights of stairs, he entered the neglected library.

Shuffling along the dusty shelves, he searched here and there until he grasped a stained, broken-backed directory. He thumbed the pages until he came to the index, and ran his eye down the alphabetical properties. Epton?

Bulloughby would – yes! – he would be heard.

Far away, within that grand house, Scrope was feeling happier. A run of winnings had thrown more finance into his hands. As for Albert and Adeline, it stood to reason that his father, growing older, would gradually but surely forget them and the child. Scrope tried to forget about Mouse too, though Button would insist on sending occasional reports.

Then an envelope arrived, written in an ugly, un-familiar scribble. Scrope read, frowning. It was a begging letter from Murkstone Hall, the very place where that brat had been sent. The so-called Headmaster Bulloughby was grumbling about the cost of looking after the boy. Ha! A simple thing to deal with, thought Scrope.

Scrope's note, when it arrived on Bulloughby's desk, curled arrogantly across the page.

'*How dare you send me your begging letters! The arrangement will not change.*'

The signature was almost unreadable. Sneep? Snip? Scrape? Scrope? Bulloughby scrunched up the grand words from the grand house and kicked them across the room.

'How dare this man tell me this! While he luxuriates in comfort, I keep the wretched child hidden from his sight.'

The more he dwelled on the matter, the clearer things became. Out in the wide world, boys struggled to exist. Here, under his very own roof, boys lolled about idly. The only person who struggled at Murkstone Hall was he, himself. Headmaster Bulloughby's rage festered and grew.

All at once, strewing papers and pens and ornaments, Bulloughby rushed to the mantelpiece. He snatched up the framed portrait of Madam Claudine and held it briefly to his chest. Then he placed her firmly face down in a drawer, under his second-best snuffbox.

'Now you have gone, I am going to do just what I like in this place, Mother, no matter what Button thinks,' he declared, full of determination. 'And what I like is that the verminous boy will not cost me a farthing-piece more. If no one else cares for the child, nor do I, and nor will I, for sure!'

Bulloughby charged along the corridors towards the kitchen. He halted by an ancient arch, from where worn steps curved down to unseen regions. The steps were carpeted with billowing clouds of steam that rose up, condensed and dripped greasily down from the vaulted roof overhead.

'If that devil ever asks, he can have the child back with pleasure. Until then, I am using that young vermin as I choose.'

He bellowed a name into the swirling mists below.

A LADLEFUL OF TROUBLE

A message came for Jarvey, calling him home. He left
without saying a word, as if it was any other day. It was
not. It was a day of changes.

As Niddle and I nibbled hungrily at the grey bread,
Bulloughby himself entered the hall. He strode to the
raised table at the far end and sat down. Picking up a
bottle, he slurped something down, then stuffed both a
gobbet of meat and a whole potato into his mouth and
chewed noisily. His eyes scoured the room.

All went quiet. I could hear every boy's heart beating, even Grindle's, though he wore a fixed grin.

Then Bulloughby rose. He put his hands on his hips
and stuck his belly out, as his gaze rolled across our
heads. Like a maddened bull he shook his head.
Though the orange wig moved a little, not one of us
dared laugh. We were all waiting. It was someone's

turn, and for what we did not know.

'Boys of Murkstone Hall,' Bulloughby roared, 'my heart is broken. For many years I cared for one of you, in hope and in expectation. But now news has come that those expectations are false. They have no substance. No glitter, no gold, no reward at all! I find I have nurtured this creature, fed him, educated him – and all for no advantage. We have an imposter in our midst, boys, and it is time this wretched creature repaid some of what he owes me.'

Bulloughby thrust out a stubby finger and pointed at me.

'Stop! Yes, you! Vermin!' he cried. 'Put down my food. Leave my table. There is only one place fit for you, and that is with the vermin you are named after. Grindle?' His son rose to his feet, grinning inanely, and loped towards me. 'Take this despicable child down to the kitchen. For years he has drained the coffers of Murkstone Hall. Now he will get the lowly place he deserves. Grindle, away with him.'

Niddle started to speak, but I was already tight in Grindle's armlock. He dragged me down the hall, down the corridors, down to the reeking, steam-filled steps. He thumped and bumped me against every corner, until we reached that arch, that entrance to the world beneath our feet, from which rattles and crashes echoed alarmingly.

'Here you are, Shankbone!' called Grindle, wary of what lay deep in that vault. Though he tried to scoff, fear shook his voice. 'Pa's sent you some help.'

Grindle shoved me forward and scuttled back up the

steps. My life in the classroom was over. I had become a servant, a scullion, a thing that lived beneath the floor.

I toppled forward and fell on my hands. Slowly, as I stood up, the steam cleared a little. The kitchen was lit by the glowing red fire of an enormous iron oven, where bubbling pots of gruel sucked and gurgled like molten lava. Several skinny cats arched their backs, hissing and waving their long tails.

Out of the gloom, a huge figure lurched at me. The firelight shone on a large balding head and a misshapen pudding of a face, which contained two fierce smoke-blackened eyes. His rough clothes were layered with grease, and what seemed to be an apron was not much cleaner than a coal sack. He paused, and rubbed one enormous hand across his forehead as if he was trying to work out what I was doing there.

Some kind of speech grumbled in the man's chest and rumbled around in his throat. Finally his mouth opened, and a terrible noise rolled out. The sound repeated and repeated, booming out of his thickened mouth.

'Oooaaaaoooo? Ooooaaaaoooo? Ooooaaaaoooor?'

Something was wrong with the man's speech. I listened and listened, and at last I worked out his words. 'I'm Mouse, Mr Shankbone,' I squeaked.

'Erk?' He peered at me suspiciously in case this was a trick. 'Erk here?'

'Yes, I'll work,' I said. Then I rubbed my bruised elbow, pointed to my arm, and knee, and cheek, and said, 'Grindle!

He grunted, nodding, and suddenly spat at the steps. Then he cuffed me playfully around the head. 'Booooaaaaaarrrrrrrby!' he roared, and laughed aloud, like an ogre in an ancient tale.

'Come!' He trudged towards a sink in the corner. It was stacked with dishes, encircled by crusted pans, all of them used many weeks before.

'This lot?' I asked.

He nodded, giving a broad grin, and held out a large wooden bucket.

I hauled the bucket to the pump outside, but as I returned to the scullery a large dog dragged itself out from under a broken bench, sharp teeth showing within its open jaws. I stepped back so fast that water slopped over my feet. I stood trembling, still shaken by my new situation, by all that Bulloughby had done, by this creature before me.

Then I thought of the old half-blind hound that lived at Roseberry Farm. He had been happy to sleep in the sun, but was wary of strangers and toddlers he did not know and could barely see. I pretended I was meeting him again.

'Good dog!' I walked steadily, keeping well out of the dog's way as I stepped past, so he knew he would not be kicked or hurt. Though he growled, he did not move from his place.

I found a greasy crust on one of Bulloughby's plates and took it out to the dog, dropping it quickly on the ground and backing away. The beast sniffed, as if people had tempted him with bad things in the past, then, with a snatch and a snap, the crust was gone. His tail did not wag, but he licked his chops and yawned.

'Aaaaaaroo?' Shankbone had shuffled out behind me. He elbowed me cheerily.

'Yes, I'm all right.'

He pointed at the enormous dog, and groaned again. 'That's Dog Bruno!' he was telling me.

Dog Bruno looked at me steadily, gave a peaceable snort and went back to sleep. We took one more breath of the fresh air outside then turned back to work.

I did what I could as best I could in that kitchen. Scraping the congealed fat off the dishes was hard and horrid work, and at first the piles seemed to grow greater rather than smaller, as Shankbone found dishes that should have been washed, once upon a time. Then the anxious feeling inside me eased.

True, filth festered all around, and there was the stench of an ill-kept kitchen, but here I was out of the blast of life above stairs. I was safe, if only for a short while. Shankbone's low grumblings and Bruno's sleepy growls reminded me of the sounds of the farm. That night, though I had to huddle close to the fire to keep out the dreadful cold, I was sorry for Niddle left alone upstairs. This kitchen was not so bad as I feared. As I worked, I felt my body and heart growing stronger.

Why had I never run from this dreadful place? Why hadn't I escaped? At first I kept a kind of hope alive, though holidays came and went and nothing changed. Button would visit, bringing no news for me, but I always thought next time, next time.

Next time never came. No message arrived, no word from Ma, no urgent call. Just silence. Maybe I was Not

Returnable. Maybe – and that was the fear – they did not want me back.

Gradually something in me shut down, and there were days when I felt my life at the farm might have been only a fantasy, a dream. I tried not to think about that time in case it had never been true.

Maybe something has to happen to make someone choose the fear outside over the fear inside. One day it would come, but not today.

I learned that each day's work was the same as the last. For breakfast we stirred a ladle around in the vast gruel pot, and for supper we stirred it again. When Shankbone had something to add – a handful of oats, a few old potatoes – he dropped them in. When there was nothing, he added jugs of water, thinning the gruel still further. The only proper meals were for Bulloughby or for Button's occasional visits. Nothing of any goodness was spared for the boys.

One cold morning I woke to the yowling of cats fighting over a pair of rabbits dragged in from the grounds. By the time I had chased the cats away, the rabbits were dead and only good for the pot. Shankbone looked at the larder where he kept the food for Bulloughby.

'Shankbone,' I said, 'the boys are starving.' The man hesitated, swaying on his heels. 'Truly,' I added.

Slowly Shankbone turned, grinned and plodded over to the vat of broth. Swiftly he took a knife from a drawer and skinned and gutted the carcases. Soon both rabbits had sunk into the grey liquid. The vat boiled and seethed, and the good meat dissolved in the broth, but not completely.

We found this out later, when Bulloughby descended the stairs. He grasped a thick walking stick, and waved it as if he was as scared of Shankbone as Shankbone was terrified of him.

Puffing himself up, Bulloughby reached into his waistcoat pocket and held up a delicate bone. 'Did you do it? Did you put meat in the boys' broth?'

We said nothing.

'Haven't I told you before? Meat is bad for boys, Shankbone. Makes them rebellious.'

Shankbone glowered and swayed to and fro.

'If you had put meat into the broth,' Bulloughby continued, 'I might not be pleased. I might even let the constables know the bad things you've done. It's a long, long list, and I know it all, don't I? Button told me, didn't he? Of course, you can explain all that to the constables. You're so good at explaining, aren't you, Shankbone?'

They faced each other. Shankbone was silent.

Bulloughby darted forward, seized my ear, and twisted it hard. 'Boys are good at spying,' he cried. 'So did old Shankbone use meat? Has he been wasting our money? Tell, boy. Tell!'

'Meat?' I gasped. 'Meat? Yes, there was meat.'

A shiver crossed Shankbone's face.

'I was watching the pot last night,' I stuttered. 'You know old Rag-Eared Tigg?' I waved my arm towards the scrawny cat that sat on a potato sack, scratching its fleas. 'Well,' I explained, 'Tigg came creeping under the table and suddenly he started up a pair of rats. They scooted up across the table and jumped over on to the cooker and up, ready to race across the saucepans. But the lid was off, sir, so those rats couldn't keep hold and – *whoomph!* – one went in and – *whoomph!* – in went the other! There's where we got the meat, sir. Perhaps I should have told you straight away, sir?'

As I finish this story, a smile filled Bulloughby's face. He was pleased to think of the boys sucking at rat bones.

'Did you want some, sir?' I suggested, keeping my face as straight as a starched cloth. 'There's some left.'

Bulloughby whirled round and glared at me, suspicious-like. He wagged a threatening finger at Shankbone. 'Take care! I'll get you both one day.' He hurried away to his own territory.

Shankbone and I looked at each other. He lunged at me and ruffled my hair, and laughter wheezed from him like a pair of old bellows.

'Mouse and rats!' he roared. 'Mouse and rats!'

CHAPTER 18

AN AGREEMENT

'The kitchen? Explain!' Button folded his arms and pursed his lips. 'Since when have you done things without asking my advice?'

'If you weren't here, I couldn't ask, could I? Did what seemed right.' Bulloughby challenged him, scowling back. 'I'm just making sure the boy gets the care he deserves, aren't I? I reckon that if I don't get much for him, he should get little from me. You of all people, Button, should understand that.'

Button scratched his chin, unwilling to rearrange the profits within his own coffers.

'The brat's useful down in the scullery,' Bulloughby stated, 'which he's not up here – and no more likely to come to any harm, not unless it's his own stupid fault. I'll write news of him, same as usual.'

'But what would you say if the child was asked for?'

Button's eyes narrowed.

'Huh!' Bulloughby held up one hand, spreading out his fingers and thumb. He thrust them at Button. 'See them? Five! That's how many times a Murkstone boy's been truly asked for, been truly Returned in the last three years. Boys get sent here so people can forget 'em, don't they? You knows that as well as I do, Button. So I'm not worried. Are you?'

Button silently weighed up the situation. Maybe, with Bulloughby so unpredictable, it was best to let the boy stay where he was.

'No,' said Button, 'I'm not. But if there's any trouble, Bulloughby, I'll swear it was all your fault, and that I knew nothing about it. Understand?' Button drew himself up as tall as he could, and leaned over the seated Bulloughby. 'Just don't rearrange things without checking with me. Never again!'

Bulloughby gave a careless shrug.

CHAPTER 19

HIDDEN WORDS

I was scrubbing away at the kitchen table when I felt someone behind me.

'Hello, Mouse,' said Jarvey. 'How are you?'

My scrubbing brush shot to the floor. 'What are you doing here? When did you come back?'

'Only this morning, Mouse,' he said. There were dark rings beneath Jarvey's eyes, but the visit to his family, wherever they were, had brightened his smile. 'Niddle told me that you didn't come to classes any more, so I came to find you.'

I begged. I pleaded. 'Don't take me back upstairs, Mr Jarvey. Don't know what I did wrong, but it's all right down here. It's better.'

Shankbone shuffled forward out of the gloom. He raised a ladle protectively and made his odd grumbling sound. 'Who's this, Mouse?'

Jarvey understood. He pointed upwards. 'I teach the boys,' he said. 'Upstairs.'

'Heh-heh! Hard job,' Shankbone chuckled. 'Bulloughby don't want boys to eat much, and he don't want them to learn much either.'

'I think you're right there,' agreed Jarvey.

'Sir? Why'd you come back?' This mystified me.

'A man must do something, and not be a burden,' Jarvey said. He glanced cautiously back up the stairs and leaned towards me. 'I discovered something before I left, Mouse.'

'What?'

'I went into Bulloughby's parlour to get the wages he owed me.'

Shankbone clapped his rough worn hands against his thighs, laughing noiselessly. 'Money? From him?'

'Wait! That's not the story,' whispered Jarvey. 'He flew into a foul temper, saying he had no money left to give me. He dragged out desk drawers and scattered papers everywhere.' Jarvey looked at me strangely. 'I picked up a handful to give back – and they were about you, Mouse.'

'Ma?' I cried, as if I'd fallen. 'Were they from my Ma?'

'No. These were scribbled reports *about* you, to be sent to somebody else.'

'Who?'

'That's it. The papers were only drafts with no names. Bulloughby grabbed them from me and thrust them away.' My face must have shown Jarvey how I felt. 'Sorry. Not much information,' he added, 'but I thought you should know.'

I turned away. I didn't answer. I honestly didn't care about whoever it was that Bulloughby was writing to, because I'd had – for a moment – such hope of hearing from my Ma. To find there was not a single word filled me with such a homesickness and longing that I could not bear it. I stomped away into a corner of the kitchen. I did not even want to look at Jarvey. How could he have disappointed me so?

'Mouse, come and speak to me.'

I did not. I'd tried to get over everything, to survive these endless days, but Jarvey's information had made my heart feel as raw as the day Button brought me here.

'Take good care of him, Mr Shankbone,' said Jarvey at last, and left.

I stacked up logs for the fire, furiously asking myself why I hadn't questioned Jarvey further. He might have recalled a word, a phrase. He might even have seen an address. I did not ask because I was angry with him, and angry with myself for letting Bulloughby have power over me.

I thumped the basket down by the oven and went back to scrubbing away at the stone flags. As the grey suds bubbled around my boots, I thought about Bulloughby's words as he sent me down to the kitchen: 'An imposter in our midst, boys.'

That dull-brained, orange-wigged oaf had some sort of secret about me, and I didn't know what it was. All I had was a single stupid medal that stuck into my bony ribs whenever I pulled the sacking around me in the cold of the night. That night I truly felt lost.

CHAPTER 20

STRANGE FRUIT

The days struggled on. I sloshed around below the stairs, preparing the everlasting school gruels and broths, and the greasy chops that Bulloughby crunched through each day. I waded through peelings and bones and swill and ash. I measured out cupfuls of damp flour and slapped the grey bread into shape.

While we worked, Shankbone liked me to tell him stories, especially if there was food in them. So I told him all the old tales I'd heard from Ma and Isaac and from Jarvey, making the crusts into meals, and meals into feasts, and feasts into enormous banquets.

I told him about magical mixing spoons, and huge pies full of blackbirds, and gingerbread mansions, and vats of everlasting, ever-increasing porridge, thick with cream. I described great mayoral banquets put on by the rich Dick Whittington, and the feasts of the gods in Ancient

Greece, and the celebrations at King Arthur's Round Table. I even told him about that once-upon-a-time fruit dropping from the branches in the Garden of Eden.

There was a lot more food in my imaginary tales than in any versions you might know, but the happiness and plenty seemed to nourish Shankbone's mind, and he hummed cheerfully to himself as he stirred the scum on his watery broths.

Now and again Mr Button liked to check on things around Murkstone Hall, including the kitchen. He usually appeared at the top of the kitchen steps, nose wrinkling in disgust, and flung a few coins towards Shankbone. This cash was for next Higgins's day, which was when Shankbone was supposed to refill his bleak, empty larder.

Higgins, with his greasy cap and once bright waistcoat, must have been a proper trader at one time, but he had sunk to carting scraps and rotting vegetables – collected from who knows where – to places like the kitchen of Murkstone Hall.

Button liked to check on Higgins's visits too. His round face appeared in the window above the yard, and his hard round eyes squinted down so he could see the contents of Higgins's cart.

'Nosy one, that!' sniffed Higgins, as he haggled with Shankbone for old times' sake, so we knew he did not like Button much.

Higgins was cursed by both his memory and his imagination. When he hauled sacks of woody carrots into the larder, he sighed for the sweetness they would have had when they were fresh-grown. As he swung sacks of wrinkled, rotted pippins, he remembered the scent of apple-blossom orchards. He knew his third-hand goods were fit for nothing but Murkstone's mean vats, but Higgins was as much a dreamer as Shankbone, and as such they looked forward to meeting and sharing their grumbles.

Now it so happened that as Shankbone and I were outside, lugging in some logs, a window crashed open overhead. We heard yells and shrieks above, then a shower of illustrated pages fluttered down, crumpled and torn. Grindle and his gang were rioting up there in the library.

I ran and scooped up a batch of the pages, before the wind could carry them away, and pushed them inside my shirt to read later. Very slowly, Shankbone bent down and picked up a page. He cupped it in his hand as if it was a great mystery and then, bewildered, held the page out to me as if for help.

What Shankbone revealed was an illustration. It was of a strange fruit, spiked and golden, and crowned with a tuft of green leaf blades. Beside it, on a great dish, lay another such fruit. That fruit was cut through, and each slice was edged like the cogs that had once turned the roasting spit. Syrup oozed like honey from that painted yellow fruit, and our mouths watered just looking at it. No fruit like this had ever grown on Roseberry Farm.

Then the strangest thing occurred. I knew what this thing was, and not from one of Jarvey's books or stories.

Suddenly I had a scent of this fruit in my nostrils,

and a taste of it on my tongue. Sometime, somewhere, I must have seen one, eaten one, but where? I had never lived anywhere where such fruit grew, not that I knew about. Shankbone hid his picture greedily away, but I couldn't hide away my mystery.

That night the dazzling dream came, as glorious as an Aladdin's cave, a palace where I had and had not been. At first I resisted. I wanted my dream to be of the farm and Ma and Isaac and all I knew. I would not go where these thoughts were taking me.

But my feet pattered into the dream, across an expanse of black and white tiled floor. I looked up, entranced at this marvellous place. The sunlight burst through a canopy of wide, gently waving leaves and flickered through creepers cascading from a high glass sky. Brilliant birds screeched and flew from branch to branch, and small green frogs leaped into deep moss-lined pools.

As I pushed aside the soft ferns, each frond glistening with drops of moisture, my hands took hold of a wonderful iron ladder. Its narrow, white-painted rungs circled around a tall fluted pillar, rising up to where the cogs and rods and spokes were turning, shifting glittering panels of glass that let in the cool breeze. Up I went, one rung, two rungs, three, four, five. My feet seemed those of a much smaller child.

Just as I thought I would reach the top and understand everything, I was lifted down, and someone with a gentle voice popped a thin slice of this yellow fruit into my little mouth.

'Pineapple!' I said, as my eyes flickered open on that stinking, greasy kitchen.

The exotic fruit had enchanted Shankbone too. Each night, when the worst of our work was done, he took out the crumpled page and gloated over it. As weeks passed, he became miserly and watchful. He snarled at me if I wasted the tiniest scrap or peeled any vegetable too thickly. He had a plan.

The next time the cart arrived, Shankbone pulled Higgins close under the outside wall, out of sight of the nosy-parker window. He whispered urgently, desperately. Higgins nodded briefly. His wrinkled-walnut face broke into an amused smile. Higgins had heard the voices and sounds of Murkstone Hall on his visits, and would not want to work here, not he. He was happy to help.

Eventually, another day came, and another Higgins's cart. As the usual delivery of shrunken turnips and withered greens took place, Shankbone glanced warily up at Button's usual window.

'Now,' he rumbled.

Higgins grabbed a bundle of stained sacking from under the cart and handed it across. Shankbone held the bundle as carefully as if it was a baby, and I saw tears in his eyes.

'Right then, my old mate. See you next month. There'll be more rotten apples about by then,' Higgins said, winking, trundling his cart away. Shankbone, trembling with anticipation, carried his prize indoors.

We went through the scullery, into the kitchen, and

there was Button, gloating and smiling. He stepped forward, intending to discover whatever was inside Shankbone's bundle. As his pink fingertips felt the knobbly ridges beneath the sacking, I spoke up brightly.

'It's a fine sheep's head, sir!'

Button recoiled, disgusted. He glared at us, then whirled on his heel and left.

I heard a deep grumbling noise behind me. 'Thank you, Mouse,' said Shankbone.

That night, when all above was still, Shankbone uncovered his jewel, his golden fruit, his prize of the orient.

'P is for Pineapple,' I said, suddenly, and that was odd, for the voice in my ear was not Ma, who would have had her P for simple Plum Pie, nor was it Madam Claudine, for her P was for Porcupine. Whose voice was it?

The honeyed scent was strangely familiar. As we sucked at the shreds of the great fruit, I knew it was a taste I had met before.

''Tis a gentleman's fruit,' mumbled Shankbone, sipping the sweet-sour juice.

But I was too young to have been a gentleman without noticing, so how had I got this knowledge? If ever I got back to Roseberry Farm, I would ask about this, and the thousand other questions that had been piling up in my mind. What else had Ma never told me, and why?

Soon enough, Shankbone's magical fruit was gone and our hopeful excitement ended. The days trudged on, wearying me as sorely as Shankbone's cast-off boots.

The weeks, in their greasy grey aprons, arrived and departed.

One dawn I lay and tried, as I often did, to remember the places I'd passed on my long-ago journey. So many days I'd travelled through that list, but now the names and pictures were fading, and my imaginary map was full of empty spaces. Would I ever – and this shocked me – be able to find my way back home again?

Maybe the desperation of that moment was why things started to break apart. One thing certainly broke most dramatically.

For years the huge vats had been hauled up and down the service shaft by chains clanking round an ancient pulley wheel. This device wound and ground, taking up food, returning discarded dishes to the depths where Shankbone and I toiled in our grubby contentment.

One night, as I waited at the foot of the shaft, listening to Bulloughby's voice ranting above, everything halted. The descending tray tilted, sending crockery and cutlery clattering down. Then, with an awful grating sound, the great wheel above gave way. Worn chains broke free and came rattling down the shaft swift and deadly as an iron snake.

I leaped back just in time, as the rusted links slashed at the brickwork and cracked the flagstones on the floor. Grease and shredded food came splattering after.

Above, Grindle and his gang howled down the shaft, mocking the mess. Then Bulloughby joined in, shouting curses, while Shankbone and I toiled to clear what we could, dragging the chains away into the corner by the swill buckets.

When all was quiet upstairs, Shankbone and I went to see the damage. The huge wheel hung loose from the wall, and the plaster was a web of cracks. The hoist would never work again.

Shankbone peered about with big, baleful eyes, like a creature wary of his surroundings. 'Bust and broken, Mouse, and us with it,' he said, wringing his great raw hands.

From now on all the food would have to be carried upstairs, to the very place where Grindle and his gang lorded it over the others. Shankbone hidden in his gloomy lair could be feared, but up in the hall he'd be at the boys' mercy.

He shook. 'Mouse, I can't do this. I can't come up here.'

It was true. Shankbone, with his smashed voice, whose groans I hardly even noticed now, would be like an injured hound in a dogfight.

'Then I'll do it,' I said. 'I'll come up here.'

I could bear it, I told myself, if I took it one meal at a time. That was how I would manage.

His face was wreathed with gratitude.

The first meal was not easy. I struggled among the tables, handing out dishes and bowls.

'Who said you could come back up here, Vermin?' Grindle yelled, his gang squeaking at me in mockery.

'Your schooling's stuck in the slop bucket now, mouse-brain.'

Grindle flicked a chewed crust at me, which started the others pushing and shoving at me as I staggered with trays between the rows.

If I retreated, as I longed to do, I'd be letting down both Shankbone and the small boys who sat with hunger in their eyes. Once I was their size, wasn't I? I hadn't forgotten that lonely emptiness.

'Mouse?' said Niddle, who sat there helping them. I paused, trying to reply, but too much had changed, and I turned away. Pinched and punched along each row, I set dishes down and went back for more, and more, and more. As the mouths filled, the name-calling ceased, though I was soured with anger. I did not know how long I could stand it.

The days became weeks, and weeks became months. Then one afternoon, as the sky darkened outside the kitchen window, I caught a reflection in the glass. At first, I did not recognise what I was seeing.

The boy was taller and older than I expected, and as skinny as two crossed broomsticks. The filthy sleeves on his worn-out shirt reached halfway down his arms, and his brown eyes, rimmed with dirt, peered out of a thin, pinched face. Two grubby ears stuck through fronds of tufty, matted hair.

Was this sad, greasy creature who I wanted to be?

SILENCE BREAKS

The old man had been ill over the winter, but as the trees covered themselves with green leaves, and the sun shone across the lawns, old Epsilon remembered a life other than his own.

He turned his face towards Scrope. 'The boy?' he asked, as if time had not gone by. 'Where is he, Scrope? I need to see him. Bring him to me.'

'Father?' Scrope said, astonished.

'Now, Scrope! I want to see Mouse,' insisted the old man, tugging angrily at the blankets covering his bony knees. 'Do you never listen? I want him here! You do such things for me, don't you? You are always fussing, arranging my life and my lands, aren't you? Get the child. It will be the worse for you if you don't!'

Scrope bit his lip. The imp in his head mocked him as he thought of Murkstone Hall. 'The boy is away at school, sir. Don't you remember? If you wish, I will happily bring him back.'

With luck, the journey would give him time to get some kind of story straight.

'Good.' Epsilon sniffed. 'Do it.'

Scrope, his mind in a turmoil, dipped his pen in the inkwell and scrawled a bitter message direct to Murkstone Hall.

'Bulloughby, be grateful, your task is ended! The old man wants to see the child, so I will be sending Button instructions for arranging the boy's return.'

Scrope blotted the letter.

So what did the boy look like now? Did he still have Albert's ears? Did he have Adeline's bright brown eyes? Even more worrying, what did the boy know about him, his kindly Uncle Scrope?

'Mouse,' he whispered. 'Young Mouse.' He had not spoken the child's name for a long time. 'What will I do with you?'

Folding the note firmly, he thrust it into an envelope. He would decide what to do when the wretched child was eventually brought home. Or should he decide now?

Scrope hesitated for a full day before he sent the envelope off on its journey, and that was one day too long.

THE LAST COURSE

I move. The rough sacks scratch my cheek. A family of cats, thin and hungry, slip down from the curve of my covers and away. They are not pets. They are angry and hungry, and they sleep against me for warmth. Do I mind? No, I do not, for the nights down here in the depths of the school are so, so cold. As the cats slink away, their eyes shine, for they are off to scavenge the corridors of Murkstone Hall.

But I am lying wide awake now, and it is because the dream came again tonight. Not that strange bright dream, which is happy, though I do not understand much about it. No, it was the bad dream. I understand the bad dream very well, because it is from the time when I was first brought to this place.

I hold up my hand, stretching it out against the pale grey square of light that is the scullery window. I see my hand, as it is this morning, grimed with cinders, stinking of onions and dishwater. Nobody can keep clean down here in the kitchen, not me, not

Shankbone, not a single dish or kettle or spoon. Nobody cares, certainly not Bulloughby or Button.

The hand in the bad dream is almost clean, and it smells of hay and horses and the open air. It is a small child's hand. It is my hand as it was when I was taken away from the sweet life of Ma's farm. It is the hand I had when I trusted everyone.

All at once I long for that place so much. I long to see it again, and Ma and Isaac, no matter that somehow I have been deceived. I long for my life as it is now to be ended.

Overnight, as if there was a change in the wind, something shifted in my heart. The dream of the farm came too often to shake it away during the day. I no longer cared about surviving in Murkstone's depths. I needed to be gone.

For so many years I had dreamed about creeping out of the school while others were sleeping, but the kindness of Niddle and Jarvey and even poor Shankbone had tugged me into staying. Now my dream haunted me night and day, and escape clanged every minute in my brain.

On a day that began like any other, I carried a tray into the dining hall. I put down the food, then returned with more. The small boys snatched for pieces of broken bread and grabbed at the half-filled bowls.

As I came to Grindle's table he hissed, 'Collecting crumbs from the rich man's table, poor Mouse!' and he urged his gang to pay me secret pinches and punches as I went up and down.

I returned with yet another awkward tray, and Grindle stuck his foot out to trip me up. I tried to right myself for a moment, struggled to regain my balance, and did.

Then, all at once, I had had enough.

I tossed the tray and the plates up in a spinning arc, high above the heads of Grindle and his gang, so that a glorious shower of greasy gravy and lumps of gristle poured down, splattering across the table, pouring into their laps.

In one triumphant glance I saw the faces from other tables grinning with shock and delight, all wishing ill on the astonished Grindle. Some started cheering and stamping, but I waited no longer.

The urgent clanging of the dinner bell brought Mr Bulloughby hurrying from his room, so that he stood, arms outstretched, to block my way. With the roar of Grindle's gang growing at my back, I turned and raced off towards the stairs, legging it up all five flights to the bell tower.

The stone steps became narrow toeholds as I stumbled and scrambled up the twisting stairway. It was so dark I could hardly see where I was going, but I cared for nothing. Once or twice I fell and skinned my knees and elbows, but I pushed upwards, higher and higher.

At last daylight rushed into the stone turret. The narrow door above me hung half off its hinges. It swung with each gust, sending dry leaves swirling in the stairwell. I leaped up the last steps, through that bright rectangle of light and out on to the roof.

I paused, almost unable to believe the wide sky that now burst around my head or the wind that gathered up my breath. The world beyond the parapet wall whirled around me and made me stagger, and for a moment the tops of the nearest trees quivered with each gust, inviting me to step out into the weightless air. No. No. That long final drop was not what I wanted. That was not an answer.

Bulloughby was scrabbling way down in the stairwell. 'Get back here, boy!' he shouted. Grindle's curses came close behind, but excited calls and laughter rose up like a chorus of loud angels from within the building, bursting from every window.

'Go on, Mouse! Faster! Faster!'

'Get away. Please, please.'

'Good luck, great adventures, Mouse!'

'Remember us!'

'Run, run, run!'

Run? Of course, but where and how? From high up on the cracked bell tower, I saw the woods that surrounded the school, and the rough road beyond the school gates, and the empty moors. There was no living person in sight, only the dull known horror of Murkstone Hall below my feet. I had wedged the warped door shut with a loose tile, but it would not hold Bulloughby nor Grindle back for long.

A stone griffin, almost my own height, guarded one corner of the tower, its beak and wings powdered away by the weather.

'Vermin! Vermin!' Bulloughby roared, almost at the door.

I put my hand against the carving and felt the monster sway, loose at the base, ripe and ready to crash to the ground below. Winding my arms around it tightly, I heaved, and the griffin fell backwards.

'Thank you, Shankbone!' The kitchen work had given strength to my arms.

The griffin rolled – with an extra shove from me – up against the door. A monster to hold a monster, if only for a while.

I paused, glad of a moment of safety. If you can climb the walls for Grindle, you can climb for yourself, Mouse, I thought.

'Come back, come back!' Bulloughby whined, thumping at the door as if it mattered to him whether I climbed or tumbled.

But I would not come back for Bulloughby. I would not go back to him or Grindle or Button. Jarvey must take care of Niddle, and my poor friend Shankbone would have to look after himself.

I lowered myself over the parapet until my toes touched a narrow ledge, praying that the weathered stones were more secure than my toppled griffin. One hand followed another, one foot after another dug in, and down I went.

Bit by bit, like a child clinging fast to its parent, I edged down the lichen-covered tower until my boots nudged the firm ridge of roof tiles. My shredded fingernails were bleeding, but the hard climb was over. I was not big, nor mighty, but I was still definitely Mouse, unafraid of any height.

I slid down the far side of the roof and gained the old wing of Murkstone Hall. I scrambled down the twisted ivy and ran across the empty yard. I shinned over the

gate, plunging away through moor-grass, dropping down through hollows and dips among the furze and bracken. As I ran, almost sure now of my escape, a question came with each panting breath.

'Where are you going to, Mouse? Where are you going?' I asked myself.

And I knew the answer. I was running for my life. I was running home to Ma and Isaac and Roseberry Farm.

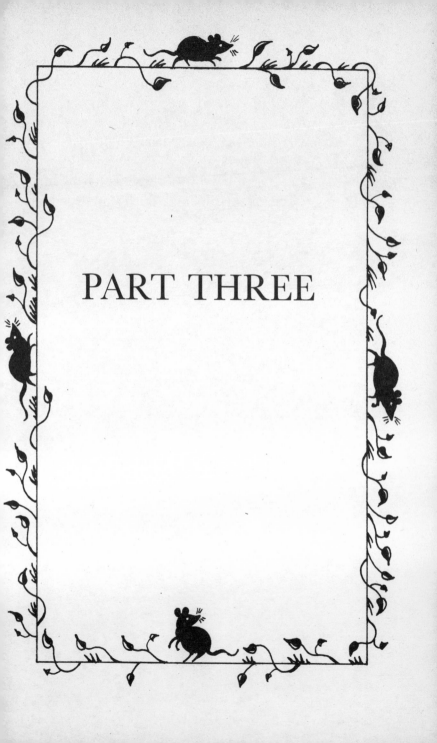

PART THREE

HOME

My journey back was long, and full of hail and rain and storm. My memories helped me in some places and led me astray at other times.

I hitched rides on carts. I stowed away on the top of slow, swaying coaches. I followed rivers busy with boats and barges. I walked and walked until my ankles were raw and my toenails blackened and fell off my feet. Some folk helped me; some didn't.

I plodded through mud and sheltered under trees and slept in sheepfolds. I drank from small streams, snatched food from fields and gardens and stole from markets and passing cartloads. My education had taught me well, and my climbing and clambering got me over walls and away from watchmen and constables more than once. Somehow I survived, and I felt the air grow warmer with each day's travelling.

I saw the chalk horse on its hillside, and that abbey with its square tower. I found some of the inns and market crosses and wells. I crossed old heathlands and ancient commons, though now they were stitched down with newly hedged fields and fine new-built houses and crossed by the cuttings and iron roads of railways.

I cannot tell you how far I walked, though it took day upon day. How far have you walked? Can you remember a time when your whole journey shrank down to one step and then another step?

It was a hard time, and a hard journey, even though Bulloughby and Grindle were far away. Hardest of all was the thought of my lost friends, of Niddle and Shankbone and Jarvey, left behind in that dreadful place.

Even so, I was excited because soon I would be with my own family once more.

At last I reached the once familiar crossroads and set off up the happy hill to Roseberry Farm. I was hurrying, for I was so close. I even forgot the pain of walking. I could not help stretching a smile wide across my face. I was coming home, after so long!

The dusty road sent up warm yellow clouds that powdered my broken boots. The old milestone leaned even further to one side, and thin saplings had become young trees.

I rested for a while in the shadow of an old elm, sucking at a long grass, partly to keep off hunger and partly to savour this sense of a joyous return. Larks were singing in the fields around, and even I could sing aloud again. I was about to walk into the dream I'd held tight for so long.

I set off again, walking, walking, and reached the very, very top. I went over the final ridge.

Roseberry Farm had been burned to the ground. There was nothing there – no animals, no Isaac, no Ma – nothing of my long-lost home but a blackened shell where the farm had once stood. All those years, while I had dreamed day and night about returning, the dream did not exist. Instead I saw a skeleton of low broken walls, crumbling stones and fireweed. Something rose up my throat, and I retched until I was sick.

I stumbled around the site, tracing what remained of the old buildings. I wandered through the tumbled walls of the cow byre and stepped over the remains of the stables. Small spiders had spun webs in the heat-cracked bricks, and nettles and tall weeds had taken over the deserted rooms. As I disturbed the bracken shoots, the scent of soot and burnt timber filled my nostrils.

My face was wet. What about Ma and everyone? Were they alive or dead? What could I do? Where should I go?

I was numb in head and heart. I searched as if searching could change what I saw. But everything stayed mercilessly the same. I turned around and around, hoping to find all was well behind me, but Roseberry Farm as I knew it had gone.

Twilight came. Evening came. Night came. I curled myself up in a ferny hollow and howled. Instead of lying under a soft cover, gazing up at Ma's whitewashed ceiling, I watched an owl swoop overhead, its two huge eyes searching for a mouse.

Daybreak. I lay among the bracken, unable to move or do anything. I did not want to eat, to speak, even to exist. I had not planned any next stage to this journey. This was to have been my happy ending. Now there was nothing and nowhere else to go. I had never felt so alone. All my memories of Ma seemed to mock me.

My mind was blank. I was totally hollow. I did not even worry that someone might have been sent after me. I lay, watching insects climb blades of grass, and fall and climb again, the foolish crawling things. Morning. Noontime. Afternoon. Hours passed.

A second evening. The setting sun burst into flame across the horizon, turning the clouds into wreaths of crimson fire. I sniffed, as the faint scent of burnt wood grew stronger. I breathed in again, and it was not the dead, damp scent of old soot. Hot smoke tickled my throat. Someone had lit a campfire nearby.

Then a sad tune rose up in the air, haunting the desolation like a ghost. I struggled to unfold my aching limbs and stood up on my two battered feet. I stumbled towards that penny-whistle tune, the very song I'd heard long, long before.

Within the ruins of my farm sat the old wayfaring tramp. Sheltered by a broken wall, he watched his evening fire. As I staggered through the tangled weeds towards him, he gently laid down his pipe and gestured for me to sit beside him.

'Who are you, boy? I seem to know your face.' The breeze lifted the long wisps of grey hair from his forehead, and his sun-brown face was open. His eyes were calm as a summer sky.

'Mouse,' I stammered.

'Ah! You came back then? Were you sent or did you run away, child?' His eyes crinkled up at the corners.

'I ran. Escaped. I want to see Ma.' It was obvious to anyone that was what I would be doing.

'Best to warm yourself before night comes, Mouse.'

'But Ma? What about my Ma?' I asked, starting to let the terror loose from my mind.

'Your Ma? Ma Foster? A fine woman,' the tramp said softly. 'She was Ma to so many little fosterlings. Many a mother must bless her, though she had none of her own, poor woman.'

'She did! She had me! I was her own special child!' I shouted at the stupid man. 'She was my Ma! Mine!' I fixed my eyes on him angrily. 'Don't you remember me being here?'

He squinted at me again and smiled, amused. 'Weren't you the tiddly climbing one? Squirrel, or rat or something?'

'I'm Mouse. Mouse.' My voice rang hollow. I wondered if, like the farm, I no longer existed.

'Don't take it hard, boy. We don't know everything in this life.' He handed me a mug of tea. 'Sup this.'

'No!' I yelled, as if I was an infant again. 'I tell you, Ma was my mother. She said she loved me best!'

He raised his mug, as if in salute. 'That good woman loved all her little ones,' he sighed. 'She was very kind to wanderers and even to old tramps like me, Wayland. It is a pity she has gone.'

Gone? Gone? I burned with anger. Had my Ma betrayed me? Maybe she was waiting for me to go, so she could run away. Maybe she was in league with Button Man and Bulloughby all along. Maybe she knew about all that had happened to me at that awful place. Maybe she was the one who burned down the farm so I could not find her. What did I know about my Ma anyway? Maybe, maybe . . .

I ranted and raved and accused my dear Ma. The lock that had kept my anger shut down so long at Murkstone Hall had snapped. I burned with fury. I raged and stamped about, making the sparks whirl up around old Wayland's fire. I might even have hit him. I cannot tell you what I said, what I did, only that it was all in anger.

Eventually I stopped, and wiped my face on my sleeve, so the tears made long sooty smudges on my cheeks.

'Did you mean all that about her, boy?' Wayland asked.

I could not speak. I shook my head.

'I thought not.' He offered me the mug again, and this time I took it and sipped, drop by drop. 'Want to know what folk say happened?'

'Please,' I whispered.

'Some say a new gentleman had got the lease of Roseberry Farm.'

I had always thought the land belonged to Isaac, but now that felt like a silly child's hope.

'When the next rent day was due, Ma and Isaac were told that they'd have to leave the farm. Some stuff they sold, and some they gave away.' Wayland's voice faded, as if he had remembered moments he didn't want to tell me about. He gazed bleakly ahead. 'All Ma and Isaac took fitted into their one cart.'

'Were you there?' I asked, sure he had been nearby, though he was trying to hide it from me.

'Not there in time, Mouse,' he said, hesitating. 'A gang of four ruffians were there, seeing them off the farm, and joking as Ma brought out her last bundles. Isaac would have laid a whip on them, but Ma stopped him. "Too late now, my love," she said, and sat with her head bowed as Isaac shook the reins and let his two horses take them away from the farm.'

'But none of it makes sense,' I said. 'Why burn the farm to the ground? Why?'

'Don't know,' Wayland murmured. 'It was a cruel act.'

It was if someone had wanted to wipe Roseberry Farm off the face of the earth. How could someone have hated Ma and Isaac so much, and why? It was impossible, but it had happened.

'Where did they go?'

'Where do people go when they've nothing left?' he sighed. 'The city, of course.'

'Didn't you even speak to Ma?'

'I got to the gate as the cart rattled through. The villains were whooping and yelling, but I'm sure Ma Foster called out something about searching for a house.'

'How long ago was this?' Willowherb grew in billows among the broken walls. Was there some clue I couldn't quite find?

The tramp pondered, poking his fire. 'About two years ago, I reckon, just when Michaelmas rent was due. She was a fine woman, and it makes my heart sad to camp here now, Mouse. That's the truth.'

Two years? I stamped more paths through the nettles and the weeds. Wasn't it two years ago when I was shoved into Shankbone's strange care? And what had Ma said as she was leaving? Had she talked about a house, or a mouse? Was she setting off to search for me? This was too, too much. I stood there shivering with tiredness.

'Rest, boy. Come here. Eat this.' Old Wayland handed me a lump of bread. 'Enough is enough, Mouse.'

As I filled my empty belly, the night darkened around us. I was glad the night had come. I had had enough of everything.

All the same, the next morning arrived, and the farm was still as burned and broken as before.

Wayland shook off the night's sleep and brushed the leaves from his long coat. Dew-starred cobwebs stretched across the stonework, and birds searched for insects in the sooty cracks.

Roseberry Farm was no longer a place for me. I had nowhere to go, but I wanted to go nowhere else. I crouched there, rocking, as dull as a lump of clay.

'Get up, boy,' Wayland said.

'No.'

Wayland ignored my reply. He dragged me to my feet. 'Walk!'

I slumped down.

He lifted me up again. 'Walk!'

'Why? Where?'

His voice was harsh. 'Because I'm telling you. Where don't matter. Just walk!' He shoved me ahead of him, along the winding path, making me leave all that I once called home, though it was that no longer.

'As easy to go as to stay,' insisted Wayland. 'Move. On!'

We walked. On and on. Whenever I slowed down, he pushed me forward. Whenever I tried to turn back, he refused and blocked the way, eyes shining hard.

I cursed. I barely looked where I planted my boots. I tripped over clods and flints and tangled myself in thorns. Whenever I tried to sit, to slump, Wayland hoisted me up and marched me on, mile after mile. At the end of that first day, I crumpled asleep, even though there was bread in my mouth.

Wayland lifted me up again well before dawn. He pushed me on as the path rose steeply. We passed stone walls and sheep pens and huge boulders. We plodded past ancient rocks standing deep among dark trees. Whenever the way grew steep, he dragged me with him.

Just after noon, when my breath was scouring my chest, he paused.

'Look you.'

Ahead, the sky had turned dark as night, and already the wind was rising.

'Storm coming, Mouse.' Wayland smiled grimly. 'No sheltering. We walk. We keep walking. This time you've got to face it, boy, got to face it down.'

When the storm hit, it was a fierce one. The wind grew to a gale, water streamed in torrents from the sky, lightning flashed and thunder crashed. Still I was pushed onward by that unrelenting hand.

'Tell me,' called Wayland. 'Tell me all about what happened to you. Tell me about wherever you were, Mouse.'

So I opened my mouth, and the water drizzled between my lips while I thought about the carriage that came, and the Button man. I mumbled something, a word or two.

'Didn't hear. Louder!' shouted Wayland.

I told him about the coach again.

'Louder!' shouted Wayland. 'Tell me again, Mouse.'

Was he deaf on purpose? 'Listen. Listen, you stupid man! This is how it was! This is what happened!'

And this time I shouted about that dreadful day, about that dreadful year, about that dreadful time. I shouted and yelled and shrieked about all that had happened, and how, though I tried, Murkstone Hall had been more than I could bear. I trembled with rage and shame and my entirely broken hopes.

While the rain fell like punches, and streams poured from the rocks, I stumbled among stony crags, telling the wind, the gale and that pushing, tramping Wayland about my desperate life. I almost acted out those scenes and horrors. I shrieked until my words scratched my throat. Wayland kept up his fast pace at my heels, while all I thought about was the step ahead of me and that terrible, cruel place.

On and on I shouted, louder than the storm around

me. I told all the bad times, every one of them, every moment. The climbing that was half pleasure and half agony. I told poor Niddle, and my friend Pyeberry, whom I had never seen again. I told Grindle. And I told the long, long journey home to Roseberry Farm.

By the time the storm had passed us, I could only gulp at the air, mouthing single words and odd sounds, and I was tired, so tired.

I stumbled into a half-walled hollow, and this time Wayland caught me by my shoulders so I did not fall. Carefully he lowered me on to a stack of bracken and wrapped his own cloak around me.

'Well done, Mouse,' he said gently, and smiled. 'Well walked, well told. You have thrown your story to the wind now, and it is time to be at peace. Don't let the bad things in your life keep you imprisoned, child. Live free of them. Understand?'

He lit a bright new fire and brewed a tea of herbs and honey. I felt empty, gathering up the few good moments, the few good friends, and the sorrow. The rage had passed on and away, and I knew finally, deep in my heart, that Murkstone Hall was not my fault. I had not deserved that life, not at all.

I dozed, and woke just before dusk to the sound of Wayland's solitary music filling the calm after the storm. I watched the birds looping in gathering circles around the sky before returning to their nests at last, to rest.

When I woke again it was to a bright new day. I could not forget all that had happened, but I would travel on, and would find Ma.

'Thank you for looking after me, Wayland.' I was sorry for my anger.

'Such wild walking has helped me too, Mouse,' Wayland answered, and I wondered what his own life held that kept him always journeying.

There was still plenty of hard walking to do. Three more days and nights we travelled along the high ridges, where the ground grew rocks and the air was fresh and clean.

On the fourth day we crested a gentler hill and I discovered that a valley was spread below our feet. Wayland hesitated, reluctant to leave the high land, but down we went. This new track led into a wood scattered with fallen leaves, then out along the banks of a stream where trout swam like silver shadows within the deep pools.

'A good place,' said Wayland, setting down his bundle, 'for tonight's camp.'

After we had eaten, and settled for the night, he took out his pipe and played a softer tune.

'Mouse,' said Wayland, as dawn woke us and set the birds singing in every bush and tree, 'you still set on following Ma Foster? Whatever you might find?'

'Yes,' I said, after thinking on that awhile.

'Then there's your road, boy.' He pointed to a gap in the trees.

A single track ran through the fields, gradually growing into a wide, well-trodden path. The path became a lane marked by hedges, before, at a crossroads, joining a road that led to a distant highway. Soon the summer's day would dot that landscape with people and beasts and carts and carriages, all going to or from the far-off city.

'Stay for a bit longer, Mouse,' said Wayland. Lifting his head, he whistled loud and long into the breeze, five times in all, then paused, as if he was waiting. Eventually he whistled again. Whatever it was he was expecting, nothing happened, not then.

So we went further down the track, until we reached the lowest edge of the woods.

Wayland halted again where a narrow plank bridged a brook and pointed out where a kingfisher darted bright blue above the water. He rocked to and fro restlessly, as if he was unwilling to leave his hidden life.

'I can't come with you, Mouse,' he said eventually. 'I am not one for people and their busyness, or their buildings. Folks in towns don't smile, don't give you the time of day, and worse, much worse.'

I straightened up, determined. 'Wayland, I can go on by myself.'

'Let us wait a bit longer. Let's see.' He whistled again, the same as before, but this time we heard a dog barking in the distance, quick and sharp. A broad smile spread across Wayland's face.

'Ah! My ears have heard our salvation.' He was full of smiles then, as if he had some happy knowledge.

'What is it?' I asked.

'Patience, Mouse!' He glanced at me, amused. 'A visitor is about to arrive.'

We waited, and eventually a patch-faced terrier shot out of the hedgerow. It scampered across the fields towards us, dashing up to Wayland.

The tramp greeted the small dog and rubbed its round belly. He murmured, and the dog's ears pricked up as if he understood all he was being told.

'All is well, Mouse. Toby will take you to an old friend of mine,' Wayland said sadly, 'and now it is truly time for us to part.'

He stretched out his weatherworn palm, and we shook hands very formally. 'Take care of yourself. If you do find your Ma Foster, I promise she'll be wanting to see you again, whoever you are to her. Farewell, young friend Mouse. Journey well!'

Then Wayland turned, and he went back up into the shadows of the trees, towards the higher land. Already his step was lighter, swifter, glad to be returning to his own wilderness.

Little Dog Toby gave a funny little growl, half a bark and half a grumble, and trotted back along the downward path, so I followed on to whoever and wherever he was leading me.

CHAPTER 24

A CHANGE OF PLAN

'Gone?' snapped Button. 'Just when the boy's wanted again?'

'Yes!' Bulloughby growled. 'Vermin's run off!' He stared back at his neatly suited accuser. 'Not my fault, Button. You knew the boy was down in the kitchen,' he added, as he adjusted his ill-kept wig. 'Scrope said you'd be coming. You shouldn't have waited so long to collect the brat, should you?'

'Scrope won't be happy to know the boy's disappeared.'

'Scrope won't be happy?' Bulloughby echoed mockingly. 'Worried he'll be cut out of some family fortune if the brat isn't found? Serves the rascal right.'

Button ignored Bulloughby and concentrated on what opportunities this new situation offered.

'And not only that –' began Bulloughby.

'Bulloughby, be quiet, can't you? Just shut up! I have to work this out.'

At that moment a boy backed in balancing a pot of stewed brown tea and a dish of four rock-like scones, which he placed before the men. The boy was covered in grease and grime.

'Back to the kitchen, Niddle,' Bulloughby shouted irritably.

Button bit into a scone, grimaced and absent-mindedly returned it to the plate. While Mouse was kept alive at Murkstone Hall, he could threaten Scrope by the precious child's very existence. Now that the child was most definitely Returnable, the boy was more valuable, very much more valuable.

'Decided. I'm going after the boy myself,' Button said.

'You and me both.' Bulloughby stood up unexpectedly and dragged a disreputable travelling bag from the top of a cupboard. Hunting for Mouse held far more attractions than Murkstone Hall's dull gloom. 'Jarvey can look after this damned place for a while.'

Button eyed Bulloughby. The stupid fool, even with his red wig set at a jaunty angle, might be useful.

'Let's go!' Bulloughby urged, trembling with excitement, then paused. 'But where will Mouse have gone?'

'Roseberry Farm, I expect,' Button told him, 'though much good will it do the boy when he gets there.' He recalled his thugs' enthusiastic description of the fire.

When Niddle returned, somewhat warily, to carry away the tea things, he was interested to find Bulloughby's parlour empty. Button's beetle-black carriage had left Murkstone Hall, and the quest had begun.

Niddle, meanwhile, was glad of the four tough scones. His teeth were young and strong.

PUNCHMAN

Dog Toby took me into the Old Bell Inn, where the bar-room was crammed with jostling customers. Dodging through, he led me out and across a yard where carters haggled about loads and journeys and over to a small grassy patch where a pair of donkeys grazed under the apple trees.

A crowd of giggling children were milling about a canvas booth, shrieking at a strange high-pitched squawking noise.

'That's the way to do it! That's the way to do it!' cried Mr Punch, smacking his stick so enthusiastically on the white-painted ghost that its wooden skull rattled.

A cheer went up as the skeleton disappeared.

I laughed aloud. I was Mouse out on the road, eager for what good things might come. I was looking for my

Ma, and I would be as bold as Mr Punch with his rude, red-nosed face.

'That's the way to do it!'

The two puppets raced backwards and forwards, the shrieks mounting, until Punch whopped the ghost one final time. The skull-head was whisked behind the curtain, leaving Punch to parade to and fro, bowing delightedly to one and all.

'Oh, oh, oh! Lookey, lookey, look! Do I spy my dear little Dog Toby down there?' Punch cried in his strange, buzzing voice. 'Where have you been, my naughty, naughty boy?'

Toby darted forward. He bounced up on to his hind legs in front of the booth, and yapped in the friendliest way. With his tongue hanging out, Toby looked as if he was laughing too.

'And how many sausages do you want tonight, my dear little puppy dog?' asked Mr Punch.

Dog Toby sat on the ground, and barked as if he was counting.

'One? Two? . . . Eight? Nine? Ten? Ten sausages? Ooooooooh! Greedy, greedy Toby! No sausages at all for you tonight!'

Toby whined in a wonderful display of sorrow.

'Maybe I'll give you a sausage now. Come closer, come closer, my little pet. Now close your eyes.' The puppet's evil face leaned over. As Toby closed his eyes, the hook-nosed figure raised his cruel stick.

'No, no!' shrieked some children, unable to bear wicked Mr Punch a moment longer.

But with a quick, artful jump, Toby skipped back and

Mr Punch missed and ended up hanging over the play-board, his little legs swaying. Everyone clapped and laughed. Then Mr Punch righted himself, made friends again with his bold little dog, and the children joined in one last song. All at once, the scarlet curtains closed.

As Mr Punch's song ended Toby reappeared, holding a velvet collecting bag edged with bells and tassels in his sharp white teeth. Hopping on to his hind legs, he carried it round the crowd, dancing in front of people until they dropped a couple of coins into Punch's pouch. His whines shamed those who tried to leave without paying.

I watched Toby carry the jingling, jangling bag back under the canvas. Now what was I to do? Then, as the crowds wandered away, a finger reached out of the booth, beckoning me inside.

Sunlight slipped through gaps in the canvas tent, making it easier to see out than to peep in. I blinked as I entered, and saw a man perched on an upturned wooden box. His thinning curls were streaked with grey, and his face was like that of a kindly woodland imp. He gave one last squawk and removed a wooden reed from his mouth, slipping it securely within his yellow waistcoat.

'Charlie Punchman. Pleased to meet yer!' His eyes twinkled as he fished around in his green jacket until he found a bottle. He uncorked it, swigged a few drops down, then stowed his medicine away. ''Scuse my brandy and water,' he said. 'Any man who strains his voice box like I do needs strong physic. Now, who do we have here?'

He slapped his knees and studied my face, turning his head to one side and then the other. 'Hmmm. You don't seem to be a very terrible villain. Mind you, you'll be even finer once you've thanked Dog Toby for hearing Wayland's call.'

Embarrassed, I shook the dog's offered paw and was rewarded by a friendly bark.

Punchman grinned and rolled his eyes thoughtfully. 'Though we does wonder exactly why that old wanderer Wayland sends Charlie Punchman a runaway boy. What say you, my wooden friends?' He addressed the gallery of puppets that hung from hooks around the wooden frame. 'Shall we let him stay? Speak now, folks, if you have anything against the child. It is your right.'

Was my fate to be decided by the gaping skull of a ghost, scarlet-cheeked Mrs Punch, a bawling baby in a shawl, a stern constable, a frowning judge, a hangman and the click-clacking jaws of a green crocodile?

'No answer, eh? I take your silence as assent, friends. Thank you for your advice. Boy, you is approved of. Now, what's your name?'

'Mouse,' I mumbled.

'Mouse? A remarkable name for a remarkable guest, ain't that so, friends? Well, young Mouse, you've arrived at the right place. There's nowhere so quiet as the inside of Punchman's private castle when the guests has gone. Want some lunch?'

Fumbling in a bag, Punchman brought out hunks of cheese, cold chicken legs and fragments of leftover pastries.

'Not exactly unthumbed, Mouse, but mostly vittles of

the highest quality,' he informed me. 'Tuck in.'

So I munched away, with Mr Punch and his painted gang staring at me from their hooks. Dog Toby bolted down his share, then squeezed beneath the canvas so he could investigate the orchard. Charlie opened up the flaps of the booth a fraction, tying them into place, then leaned back, full of ease, beaming.

The day was softly warm, and I smelled the sweet grass of the orchard and heard the donkeys' gentle braying. Though Ma and Isaac still hurt in my heart, a smile crept on to my face. Silently, I thanked Wayland from the bottom of my heart for sending me to this new companion.

'You stay in here, boy,' Charlie Punchman said, once our meal was well digested. 'Got a bit of business to do.'

He returned after a while, carrying a neatly patched shirt and a ragged oversized jacket he'd wheedled from a widow woman he knew.

He winked. 'Put them togs on soonish, and keep them on. If wise old Wayland sent you to me, sure as eggs is eggs he thinks there'll be someone coming after you.'

He also handed me a battered top hat, so large that it fell down across my forehead and rested on my ears. Dressed in my new garb, I felt brave enough to snooze under the apple trees while Punchman performed another show.

Then we ate half an apple pie, and later we had supper too. What a life of plenty was this, after Murkstone's thin meals!

Overnight we slept in the widow-woman's shed, and were back on the road early next morning with the booth and puppets packed into the deep basket that Charlie Punchman heaved up on to his back.

'Let me help.' I reached out, but he refused.

'No, Mouse. Not yet, boy, but thank you,' Punchman said, shaking his grizzled curls. 'Might weaken my poor old sinews.' Panting slightly, he lurched forward along the road. 'Besides, if I can't do this on a fine spring day, I'll be finished, won't I? Eh, Toby? But I'll be most glad of your company as we go, boy. Now, let me tell you about this Punch and Judy lark . . .'

And so I started on a strange new life, a time when I played with puppets and talked to wooden dolls.

Charlie Punchman was peaceful to travel with. He and his gaudy family didn't ask anything of me. He didn't ask why, or what, or who, or anything I didn't want to think about, such as where had Ma and Isaac gone. Nor did he ask why Wayland believed that someone might come following me. I was glad to live day by day and let my head be like the wooden painted puppets, feeling nothing.

I learned plenty from Charlie Punchman. I learned all the lines and gags and songs of his old familiar show. I learned how he turned crowds from bewilderment to laughter in a moment. I learned to read Toby's barks, both the quick yaps that were part of the act and the growls that warned us when pickpockets were about.

I began to be a real help to Punchman. At first I

watched out for any too-happy farmhands who might barge into the booth and spoil the show. Then Punchman sent me around with Toby and the jingling purse, which taught me to watch every hand, because some fingers slipped more coins out than they slipped in.

In my brash rig of clothes I felt altered enough to bark up Punchman's trade. Over the weeks I learned how to call up audiences, whether in noisy markets or on calm village greens. I learned to parade about boldly in my baggy jacket and tall top hat. Niddle would not have known me now, with my face browned by sun and wind, and the miles I'd walked and the food that put strength in my bones.

Once Punchman began to let me help with packing his bag of puppets he had more breath for his tales, and gradually he heard some of mine. One day he learned rather more.

The dust was thick around our ankles as we arrived at a village for the annual feast. The journey had been long and tiring.

'Should be a good day, Mouse. Feasts and markets are most profitable occasions.' Punchman pointed to the village green. 'See that spot over there? That's our site today. Big old oak will give us shade or shelter, no matter how the day turns out.'

The crowd collected around us before Punchman had unpacked his cast or hung them up for their parts, and he was more tired and slower than usual setting up.

Some folk started to shout out, demanding that the

show begin, and a pair of drunken lads threatened to break the booth apart. Some of the waiting children cried and grizzled, like those babies back at the farm, and I saw customers turning away for their homes.

'Oh Lord, I'm too old for this today,' groaned Punchman, 'and I think we're in for trouble from this lot. Heaven help us, boy.'

The crying and grizzling reminded me that I, Mouse, was not helpless.

I snatched a spare swozzle out of Charlie's pocket and sprang up, crowing and bowing and waving my hat in the air. I did the old running-around-on-the-hands trick, and then covered the ground with somersaults, one, two, three, ending on my feet.

'That's the way to do it!' I squawked once the swozzle was tucked inside my cheek, so I sounded like Mr Punch myself.

I did one-hand and two-hand balances, and rolled into somersaults and did high handsprings. I shinned high up the oak tree and walked along the branches, all for the joy of it, and with no Grindle threatening me this time. I balanced one-handed on this bough, then hopped across to another, swinging round it.

Down in the green shade, the faces looked like newly fallen apples scattered across the grass. I crowed out at the people, making them laugh, and I sang one of Mr Punch's songs.

Then down I came, scampering from branch to branch, leading everyone's eyes back to the booth, because by now Charlie and Mr Punch were ready. The show started at full tilt, and everything went well.

'Mouse? They named you well, my boy,' Punchman chortled as we counted up our takings. 'You're as nippy and quick as a mouse all right! Well done!'

From that day onwards, whenever we were pressed, Charlie asked me to do my somersaults and hand-walking and balancing along fences or walls to attract the punters to his little show.

'But no acrobaticals on church gates or holy market crosses,' Punchman insisted. 'Them vicars and parsons won't be pleased to see a travelling lad upside down on their property. A show of respect is important in this line of business, Mouse, if you want to stay clear of trouble.'

So I travelled on, spending days and nights in the company of Mr Punch and his friends, as if that was where, for now, I was meant to be. No matter what Wayland feared, nobody did come asking for me. I almost stopped watching every shadow, and pretended that this was how I could live, although the leaves and skies told me the season was changing.

It was no different to any other day when it happened. A small crowd had gathered round the booth we'd set up in the stable yard of a tavern, near where the horses were being led in and out. As we began our show, a straw-haired stable hand wandered out and leaned against an upright beam.

I stared. He bent down and whispered to a young woman beside him. The fellow had the same wide, innocent smile as Isaac. Though he was not Isaac and she was not Ma, I remembered. I remembered too much, and was afraid that I had forgotten my search. I felt empty inside.

That night, as we sat over our supper, I was silent.

'Is it come then, Mouse?' said Punchman.

'What?' I faltered.

'Your time to go? To move on? I knew it would one day.'

'But I won't . . .' Words were like chalk in my mouth.

'Mouse, not everything happens as we most want it to happen. If it is time for you to be on your way, then that is what you must do. We have had good times together, so let us be thankful for such happy days, even if they must end. Let us be glad to have been happy, and enjoy this last night together.'

He took a deep swig of his brandy and water. Then, as we shared slices of fine strong cheese and plum cake, he added, 'You know, Mouse? I think I might try that nice widow woman again. Old Punchman will want somewhere warmer than a hedge to sleep under once the winter nights are here.'

Dog Toby nuzzled my hand and snuggled tightly against me.

'Don't you fear! The road to the city ain't far off, Mouse,' Punchman murmured as we drifted off to sleep. 'Every show must have its ending.'

We parted, eventually, at a crossroads beside a steepled church, with autumn just about to begin.

'Who knows, Mouse? We may meet again,' he said, but I could not give any answer. I felt sore about leaving him and his wooden family because, for a while, they had given me another, happier life.

Punchman looked proudly up at my tanned, outdoor face. 'You done well by me, boy, and I will always remember you,' he said briskly. He whipped out a bright silk kerchief from his pocket, tied it around my neck and patted me on the shoulder. 'Bye now.'

'Bye,' I said, as he hugged me quickly.

The last I saw of my good friend was a tiny figure, weighed down by his booth and puppets, travelling back the way we had come. I was glad I had shoved my worn, warm jacket secretly into his pack, for Charlie Punchman might need it in the cold times coming.

Then I took the road to the city, and to what I would find there.

THE CITY

The dome-crowned city! Do you know, I was dazzled by it. And I was scared by it too, if I am to tell the truth.

When I first saw the great conglomeration from far off, high on the misted heath, it seemed a magnificent place. There, where fog and ferns surrounded me, the distant city seemed full of hidden promises, but whether for good or ill, I could not tell. Perhaps I would know by the time I saw the wide silver river. There was a long way still to go. With Punchman and Toby far behind me, this last part of the journey seemed endless and uncertain. If I ever met Ma, would she even know me? Would I know her?

'Ma, Ma, whoever you are . . .' My boots trudged on, taking me with them.

Then I heard a cart coming closer, jolting and rolling across the ruts, bound for the city market, and bound to save me too, though the driver would never know it. He let the reins slip so he could refill his baccy pipe, and the horses slowed their pace.

Up into the back of the cart I scrambled, pushing myself under the sacking, in among the vegetables. The sacks of spuds and turnips would not budge, so I squeezed in among the knobbly cabbages that oozed claggy water and occasional thin, pale worms. Closing my eyes, I slept for long, sweet miles, and so I was brought to the city.

'Hey up! Hello, Joey boy!'

'Hallooo, Gringold, you neep-head!'

'Hey there, Lucy, my dear one, my darling!'

'Steady, steady!'

The shouts were what I heard first, as drivers urged their horses into the surge of traffic. We were jolting along a wide befouled road, where wagons and carts and omnibuses and cabs filled the highway, and on either side the pavements streamed with hurrying crowds.

I lifted up the crusted sacking and stared around at this new world of mine. The spires! The domes and towers, and the high roofs and the chimneys, the many hundreds of chimneys!

A mighty train, with its own blazing chimneys, rushed across an iron bridge overhead, enveloping all below in a swirl of smoke and smuts.

We passed buildings and shops and pubs and stalls and penny gaffs and street pedlars offering their wares. There were calls and cries at each corner, and so many, many people, so much noise. Was this web of noise what Wayland hated?

The streets of cities in stories are paved with gold, but not this one. All was mud. Ragged children darted into the mire, armed with brooms and buckets, eager to sweep a crossing for a few coins or to scoop up dung and droppings to sell on where they could.

At once I was happy, and hopeful. If there were horses, then surely I would find Isaac. And Ma.

Another cart ran too close to the vegetable cart, wheels scraping. 'Get out of my way! Move yourself, you spotted oaf!' my driver roared, lashing to the side with his whip.

Move yourself? Move myself? I would, I would.

I moved. I jumped out and scarpered away. It was me, Mouse, darting off into the city, with harsh words slapping at my back, but what did I care about such names in that great moment? Nothing!

And what did the city care about me? The answer to that was also nothing. Soon my running turned to a walk, and then to a trudge. I realised I did not even know what I was looking for, and a dull anger rose in my heart. Suddenly my hope of finding Ma and Big Isaac was like believing in fairy tales.

Stories describe cities as places of order, but this city was not a neatly settled place. The streets were being ripped apart and old patterns of stone were being broken. Bridges were half-thrown across roads, and great holes were being dug into the ground. It was as if giant invisible moles were burrowing through the whole place. This was a city that moved and grew with each passing day.

Some of it was beautiful. I wandered along fine, swept pavements and spied tree-filled garden squares surrounded by high spiked railings. The grass within would be sweet as a meadow for a night's sound sleep. I paused.

As a church clock chimed, a uniformed man with a bristling moustache strutted from the area of one of the tall houses and entered the garden. He must have just drunk tea with sour milk, because he searched every inch of the garden. He thrashed his cane under bushes and behind trees, to drive out anyone hiding there. He took a watch from his top pocket and checked the time. He left abruptly, locking the gate behind him as if he was the very angel at the Gates of Paradise. I would not be sleeping under those sweet roses that night.

I walked on, afraid of the weariness sweeping over me. I had no Wayland or Punchman at my side, and no Dog Toby. Where could I go? To the workhouses? I had heard of them. Once in, never out, and if Murkstone Hall was called a school, what must life in a workhouse be like? If I was caught and locked up in such a place, I would not be able to find my Ma.

On and on I went. The fine gardens changed into stench-filled streets, the tall houses became shabby tenements. I saw warrens of foul alleys, full of filthy puddles and ragged children. Their bitter, grey faces reminded me of Grindle, ready to attack, so I turned, and went another way.

On every crowded street, a patchwork of scents and smells wrapped around me, teasing my stomach. Dark velvety aromas wafted from coffee houses. Rowdy pie shops offered warm, oniony greetings. I sniffed the air greedily, as if this would cure my hunger.

Sweet scents rose from the trampled blossoms around the flower stalls, but not all was delightful. Acrid stenches crawled out from slaughterhouses and glue factories and tanning works and midden heaps. The people who lived here must have no need for street names or maps. Their noses would tell them where they were.

The dusk turned into night, and the crowds were going home. Shop after shop turned off the globes of their gas lamps and locked their shutters. The tumult of carts and coaches quietened. Elderly link-boys passed me, lifting their long poles to extinguish the lamps. There was no need for light when all good folk were safe indoors and only wanderers and vagabonds were outside.

I had nowhere to go. My feet were rubbed raw inside my boots, so I had to think before making every step. I had no idea what to do.

Outside the Red Lion several large barrels had been stacked, waiting for a dray-cart that hadn't arrived. I sneaked between their oak bellies and crouched down. They stank of stale beer, but I was weary to my bones, and my eyes drifted to a close.

A vile mist rose from the drains, creeping like doubt. How had I thought I could find Ma and Isaac in this huge city? It was all too vast, too impossible. My plan was only a dream, a pretence. I bit my sleeve to stop my teeth from chattering, and dreaded the hours ahead.

*

Well after midnight, shrill, childish voices woke me. Two small girls appeared around the corner. Rough wool shawls were gathered over their trailing gauzy skirts. Giggling and singing, the little girls danced over cracks in the pavements and hopped along the kerb, their legs thin as those of foals on a farm. Tinsel strands sparkled in their hair, and their cheeks were smeared with paint.

Out of the night, a large coach rattled into view, pulled by two well-groomed horses: a gentleman on his way home. It kept close to the kerbside, and the hoof-beats slowed to a walk. I had reason to be suspicious of carriages, and this one was slowing almost to a stop. The cab door opened. Someone reached out, inviting the girls to come closer, to come inside.

'Watch out!' I yelled, darting out and dragging the two girls back to safety. I slammed the door hard against that beckoning arm. A voice inside yelled in pain and shouted to the driver. The carriage moved off at a brisk pace.

Turning to the small startled girls, I smiled in as friendly a way as I could. 'Don't worry. The man's –'

'Got you, you pig!' An enormous bag of laundry shoved me down against the paving stones. A girl about my own size was pummelling me violently, her long plaits flying about in fury. As I squirmed, she landed a fierce punch on my nose. 'Don't you dare hurt my sisters! You vile serpent! You spotted toad!'

The two tiny ones howled like banshees.

'Didn't hurt them!' I mumbled. My mouth was stuffed with cloth, but the thumping continued.

'Just because they're younger than you, you sneak-thief, you cutpurse, you filthy beggar! You'll be sorry you ever went near them —'

'Kitty, please,' one small girl screeched, 'it wasn't him.'

'What?' The attack ceased.

'This brave boy saved us from a nasty man in a big coach,' said the other, 'so please don't keep hitting him.'

Kitty removed the bundle from my chest, but kept her hand raised, ready to strike again. 'Why didn't you say?'

'Mouth full,' I mumbled, pointing, 'of shirts.'

'Stand up then, whoever you are,' said Kitty, rather awkwardly.

I sat. I stood, eye to eye with Kitty. Then I swayed and blood gushed from my nostrils. Everything circled around me.

'Kitty! You've done a murder!' The small girls howled in fear and grief.

'Shut up, Dora. You too, Flora. Of course I haven't.' Kitty glared at them. 'And it's your fault for running ahead of me anyway. I told you not to go so fast.'

I mopped my gory face with Punchman's bright handkerchief.

'Fancy silk and all,' she said. 'Must be a thief!'

'Somebody gave it to me,' I sniffed, as the blood dribbled down my chin.

'Oh heavens! Just take this, boy.' Kitty dragged a half-clean shirt out of the bundle and dabbed at me, even though I was caked in dirt already.

'Thank you,' I muttered.

Small Flora patted my hand sympathetically, as if I

was an injured pet or a lost soul. 'Shall we take this kind boy home, Kitty?'

'Maybe he's a poor runaway orphan lost in a deep, dark wood,' lisped little Dora.

'We're not in a pantomime wood now, Dora. We're in the middle of a blooming big city,' Kitty snarled. 'Fairy tale's over. I'm sorry, boy, but we have to go.'

The cascade of blood had stopped, but my head was buzzing. 'Help me,' I begged, 'please!'

'Oooooh! Yes, yes, yes! Let's help him!' cried the little ones, delighted with such a plot. 'He did save our lives, didn't he?'

'Maybe he's an escaped prince,' Flora added, peering into my eyes. 'Are you under a spell, boy?'

'Silly! He'd be a frog.' Dora nudged Flora with her elbow. 'Or a pretty bird.'

'Please, please! Let us take him home with us, dearest Kitty,' they pleaded.

Then Flora's baby-sweet eyes glinted with cunning. 'Or we'll tell the Aunts that you weren't looking after us properly. Won't we, Dora?'

'Mmmmmmm.' Dora nodded. 'We would.'

This threat hit Kitty hard. 'Be quiet, you two,' she said, stuffing the bloody shirt back into her bundle. She hoisted the weight up on her back again and glared at me. 'You! What's your name?'

'Mouse.'

The girls giggled.

'Mouse! Honestly, it is,' I added, and had to admit to a fact that has puzzled me more and more, 'though I don't know why.'

Kitty's brown eyes viewed me with curiosity. She almost smiled. 'Well then, you homeless Mouse, if you want help you'd better move those ugly boots of yours. One chance. Come on, girls. Quick march!' And she strode off.

I could not help Kitty with the bundle. I could barely hobble along, but I had to keep up or be lost in a warren of streets and alleys. Her figure, in a dull grey dress, marched ahead, while the little girls skipped on either side of me as if I was some sort of prize.

'Don't worry, Mouse,' said Dora. 'She's nice really.'

'No, I'm not!' Kitty snapped back, without turning round. 'Hurry, all of you. The Aunts will be waiting.'

CHAPTER 27

BITER BIT

'Where is the boy?' Old Epsilon's question had turned into a continual drone. 'I want him here. I need him . . .'

Scrope dragged his topcoat from its hook, put on his boots and hurried outside. He would go himself. He would search for that faraway school, and find out what was going on.

He had just ordered his roan mare brought from the stables when an elderly man ambled up on a weary old nag.

'Message for you, good sir,' he cried, and handed Scrope an envelope.

Having sent the messenger away, Scrope rested against the mounting block to read the letter, expecting to see that the boy was about to arrive, but some unwelcome words appeared.

. . . I suspect, dear Scrope, you do not want your father to know about your plans for the boy. You always had so many plans and wishes and, by chance, I have kept all your letters as proof.

Alternatively, you might prefer the child to perish before the loving reunion you mentioned. I am happy to remain quiet about either scheme, but my discretion will cost you.

One important point: up till now you have been lazy about your debts, all borrowed on promises of Epsilon's riches. I am a little weary of waiting, so from now on I expect all moneys to be paid promptly . . .

Scrope felt sick to his stomach. The deceiver! The traitor! The turncoat! Yet, deep inside, Scrope knew that he should have seen this all along, this truth behind Mr Helpful Button, with his red-cheeked smile and his busy little notebook.

Scrope thought and thought . . . and thought. Maybe it was best to do the simple thing. He could go to this Murkstone Hall and get the boy, and then he could sort out things with Button.

If the little man was there at the school, Scrope would have the benefit of surprise. If not, collecting the boy would be an easy enterprise.

But those last words? Paid promptly? Maybe it would be best not to go empty-handed, just in case things became awkward. Scrope returned to the house to find what he could find.

A Place of Great Cleanliness

We crossed an empty marketplace, where skeletal dogs and cats fought for the last grisly scraps, and rats, eyes shining, ran along the drains and gutters. Water, oozing from a cracked horse trough, made foul puddles among the dung.

'I'm so thirsty!' Flora sighed dramatically, pulling Dora towards a dripping pump stand.

'No! Don't you dare!' Kitty scolded, marching us on. 'And keep your skirts out of the muck!'

We passed beggars huddling against the warmth of a baker's shop. Was that was where I would be tomorrow night? A bridge took us over a darkly glittering ditch, and then we came to a row of shuttered shops and a broader, kinder street.

'This way!' Kitty said, as we turned down an alley and entered a tiny square. 'Welcome to Spinsters' Yard.'

The faded buildings staggered this way and that. Some seemed so ancient that only their timbers held them upright.

Kitty slipped a key into a tall gate in a wall, jiggled it until a latch clicked and we were through to a big backyard.

I stumbled at this gateway, and in that pause I was lost, trapped in a maze of washing lines and clothes props. Wet cloth flapped and slapped and cracked against me, suddenly parting to reveal the three girls mounting six stone steps, to where a woman with a lighted candle held open a door.

'At last!' she called. 'We were worried.'

Afraid that the light would vanish and the door shut against me, I dashed forward through the washing. Kitty waited, with a half-smile, then grabbed my wrist and pulled me through into their home.

What? I had arrived in a giant wardrobe, where there were more garments than any one person could need. Shirts, gowns, chemises, petticoats, drawers and pantaloons were everywhere. Some hung rudely from long racks suspended from the ceiling. Some were folded in neat, pious stacks. The air was warm with the scent of lightly scorched cloth and hot irons.

Flora sighed impatiently. 'Do come along! We're in the next room!'

'Here he is,' Kitty said, pushing me forward. 'Boy, meet Aunt Indigo and Aunt Violet.'

Aunt Indigo stood tall as an ancient empress. Replacing the candlestick on the mantelpiece, she stared down at me sternly. Aunt Violet, an oil lamp glowing at her side, sat holding a piece of fine needlework. Behind her wire spectacles, her gaze was as steely as that of her larger sister.

'Who on earth is this, Kitty?' Aunt Indigo frowned.

What did I look like to these women? My garments steamed with the sudden warmth. More than ever before, I felt my clothes were tattered and filthy from my outdoor life. I was ashamed to be indoors, in their clean, crowded room.

'I am sorry,' I muttered, almost too low for them to hear.

Kitty glanced at me, and almost grinned. 'He needs a place for the night, Aunts. I think we should help him.' Her voice was firm and steady.

'Truly, truly, we should because . . .' Dora started, but Kitty glared at her fiercely.

'How did you meet him?' Aunt Violet asked.

'On the way home, Aunts.' Kitty's brown eyes flashed me a message: 'Don't tell them what happened, Mouse. Don't!'

Desperation echoed in my voice. 'Please? I've got nowhere to stay. I've only just arrived, and I'm not in trouble or anything. I'm here because . . .'

How could I explain? How could I admit to asking about my Ma, when I wasn't even sure of her name, or who she was?

'I'm looking for a lost relation,' I said, feeling dizzy. After so long on the road, this clean, pleasant place was weakening me. 'Let me stay for one night?'

'And your name is?' Aunt Indigo had crossed her arms over her dark blue bosom and was tapping one foot sharply beneath her long skirt.

'He's Mouse.' Flora and Dora giggled hysterically.

I nodded and shrugged. 'Yes. Mouse. That's what I'm called.'

Raising one eyebrow, Aunt Indigo cast a querying glance at her sister. Aunt Violet smoothed the long fringes of her mauve shawl, adjusted her glasses and regarded me intently. Her look was more kindly than that of once-upon-a-time Madam Claudine, but I shuffled awkwardly, feeling wretched as a beggar's dog.

Suddenly Aunt Violet smiled, and all was decided. 'Well, young Mouse, you look honest enough, and if we don't take you in tonight, nobody else will. We will worry about tomorrow, tomorrow.'

'But you'll have to sleep down here, in the armchairs,' added Aunt Indigo. 'Kitty, get the boy some blankets. Little ones, go and help her.'

Clearly the Aunts wanted to speak to me alone. 'First things first, Mouse. You have been travelling for a very long time, haven't you? Have you got any luggage?' asked Aunt Indigo.

'Nothing.' I spread out my hands. 'This is all I have.'

'Furthermore . . .' Aunt Indigo approached me and sniffed. 'Exactly as I thought. We have a certain requirement.' She pointed at the door leading back to the yard. Was she sending me away? 'You need a wash, boy.'

'We'll find you something clean to wear afterwards,' added Aunt Violet quickly, seeing my alarm.

Aunt Indigo whisked me across the flip-flapping yard and into a small outhouse. She lit a candle-stub, revealing jugs and buckets, scrubbing boards and mangles, and one vast wooden tub full of almost warm rinse-water. A copper boiler sat in a corner, steaming gently, though the fire underneath had been damped down.

'Get in the tub, Mouse,' Aunt Indigo said, handing me a block of soap, a scrubbing brush and a clean rag. 'Leave your clothes on the floor. There's a towel on the hook, and we'll bale out the water in the morning.'

I was left alone. Glad of such practical kindness, I removed my crusted garments. My tarnished mouse medal still hung around my shoulder, but as I pulled at the fraying string, the threads broke. Catching the medal before it slid into the water, I placed it on a safe shelf. Then I plunged into the tub and washed away all those years of filth and wretchedness.

Eventually I was scrubbed and dry. Looking away from the scummy tub, I tugged on the clean garments Aunt Indigo had flung through the door. With my silver medal down deep inside my sturdy breeches pocket, I scampered across the yard and back into the warm house.

Ma, I thought, if I was running to you, would it be to a place like this? Or where? And would you still welcome me in?

I saw Aunt Indigo handing round cheese on toast, and my belly grumbled with hunger. Side by side, Dora and Flora chewed, eyes closed and almost asleep.

'Help yourself, Mouse,' Kitty said.

Blinking back tears of exhaustion, I reached out for the plate so fast I was almost snatching.

Aunt Indigo tapped me on the shoulder, not

unkindly. 'Don't eat too fast, boy, or too much, or you'll end up with pain in the stomach. There'll be more in the morning, when you'll want it.'

The clock on the mantelpiece struck twice. 'Say goodnight to everyone, darlings, and take the tinsel out of your hair before you go to sleep,' Aunt Violet said, shooing the little ones upstairs to bed.

At last I could ask. 'Please? Where have Flora and Dora been? What have they been doing? Do parties go on so late in the city?'

Kitty and Aunt Indigo stared at each other as if I'd asked something so obvious they didn't understand me, then they started to laugh.

'Children's parties? Oh, Mouse!'

'Mercy me!' said Aunt Violet, coming back downstairs. 'We forget that we live a rather strange life, don't we?'

'And we'll tell you about it tomorrow,' yawned Aunt Indigo, dragging two chairs together and flinging down an old velvety cape for me to use as a cover. 'Time for our own beds too.'

'Goodnight, Mouse! Sleep well!' Kitty, beaming jauntily, followed her aunts upstairs.

I lay there, in the darkness. I smelt the soap in my hair, I heard the Aunts snoring gently overhead and I pinched myself. What kind of good wishes had Wayland and Punchman sent after me if they had brought me to this comfort? I hardly knew myself that night.

I woke, unwillingly. I had not slept so deeply since my long-ago life at Ma Foster's farm. I wriggled about under the crimson velvet cover, feeling easy, clean and happy, and trying to keep the search for Ma and Isaac quietly at the back of my mind.

'Hello, boy!' Flora and Dora, their curls tied in rags, peered at me over the arms of the chairs. Though the sun shone brightly through the window, they were still in their nightdresses. The little girls beamed at me.

'We saw your eyelids moving,' said Flora.

'So we didn't actually wake you up, did we, Mouse?' said Dora. 'Come on, sit up, do!'

'Did you know we're fairies, Mouse?' Flora told me importantly.

'We are fairies almost every night,' Dora added.

'What? You pretend to be fairies?'

'No! Stupid boy! We *are* fairies!'

I could not work out what they were talking about. 'Pardon?'

They giggled. 'We are fairies at the famousest theatre in the city, silly Mouse.'

'Tell me. What exactly does a fairy do?'

Flora began. 'Well, we make sure our hair is clean and curled and everything, and then we go to the theatre, and get told what to do, and we wear pretty dresses, and shoes —'

'— and wings. Don't forget our wings!' Dora fluttered her arms to demonstrate.

'Then we do the proper dancing, and smiling —'

'And sometimes singing —'

'And then we do lots and lots of curtsying at the end.'

'Then we do it again the next night, and the next.

Though sometimes we have to be heavenly angels,' sighed Dora, raising her eyes piously.

'Or dark and midnight spirits.' Flora's voice became spitefully doom-laden and she put out spiky fingers. 'But mostly we're fairies,' she ended brightly.

'Is Kitty a fairy too?' I asked.

They frowned, aghast, and covered their mouths. 'Don't be silly. Our Kitty can't be a fairy any more.'

'Has she been a fairy, then?'

'Mouse, Kitty was the most famousest fairy that ever lived!' Dora whispered. 'She was wonderful!'

'But she isn't a fairy now,' Flora declared, finger on lips. 'Now she just helps with things that have to be done.'

This was mysterious. 'Why isn't Kitty a fairy now?'

They sighed very deeply. 'We don't know, exactly,' Dora told me.

'And we do know almost everything!' Flora confided.

'But you could ask Kitty, and then you could tell us . . .' Dora mused, smiling sweetly at me.

Flora warned me, eyes wide. 'But don't do it unless she's in a very, very good mood. Kitty can be really, really cross sometimes!'

'We did ask her once, but it made her sad,' Dora said. 'Like you looked sad when we met you.'

Aunt Indigo burst in briskly, folded washing in her arms. 'Girls, that's enough. Go and help with breakfast, you chatterers,' she ordered sharply. 'You mustn't believe everything the twins tell you, Mouse.'

CHAPTER 29

BENEATH THE CUPBOARD

Scrope hurried beneath the huge portraits, towards the main door of Epton Towers. As he went, he tumbled the contents of an old jewellery box into his open travelling bag. Maybe it was the thought of Button's threats that made him stumble suddenly on the mat?

The bag dropped, catch undone, and a single ruby brooch spilled out. It danced across the tiles, sparkling in the rays of light, then rolled beneath the heavy cupboard that held the post tray, where letters were left.

Scrope looked about him, but saw no servant. Dropping down on to his hands and knees, he peered deep into the dark narrow space but could not reach the brooch. He seized the paperknife from the tray and poked it into the gap. Though the blade tapped against the brooch, it met something light and papery too.

Scrope flicked the paperknife, and the ruby brooch

skimmed out across the tiles, along with a long-hidden note whose cobwebby edges had been chewed by mice.

Scrope caught sight of his own name, written in Adeline's looping script. Trembling, he unfolded the note and glimpsed the date when it was written. So many years ago!

Dearest Scrope,
How can I thank you for all your kindnesses to me ? If there was ever a noble soul, that is yourself. Soon you will be my own true and trusted brother, someone who I know I can ever rely on . . .

True and trusted? The words burned like acid. True and trusted? Scrope's head whirled with memories and he groaned.

What had he become since that day, since he first knew Adeline? How had he behaved since then? Scrope sat like a child on the tiled floor, going over and over her words, seeing himself as Adeline saw him. His spirit shrank within him. *True and trusted brother . . .*

One of the footmen appeared tactfully at Scrope's side and helped him to his feet.

Scrope walked to the door as if in a trance. He mounted his waiting horse and sat unsteadily in the saddle. All he could think about was Adeline, and Adeline's words.

Trusted brother? Untrusted enemy? Which one was he? After a while he set the horse trotting on.

The footman told all the other servants that the young master's face looked as if he had seen a ghost, and that, unbelievably, Scrope had thanked him for his kindness.

NEW FACES

Out in the wash-house, Aunt Indigo was bellowing hymns as she beat out the dirt with the dolly-stick. Aunt Violet's sewing machine was thrumming away in her sewing room.

Then a neighbour, Mrs Orpheus, arrived, as I learned she often did. She stood two irons in front of the fire to heat and spread thick ironing blankets and cloths over the table. Soon Mrs Orpheus's irons thudded and thumped, smoothing the crumpled shirts beneath their weight. When one iron cooled, she put it before the fire again and took the other one.

The only place where Kitty and I could talk was in the scullery, while she sorted out the contents of last night's bundle.

'Adnam's shirts, six, two gory . . . Adnam's plain cravats, six . . . Adnam's stockings, silk pairs . . .

Adnam's . . . Ooops!' Kitty thrust a pair of gentleman's drawers into the washing basket.

'Who,' I said at last, 'is Adnam?'

'What? Hugo Adnam? Don't you know anything about the theatre? About plays? Adnam is only the most important actor of all time!'

Plays? Jarvey had read plays with us, but I wasn't sure that counted. 'Not much,' I said, unwillingly, 'but I do know about Mr Punch.'

'Ha!' Kitty cried disdainfully. 'Mr Punch? He's not a real actor. He's a wooden doll.'

'Well, let me tell you, Kit . . .' I began.

Without giving her a moment to argue, I rattled out everything about my time with Charlie Punchman and Dog Toby. I told her about the shows and the crowds, and I knew those months were true, unlike some parts of my life. I left out any talk about handstands because Kitty, the once famousest fairy, might not be very impressed with my skills. Eventually I paused for breath.

'Enough, Mouse, enough. Maybe Mr Punch is a *sort* of actor, after all!'

We laughed for a moment, friend to friend, but once the brightness of my story was done I shut up. My mouth felt full of ashes, for I had remembered Roseberry Farm all burnt out, and Ma gone, and all those other thoughts. Too much, too much.

Kitty eyed me expectantly, longing for another adventurous story. 'Who are you looking for, Mouse?'

'No. Doesn't matter, Kit. Tell me more about your grand Mr Adnam instead.'

Kitty stood up proudly. She paced about as if she

was on the stage, eyes bright with enthusiasm. 'Hugo Adnam is the Greatest Actor that ever lived. He *is* the Albion Theatre – that's what everyone says.' She put her face close to mine, making sure I did not miss the importance of her words. 'Mouse, Adnam does just about *everything*. He manages the actors and musicians and dancers and the scenery. Everything!' There was such longing in her voice.

'Really?'

'Well, he doesn't do the tickets and playbills and that front-of-house stuff. The General deals with that, but he does everything else. Mouse, you should see the place, full of people, stagehands and actors and Hugo and . . . and . . .' Her face darkened as she muttered, 'And Bellina Lander.' Now it was Kitty's turn to be silent and angry.

'You win, Kit.' I tried to make my voice cheerful. 'Adnam sounds much grander than wooden Mr Punch and his swozzle.'

She smiled a little, but her whole body drooped.

'So that's what you were doing last night?' I persisted. 'Bringing the girls back from the Albion?'

'Mmm. They'd been dancing.'

'And you?'

'Enough, Mouse!' she spat. 'They dance onstage; I don't. Understand that?' She flounced out angrily, carrying the dirty shirts to the laundry.

Whoa! If Kitty turned against me, I wouldn't last long at the Aunts'. I waited till she returned. It was time for a touch of truth.

'Want to know why I'm here then?' I swallowed

hard. 'I'm trying to find my Ma.'

'Your lost Ma?' Kitty was fascinated by the idea of my own drama. 'Where does she live? What's her name? Tell me all about her!'

It was a mistake to hear these questions that I'd so far only thought for myself. 'Ma might not be my mother, Kit, just somebody where I once lived. Don't know much about her really.'

'Then how are you going to find her, Mouse?' Kitty asked, her eyebrows arching. 'What facts do you have?'

What facts indeed? Ma Foster? I had begun to lose trust in that name. There was some other name that Isaac used, but what was it? Annie? Harriet? How could I not remember it?

'None, Kit.' I shuffled awkwardly, then spoke brightly, as much to myself as to Kitty. 'Maybe I'll just see Ma out there on the street and know her as soon as I see her.' This sounded a pitiful hope. The Ma in my head was Ma as she looked when we were happy at Roseberry Farm. What did she look like now?

Why, Mouse? I asked myself – before Kitty did. If you knew so little, why are you here? Because this was the one place where there might be hope? Because I had nowhere else to go?

'That man in the carriage last night –' I said, changing the subject '– did you know him?'

Kitty gave an exasperated breath. 'Course not. It was just something that happens, one of those nuisances I'm always warning the girls about, like drunkards and pick-pockets and dogs foaming at the mouth. I'm really glad they got scared, Mouse. It's dangerous so late at night.

Perhaps it will stop the silly things running on ahead next time.'

'Why don't you tell your aunts? Surely Aunt Violet would tell them to behave?'

'Idiot! If I tell the Aunts, they'll have to stop the girls dancing, and what would we do without the money they bring in? We'd probably be out on the street.'

'Like me?' I asked.

Kitty blushed. 'Sorry. But don't say a word about last night,' she begged. 'Please, Mouse.'

And a loud scream made us rush into the yard.

Catastrophe among the washing lines! Aunt Indigo, like the captain of a storm-tossed sailing ship, was battling to keep the masts of her clothes props upright. The washing flapped like loose sails, ready to plunge down, but their fall would end in murky puddles instead of bright waves.

'Do something!' Aunt Indigo shrieked, as one clothes prop crashed to the ground, and the line sagged lower.

Mrs Orpheus, iron in either hand, gasped fishlike from the steps. Aunt Violet hopped across the pools of water and joined Indigo in lifting the dripping cloth.

'Oh heavens! If another line goes, we'll have to wash it all again,' gasped Aunt Violet. 'As if there isn't enough to do already! Kitty, child, help!'

Up on the house wall, just by a nailed-up window, was the small iron wheel that the lines ran through, so tightly jammed it would not slip forwards or backwards.

Kitty dragged a ladder out of the wash-house. 'It won't reach,' she cried angrily.

Thanks to Grindle's training, I knew how to reach that washing line. Despite Punchman and his pies, there was still not much weight about me, so I shinned easily up the nearby drainpipe.

'Let me look a minute,' I called, and examined the wad of frayed thread that stopped the well-worn pulley wheel from turning.

'Lift everything up, high as you can,' I shouted. 'Up! Up!'

Kitty, Indigo and Violet balanced the wooden props aloft as if they were bearing celebration banners for our good Queen's birthday. I picked away at the matted threads until at last the wheel was cleared and the line started to run easily through the rolling pulley.

'There she goes!' I shouted.

Quickly Aunt Indigo adjusted the props and lines and tightened everything up carefully. 'Excellent work, Mouse.'

I clambered down the drainpipe, to where the Aunts were almost giggling with relief. Aunt Indigo slapped me on the back. 'Saved us two days' work, lad. Saved our shirts and sheets! Well done!' She raised her hand to her forehead. 'Heavens, Vi! We've got to get new lines, no matter how much they cost.'

'So very, very glad you were here, Mouse,' added Aunt Violet, bright-eyed.

That morning I was the very hero of the wash-yard, but would I seem such a hero to Ma? I tucked away that prickling thought because everyone was glad I was there. Even Kitty was smiling at me.

*

Aunt Indigo spread jam on slices of bread and handed them round. There had been a family meeting. Once we had eaten, the Aunts nodded at each other and began.

'We are in your debt, Mouse,' declared Aunt Violet, 'so listen. The show at the Albion is already dressed, so we can let you stay on here for a day or two.'

I thanked them, not quite understanding, and wondered what was coming next.

Aunt Indigo sighed. 'You see, Mouse, once Adnam has chosen his next play, there'll be cloth and clothes everywhere, costumes in every corner, and more bodies here helping,' she explained. 'No space to live. No space to lie down. No room or time for anything else, day or night. It will all be rush, rush, rush, even for our three girls!'

Everyone nodded emphatically.

'I wish we could think of somewhere for you to stay for longer, Mouse,' continued Aunt Violet.

'But you can certainly stay tonight!' Aunt Indigo added insistently.

'Thank you,' I answered. Even one night in the warmth was better than a night in the gutter and, besides, I was supposed to be finding Ma, wasn't I?

As we all sat there rather awkwardly, the brass clock on the mantelpiece struck the quarter-hour, and Aunt Violet clapped her hands merrily. 'I have the solution. Why not Nick Tick?'

'Nick Tick?' Kitty hesitated. 'Surely there isn't any room with all his family, is there?'

'Then you must persuade him he can find a spare

corner, mustn't you, Kitty?' replied Aunt Violet, shooing us towards the door. 'Hurry, hurry! The girls must soon leave for the theatre.'

'Nick Tick?' I wondered.

Close to Spinsters' Yard, on the paved thoroughfare, was a narrow old-fashioned shop, with two narrow bottle-glass windows and a narrow door. Kitty turned the handle.

'Watch where you step, Mouse,' she warned, as the bell on the shop door jangled, and we were surrounded by a loud chorus of clicking and whirring and ticking.

Nick Tick's mechanical choir was composed entirely of clocks. Grand and small, round and square, wide and slim, row upon row of dials gazed down from all sides.

There were miniature clocks, grown-up clocks and grandparent clocks. There were clocks with blunt solid hands and clocks with ornate squiggly pointers, large clocks in tall mahogany cases with polished pendulums and flashy clocks gleaming from bright brass cases.

Some fanciful clocks had sneaked in among the plainly dressed timepieces: wild piratical clocks, where painted sailing ships rocked on aquamarine billows, and handsome sporting clocks, where sprightly horses leaped endlessly over emerald-green hedges and peacocks flew across palace lawns.

'Mr Nick?' Kitty called. 'Can you help?'

'Hello? Hello? Who is it?' From the rear of the shop appeared Mr Nick Tick, peering at us through two sets of glasses. His old-fashioned waistcoat, looped with several watch chains, reached to his knees. 'Kitty, my dear girl!'

he cried, pushing both pairs of spectacles up on to his balding head. 'How pleasant to see you.'

'Mr Nick, I've a message from the Aunts. This boy here needs somewhere to stay.'

Nick's smooth brow furrowed, as if he was weighing the problems my presence might cause to his clocks, so Kitty added hastily, 'The Aunts will feed him, of course.'

'I'm hoping to find a lost relation very soon,' I added, in case this would reassure Mr Nick that I wouldn't be under his feet for long. I stuck out my hand. 'They call me Mouse.'

'Mouse? Mouse?' Nick Tick bubbled with laughter and shook my hand hard in return. 'Well, dear boy, I have somewhere that might do, but I am not sure if my little shop is quite quiet enough for a mouse.'

As if to demonstrate, the shop exploded in a cacophony of chimes and clangs. The hour had arrived, and each clock shouted out its own particular tune. Floorboards shivered under our feet, cupboards swung open, and small tools trembled on their hooks. Kitty and I clamped our hands over our ears.

Could I manage to live in this noise? Could I sleep through so much sound? I'd managed to live through some very unhappy silences. 'Thank you. I'm sure your clocks won't disturb me much, Mr Nick.'

'That is good,' he said, smiling, 'because now, Mouse, I shall show you where you can hide.' He toddled towards the back of his shop and indicated two wooden panels in the wall. Sliding them apart, he revealed a narrow box of a bed, with a good thick mattress. I saw there were even some narrow shelves in the alcove, and a few old, well-worn volumes. 'It was my own bed when I was but a boy. What do you think, Mouse? Yes?'

'Thank you so much, Mr Nick,' I answered, anxious about what I had to say next, 'but I cannot pay you anything. I'll help you with anything you like, Mr Nick, I will!'

'Then, Mouse, this meeting is most timely,' he said. 'Look!'

He drew a line in the dust on the floor with the toe of his much-mended shoe.

'As you can see, I am in need of a little assistance myself. So you can help me, and I can help you, and that seems to be a most successful arrangement.' He grasped my hands again and shook them in an even more lively manner.

'Thank you, dear Nick,' said Kitty. 'We'll go and tell the Aunts.'

'One precise second!' Nick Tick rummaged in a jar and extracted a key. 'For you, Mouse,' he said. 'Come and go when you want, and I trust you not to slam any doors or suchlike, eh? My family easily becomes unbalanced. Now go, go! I have work to do!'

Mr Nick flapped his hands to send us away, then picked up a timepiece as fat as a currant bun. 'This special friend needs all my attention, don't you?' Nick Tick clicked the catch, and the watch sprang open.

As we went out, he was humming. 'Hickory, dickory, dock . . .'

*

'Kitty, Kitty! Where were you? We'll be late!' Dora and Flora danced from foot to foot, desperate to be taken to the Albion Theatre. 'Now, now! Let's go!'

Their hair, still twisted in tight rags, was hidden under their bonnets, to make sure it would fall in beautiful curls for the show. Kitty's own hair was tied plainly out of the way in a tidy plait. Hearing their excitement, her dull, angry mood returned.

'Kit, can I come with you?' I asked. The sooner I learned my way around this city, the sooner I could start looking for Ma.

'Yes, yes, he can. Can't he, Kitty?' cried Flora and Dora.

Kitty hesitated, looking at me uncertainly.

'Double load of washing to return,' hinted Aunt Indigo.

'All right. But don't you go expecting any omnibus ride back, Mouse.' Kitty sniffed. 'We walk there and we walk back.' She glared at the little girls. 'And you two had better not give me any trouble tonight. Understand?'

Off we went, me hurrying after Kitty as she steered Dora and Flora through the crowds. So many people, so many streets, so many buildings! How could I ever find my Ma in this place? Was I right to be searching here?

CHAPTER 31

FOLLOWING ON

The two men reached the overgrown walls of Roseberry Farm.

'How do we know the wretched child came here?' Bulloughby grumbled.

'Make a change if you knew anything,' said Button rather coldly. Travelling with Bulloughby was a distasteful experience. Why was he, Button, surrounded by people who complained all the time?

Button viewed what was left of the site. Scrope had asked him to punish Hanny, and his hired thugs had obviously been rather enthusiastic, but Button had no time for guilt. Besides, if the boy had seen this burnt-out shell, he'd not hang around. He'd be off again, fast.

Button patted his hands lightly against his stomach and smiled. The city, of course! Searching for people was very rewarding. Hadn't that stupid nursemaid believed she was safe in this quiet place? He'd proved her wrong.

'Mouse will be trying to find his old nurse now,' commented Button, 'so we will travel on to the city too.'

Bulloughby huffed and groaned his way into the carriage and spread himself across one side. Button climbed in, exhaling displeasure, and sat as far away as he could on the opposite seat. Bulloughby's own particular aroma, a mix of long-worn clothes, snuff and a strange vegetable scent, spread through the carriage.

Pressing a handkerchief precisely to his nostrils, Button tapped a signal to the driver. Off trotted the horses, following the very route Ma and Isaac had taken to the city.

As the miles passed, and the coach swayed, Bulloughby beamed inanely, happy to be away from the burden of his dreadful school.

Button's lips were curved, but because of the oaf he was travelling with, this man so easily led by his emotions. What fools some people were! Rather like Scrope, thought Button. That one had a clever mind, but it was twisted out of shape by his jealousy. Which was, all things considered, rather beneficial for Button.

'Good, this is!' Bulloughby grinned, and belched.

Button's eyes glittered, like a spider content to wait in the darkest corner of his web.

CHAPTER 32

BEHIND THE SCENES

'What do you think then, Mouse?' Kitty said. I could not speak. So this was the Albion Theatre, with its green copper dome!

It was like an ancient temple I'd seen in one of Jarvey's illustrated books. Eight pillars guarded the entrance, holding up a triangle of stone within which carved gods and goddesses lounged about lazily, as if they too were waiting to see Adnam's next show. Below them, on the wide stone steps, flower sellers and apple-women gathered and gossiped.

'No, Mouse! Not that way. That's for the audience.'

We went to the back of the theatre, which dressed only in plain, everyday brick, and up to the stage door. It had no handle, so Kitty rapped three times and an eye appeared in a spyhole. The door opened, revealing an ugly, crop-headed man.

'Hello, Smudgie!' Flora and Dora said sweetly, patting his hand as they passed.

'Hello, Smudge,' Kitty said. 'Meet Mouse. The Aunts have sent him to help me.'

Smudge had the thickened ears and knuckles of an old boxer. 'I'll be watching you, boy,' he growled.

Inside were bare echoing corridors and steps that led up or down to hidden places, not beautiful at all.

'What's down there, Kit?'

'Cellars full of old scenery and props,' Kitty replied. 'And spiders, of course – thousands of enormous spiders,' she added mischievously. 'Maybe a few ghosts. Not many people go down there.'

Flora and Dora squeaked and shuddered with delight, but I couldn't tell whether Kitty was teasing or not.

We went up, not down, climbing five flights of stairs lit only by occasional hissing gas lamps to get to a large chilly studio, lit by a large skylight.

'The fairies!' cried Flora and Dora ecstatically, though whether this joy was because they had missed their lessons I could not quite tell.

The fairies were wiping chalked proverbs from their slates and giving them to an older girl to stack, happy their schooling was done for the day. Now it was the time for proper lessons.

Fussing and chattering, the young dancers rushed around a graceful young woman with a stern face. Her frothy hair was tied up in a black velvet ribbon.

'Get ready for your practice, girls,' the woman called. 'Smallest at the front. You big lasses at the back!'

This teacher wore a high-buttoned blouse, but her

embroidered skirt was so astonishingly short that I could see her ankles.

'Stop staring, Mouse.' Kitty nudged me quickly.

I should add that the woman was also wearing a big knitted muffler and fingerless mittens, and that the dancers, when not actually dancing, clutched thick shawls around them.

Flora and Dora hurried across to their dance teacher too and pushed forward. 'Miss Tildy! We're here at last.'

'Are you now, my little ones? Good. And have you remembered those new steps, young lasses?'

'Yes, Miss Tildy.' The twins showed off the pattern of their steps with glee.

'My, haven't you done well, bairns? But did you also remember that you must dance a wee bit further over towards the wings? We don't want to upset the fine Miss Bellina Lander once she joins us onstage, do we? She'll want some space so the grand gentlemen can admire her, won't she?'

'Yes, Miss Tildy,' the two girls chorused, dropping rapid curtsies, and ran off to join the gaggle of tiny dancers.

Kitty growled under her breath.

'So how are you then, Kitty?' Miss Tildy asked gently.

Kitty tossed her head and sparked back, 'Fine as ever, thank you, Miss Tildy.' Tilting her head in my direction, she added, 'I must go. I have to show Mouse what work needs doing.'

'Nice to hear that, Kitty. You will take care your young friend is no trouble to anyone, won't you, dear?'

'Certainly I will, Miss Tildy,' Kitty said. She stormed

off, muttering, 'Stupid, stupid, stupid,' and I followed on her heels.

As we left, Miss Tildy called out the name of a tune to the elderly woman poised at the piano, and announced, 'First position, girls!'

Quite soon, the Albion's cast of actors would arrive, Kitty said, so we needed to deliver everything to the correct place.

It was too early for anyone to be in the green room, waiting to go onstage, so Kitty thumped fresh linen napkins and towels down on the table.

'Hate it when an actor spills food down their costume just before they go onstage! Some get so occupied looking at their lines that they forget the pie-gravy slipping down their shirt.' She added, 'Though most poor souls get too nervous to swallow a thing.'

We went up the men's staircase first, starting with the dressing rooms of the important actors. The names were inserted into the polished brass holders on every door. Hugo Adnam's name came first, though he had a suite of rooms. Charles Knightley was next. The next flight up was more dressing rooms, including Arthur Boddy's cosy corner.

'Poor Arthur's puffing like a steam train by the time he gets up here,' Kitty said. 'Arthur does comic parts. And here's Ned and Fred Horsely's.'

These names were tacked to the door with drawing pins. In each room Kitty left a stack of clean shirts and towels.

'Done,' she said briskly, as we hurried downstairs

again and picked up more piles of linen. 'Now for the ladies' staircase.'

First we came to the large dressing suite kept ready for Miss Bellina Lander. Kitty kicked the door roughly ajar.

'I just know that woman will arrive for the very last rehearsals, ready to make problems for everyone,' Kitty said, dark eyes flashing angrily.

Next flight up, there was Marianne Day's dressing room, and then Sophie de Salle's room. Minnie Flowers and Tilly Tibbs shared a room up on the third floor. No brass name holders here, but they had two saucy lace-trimmed postcards pinned to their door.

Kitty took me to other rooms, far from the stage, where the lesser actors had to squash and share. The linen she delivered to these unnamed rooms was full of darns and patchings.

'Doesn't look very exciting while it's empty, does it, the theatre?' said Kitty.

But to me it did. Some dressing rooms held swords and armour and heroic banners. I saw embroidered robes draped over tall screens, and velvet fur-trimmed cloaks rather like the one the Aunts had used last night as my bed-cover, hung on hooks along the wall.

There were shelves filled with hats and crowns, and baskets containing wigs and coils of coloured hair. Trunks and hampers were stacked in corners, overflowing with bright garments and belts and scarves. Some trunks were named and very securely locked.

'They worry that their most precious treasures might get nicked,' Katie informed me, amused. 'Careers have been made with the help of a few good personal props, especially someone else's.'

Mirrors shone on all sides, making the poky rooms seem larger. Each dressing table had a small face-mirror, surrounded by pots, brushes and powders and glue, and taller mirrors stood here and there, so that whole costumes could be seen.

In the mirrors I suddenly I saw myself again: Mouse in the city. Such a strange sight it was. No longer was I the grimy kitchen mouse, or Punchman's boy in a battered hat. My brown hair stood in soft tufts, and my ears and face and clothes were clean. So this was me: an almost respectable Mouse, apart from the wary look in my eyes.

Kitty paused and stood beside me, our heads level. 'You're not taller than me yet, Mouse,' she said wryly.

Was this city Mouse someone that Ma might recognise, or not? I had not forgotten my quest, not at all, but I needed to feel my feet on firm ground first. I leaned over and grimaced at the mirror.

'Don't touch!' Kitty warned. 'If anything's out of place, I'll be in more trouble.'

More trouble? Whatever had happened before? But by now everything was done. We hurried down stairs and around stairs to a tiny uncomfortable room filled with boxes and a slight smell of cheese.

'The boot room,' said Kitty.

Kitty lit a small oil lamp, dragged down a sack of satin dancing slippers, opened a sewing box and began darning.

'That lot will need polishing, Mouse,' she told me, nodding at a tub stacked high with dusty shoes.

What a strange collection! I had never seen anyone wearing shoes like these on the street.

'The actors need the right shoes for the right roles,' Kitty explained. 'Neat shoes with metal buckles are for lawyers and vicars. If you're acting a hero or a villain, you wear knee-high boots, but if you're a bishop or an ancient king you'll wear those paddling fat-toed leather slippers. The top actors have their shoes specially made.'

'And these?' I held a pair of fancy high-heeled shoes made of stiff patterned brocade. They looked quite large.

'Old-fashioned court gentlemen and pantomime dames,' Kitty commented briskly. 'No polishing. Just brush off the dirt as best you can.' She paused and added, 'Thank you, Mouse.'

Crouched over the tub of shoes, I thought about Shankbone's vats of broth and boxes of vegetables, and how good he had been to me, in his way. Then I thought about Ma, and how she was even better, even though I did not know what to believe about her any more.

'Kit, where's your mother?' I asked.

She replied simply, as if she'd explained it too many times, 'Haven't got one. She died when the girls were born. Now we have the Aunts, and they look after us, and that's enough.'

Then she added, so quietly I could hardly hear, 'When I was a little girl, we used to have Hugo Adnam too. I remember him visiting our house, playing with me, and talking to my Ma and the Aunts about costumes and scenery and all sorts of theatre things. Then, once the twins were born and my mother died, Adnam stopped visiting. He left us alone. Don't know why exactly.' Kitty frowned. 'Sometimes things just happen, don't they?'

Slowly the whole theatre began to come to life. The sounds within the building grew louder, so we heard footsteps and shouts on the stairs, and greetings above, and the banging of doors. The cast was arriving and going to their rooms.

After a while, faintly and far away, instruments shrieked and shrilled as the musicians started to warm up, and the building began to hum.

'Audience,' commented Kitty, taking another slipper from the basket.

Then the orchestra burst out, and this time voices joined in, each one a different rhythm. We heard a run of laughs and shouts, and the audience bursting into applause.

'Arthur Boddy,' said Kitty. 'Same act, same jokes, but they love him.' Then there was a gallop of lively music, dotted with cymbal clashes. 'Acrobats,' she said. So it went on, one act after another. Kitty grew quieter and quieter.

Eventually the orchestra swelled in a new melody. We heard small feet pattering above us, as the fairies got ready for their act.

Kitty stabbed her needle into the satin slipper, flung

it into the basket and closed the wicker lid. 'Untangle old ribbons, sew on new ribbons, darn the wretched toes and heels. Not even a glass slipper among them. Oh, Mouse, life is rotten sometimes.'

'What is it? Tell me, Kit.'

But she didn't. She sniffed and wiped an arm across her eyes. 'Want to see the girls onstage, Mouse?' she asked almost cheerfully.

Now, with the place all darkness and brightness, and me blinded and blinking, I had to take care where I stepped. The audience could only see the stage. I saw how vast the Albion really was. Punchman's little booth would have fitted in a thousand times.

On either side of the stage itself were spaces almost as huge, where the scenery and props waited their turn. As Kitty led me past painted backcloths, she showed me to watch out for the weighty sandbags that kept the scenery ropes taut. We stood a little way back in the wings, and now my eyes, used to the dimness, saw the stage crew moving silently among the canvases and padding along the high walkways above us.

Above the stage was a space as huge as the inside of a tower, with backdrops and other scenery suspended on long poles, ready to be flown down between the acts.

Kitty tugged my arm. "Watch how they change the stage, Mouse!' she whispered.

The orchestra, hidden below our sight, proclaimed another tune, and the young woman onstage began to sing. A beam of lantern light shone directly on her white arms and tumbling golden curls, as she bewitched

the audience with her melancholy tale.

'Sophie de Salle!' Kitty breathed admiringly. 'Such a voice!'

Midway across the stage hung a vast gauze curtain, but the bright lights did not reach the dark space behind the gauze. Here, as the music pulsated louder and louder, the stagehands worked, sliding more painted flats into place and lowering fresh scenery from the fly floor overhead. The ropes slid within their runners with a faint rasping sound.

Just as Sophie's voice soared to its most piercing pitch, one of the crew gave a thumbs-up. Bushes of artificial roses were speedily wheeled on to the boards and sandbagged into position.

A soft rustling told us that the tiny girls were waiting elsewhere in the wings, listening for their cue.

'Go, darlings!' whispered Miss Tildy as the music's mood altered.

Each little dancer tiptoed rapidly on to the stage and into her pose, just as a new set of lanterns blazed down behind the gauze, revealing the new scene. The audience gasped.

Sophie's lonely setting had been transformed into a painted garden, where Flora and Dora and the other small girls sprang around in sparkling sequins, fluttering their wings.

Smoke streamed from machines either side of the stage, both before and behind the gauze, billowing beautifully. In truth, the smoke was cold, uncomfortable stuff, damp as the dormitories at Murkstone Hall.

A pair of stagehands pumped energetically at a tin

canister, casting a small cloud of dense dusty powder into the centre of the stage, concealing the figure rising from the trap in the stage floor.

As blue light picked her out, she moved her transparent wings slowly back and forth, gesturing to the applauding audience as if she was floating in the air just for their delight. They gave one huge gasp of happiness and clapped harder. This girl was the most important fairy on the stage. I felt my hands wanting to applaud too, although I knew I'd seen her tidying up Miss Tildy's schoolroom slates less than three hours ago.

Kitty tugged at my arm. 'Let's go, Mouse,' she said.

Back in the boot room, Kitty dragged out a sackload of peasants' clogs and insisted we clean them at once.

'Never know when they'll be needed,' she said, scrubbing furiously at the wood.

So what happened after the arrival of the important fairy I didn't ever discover. At last the show ended, with a final roaring from above. That – so Kitty told me – came after Hugo Adnam had recited one of his most well-known speeches.

'Shakespeare,' she said. 'Macbeth. And I know who's the missing witch.'

'Eh?'

'Never mind, Mouse. You will. She'll be back soon.'

*

With no bundles to carry, the walk home didn't feel as long as the night before. No dark carriage alarmed the little girls, and my feet didn't hurt as badly, but Kitty was very, very quiet, and so were we.

IDLE WORDS

No news of Mouse. The roads were dull, the journey was dull and the talk was worse than dull. Button and Bulloughby rested in a village inn, where a roaring fire thickened the air and stifled the breath.

Bulloughby, with two large pork pies secure beneath his belly, slumped against the settle. Eyes closed, he snuffled into a dream.

Mr Button wiped the corners of his own mouth very clean with a folded napkin. Neatly and quietly, he placed it beside his knife and fork. Nobody would know it, but Button was listening extremely hard.

In the corner of the bar, three old farmboys gossiped over tankards of ale. The oldest scratched his bristled chin and sniffed sadly. 'All the old things are going. Last village feast weren't as good as before. We never got that big bear that used to come a-rattling his chains.'

'Old brute frit maids something terrible, he did,' the second laughed wheezily. 'Got me an extra cuddle if that great scary Bruin was around.'

'That's enough of your saucy talk, young William,' grumbled the third glumly. 'That ill-tempered beast whopped my terrier across the bear pit and fair broke its back. Lost a sovereign there, I did.'

'Reckon poor old Bruin's dead by now,' the first man declared. 'Some of the old acts came this year, didn't they, Seth?'

'Aye, Nathan's right,' agreed Seth. 'We got the old peg-leg sailor with his hurdy-gurdy music and monkey, didn't we?'

They maundered on through old songs, humming words they had forgotten. Button smiled almost benignly at the tuneless trio, who soon ordered more ale.

'I've thought of another one who came. Old Punchman!' Seth said triumphantly. 'Him with Dog Toby and his rattling painted puppets. *That's the way to do it! That's the way to do it!*' Remember?'

'Were even better this year. He had that boy helping him. Tufty-headed lad, skinny little thing, and such sharp brown eyes! Bet Charlie Punchman was glad of that lad, skipping and dancing while the booth was being put up!' said William.

They all nodded and clapped their hands together at the thought.

'Hee hee! The little rascal clambered along the blooming boughs as if he was a blooming little mousekin,' Nathan cried.

'Hee hee hee!' they wheezed.

Seth turned to Button. 'You should have seen that boy, mister! Life and soul of the show he was.'

'Indeed I should.' Button was full of fun too. 'In fact, I'll make it my task to look for him right away. Do any of you smart fellows know where this merry Charlie Punchman might be found?'

TIME PASSING

Nick Tick had simple habits – just one boiled egg and an apple for breakfast, and a pot of tea and sponge cake for supper – so I was very glad I was going to eat with the Aunts in Spinsters' Yard.

I had swept the shop floor with a damp mop, to keep the dust down from the clocks. My insides rumbled for breakfast, but Mr Nick called eagerly, 'Come, Mouse!' With a key in his hand, he was almost ticking with excitement. He wanted to share something with me.

We went through to a secret room, tucked even deeper away than his workshop. This was Nick's treasure house, where he kept his most precious tools and minutely written notebooks, and his cleverest metal-boned children.

Nick Tick, their creator, was showing me his world of tiny machines. He darted among the magical metal

215

toys like an inventive elf.

'Ready? Watch!' One by one, all Nick's inventions moved into motion. Pendulums shone like tiny suns. Lead weights rose and fell, cogs turned and rods twirled and twisted. Long chains ran up, down and around, muttering gently to themselves. Metal arms signalled or stretched. It was amazing!

'See, if I turn this switch, how this spindle moves in another direction,' he sang, hurrying up and down his workbenches, commenting as he went.

An old tea caddy, dripping with tarnished silvery chains, stood on a shelf, and I was reminded of my night in the Aunts' wash-house. I waited until Nick Tick's display had ended.

'Mr Nick, please could I have one of those chains?'

'Certainly, though for what purpose exactly, my dear boy?' Nick pushed his glasses up on to his forehead, very precisely. 'What weight? Length? Type of catch? What is needed?'

'It's a small token that I've promised to wear, but the string has snapped. I think it's some kind of medal.'

'Well then, dear boy, you don't want any of those chains. Poor quality. Links too frail, metal too soft. Try one of these.'

Within a drawer filled with dismantled pieces, springs, links, screws and cog-wheels of all sizes was a box of sturdier chains.

I hesitated. 'I'll pay you back when I can, Mr Nick,' I said awkwardly.

'I know you will, Mouse,' he answered. 'May I see this important item?'

Could he see it? I had kept my medal secret through all the gloom of Murkstone Hall, and through all my time on the road, just as I promised Ma. I had, I had, I had. But now I didn't know who this Ma was. To whom exactly had I made my promise?

I was so tired of secrets, and if kindly Nick Tick couldn't be trusted, who could? I placed the tarnished medal in his hand.

'I was given this long ago by . . . by a friend. It's my secret,' I said, 'and please don't tell Kitty or the Aunts about it.'

I wanted to keep my secret to myself. It was my one true clue, one that my fingers had read like a book in dark corners and had held tight in times of trouble.

Now, as the medal glinted in Nick Tick's palm, my neat namesake looked almost unfamiliar. I could see that some of the careful detail of its fur and whiskers had been smoothed by so much wear.

'This is most remarkable,' said Nick, reaching for a magnifying lens. He turned the disc one way, then another. 'Fine, fine indeed . . . Aha! Very, very clever!'

Nick slid a practised fingernail along an invisible groove in the medal, and one half flipped open, revealing a floating arrow rotating within a glass disc.

'What is it?' I squeaked.

'This, Mouse, is a pocket compass, and probably made for a grand lady.' He turned it over. My name, engraved in curling letters, appeared. 'Intriguing, isn't it, my boy? A compass is a strange gift for a sweetheart. Do you know who owned this before you?'

I shook my head. Not my Ma, for sure, nor Isaac.

Nick Tick selected a chain, running the links through his fingers and tugging it to test for strength. 'A satisfactory chain for a remarkable piece,' he said. 'Here you are.'

'Thank you, Mr Nick.'

Wasn't a compass something that helped you find your way? I'd been carrying this device for so very long, but my life had no sure direction. Was Ma, whom I knew so much and so little about, truly where my path was pointed?

'There's damage along the edge,' Nick added. 'If the hallmarks had been clearer, I could have traced it back to where it was made.'

'Oh!' Quickly I threaded the chain through, hung the compass round my neck and slipped it back under my shirt. Was it stolen property? My Ma could not be a thief, could she? Or Isaac? Surely not.

'Don't worry, Mouse.' Nick put his finger to his lips and winked. A quizzical smile lit his face. 'If I say a word about your medal, may my clocks never strike again! Now off you go and see young Kitty,' he ordered. 'Ever since that bad thing happened to her, she's needed a good friend.'

'What thing?'

'That's Kitty's secret, and no doubt she'll tell you one day.' Nick turned back to his workbench and was immediately lost in his clocks again, coaxing a mechanical bird to sing the hours.

For me, this was a new kind of life. I got used to being clean, to eating and to watching the scars heal on my shins and arms. I helped the Aunts by doing odd jobs, and helped Kitty take Flora, Dora and the laundry to the theatre and home again. It was a life that felt comfortable.

I helped Nick Tick, but what he liked best was having me at hand to chat about how one or another of his small machines worked and could be made better. I think talking helped him think things through.

'Here, boy.' Nick would open up his notebook and draw a rapid diagram across one of the pages. 'Now this is what I mean. Do you see?' And then we would discuss his idea.

As I was interested, he gave me a notebook too. 'Take it, Mouse. Sketch, draw, write. Whatever you will. Do not let your mind grow idle.'

Nick said that we were living at the start of a great age when machines would help mankind to build an organised, punctual world. He talked about steam engines, and telegraphy, and about an invention made by a certain Babbage that might one day count until time itself ended. Nick believed each machine was a small miracle, and that gradually they would create a world of precision and perfection. These were odd imaginings, but I'd known people with far worse intentions, hadn't I?

So I was glad to listen to Nick's dreams. I was glad of the Aunts, and Flora and Dora, and Kitty, and the comfort of their home. I was not unhappy with this new life that had wrapped itself around me.

Yet when I least expected it, memories rose up, ready to drag me down. As we gathered for supper around the friendly hearth, my mind flashed back to long-ago suppers with Ma and Isaac, and often in the early hours, when I was alone in the shop, I woke trembling from dreams of fireweed and burnt buildings.

It was time for me to search until I knew the truth about Ma, about the compass and about myself.

'Kit,' I said, as we came to the Albion one morning, 'I have to go and look for Ma.'

'I'll tell Smudge to let you in later.' She gave a smile and patted my arm. 'Good luck, Mouse.'

So my search began again. I walked through the streets and alleys and nooks of the city, looping further and further. I traced and retraced my steps, wondering what clues I should be seeking. So often I thought I'd seen Ma or Isaac, but when I sped after what seemed a familiar figure, I'd discover that I did not know them at all. I would follow an easy country lope that could be big Isaac's walk, but as I passed and swung around to stare, the face showed me at once I was mistaken. Nor were the women ever Ma.

Every time this happened, it was like Grindle punching me hard all over again. I had to rest and catch my breath.

I searched some of that week, and the next, and the week after. Occasionally that long-ago time at Roseberry Farm seemed so hazy that I was not sure it had existed at all.

How would Ma and Isaac live, here in this city? If I could guess that, I might have an answer. Were Isaac's great and gentle horses pulling around some mighty load, or had they already gone to the knacker's yard? Were Ma and Isaac toiling in some busy factory, or were they paupers, one in each wing of a workhouse, never to meet again? Or were they . . . ? Yes, there were other things I imagined too.

I hated the crowds who got in my way and the people who obscured my view. I hated the excavations that blocked the paths and scratched out the landmarks.

People said that this was a modern time, that we had the penny post and bicycles, steamships and railways, tunnels under the ground and manufactories larger than cathedrals. But in such a marvellously modern time, why could you not find someone when you really needed to?

CHAPTER 35

A DIFFERENT LAUGHTER

Mr Punch proudly took his final bow, and the show was ended. Charlie Punchman hung up his puppets, and stepped out into the yard. Dog Toby waltzed around on two legs, encouraging the crowd to drop their coins in the velvet purse, while Punchman beamed at one and all.

He greeted the giggling children, the pigtailed girls, the crop-headed boys, the big sunburnt lads and lasses leaning against the wall, the wives glad to be away from their hearths, the men young and old, all cheered by his show. He felt the weight of the purse that Toby returned to his hand. Today life was good to him.

As the crowd thinned out, Charlie Punchman saw two smiling faces waiting at the back of the yard: a large red-faced fellow, rather too full of beer, and a small neat man in a beetle-black coat whose small eyes glittered and whose mouth widened into a somehow sinister smile as they approached.

They beckoned Charlie Punchman. Maybe he was too tired to think. In any case, he went over to meet them. His little dog ran too.

Suddenly the big man grabbed Toby's collar, so the dog twisted and turned but could not get free.

'A word with you,' said the small man, 'about a certain boy. I want you to tell me everything you know.'

Punchman's mouth closed tightly.

CAUGHT IN THE ACT

On the Albion stage, I saw Chinese acrobats balanced in pyramids, gypsies hurling knives and eating flames, magicians plucking doves from thin air, funny-man singers in the gaudiest of outfits, and performing parrots and monkeys who cried from the stage for their lost jungles.

Between such acts, Flora and Dora and the littlest girls flitted prettily around the stage. The older dancers trailed around in romantic gauze, or hopped and skipped in comical cottons and clogs. Whatever the dance, whatever the night, the orchestra kept on playing.

After the interval, when half a hundred gas lamps flickered and glowed, came the most important part of the night: the play. It might be a scene, an act, an important speech, or, best of all, a play whole and entire. These were the best. These were proper stories.

Kitty and I often crept backstage to watch the actors at work, but not always.

'No. Why should I spend my time watching their silly faces?' she told me, grieving because she was not part of the show. 'Go up there by yourself if you want to.' So I did, and that is how I first saw part of a famous play.

Miss Day and Mr Knightley were onstage, limelight softening the paint on their faces. Marianne Day was acting Juliet, the heroine, and Knightley was Romeo, her sweetheart. After long speeches between them, Knightley climbed up the rose trellis towards Juliet on the balcony. The conductor urged the orchestra to play louder, because they had orders to hide Romeo's creaking knees.

Knightley made Romeo's words resound mightily, which was very much needed, because some of the audience booed and called for Hugo Adnam to speak the speech instead.

Romeo and Juliet was a famous play written many years ago by someone called Shakespeare. It was a good play because it had exciting sword fights and midnight meetings and poisons and daggers. It had death scenes where everyone thinks the lovers have died, but in fact, when Knightley acted it, they woke up and lived happily ever after.

Kitty and the Aunts argued about this play. Apparently Adnam wanted to put on a new, true version of the play one day, where the lovers do die, just like Mr Shakespeare said.

However, the Aunts insisted that people liked happy endings best. Aunt Violet said that maybe Shakespeare did not understand how to write plays that people enjoyed. Aunt Indigo thought that Shakespeare had probably written a happy ending, but that it had got lost.

What interested me was this whole backstage world, so much bigger than Punchman's canvas booth. How did everything work within the great Albion?

So I kept my eyes open wherever I went. I saw the low trolleys that could wheel leafy trees, golden thrones or tumbledown hovels onstage at a moment's notice. I discovered the enormous wheel that raised the velvet curtains. I found the wheeled boat that usually appeared among rippling waves of cloth, rocking as if it was atop real waves, while the giant metal sheet hung in the wings roared out its thunderstorm. The Albion was a place of trickery and craft, where plain, ordinary materials were turned into a moment's magic.

As often as I could, I sneaked up one of the ladders and on to the fly floor. Up there, in the vast space above the stage, drops of cloth hung suspended like banners. Gauzy screens were ready to descend, trembling, and transform the stage. Up there, where the lantern's beam was changed by artful filter glass, the stagehands ruled the walkways and gantries, to create the world the actors inhabited down below. How Mr Nick would love to see all this cleverness!

Hah! I was not concerned with Romeo or Juliet. Sketching and scribbling, I captured tricks and devices to share with Mr Nick. I filled page after page of my notebook. I even copied down the running lists nailed to the wall for everyone to see. Here the cues and changes, scene by scene, were written down. Here were the lists that explained how they managed to make the Albion work like . . . like . . . like *clockwork*. That was what I wanted to tell Mr Nick.

Then, as I turned a page, a large hand clamped itself over my face. I could see nothing, and I felt myself carried away roughly. The performance was still going on, so I dared not shout. Someone carried me lurching and bumping, along echoing corridors. Then there was light.

CHAPTER 37

ELSEWHERE, A CART STOPS

Elsewhere, a cart stopped. A driver climbed down to see what lay in the ditch by the roadside.

He discovered an old man, his curly hair crusted with mud and blood. Although the man had been battered about the face and body, his knuckles clutched a bag and a tattered basket. A small dog worried and whined anxiously at his side.

'Take us to the city, friend, for pity's sake,' the old man begged, giving a faint smile. 'Me and Toby.'

As the kindly driver lifted the old man into the back of his cart, a host of painted puppets, smashed and broken, spilled out of the basket.

The old man groaned fretfully and tried to get down.

'Wait, sir, wait. I'll pick up your wooden babbies for you,' the carter said soothingly. He picked up the strange collection and placed them back in the old man's basket.

'Thank you, sir,' the man gasped. As he clutched the puppets tightly, his face contorted with pain. 'No, I don't want any help,' he wheezed. 'Just take me to the city.'

The dog jumped in beside him, and the cart jolted off down the road.

Struggling, the old man dragged a filthy jacket out of his bag and pushed it close to the dog's nose. 'You remember who wore it, don't you?' The little dog barked softly. 'That's right, Toby,' said the old man. 'We'll go and find him and warn him, wherever he is.'

Patting that warm furry head, Charlie Punchman drifted off into a painful sleep.

HIMSELF

I saw, across a large dressing room, a tall man in full stage make-up and black velvet costume. Scarlet-rimmed eyes glared at me from a powdered face. Dark lines transformed the backs of his hands into predatory claws. It was Hugo Adnam himself. Beside him stood his dresser, a long velvet cape hanging ready over his arm.

'What is going on, Vanya?' Adnam's rich voice sounded cold. He glanced up at his dresser. 'Do you know anything about this, Peter?' The man shook his head.

'I have something to show,' said Vanya, keeping one hand gripped on my shoulder. My huge bearded captor spread my notebook across Adnam's dressing table, between the greasepaints and brushes. 'Is this!' he growled.

Impatiently, Adnam flicked through my sketches and scribbled notes, ignoring the untouched meal of cold chicken and champagne that lay within easy reach. 'Interesting,' he remarked.

A burst of muted applause revealed that Romeo and Juliet were now living happily, and a stalwart marching song began.

'Five minutes,' the call came outside the door.

'Five minutes, Mr Adnam,' the dresser echoed softly, shaking the folds of the cape.

'Thank you, Peter,' Adnam said. 'I will be there for my cue.' He slammed the book shut and leaped towards me dramatically.

'So! A spy lurks in the Albion's wings, noting down all the secrets of my theatre. Who do you work for? Who let you in? Which theatre sent you, boy? Tell me! Disclose!'

'I'm n-n-not a spy, Mr Adnam,' I said, stuttering. 'I don't know about any other theatres. This is the only theatre I've been inside. I wanted to show these drawings to Nick Tick –'

'So what theatre is this Tick fellow from? Where does he act? Who is his manager?' Adnam's eyes glowed villainously.

'No, you don't understand.' I almost laughed. 'Nick is just a watchmaker.'

'A watchmaker? Hah! So you say. Remember, boy, I am an actor,' Adnam sneered, 'so I know how easy it is to lie.'

What could I do or say without getting Kitty into more difficulty than she was in already?

'Two minutes,' someone called, knocking at the door.

'Time to go, sir,' said Peter, opening out the dark wings of the cape. With a weary sigh, Adnam let the dresser fasten it around his neck.

'Vanya, I will leave this matter to you. If you are worried, keep this thief close until the end of the performance and we'll hear what he says then.'

Abruptly Adnam lunged at me, dagger in hand, its point glittering sharply. 'Listen, you spy, you snoop-merchant! If tonight's audience is not good, I will be in an even worse mood by the end of the play, so beware, boy. Peter, door!'

Adnam exited towards the green room, the cape swirling behind him and Peter running after with a silver-backed brush and comb.

Vanya's bushy eyebrows met in a frown.

'We go elsewhere,' he decided, thrusting my notebook into his pocket. His hand gripped the nape of my neck as he escorted me along several corridors, down some steep wooden steps and into a large vault somewhere below the theatre. The great roar of applause that met Adnam's entrance onstage faded swiftly away.

Vanya's musty lair was stacked with oddments of props, complicated fragments of scenery and pieces of wood. Despite Kitty's earlier tales, I sensed no ghosts, though the man in front of me was scary enough. His fists were like boulders.

Vanya shoved me down on a large stuffed cushion and plonked himself on a chair. Then he took my notebook from his pocket and, by the light of an oil lamp hanging from the wall, read it through carefully. He turned the pages this way and that, studying my sketches from all angles.

'Not bad, spy-boy.'

'I've told you, I'm not a spy. I don't know enough to be a spy. I was just interested in the machines you have in this theatre, and that's all. I wanted to let Mr Tick know about everything that you've got here.'

'Let's try again,' Vanya growled. 'What theatre does Mr Tick work for? Lyceum? The Royal?' His face was so far forward, his nose almost touched my own. 'The Peacock? The Apollo? Speak.'

'Mr Tick works as a clockmaker. That's all. I lodge in his shop.'

'You expect us to believe such a story?'

'It's the truth!' I said again.

At that moment Kitty rushed through the door. 'Mouse!' she gasped. 'Peter told me you'd been brought down here.'

Vanya turned to her. 'You know this sneak?'

For a moment Kitty had a chance to avoid the situation, to keep out of trouble.

'Keep quiet, Kit,' I mouthed.

'Of course I do,' she said. 'He's a friend. He's staying with my neighbour –'

'Who is this neighbour?' Vanya asked. 'Quickly.'

'Nick Tick. He's a watchmaker. What has that to do with things?'

'Aha! So one part of the story is true.' Vanya sighed and dropped his huge head down between his hands. 'Kitty, this boy has made Mr Adnam very angry. He was spying on the play. Look at this book.'

'No, no. Mouse wouldn't,' she said. 'Not spying. He's just nosy about machines and so on. Look at these first pages, Vanya. These are drawings of Mr Nick's clocks.'

'Please, Mr Vanya,' I said wearily. 'I apologise most sincerely, honest. And I don't understand all this talk about spying. Besides, who'd want to spy on a theatre? This isn't a war, is it?'

'Yes, of course it is!' they hissed, like a pair of furious geese.

234

CHAPTER 39

MEANWHILE, ON A SMALL ISLAND

Two days of unexpected gales and a strong current forced Captain Marriner's vessel well off her usual course.

When all was calm again, he studied his sea charts and re-plotted the voyage. By his measurements, the ship would be back on her usual route within several days, as long as the weather held, which it should because the ocean was as blue as his own daughter's eyes.

Just then the cabin boy burst into the Captain's cabin, bringing word of an unexpected sighting on the horizon.

Captain Marriner returned to the deck and lifted a telescope to his best eye. Exactly as Second Officer Quinn had observed, a thin plume of smoke was rising into the tropical sky. Surprisingly, the smoke came from an island that, until that moment, had always been just a dot on the charts.

'Do we have any records of habitation there?'

'None that I know, Captain.'

'Then it is our duty to investigate. Prepare the long-boat and have some marksmen ready, in case of danger. God Save Her Royal Majesty.'

A dozen men leaped from the longboat, guns at the ready, and waded through the lapping turquoise waves towards a wide crescent of yellow sand.

Among the palm trees they saw a ramshackle shelter constructed from driftwood and branches. It seemed to be encircled by small plants, sprouting twigs in baskets and assorted leaf-wrapped packages.

The trail of smoke came from a cooking fire set in a dip in the sand. The glowing cinders were tended by two figures – a man and a woman. Their clothes were worn thin, and the hair on their heads was bleached by days of endless light.

As the sailors approached, the couple rose up like ghosts, and stared steadily at their rescuers. Two pairs of eyes – his pale blue and hers brown as hazelnuts – peered out from faces weathered by sea salt and sunshine.

The woman took hold of the man's arm. 'Is it a mirage, Albert?' Her voice was quite calm.

'No, Adeline, my dear, I don't think so. In fact, I have hopes that it may be time for us to go home.'

'That will be most pleasant, my dear one.' She gave a confident smile. 'I do hope there will be room on that ship for our plants. They are growing so nicely now.'

The ragged man approached Second Officer Quinn. 'Thank you for arriving at last,' he said, giving the armed sailors a puzzled glance 'but won't all that armoury stop your men loading our plant specimens speedily?'

'But –'

The woman stepped forward briskly, her dark eyes determined. 'No buts, young man. This gentleman is the renowned botanist Albert Epton, and I am his wife. We wish to talk to your captain. Now!' The sea breeze tugged at the threadbare lace of what had once been an elegant gown.

Without intending to, Second Officer Quinn found himself saluting Adeline.

Cloaks and Daggers

'Of course it's a war, you idiot!' Kitty raised her hands in the air, exasperated. 'Mouse, don't you realise? Hugo Adnam is probably in debt to his eyeballs. If the Albion doesn't stage the most spectacular show in town this season, he'll be ruined.'

'And if a boy like you,' added Vanya, 'steals the secrets of our productions and sells them to those no-good theatres around us, you bring about our ruin too.'

I was amazed. 'I wouldn't do that.' There was a long pause.

'Good,' Vanya said, his huge bulk overhanging his chair. 'That is very good. Because if you did, I should not be pleased, and that would be most uncomfortable for you, though not for me!' Clasping his hands, he rolled his strong thumbs round each other menacingly.

If anyone was uncomfortable it was Kitty. She

jumped every time any footsteps passed the door.

'Mouse, I must go. Tildy said Miss Lander might call in at the theatre tonight. She mustn't see me. Anywhere.'

She hugged the big man reassuringly. 'Vanya, Mouse is telling the truth, I'd swear on it. And I'm sure Mr Tick has no thought of stealing ideas from your theatre. So please tell Adnam there's been a mistake, won't you?' She darted off, adding, 'Mouse, see you soon.'

'So, Mouse-boy, it seems Miss Kitty means us to be friends.' Vanya gave a slow grin, and it seemed my name had been cleared. 'I shall look again at what you were doing.' This time he turned the pages of my note-book with some care. 'Hmmm. Not bad. I like this.'

I leaned over and saw my drawing of a wind machine. 'Yes. That's a very clever idea.'

Vanya beamed with pride. 'It goes from a breeze to a wind to a fearsome gale with no trouble at all. And it is my triumph, my invention, Mouse. Mine!'

He held up his two huge hands and stretched out his thick fingers. 'These two hands don't look clever. They look like hands of an idiot, a simpleton, an ogre. Like hands that can do nothing much.' His eyes shone brightly. 'But I tell you, Mouse, these so-stupid hands can make *magic*!' He tapped his head. 'And this thick head too is not so dumb.'

I wasn't going to let my own friend go undefended. I held out my own hands. 'Nick Tick's hands are smaller than these, but he can make magic too.'

Vanya tugged thoughtfully at his beard. 'If it is as you say, Mouse-boy, then I have a test for the clever Mr Nick I hear so much about tonight.' Grunting, he reached deep inside his coat. 'Ask your mechanical Mr Tick if he can mend this piece for me.' His giant hands held a tiny watch, studded with stones. 'Tell him it belonged to my mother. Tell him if it goes good, I will pay.'

The performance was over, the applause had died and the auditorium was empty. Adnam sat in front of his mirror, wiping the paint off his weary face and listening as Vanya explained the situation.

'Boy, I may have accused you wrongly,' Adnam said, and rested his head on his arms, exhausted. After a while he lifted it up again. 'Ah, you are lucky, child. If I do unexpected things, the crowds are not so quick to forgive. Go!'

As Vanya pushed me out into the corridor, he gave me back my notebook. 'Come see me soon, boy.' He gave an amused growl. 'I am awaiting your so-clever Mr Nick's work.' I turned to go and he dug me gently in the ribs. 'And bring me more of drawings too. I like a boy who is interested in such things.'

When Nick saw the watch, his eyes sparkled brighter than the stones. It was as if I was giving him a present.

'Such a watch! I will do my best for this friend Vanya,' he said, holding up the watch so that it shone in the candlelight. 'Now, my beautiful silver lady, tell me your troubles . . .'

So my life went on. Most days I felt glad of my luck, especially when I passed stray waifs begging on the street, because that's where I could have ended. Though my lodging was spread between the Aunts' clean rooms and Nick's cramped shop, I was in a far better place than I had expected when I set out from Roseberry Farm.

I tried not to be a burden. I tried to help. I baled out washtubs and carried coal to the copper for the Aunts. I amused Flora and Dora, or let them amuse me. I helped keep Nick's floor clean and his shop in order. I swept out the litter from between the rows of seats, helped around the theatre and listened to Vanya's tales of his machinery. It was all good, but it was not enough, because I still had a burden of my own.

Where exactly was Ma? I had come to search for her, to tell her I had not forgotten her, whoever she was. Sometimes my heart felt so sore that all I could do was curl up and speak to no one. Sometimes I got angry. Why had Ma told me so little? If I did not belong to her or to Isaac, to whom did I belong?

I looked and looked, walked and walked, asked and asked, but there was still no clue. Whenever I could, I visited the horse-fairs and hack-yards and coach-stands. I checked the fine carriage horses, the street-worn mares and the broken-backed nags ready for the knacker's yard as they stumbled through the city streets, but there was no sign of big Isaac among those horses, no sighting anywhere.

I haunted the banks of the great river and gazed towards the great docks, wondering if Ma and Isaac had bought a passage to a new land. The tide flowed up the river and ebbed down the river, carrying flotsam and jetsam and all manner of rubbish. Even when the tide went out, the rubbish was still there, lying on the shores.

Gangs of mudlarks, poor children, flocked along that filthy shore, searching for any valuable find to take to their masters. Often their cries of delight turned to curses or tears as the bright stuff they'd spied in the knee-deep sludge turned to broken glass and was not the diamond they dreamed of finding. Still they searched on, bending and stooping.

How could I search out my Ma? How could I capture my bright dream when all was changing about me? The seagulls bobbed on the grey water, and the cries were mocking.

CHAPTER 41

A SMALL VISITOR

Something pushed the door of the hospital ward ajar. A dark nose poked round it, sniffing as if trying to discover something or someone. The burly nurse, busy filling bottles in the dispensary, did not see the small creature scamper through the narrow gap. Dog Toby wriggled beneath one bed and another and another until at last he reached the bed in the corner. Standing on his hind legs, he tugged at the blanket, whimpering softly.

The old man woke. 'You?' he said, and smiled. He reached to stroke the dog, burying his bony fingers in the warmth of that furry coat.

Then, with a great effort, the old man rolled over to rest on his elbow. He rummaged in the bag stowed under his pillow. Gasping painfully, he dragged out an old jacket and held it to the dog's nose.

'The boy,' he wheezed. 'Remember the boy? We must keep trying, Toby.'

The dog wagged his tail and sniffed and sniffed. This city was so full of interesting smells that it was hard to track down a scent, even one he knew well, though that particular memory seemed fainter each day. Besides, he did not want to leave his master, so he sat watching as the old man dropped into a doze.

As footsteps came down the ward, his master stirred and grimaced at the little dog. 'I told you, friend. Go!'

The dog's ears twitched and he tried to jump up on the blanket.

'No, boy. Go! I'm telling you to go and find him. Go!'

Uncertainly, the dog pattered away, then turned back. Was this really what his master wanted?

'Yes, that's right. Go! Good boy!'

The dog's tail drooped for a second. Then, with a sigh, he turned and hurried off, doing Punchman's bidding one last time.

FOUND AND LOST

Miss Tildy was too busy to teach the girls today.

'I'm sorry, darlings, but I have been asked to help someone with an important part,' she said coyly.

'Bet I know who that is,' hissed Kitty.

'Miss Lander's back,' Flora and Dora informed me. 'She is very pretty, but she can't dance.'

We sat on the theatre steps munching on cold slabs of Aunt Indigo's pie. When they had finished, the little girls ran around feeding crumbs to the pigeons, and Kitty chatted to the apple-women.

I was too tired to go searching for Ma that day. Nick Tick's clocks chimed constantly, night and day, and it was sometimes hard to sleep through them. I sat there yawning and gazing dismally at the crowds.

A small dog pattered out from among the hurrying feet. It paused. It sat on the pavement and sniffed the air. It stretched its nose in my direction, and then its whole body. Then it moved. Slowly at first, then faster and faster, it came running towards me. Sniffing, snuffling, bouncing, barking, the dog raced round me, jumping up again and again, tail wagging.

Punchman's Toby!

'Whatever are you doing here?' I bent down, and he rolled on his back so I could tickle him, though he showed his starved ribs and his dulled, dirty fur. 'You poor boy!' I said, petting him until he wriggled to his feet again.

All at once Toby danced away, and back, and then away again, wanting me to follow him. I got a very bad feeling then, hearing Toby's whimpers of distress. Punchman was in the city, but something was very wrong. He would never willingly let his dog get into this condition.

'Kit, I've got to go with Toby.'

'We'll come along with you,' Kitty said firmly, 'for a while at least.'

'We'll see Punchman's puppet show?' said the girls, who had heard my tales of Dog Toby. They linked hands and put on their good-as-gold faces.

I didn't laugh at their cheekiness. I didn't even care. I was too worried. They could all come if they wanted. I was already off, racing after poor little Toby. I had to keep up with the scampering dog. I needed to know where Punchman was, and why he was here.

The very worst of news. Toby took us through a warren of streets right to the gates of a charity hospital. It was a mean, cold place, close to the river. He waited for us, shivering.

'Poor thing!' Kitty scooped Toby up and wrapped him deep in her shawl, hushing him as if she was carrying a baby. Flora and Dora walked very close to Kitty's heels, holding her skirts anxiously.

At the entrance porch, a porter with a face like boiled pudding tried to turn us away.

'Oh, please let us in, sir,' Kitty pleaded, so sweetly you could not have imagined her as anything other than meekness itself. 'Please help us. We are searching for our poor lost grandfather. We will be as quiet as the tiniest of mice, sir, and our mama has always taught us to be good. Alas! There's only mama, my brother here and me, and we must care for these two tiny sisters and our baby brother.' She peered into the shawl affectionately.

'Go on then, miss,' Pudding-face said, as a tear welled in his eye, 'but be quick about it. Second corridor on the left.'

We found a long grim room filled with low cots, where rows of men lay staring or moaning. This was not a place to play with puppets, or joke about a clattering wooden skeleton.

Punchman's bed was at the far end. His face was bruised, as if he had been beaten. His shivering hands clutched and picked at his blanket, and his shocked eyes watched out for something far away.

As Kitty put Toby down, he nudged his furry nose against the old man's hand. Punchman turned his bruised face, and his eyes twinkled.

'Hello, Punchman,' I said. 'Came to see you.'

'My boy Mouse!' His once strong voice was as thin as a thread. 'What a welcome sight! I knew I could trust my good little dog.'

I nodded and smiled. Words stuck in my throat.

Punchman patted and praised Toby for finding me. Then he said, 'So that pair haven't found you yet? That's good, that's good.'

'What? Who?' I turned cold. 'Who wants to find me?'

'The big 'un and the little 'un. Them two who are after you.' He coughed painfully. 'Vicious, they are. Little 'un said they were going to find you first, before someone else does. Not nice men at all, Mousey, so you'd better be careful. We came here to tell you that, didn't we, Toby?'

Kitty glanced across. 'What does he mean?' she mouthed.

It was too late. Punchman's mind had drifted on, and for a while his mumblings made no sense. Then another anxiety surfaced, and the old man tried to drag a grubby sack from under his bed. 'Mouse, help me. Let me see them again.'

One by one I took out Punchman's puppets so that he could see each familiar carved and painted face. He raised a hand to each one, and nodded, giving shallow, contented sighs.

'Look after my wooden friends for me, won't you, my boy? Won't be using them for a while.'

Suddenly his feverish eyes gazed beyond me, at little Flora and Dora with their shining golden curls.

'The Lord be praised. It's the blessed angels come for

me after all, Mouse, my old friend. Two pretty little cherubs, come to take me to heaven. Keep safe, my dearest boy,' he whispered. 'Keep happy.'

Punchman smiled, and it was a moment of great joy. Then he was gone to his peace.

We carried Toby away with us, holding the shawl tight around him so he could not run back.

Kitty looked at the girls sternly. 'You say nothing to the Aunts about where we've been.'

'Not even that we are angels?' Flora asked.

'Not a word from either of you, or you'll never live to be angels. The Aunts would be worried.'

The girls were not worried about poor Punchman. Hadn't the old man gone to heaven to be an angel, like their mother did when they were born? I, Mouse, had a sackful of the old man's puppets, so they would be able to see a show after all. Best of all, we now had Dog Toby to look after. The dog was only one of my worries.

'What did he mean, Mouse, about the men after you?' Kitty asked quietly.

I dared not reply, because the more I thought about Punchman's bruises, the worse I felt about whatever I had brought my friend. He spoke of a big man and a small man. They could only be Bulloughby and Button.

Dread wrapped around me. I walked back to the theatre in silence. How could I explain those men to Kitty without worrying her? Why did they want me anyway? Bulloughby had no reason for wanting me back at Murkstone Hall, and I could not imagine that I mattered much to Button.

Next day I said another goodbye to Punchman. He was buried just outside a churchyard stuffed with upright slabs and smug angels. I had groomed Toby as best I could, and I prayed as best I could, in the words Ma taught me, with Mr Punch peeping out of my coat pocket.

The parson, uncomfortable about being seen in the pauper's corner, gabbled through the prayers. I placed a bunch of violets on the bare mound of earth in feeble farewell.

As I strode back to the Albion, Punchman's words chattered in the back of my mind: 'Going to find you first, before someone else does.'

All these months, while I had been searching so unsuccessfully for Ma, someone else was searching for me. I wanted to be ready for whoever it was. Maybe my lost Ma was the only one who could explain.

So I tried harder to find her. I got up early, to grab hold of the ordinary dawn-lit everyday world as well as the half-pretence of the Albion's night-time world. I discovered nothing new, except that I was growing tired to my bones.

I hung round all the carriage stops, enquiring. I peered into the speeding flies and the slowly rolling carts. I jumped on the running boards of the hansom cabs, asking the drivers if they had seen someone like Isaac in any stables.

When the omnibuses stopped, I watched every face. I studied the Sunday folk coming from steepled churches, dressed in heavy silk and bombazine, and the chapel folk, buttoned into their simple best as they scuttled towards their own Sabbath service. No Ma or Isaac there.

This city had become such a big, big place. Since meeting poor Punchman, my fear of shadows had returned. I grew ill-tempered, unable to chat and joke with Flora or Dora. Their wide hurt eyes followed me, silently asking what they had done wrong. I even avoided conversations with Kitty.

Though Dog Toby followed at my heels, my searches made him anxious for his lost master, and he howled if he was left alone among the boots and shoes at the Albion. After he'd gnawed his way through two misshapen pairs, I left him behind, at Nick Tick's feet. Toby snoozed, content, in the warm shop, but he met me with a wagging tail whenever I returned.

I could not help him. I could not help my friend Punchman, could I? I didn't even want to help myself. I curled up in my small bed in Nick Tick's house, and longed to disappear. I closed my eyes. Ma, where were you?

In a fitful dream, three leering strangers knocked the door down, calling me by a name that was mine but not mine.

'No, no!' I yelled as they reached for me, and woke. Kitty was thumping the pillow by my head.

'Sit up!' she said.

'Go away, Kit,' I grumbled.

She pulled the covers off, making me face her. 'Mouse, why are you being so horrible?'

I glared. I waved my hand dismissively. 'Leave me alone.'

She stood there defiantly. 'Listen, Mouse,' she said, 'I got the Aunts to take you in. I got you work at the theatre, even when I wasn't in the best place there myself. I told Vanya I trusted you, and I got you out of trouble with Adnam. I even went to that filthy hospital to see that poor old man. But all this means nothing, because you don't trust me. What on earth is wrong?'

'Secret,' I muttered.

'Pah! Everyone's got secrets. Please, Mouse, tell me.'

So I did. I admitted my search was getting nowhere, that I was bitter that Ma lied to me, that I was a silly little boy who got taken from his home like a fool. I told her about Murkstone Hall and Grindle. She listened without interrupting, and I dared to hope she understood.

Finally I explained what Punchman had told me. A pair of men were following me – one big, one little. I paused, then added that they wanted to find me before someone else did so. Just saying those words made me afraid.

Kitty stared at me, her eyes filling with concern.

'Don't know who this other man could be, Kitty,' I said. 'Don't know what he wants. Don't know what any of them want.' The thoughts kept going round and round in my head. I needed to think about something else.

So I turned the tables on Kitty. 'Now you tell,' I said. 'Why do you skulk around that theatre, acting as if you're invisible?'

"No. One thing at a time, Mouse,' she said briskly. 'Tell me.'

Her plait flew from side to side as she shook her head. 'Not now, Mouse. Besides, I've come to tell you the Aunts are frying up some sausages, so don't sit there like an idiot. Get ready. We miss you. Hurry up!'

She left me there. I suddenly felt so glad that I'd told my tale that I laughed. A plate of sausages? Toby looked up hopefully, tail wagging, and barked five times.

'Hope the Aunts have plenty of sausages then,' I told him.

SOME WORDS OF DIRECTION

Button's smile creaked on his face. Bulloughby's presence was hard to endure. Though the oaf had suited his purpose back at Murkstone Hall, the Punchman incident had made Button see the boastful headmaster as a liability.

When they'd got Punchman on his own, Charlie had fought back so fiercely that Bulloughby had backed away. Who would have thought the little puppet master had so much fight in him? And then, with the sound of other wheels approaching, they'd flung the little man down among the reeds, in the hope that he'd drown in the ditchwater before he had a chance to wake – and all this without getting any information. That had really annoyed Button.

An even worse annoyance was that Bulloughby was not a pleasure to be with. The big man sniffled and

snorted like a walrus, complaining loudly and continually, no matter where they were. Bulloughby had a habit
of drawing attention towards them. This was dangerous.

Mr Button was a man who needed to be discreet. His
kind of work was best done quietly, and Bulloughby was
disturbing his mood.

Down the city street the big man and small man
walked, passing costermongers' carts and pie shops and
noisy pubs where songs burst out from doorways, filling
the night air with sound.

Button stopped, looked left and right, then turned
into a quieter road. 'Remembered a short cut,
Bulloughby. This way.'

The two men walked on and soon came to an exca-
vation site fenced off by wooden palings. Within was
one of the vast tunnels that engineers enjoyed hollowing
out beneath the modern city.

No navvy gangs toiled down there now. They were
busy drinking and brawling elsewhere in the district. A
dim lantern light hung outside the watchman's rough
shack, but from within came the sound of snores.

Button froze, suddenly. 'Quick! There!' he whispered.
'I saw him, the wretch! I saw Mouse!'

'Where?' Bulloughby swaggered forward, chin and
fists stuck forward. 'I'll grab the vermin.'

Button pointed to a gap in the fencing. 'Ran through
there, he did. Expect he thinks he can hide from us, my
friend.'

'But he can't,' Bulloughby said, pulling the palings
further apart. He stepped unsteadily through.

'A bit further over, my friend,' urged Button. 'I'm here, right behind you. Just wait till we get hold of him! Then you'll be able to learn the brat, won't you?'

'Mouse,' Bulloughby called, 'I'm coming to get you, and this time you won't get away from me. I'll learn you and I'll learn you and . . .'

The last words were rather more indistinct because Bulloughby felt such a sharp crack on his head that he found himself plunging down the shaft, way down into the belly of the tunnel, and entering the pool of seeping water that lay at the bottom.

'Such clever engineers we have nowadays!' commented Mr Button, as he slipped his lead-tipped life preserver into his coat and walked briskly down the quiet street, at peace and alone.

A REQUEST

Vanya grabbed me and pulled me into a shadowy niche.

'Your Nick Tick, he is not blabbermouth?'

'No. Of course not.'

Vanya's words rushed out in a mix of excitement and fear. 'It is this, Mousekin. I have a teeny tiny idea buzzing in my brain. It is only a pinch of a plan, an inch of an invention.' He hit his forehead forcefully. 'But my brain is made of wood. I cannot see the whole picture.' His arms stretched out as if he wanted to demonstrate the vastness of the puzzle. 'Mouse, soon the great Adnam will say, "Vanya, my dear friend, the one I rely on, what great surprise is there to use in my next play?"'

A vast sigh rose from his chest. 'So help me, boy, I have nothing to tell this magnificent man. I need another head to help me.' He placed his hands on my shoulders, and stared down at me, his eyes hopeful. 'Mouse, maybe your Mr Tick is a man who can help me. He made my mother's watch work again. Will you ask him for me? It is most urgent.'

'I'll ask him tonight,' I said.

'Good boy!' he said, beaming. 'But do not give too much away, will you? This is our big, big secret!'

Vanya placed one finger to his lips and padded off to attend to the latest delivery of scenery.

Vanya's forceful knock set the doorbell clanging, making Mr Nick open his door very quickly indeed.

'Humble apologies!' Vanya whispered, closing the shop door very gently. 'Forgot.'

Dog Toby crouched against the floor, growling. 'Shh!' I said, and stroked his furry head.

'You are most welcome, Mr Vanya,' Nick said. Nervously he led this huge bull of a man among his precious clocks. Vanya trod slowly, one pace after another. Then, carefully lowering his head, he entered Nick's small workroom with its miniature machines.

'A very wonderful sight!' Vanya shook like a child entranced, but he touched nothing. 'It is just as Mouse described. You are an extremely clever man.' He grasped Nick's neat little hand in his huge paw enthusiastically. 'Mr Nick, I am most delighted to meet you. Such miracles you've made!'

'Delighted myself, Mr Vanya.' Nick blushed, overwhelmed by Vanya's joyous response. 'Now, to business. You have an idea that you need to discuss?' He indicated a sturdy wooden chest. 'Sit down, Mr Vanya, do.'

'An idea? That is what I do have! A marvellous idea,' beamed Vanya, sitting. He brought out a pocket flask and two small metal beakers, which he filled. 'We will be good friends, Mr Nick. Now drink!'

'Cheers!' Nick sipped, then gasped for breath. 'Somewhat strong for a chap like me, I'm afraid,' he gasped. 'So? Tell me all about this idea of yours.'

Vanya whispered something in Nick's ear. 'It will be stupendous,' he concluded, rolling his eyes.

'It will be that amazing?' Nick said, bright as a sparrow that has seen a fall of fresh crumbs.

'Amazingly so. It is a flying machine that will let the actor move this way and that, free like a bird, free like angel flying.' He tugged some folded sketches from his pocket and smoothed them out across his knee. 'You see how it goes? You think it good?'

Nick peered at the heavily annotated and pencilled diagrams. 'I think,' he said, 'this is a very excellent idea, though there is this, which must drop down, and this, which could be better . . .'

'I knew your brain would be the right one to help me,' Vanya rumbled, and so their happy conspiracy began.

All that week, I caught Vanya gazing up into the fly-tower, where the scenery hung, or vanishing away into his under-stage vault. When Friday came, he handed me a sealed paper. 'For Mr Nick,' he whispered.

On Monday, a securely tied note from Nick was tucked into my jacket. 'For Mr Vanya,' it read.

*

The next time they met, Vanya entered very, very softly, and within a moment he and Nick sat, heads together, in Nick's tiny shop, studying an unusual mechanical device constructed from thin cane, clamped fast to the workbench.

At one end of the invention was a small pendulum, and some small gears and joints that worked a long extending arm. With its dangling thread and hook, it looked almost like a miniature crane.

'Will it work?' Nick's eager grin must have raised his ears two whole inches higher on his head.

'Ah, who knows?' Vanya sighed, a smile appearing beneath his beard. The huge man glanced at the tiny man and they chortled. 'Shall we see?'

Vanya hung a pippin apple, wound round with thread, on the hook. A lever was released, and somehow the whole mechanism slid into motion. Gradually the long arm extended forward, further and further. Nick released another spindle, and somehow the arm moved from side to side, swinging from its one fixed point. The gleaming apple followed, developing an arc that grew wider and wider as the thread was let out.

'It flies!' Vanya cried. They clapped each other on the back, applauding their own cleverness. Dog Toby, tail wagging, danced after the flying apple.

'Nick Tick, you are a master.'

'No, Mr Vanya, it is you who are the genius!' They bowed a little to each other, delighted with their experiment.

'It will need more work,' fretted Nick, 'but how can we get the thing properly made?'

Vanya laughed, and grinned in a determined way. 'Where there is a will there is a way, my friend. Just now, we celebrate!' He extracted his familiar flask and cups. 'Here, Mouse!' he called, throwing me the apple to eat.

It was one thing to share the idea with Nick, another to explain it to Adnam. As we stood outside his dressing room, we could hear the great actor shouting orders to his faithful dresser.

Vanya's mouth worked away, as if he was gathering his words there, ready to present to Adnam. Nick and I carried another model of the marvellous machine between us.

'Go away! I'm busy!' Adnam shouted.

'It is me, Vanya, with my friend Mr Nick and the boy!' Within moments Peter had opened the door, iron in his other hand. Several white shirts hung over the folds of a painted screen.

'I have only a few moments, so waste no time,' Adnam urged. His face, make-up just removed, was red and raw. 'I am due at a grand dinner immediately, where I must coax even more wealthy souls to donate money to my Albion.'

He rose and dragged on one of the crisp white shirts. Peter brought forward a set of evening clothes.

Vanya nudged Nick, who started babbling out his enthusiasm. 'Mr Adnam? You want your theatre to have a new machine? You want a special invention, a new pattern, a thing never seen before?'

'It is very, very good,' Vanya added.

'Of course I do, sir, if it is as good as you believe.' Adnam checked the time on his gold fob watch. 'So come on, tell me do, now. Speak!'

Vanya opened his arms wide as wings. 'Is brand-new way of flying. Just now all we have is the old ceiling trap opening, and the actor going up and down, up and down on a rope, like bucket in a well. Very dreary. Very ugly. Sometimes the actor swings a little left, then sometimes swings right. Sometimes the actor is pulled back up through the trap. Some big surprise!' Vanya curled his lower lip scornfully.

'But me and my clever friend make something totally new. Once the lights are low, the actor will seem like angel flying out over the audience.'

'Are you sure? Sounds impossible, Vanya.' Adnam pulled on an emerald brocade waistcoat and an evening coat.

'Think, think, Mr Adnam!' said Nick. 'Does the fisherman always stand in the water to cast his line? Show him, Vanya!'

Grandly, Vanya placed a wooden box on the table. He unclipped the lower fastenings, and lifted the lid. The new model was made of metal wire, and fine strings guided the action. Instead of that apple, a small peg-doll dangled from a silken thread. The inventors set the machine in motion.

'Please cover those candles, Peter, sir,' Nick said, pointing.

Peter did, though he huffed a little. With only two lights shining, the thread had become invisible, so the doll looked as if it was circling and weaving through the air.

'Is magic?' beamed Vanya.

'Perfect magic!' Adnam sprang up and slapped their backs and called them good fellows. As Peter relit the candles, Adnam pumped their hands. 'Yes, it will be wonderful. Make it soon, soon, but with not a word to anyone, my clever, clever friends. A wonderful invention!' With that, he pulled on his cloak and rushed out.

Peter tidied away Adnam's clothes and rearranged his dressing table. Just as precisely, Vanya and Nick repacked their little machine, and then Peter ushered us into the corridor.

'Did he say anything about money?' asked Nick, as we all left.

'Hey, that is Mr Hugo Adnam for you!' Vanya gave an enormous shrug. 'But an adventure, eh? Don't you think so, Mouse?'

'But what is the machine for?' I asked.

'For flying!'

'Flying who?'

'Who knows? Adnam has yet to name his play,' Vanya said dismissively. 'Now, we must both be busy with other work. Farewell, my dear Mr Nick.'

As he descended the steps to his lair, he turned and winked. 'Have no fear, my friend. We will meet soon, and we will build our clever machine so cunningly that nobody will work out our secret. A few cogs from this one, strong struts from that one, fine rope or wire from another. No stinking spies will discover what marvel is going to appear in Adnam's next show, not until it is too late for them to copy it! Ha!'

*

I am sure that little machine helped Adnam decide on his play, because within three days word arrived at the Aunts'. Time to prepare for the new extravaganza! Overnight, as the Aunts had told me, cabs arrived almost hourly bearing bundles of cloth and parcels of thread. The Aunts' home almost became a manufactory.

Overhead, the treadle of Aunt Violet's sewing machine whirred continually. Half-finished garments hung everywhere. Older costumes lurked about, waiting for renovation or transformation, or for cutting into useful pieces. A portfolio of Adnam's quick sketches was spread across the table, each character's costume covered with Peter's meticulous measurements and detailed description.

Aunt Indigo unrolled the bales of fabric. She measured and marked and cut the cloth, then took the sections of each garment to Aunt Violet for stitching together.

There were boxes full of dazzling silks and feathers and spangles, skeins of ribbon for folding into rosebuds, and the threatening glint of needles and pins arrayed on every surface. Dog Toby was given very strict orders to stay in his box.

'Thirty tiny fairies, plus headdresses,' said Aunt Indigo, checking yet another list. 'Twenty junior fairies, plus headdresses. Four headdresses for the horses . . .'

'Horses?' I said.

'For the golden coach, silly!' Dora sighed at my stupidity.

'I've ridden on two huge carthorses –' I began, but Flora interrupted.

'Carthorses would be much too big, silly Mouse,' she said. 'Fairy horses are very, very little.'

'So where do you get these fairy horses?' I asked, half mockingly.

'From Mr Spangle's Emporium. Where else?' said Kitty.

CHAPTER 45

Down by the Docks

Towards the wide grey estuary, where the city's distant stench mingled with the sea-salty air, ships lay at anchor, waiting to be taken upstream to the docks and warehouses. Small boats sculled here and there, ferrying passengers and urgent packages ashore.

The river pilots had brought Captain Marriner's ship to a safe mooring. His voyage was almost ended. He stood by the gangplank, duty bound to bid farewell to important passengers.

These included Adeline and Albert, who were waiting to disembark. Few people would recognise them as the pair of scarecrows rescued from a desert island now that they were dressed in the fashionable clothes of wealthy gentlefolk.

It had been a strange time, thought Captain Marriner. When Albert and Adeline first sat at his table, they had been bemused by so much crockery and cutlery silverware, and the long list of dishes appearing on the menu. Yet, within days, their true British manners and poise had returned.

The pair had sent messages from each port along on their return journey: telegrams to the Geographic Club, the Botanical Society, to Kew Gardens, and to Epton Towers. Replies had come back from all except the last.

Albert and Adeline approached Captain Marriner. The porters had already lowered their personal luggage into the small boat that would ferry them to shore.

'Thank you so much, Captain Marriner,' said Adeline. She gazed uncertainly towards the riotous wharfs and quays ahead. Her years of life on the lonely island were still very much with her.

'Definitely, definitely! Thank you so much for all your help, Marriner,' enthused Albert. 'Very well done.'

Marriner saluted, Albert raised his hat, Adeline extended her gloved hand briefly towards the Captain, and the pair descended to the sound of the ship's whistles.

Adeline, the Captain admitted, was most charming and persuasive when she chose to be. No wonder her husband doted on her every word. However, the Captain would be glad to be rid of their collection of wretched botanical specimens. The things had filled three of his cabins. He had allowed as many on board as he could, but what a fuss there had been over all the plants abandoned on the island. Adeline had lamented as if some of those plants were her children. 'Our life's work gone!' she had sobbed.

Captain Marriner turned to the next farewell and felt a reassuring surge of impatience. As soon as every passenger had disembarked, he could get his ship put in good order again. The unwelcome plants could be shipped to shore and stored in a warehouse until their destination was settled. Then his crew could set about making his vessel shipshape again. After all, he ran an orderly, sturdy ship, not a flower shop.

Busy Captain Marriner was too far away to see the newspapermen gathered on the quay. As Albert and Adeline arrived, the reporters swooped like ravens for scraps of news.

They were a little disappointed to find that the rescued plant hunters did not want fame thrust upon them, and, in fact, most rushed off to follow rumours of a murder in a local tavern.

So the news of Albert and Adeline's return was not widely publicised, though there was much amazement and joy among several botanical scientists and map-makers.

CHAPTER 46

THE EMPORIUM

'Here we are,' said Vanya, as we clattered down the broad cobbled way that led to Mr Spangle's Exotic Emporium. The yard was full of packing cases, straw poking from between their slats, and great canvas bales sewn tightly up with twine, all marked with strange foreign letters.

The Emporium was a huge warehouse of a building, with high barred windows. Kitty's eyes narrowed, and she became increasingly uncomfortable as we entered the imposing doorway. Aunt Indigo had sent her to note down the measurements needed for the bridles and headdresses of the new fairy horses.

'And we are here too because we are fairies,' Flora told me, skipping along cheerfully.

The gates clanged behind us, and we entered a realm

where enormous green plants burst out of open sacks, and palm trees rose from gigantic pots.

Being inside the Emporium was like being in one of Jarvey's stories of the jungle, a place alive with shockingly coloured birds and jewelled finches, although in Jarvey's tales the birds were not confined to wicker cages.

Screeching peacocks plunged angrily from one roost to another. Brilliant parrots, all scarlet and emerald, circled angrily on their perches, raging at the chains on their feet. Beneath their shrill calls, I heard deeper, wilder roars echoing from somewhere within the Emporium.

Mr Spangle surged out of his office, arrayed in a jacket of deepest purple and patterned with golden dragons.

'To what do I owe this honour, dear Vanya? I trust Hugo Adnam is well? And dear, beautiful Bellina?' he said with a sly look at Kitty.

Kitty shrank even further into herself at the sound of Bellina's name. She stared fiercely at the parrots.

'So, Vanya, what can I suggest for some theatrical impact? Panthers are popular this season.' He strolled with us around several cages and crates. 'I've a wonderful python over there, and six Pekinese puppies, just arrived.' Spangle paused thoughtfully. 'Best not have both of those onstage together, just in case.'

'Adnam may be interested in four ponies,' said Vanya. 'Small ones.'

'Fairy ponies,' cried Flora and Dora prettily, 'for the Fairy Queen.'

'Then you are in luck. A foursome arrived this very week, all white.' Mr Spangle rubbed his hands together gleefully. 'Expensive, mind you, but trained specially for the winter season. They'll obey a fairy princess's whisper, stand as still as sugar mice and turn on a sixpence. They're so well taught they won't make a mess onstage, not even during the finale, or so I'm told. Walk this way, sirs, ladies.'

The four ponies stood in a pen, tossing their long manes and whisking their tails. They whinnied as if they were already impatient to leave Mr Spangle's Emporium.

'Oh, they're just so pretty!' gasped Dora unwisely, before Kitty could stop her.

Vanya scowled, knowing he had to bargain with the smug Spangle. 'Huh! Silly little girl! She knows nothing. These four things look dull as boiled milk. No energy, no life. Probably poor-tempered as well.'

'No, no. They are each as sweet as honey, I promise,' oozed Spangle. 'Guarantee they'll give Adnam a stunning scene.'

Vanya shook his head slowly and glumly. 'Think these ponies will need too much grooming and powdering to be worth putting on the Albion's stage. Such preparation work takes time, and we are already so very busy. Maybe for a sum like this we could take them,' Vanya sighed, rolling his eyes mournfully as he handed Spangle a written offer from Adnam.

'My heart, my heart! Way too cheap,' Spangle bleated. 'Cheaper than I deserve, my friend. I paid far more than that for them.'

Vanya drew himself up to his full bear-like height. 'Well, that is the Albion's offer. Take it or leave it,' he growled. 'Is easy for Adnam to change script about,' he suggested, 'if ponies cost too much. Such creatures are only onstage for a moment, so they will not be missed. We have other excitements. Let us go, children.'

Mr Spangle coughed and peered at the letter again. Then he bowed and dipped and humbled himself. 'Oh, that is the number! That is what it says. My mistake!' he murmured. 'Tell Mr Adnam the four white ponies are his. I can even arrange their constant care, though I will have to add a small charge for the hay and so on.'

'I will tell Mr Adnam that there will be very small charge for such help, yes?' rumbled Vanya, with no hint of a smile. 'Delivery by Friday?'

'Just as you ask, Mr Vanya,' said Spangle. 'Pleasure doing business with you as always.'

So they shook hands, the deal was done and we wandered back through the vast Emporium, where goods and creatures from all nations of the world were gathered together behind bars.

We stopped to watch a group of small monkeys, who huddled together in a draughty cage, rocking anxiously. Their wizened keeper unlocked the door and trudged in with a bucket of water. He filled an empty bowl, threw a handful of seeds on the sawdust floor and turned to leave.

Quicker than thought, one monkey leaped through the gate, racing hand over hand up and over the cage towards the bright skylight high in the ceiling.

'No, you don't, you blighter!' shouted Spangle. There was a gunshot.

The twins shrieked. The monkey fell, tumbling, landing in the angle between two iron beams. It chattered briefly, as if it might still be alive.

The footholds only needed a glance. Up the first section of ironwork I went, and the next. Ignoring the screeches of girls and peacocks, I leaned out along the girder, put the trembling little creature inside my buttoned jacket, and came down almost as quickly as I'd climbed up.

'Well, well! Little Mouse!' Vanya's eyes were wide with astonishment. Kitty smiled at me too, as if she'd suddenly decided I was more than a friendly runaway.

Flora and Dora whimpered over the little monkey, though by now it was eager to return to the concerned calls of its tribe – and that was where it must go, for where else could it be kept?

I carried the creature back to its cage. The bullet had not injured the animal badly, just scraped away a line of fur. Jumping from my arms, it scampered, chattering, along a twisted log and sat to let its friend search its fur for fleas.

Mr Spangle groaned as he struggled back up off the floor, which was where Vanya's weighty blow had laid him.

Vanya glowered. 'You do not do that no more, Mr Spangle,' he said, handing back the gun. 'Understand? Or we do not trade with you no more, eh? Furthermore, I expect those horses to be very happy and healthy indeed when you deliver them, Mr Spangle.'

We left, with Spangle bowing abjectly.

Vanya gave me a strangely interested glance. 'I did not know you climb so good, Mouse-boy. Useful to know, very useful indeed.'

A CUNNING PLAN

It took almost a day to do it, but, among the shouts of stagehands, Mr Nick and Vanya's fantastic flying device was raised up above the stage.

The mechanism fitted perfectly into the height of the stage. The oiled gears and wheels spun silently, and the wires and ropes ran through metal eyes so they would not tangle. The rewinding wheel had powerful handles, so that the flying line could be drawn back fast. All the scenery would have to be specially designed around it, because the machine had to remain concealed until it was needed.

'If the stage was any other stage, we would be in trouble,' Vanya commented, 'but here, with the space so tall, it will go well.'

I stood on the stage, gazing up. How I admired the cleverness of Vanya and Nick, my two friends, as they stood beside me. Gradually I noticed that their eyes were fixed on me in an oddly fond way. They seemed rather on edge, as if something was about to happen.

Nick coughed, smiled and patted my arm reassuringly. Vanya breathed in, and then he breathed out and said, all of a rush, 'Mouse, we have something to ask you.'

Vanya held up the newly made flying harness, all leather and straps 'Could you . . . ?' Vanya asked.

Could I? What could I say? I'd heard Vanya and Nick working on their machine so often. I almost imagined I could draw it with my eyes closed. I trusted them, of course I did. I wasn't afraid of going up so high, though I was more than a little worried about coming down again. Could I? This was a real live theatre.

Then I felt a tingle of excitement, like the feeling I'd had when I danced on beams above Punchman's booth and the crowd cheered. I started to imagine soaring over the audience . . .

'Yes,' I said. 'I will.'

First I put on a thick cotton vest and a pair of cut-down linen breeches, and then the flying harness. Even with padding, the straps did not feel very comfortable. I strutted about, trying to get my body used to the weight.

Kitty found me a pair of soft leather slippers, tightened by laces.

'Won't my boots do?'

'Mouse, you must land like snowflake, not crashing elephant,' said Vanya. 'And what if a boot fell on someone's head?'

'What about barefoot?'

'Believe me, the stage is full of splinters,' said Kitty.

Two of the stage crew were leaning over the railing, high above me. I seized the first rung. Hand by hand, foot by foot, I willed myself up, the long ladder thrumming at each step. I reached the iron gangway above the stage, where each of the ropes that raised the scenery ran in its own wooden groove on the wall.

I stepped on to the grating and glimpsed the boards of the stage far below. What was it about this climb, with its changing pools of light and dark, that worried me so?

Trembling, Nick climbed up to the walkway after me, because he must. He had to show me and the stage-hand exactly how to clip the lines into place, and how to steady the anchor rope. He had to show me the long lines running down to the floor that would be used to haul me back from my flight. The burly stagehand far below grinned up at me. I paused and took in a deep hard breath.

Way down below, in the middle of the stage, four safety cushions had been dragged up from beneath the stage traps. Though these squabs were bigger than a king's bed, from this height they seemed smaller than Aunt Violet's dainty armchair pads.

Kitty and Vanya were watching from below, tiny as toy figures. Dog Toby was pattering around the stage, worrying in case it was my turn to come to harm.

'Mouse,' said Nick rather anxiously, 'once you are ready, imagine you are diving down into water. Don't worry about the machine. It will follow you.'

He didn't know that I had never been a swimmer.

'Are you ready?' Nick asked me. The stagehand had grasped the ropes.

'Almost.' I curled my toes around the iron ledge, getting my balance, and I wrapped my fingers around the handrail on each side.

'Good luck, Mouse-boy! Go well!' Vanya shouted, waving up at me. Toby danced about Vanya's feet, barking his own wishes. I waved back at them. If the machine didn't work, this gesture would be my last.

I spied the long limbs of Hugo Adnam sprawled in the front row of the auditorium. He was pretending to study a script, underlining parts and scenes, but he too was waiting for me to jump. The future of his beloved theatre depended on the machine's success.

When I was with Charlie Punchman, I had learned to crow and shout and prance and call up a show. Here, at the Albion, I was no singer or actor. All I could hope to do was climb, and fly. I hesitated, feeling sick. I was afraid.

'Let us see the machine at work,' whispered Nick, behind me. 'All the straps are fastened now.'

I did not move.

'Hey, Mousekin! It is time. Fly, Mouse, fly!' bellowed Vanya, his jovial face beaming at me. 'Have courage! Have delight!'

Have delight! I took a deep breath and counted, 'One, two, three . . .' and then I let go, falling forward into a downward swing. The arms creaked, the harness squeezed tight into my ribs and Vanya's lines took me arcing across the stage. Just when the rope was reaching full stretch, I heard the rollers swish along their runners and I flew further out over the seats, out above Adnam, who could not keep his eyes off me.

I swung out then back, out then back. Then the lines tightened and, like a marionette, I was taken from one side to the other in a giant half-circle.

Kitty and Vanya were clapping and dancing, Nick was cheering, Adnam was on his feet, and I swear that even the carved golden cupids around the theatre were smiling at me.

I flew, I swooped, I soared. My mind was dazzled by the flight, by the action. Whatever Vanya and Nick had told me had gone out of my mind. What was supposed to happen next?

I felt a tug at my waist, and the windlass turning, reeling in the line and lifting me up so I could land safely back on the stage.

I met the boards with an inelegant thud, as the slope of the stage toppled me backwards and I collapsed on my behind.

Everyone rolled about, gasping with laughter, but from an underlying sense of relief.

Nick's round face peered down at me. He was beaming like the man in the moon. Vanya was shouting, Kitty was cheering, while Dog Toby, responding to the atmosphere of celebration, raced across the cushions and jumped on to me, tail wagging madly.

Adnam stood, applauding. 'Gentlemen, you two are geniuses!' He reached into his pocket and flung some coins at me. 'See! The boy Mouse is hired. You can have his services whenever you want to work on your machine. But remember, it must be perfected in time for the play. The reputation of the Albion depends upon you!'

So we continued. Now the machine was truly installed, Vanya made use of me almost daily, balancing this wheel, adjusting this line, checking for any damage to the straps. Nick asked me for daily reports. The stage-hands muttered their observations as they passed.

The only one who said nothing was Kitty. When the first flight went well, she had danced around and told the little girls all about it, but since then, day by day, she had grown more distant.

'Kit, what is it?'

'Nothing,' she said, stabbing her needle into a piece of tough cloth. 'Go back to Vanya. I've got lots to do here.'

'Tell me.'

'No, Mouse. Just go!'

CHAPTER 48

SCROPE ALONE

So this was the place, Scrope thought as he dismounted. He had reached Murkstone Hall, and he would do what he had come to do. He sighed, hardly able to believe he had finally arrived.

He had known the school was far away, but he hadn't realised how far into the wilderness he would have to travel. No wonder nobody had built a railway along this route!

The journey had been a nightmare. His horse had gone lame on him and needed to be rested and he had chosen to wait till she had recovered rather than ride an unfamiliar animal. Then, in another inn, he had come down with a dreadful fever and been an invalid in bed for a week or more. The ruts and potholes were so bad he had twisted his back and could only stand being in the saddle for an hour or so a day. Finally, a river had flooded, so he had had to go many miles out of his way in search of a passable road.

Scrope knew that these all seemed like excuses for avoiding an awkward scene. But he hadn't turned back, though he could have done, and now he was here at last.

The iron gates hung loose in the pillars, and the building beyond was dark and ugly. Was this where the boy was sent?

A soft voice in his head corrected his words: 'This is where *you* sent the boy Mouse. You, yourself, Scrope!' But he could not bear to think of that, not at this moment. He was gathering his strength for what he would face.

To his surprise, a brisk command rang merrily across the cold, unfriendly landscape.

'Now, boys! Get ready! Go!'

The shouted order was almost obliterated by the joyful shrieks of a gang of assorted boys, both large and small, who came racing wildly towards Scrope.

He stood mesmerised, guilty and afraid, but they were only charging at the gate pillars. With screams of success, they smacked their hands against the stone and turned, racing back merrily the way they had come.

One last boy rested at the gate, out of breath. He grinned inanely, full of the pure pleasure of the race.

'Is this Murkstone Hall, boy?' Scrope asked hesitantly. 'Is this where I can find Mr Bulloughby?'

The boy's grin was instantly gone. His eyes were full of terror. 'No, mister, Bulloughby's not here and we hopes to God he's never here, never again.' His gabble ended in a cry for help. 'Mr Jarvey! Mr Jarvey, here's a man to see! Come quickly!'

A tall thin man loped along the path, a little unsteadily. 'Are you all right, Niddle?' he asked, ignoring the visitor.

'Yes, sir,' Niddle answered, moving close to his side.

The teacher leaned against the pillar, unable to speak until he too had caught his breath, but he fixed Scrope with a fierce eye. When his wheezing had quietened, the teacher asked 'What do you want, sir?'

'I believe,' Scrope said, 'that there is a boy called Mouse at this school.'

'There was once.'

Once?

'He ran away,' the teacher added.

'Ran away?' Scrope echoed. This was Adeline's son he was asking about. 'Was he sometimes happy? Was he treated fairly well?' he blurted out, wishing it could be true. 'Was Mr Bulloughby kind to him?'

The man and boy stared at each other, as if Scrope's questions were preposterous.

'What do you think?' asked the teacher, almost violently. 'What do you think life was like for any of these boys while Bulloughby was around? It was grimmer than the halls of hell, and even worse than that for Mouse, with Bulloughby always at his back. Thank God that man has left us in peace for a while, and all good wishes to Mouse, wherever he is.'

'Come.' Jarvey turned the boy towards the school. 'Time to go back inside, Niddle. Run. There'll be some good hot stew waiting, and this visitor must have far to travel tonight. We won't keep him.'

'Goodbye, sir,' said Niddle wistfully. 'If you see Mouse, tell him about us. Tell him his friend Niddle says hello.' The boy trotted happily back up the path.

Jarvey's eyes blazed at Scrope. 'I will tell you this, sir. Wherever Mouse has gone to can be no crueller than this place was to him, thanks to Bulloughby and that dreadful monster Button.'

'Thank you.' Scrope did not know what else to say.

'Furthermore,' Jarvey added, his words chillingly cold, 'whoever sent a child in their care to this place deserves very little sympathy. Do you understand, sir?'

He left Scrope standing alone on the stony path.

KITTY CAUGHT

Though the wonderful machine needed perfecting, I still had to earn my keep. As Kitty did not seem to need much help, I was often busy sweeping between the rows of seats in the auditorium.

Anything I picked up – anything valuable, not apple cores or trampled playbills – had to go straight to Smudge's waiting hands. I once gave a gilt bracelet in to Vanya, but that was before I understood how sweeping worked. Smudge had not forgiven me.

Then handfuls of sawdust were scattered between the rows to soak up any damp patches. I worked away with my broom, though every so often I glanced at Hugo Adnam and his cast rehearsing onstage.

One afternoon, in a flurry of expensive scent, a woman entered the theatre. She swirled past me in a neat costume of mauve satin, and her tip-tapping heels made footprints through the sawdust.

'Adnam,' Bellina Lander cried, 'it's me, darling. I'm back at last!'

Everything and everyone stopped, even Adnam.

Bellina Lander was strikingly beautiful. Her skin was ivory pale, her eyes burned like green fire and her hair was a curtain of dark silk. She attracted every eye, and every ear, and she knew it. Nevertheless, by the time I had swept five more rows, I'd realised that Miss Lander had her own way of rehearsing. She was quickly bored by anything other than her own part, and she adored Adnam and ignored everyone else.

While Bellina rehearsed her major scenes, all the actors and stagehands had to be on or around the stage to give her an audience. Whenever one of her minor scenes was in rehearsal, another actress had to stand in and read the lines for her, because La Bellina had more important things to do.

'Don't worry, Hugo! I'll pick up everything at the dress rehearsal. I've acted this part before, darling, or something like it. Must fly! See you soon.'

Meeting the beautiful Bellina Lander was like biting into a sugar bun and finding a sour lemon. So what on earth had Kitty done to upset this glittering star?

I tried asking the little ones. 'Flora? Dora? Have you always been dancers?'

'Since we were as teeny-tiny as kittens,' Dora purred.

'And Kitty danced like you?'

'Mouse, she was the very best dancer. Didn't we tell you that yet?'

'Then why isn't she onstage now?'

'We don't know, Mouse,' they whispered demurely, though I am sure they knew something was not right.

I tried Miss Tildy.

'Och, Mouse, I've only been here a short while. It's probably the usual story.' She waved one hand airily about. 'It's easy to place pretty wee bairns and babbies in a show, but it gets harder to use girls like yon Kitty. Nobody needs a fairy once she's more than elbow high, certainly not our audiences. She'll find it easier once she's a well-grown lass, I expect.'

Miss Tildy was quite determined to see nothing nasty within the Albion Theatre.

In the end, I went back to Kitty herself. She was down at the end of the furthest corridor in the hosiery room, folding up some old stockings. Her shoulders drooped, and loose strands of hair fell across her face.

I perched on a basket beside her. 'Kitty, I am sorry. I didn't expect to be the one trying out Vanya's flying machine.'

She looked up at me and nodded. 'I know. It's not just that, Mouse.'

'What happened with Bellina Lander, Kit?'

'You really want to hear the story?' Kitty took a very deep breath.

And then she told me.

'I sometimes think that Adnam keeps this theatre running on promises and dreams. Last year he had scraped out all of his pockets to keep the Albion alive.

Then we had a run of bad luck. A play intended to save our fortune was dull. A reliable actor broke his leg. An actress ran away with a lord. The creditors would soon be at the door.

'Then Adnam asked La Bellina to take on the leading role, and surely bring in the crowd. We all felt hopeful, until we heard what she was demanding.

'Don't think of her as a fragile butterfly, Mouse. Bellina decided the show should run on past midnight. That hour might suit her, but it would be harder work for all the rest of us: all the ordinary actors, the crew, the musicians and dancers, everyone. Did she think about how late they'd get home to their families and lodgings? No! Did she even consider the fairy dancers? Not at all! While Bellina would be dining with her grand friends, the little kids would be trailing home through the most dangerous part of the night.'

'That's not right,' I told Kitty. 'Anyone can see that.'

'Exactly. Especially me, Mouse. I just got angry.'

'What did you do?'

'I told her, straight out. I couldn't help it! Everyone heard what I shouted.

' "Don't you care, Miss Lander," I said, "that these little ones will be walking home by themselves? You'll be sending them into the streets when there's drunks and ruffians and night creatures about. You don't find that many constables and omnibuses about after midnight, do you? Or maybe you'd like the little girls to sleep on the steps of the theatre? What does Hugo Adnam say about this new idea? Has he agreed? Have you asked him?"

'The stage boomed as I stamped my foot, but voices were agreeing with me too.

' "How dare you, Miss High-and-Mighty?" I saw her lips shrink to a thin scarlet line. "The Albion can find new fairies any day of the week, believe me." '

Having seen the rehearsals, I could almost imagine La Bellina's face as she said those words. Kitty's voice dropped to a murmur.

'In the end, Adnam turned down her midnight scheme and wouldn't let a single fairy be sacked. But La Bellina wasn't finished.' Tears glistened in Kitty's eyes. 'She threatened to leave the company there and then if she ever saw me appearing on the Albion's stage again. With La Bellina newly advertised in all the papers, it would have ruined Adnam. He had no choice, did he?'

So that was how it was. Kitty had been shunted off-stage. I disliked Bellina Lander the moment she walked into the theatre, and now I hated her.

'Oh, Kit! That was terrible!'

'I haven't danced on the stage since. Adnam arranged for me to work backstage, because he knows the Aunts, but the rule is that I have to keep out of sight of Bellina Lander.'

Kitty fiddled with her hair and sighed deeply. 'It doesn't matter much now, anyway. Miss Tildy brought a new fairy dancer with her when she joined the theatre, so that's the end of the story. I work, I look after those two little tinselled nuisances,' she said flatly, 'and that's all. And what can I do about it, Mouse? What can anyone do? Nothing!'

CHAPTER 50

Homecoming

Epton Towers was there to welcome the returning travellers, of course.

'Father!' Adeline rushed across the tiger-skin rug and knelt by the old man's chair. 'How are you? We feared we would never see you again.' She rested her sun-brown fingers upon his yellowed, wrinkled hand.

'So good to see you, Father,' said Albert, though he was somewhat bemused by the sense of emptiness filling the house.

Epsilon's leathery eyelids blinked, like those of a tortoise waking from a long hibernation. His hands trembled and loosened their grip on the carved chair. He lifted his balding head, with its wisps of white hair, and stared at them.

Albert and Adeline smiled very earnestly back at the

old man, waiting for him to get over the shock of their return.

'I am glad to see you – very, very glad,' his tremulous voice whispered at last. 'There was news of a shipwreck, but I did not believe it. I knew you were only lost. I told Scrope that you would return. I did, I did!'

'Well then, where is my brother?' asked Albert, cheerfully and energetically. 'Where's our son, Pa?'

'Dear little Mouse! We have missed him so,' Adeline declared, dabbing her eye. 'I hope our little boy has given you no trouble.'

For a moment Albert and Adeline held hands. They thought of the baby they left so long ago, lying feverishly in his cot.

Then they listened out for the sound of a boy's running feet, but there was only a dreadful silence.

'Where is he, Father?' asked Albert, suddenly alarmed. 'Where is our boy Mouse?'

CHAPTER 51

CLUTCHING AT HAIRS

Dog Toby was sleeping warmly at the foot of my bed.
Nick Tick's mechanical family counted me steadily,
rhythmically into a long, deep dream.

Before my much younger eyes there rose the curve of
a familiar hill, wreathed in mist. I smelled the rich, new-
turned earth.

'Hello, boy!' I heard Isaac say. He was walking
beside me, though I could not see his face. 'Like old
times, Mouse, like old times.'

The huge horses plodded along the field, heads
nodding as they pulled the plough. At the end of the
furrow, Isaac steered the horses round, smooth as could
be, and we set off again, back up the field, the new
furrow appearing behind us.

'There! Told you I could turn them on a sixpence,
boy,' his gentle voice told me as the mist rolled in again,

and the dream disappeared.

I was at once wide awake. *'Turn them on a sixpence'*? Those were words I'd heard in my here and now life, but where? 'Come on!' I said, as we sped towards the Albion that day, with little Flora and Dora scuttling along as fast as their feet could carry them.

Right at the back of the theatre, where two great doors allowed for scenery to be moved in or out of the building, there was a yard for carts and a covered shed. This was where Vanya had constructed a pen for the four new arrivals.

The fairy horses trampled the straw nervously, rolling their eyes. They flicked their ears backwards and forwards, sniffing at their strange new home. Their coats shone, and their hoofs were polished. Someone who was not Mr Spangle loved and cared for them, these four fairy ponies who could turn on a sixpence.

Vanya was just opening up a sack of grain.

'Let me, Vanya?' I took a handful and held out my palm to the nearest pony. The animal whinnied, tossed its long mane and nudged closer. A second pony pushed towards me, and then the last pair moved closer.

It felt impossible, but was it possible too? I ran my fingers through the nearest mane. Yes! There it was, the single wheat-eared braid that was woven into my memory. Each one of the four fairy ponies had that thin, distinctive plait half hidden in their mane. Each wore that telltale sign.

'Who brought the ponies to the theatre?'

'Just a man, Mouse. He spoke kindly to them.'

'Who was he? Where does he come from?'

'Mr Spangle sent him, of course.' Vanya shrugged.

'What did he look like?'

'He stooped over. His hair is going grey.'

I turned angrily and put my hopes away. The man could not be Isaac, for he was tall and fair-haired and strong. That was the man I saw in my mind.

'Not so loud!' I snapped, as the girls squealed with delight at the ponies. 'You'll frighten them.'

I tried to dismiss my memories of big Isaac. I saw him holding me up high, and heard him talking me across the roof beam. Then something skipped in my heart. How long ago was that? Hadn't years passed for us all? Stupid, stupid, stupid Mouse!

'Vanya, how can I find that man?'

'So many questions from our Mouse-boy today!' Vanya raised his bushy eyebrows. 'Well, you could ask Mr Spangle, but he is not a man who likes to give out information, or . . .

'Yes. Yes?'

'This man will come back tomorrow morning. He wants to check the ponies are happy.'

I rushed at Vanya and hugged him. 'Thank you, thank you!' I cried.

At last, the night's performance ended.

'Kit, please push this note under Nick's door.' I didn't want Mr Tick missing me and raising an alarm.

'Why?' She moved closer and looked straight into my eyes.

'I'll tell you if it works out.' I did not want to share

my dream. 'Wish me luck, Kit. I can't explain now . . .'
I hesitated.

'In case it isn't what you want?' suggested Kitty.
'Good luck, Mouse. Take care.'

She gathered the girls together, warned them to be
very good, and set off into the darkness.

That night I slept at the Albion. As soon as the theatre grew quiet, I wrapped an old cloak round myself
and sneaked out to where the ponies were stabled. They
whinnied gently, glad of my company. I dozed between
the hay bales, waiting for the stooping man, whoever he
was.

A shaft of daylight fell across the straw-strewn floor. A
man leaned over the pen. A silhouette, murmuring. The
ponies trampled about and whinnied so I could not hear
his voice. I struggled to my feet, but my mouth was too
dry to speak.

'What be you doing in the straw, boy?' he said,
surprised.

'Isaac?' The stable was too dim for me to be
convinced.

'Eh? What did you say? How come you know my
name? Wait a moment . . .' He came towards me with a
lurch, his face ready for disappointment. 'Boy, is that
truly you?' he gasped.

'Yes, Isaac, I think so. It's me, Mouse.'

Then the man – the man who was like a father to
me – hugged me so tightly and joyously, as if he needed
support, and as if he could not believe what was
happening.

My dear Isaac! Trouble had lined his face, and his blue eyes, now shining wetly, were sunk under his eyelids. That sunny hair was streaked with frost, and he was no longer the man who could throw me high and catch me, but his smile was the same as ever.

'Is it truly you? Heavens be praised, boy, heavens be praised! The dear child again, after so long! How you've grown!'

I can barely speak about that long-awaited meeting. Isaac learned that I was safe and had somewhere to stay. We talked, haltingly, about long-gone days. Then we wiped away our tears and got the four fairy horses fed, and I asked him about Ma.

'Hanny is well, all told,' Isaac said, 'and she will be even better for seeing you.'

Hanny! Why did he not call her Ma? Or Ma Foster? Why did he not say 'your mother'?

It was a moment I'd imagined for years, but now the chance had come, I needed more time. I wanted to meet this lost Hanny, but felt afraid. I was still angry about the bad times in my life, but I could not bring burning rage to her, whoever she was.

'Isaac, I can't come straight away.' I glanced awkwardly away, blustering to cover my confusion. 'The Albion's very busy, and the horses are being tried out onstage today.'

A shadow of sadness touched Isaac's face. He understood. 'You aren't that small infant now, are you, boy? It's been a long parting for all of us. But remember, Mouse, when the right time comes, she will be glad to see you. Leave a message with the ponies.' Isaac stroked my cheek as if he still could not believe I was real, and smiled. 'I will keep you a secret to myself till then. But don't take too long, Mouse.'

Calmly, Isaac undid his pack and took out a brush. He started to groom those ponies, brushing the dirt from their backs and flanks as he had come to do. I was mesmerised by the sight of him still at this familiar task.

Isaac looked up at me, and his blue eyes shone as they once did. 'You still one for clambering about, Mouse?'

I blushed. 'I am. I'm helping get the flying machine ready for Adnam's new show.'

'You're not frightened of being up so high, boy?' Isaac gave one of his old laughs.

'Course not,' I answered, laughing back.

'You never was, was you, boy?'

Later that day I went back down to the ponies, but only Vanya was there, feeding the greedy things with sugar lumps. They nudged and whinnied and tossed their pretty manes, and there was no Isaac.

I felt ashamed that I hadn't rushed to see Ma there and then. Why had I turned down that chance? I pulled together the scraps of news he'd given me, but they weren't much help.

I felt afraid too. How had I let Isaac go so easily, and what would I do if he didn't come back?

QUESTION TIME

The gold-framed mirrors reflected the candles in the candelabra, but there was no mood of celebration in the dining room.

Old Epsilon sat in his chair, his face grey. The servants removed the plates. Little of the meal had been eaten.

'Father,' insisted Albert, once they were alone again, 'let us try once more. Where is our boy?'

'The nursery must have been unused for years,' Adeline said.

The old man glared sullenly, like a stubborn child. 'Don't know.'

'You must know!' Albert shouted. 'He's your own grandson. You were supposed to take care of the boy.'

Rage blazed in the old man's eyes. 'You didn't ask me to take care of him, did you, Albert? I told you I

needed you here, but you chose to go off. With her.'
Epsilon stared malevolently at Adeline. 'You went
chasing off around the globe, looking for seeds and
weeds and twigs. You left him behind.'

'That is not true. We wanted him brought to us
when he was well again.' Adeline replied as sharply as if
she'd been stung. 'We left precise instructions.'

'And then your ship sank,' Epsilon added, in doom-
laden tones. 'Didn't it? Was that part of your careful
plans?'

Albert rose from his seat and strode across the room,
clenching his fists. 'Father, did you do nothing for the
boy, even then?'

'Didn't need to. That nurse of yours took the child
away to a farm. Tip-top idea. Healthy place for a young
lad.'

'Hanny took the boy away? Hanny? Why? What was
the reason?' Adeline frowned.

'Scrope knows. He was the one who stayed here with
me while you were on your vain quest, not caring what
happened to me or to Epton Towers. He was the one
here while you were off and not doing your duty.
Scrope did what he had to do. He even arranged for the
little chap to go to school somewhere.' The old man
sniffed self-pityingly, ignoring the matter of the dreadful
shipwreck. 'Scrope is the one who can tell you everything.'

'But where is Scrope?' asked Albert, exasperated.

'Don't know,' Epsilon said petulantly. 'I did ask him
if I could see the boy, but it never happened. Nobody
does what I want.'

'Please try to think, Father. Where is our little boy? Do you have no clue at all?' Adeline begged.

'I told you I don't, and I am extremely tired now,' snapped the old man sulkily. He rang a small brass bell nearby. A servant entered and helped Epsilon off to his four-poster bed.

When the room was empty, Albert took Adeline in his arms. 'Don't give up hope, dear girl. Tomorrow we will start searching for the boy. Remember, if we were able to track down the lost blue rose of Alexandria, discovering our missing son should be simple. Have courage, my Adeline.'

CHAPTER 53

FINDERS WEEPERS

Whatever the answer was about my Ma, I needed to know. So I made the message as simple as I could, and tacked it to a beam, above the reach of the greedy ponies.

SUNDAY?

The next day, in Isaac's uneven lettering, I had an answer.

YES. NINE.

That night, dead dreams dragged themselves around in my head. Who was I meeting? Was it Hanny? My Ma? My mother? I didn't know. I didn't even know what I would say to this stranger. If Sunday's meeting went wrong, I would need someone who could help, who could explain things afterwards. I needed a friend.

Even as I asked, my voice sounded strained. 'Will you come somewhere with me, Kit?'

The streets were almost empty. All the pie sellers, potato pedlars, flower-girls and apple-women were in bed. Even those who would be going to church or chapel were still in their nightshirts. Pigeons strutted through last night's litter, cooing.

At the foot of the theatre steps, below the carved gods and goddesses, was Isaac. An ancient blinkered nag waited amiably between the struts of his cart.

'I see you brought company, Mouse,' he said. 'Good day, miss.'

'Good morning to you too, sir.' Kitty gave her widest smile.

Isaac helped her on to the cart and beckoned me up. The wooden vehicle creaked in response to its two new passengers. 'You ready then, boy?'

'Ready,' I said, but I had a question. 'Did you tell Ma I was coming?'

'No, boy. Thought about it, and reckoned we've all seen strange times since we was last together. Maybe what you needs is to witness how Hanny feels about you, for your very own self.'

He pointed a warning finger at me, gently adding, 'Just you be easy on my girl, Mouse, won't you?'

We crossed the grey river, where the masts of the ships made a forest on the water. We got out and walked beside the cart up a long hill, past streets of brick houses. Eventually we arrived at a rough heath, dotted with tethered horses, cattle-pens and a few wooden dwellings.

A track across the heath brought us to a grassier patch, where four milking cows patiently chewed the cud, and a pair of donkeys tugged at thistles. Smoke rose from the ramshackle building nearby, half home and half stable.

'That's where she is,' said Isaac, quietly holding Kitty back in the seat. 'You go first, boy. We'll follow in a short while.'

As if I was as leaden as my heart felt, I dropped from the cart and walked towards the place.

'Hello?' I called.

The top half of the stable door creaked open, and a comfortable woman with a round apple face appeared. Her features were softer, older, but there was no mistaking the tilt of chin as she lifted her head to welcome a visitor.

I closed my lids, dug my nails into my fists and opened my eyes to see it was still my Ma, blinking and squinting at the daylight.

'Excuse me, may I come in, please?' I stammered.

Ma glanced quizzically to Isaac. Then she opened both parts of the door and invited me through into their home.

At the lower end of the building was an area where the beasts could be stabled. At the other end, raised a little, was a simple space with small square shuttered windows.

A kettle sang on a hook over the hearth, and the clean-swept floor was covered with bright rag rugs. Beside the hard wooden settle squatted baskets full of logs and the brushes and grooming combs of Isaac's trade.

Now I was here, I could not speak. All I could do was stare at her face.

'What do you want then, child?' she said, looking at me anxiously.

At last I gulped and asked, 'Are you Ma? Ma Foster?'

She flinched. 'Oh, that was a long time ago,' she whispered, anxiously kneading the corner of her apron. Then she pulled herself together and peered at me, speaking kindly. 'I am sorry. I must have fostered a dozen of the poor little things. Which one are you, child?'

'I'm your best boy, Ma. I'm Mouse.' My words sounded hollow.

She studied my patched clothes and shook her head. 'No, my dear, you can't be. My Mouse was taken away from me to be made into a gentleman.'

I stepped towards her. Once Ma was taller than me. She could lean over my cradle and pick me up. Now I was taller than she was. I did not expect that.

'I am Mouse, Ma! Honest!'

Puzzled, she reached up and touched my cheek. Gently she turned my head a little this way and that, as if she was not sure about what she was seeing. Ma and me, we stared at each other as if we were frozen, transfixed, but I cannot say if it was happiness or pain.

Suddenly she gave a quick soft cry, and I recognised

my long-lost happy Ma once more, though tears glistened in her bright eyes. 'Oh Mouse! What did they do
to you, my best boy?'

'Doesn't matter, Ma.' I couldn't bear to tell her
about that time. 'I'm all right now.'

Ma held my hands tightly, as if I might disappear
again. 'Look, it's our Mouse at last, Isaac. It is, it is!' she
called. 'Can you believe it?'

'Yes, Hanny, my dear,' Isaac said, entering. 'Shall we
sit down?' He lifted two rush-seated chairs down from
hooks on the wall. 'Kitty girl, that kettle's on the boil.
Why not make us a cup of tea?'

I tried to keep calm, but the next question rushed to
my tongue even faster than I'd feared. I didn't care
about cups of tea.

'Ma, are you my mother? Are you? I went back to
Roseberry Farm and everything was gone, and I met
Wayland and heard about all the children.' Her face
had grown pale, despite the warm firelight. 'Now I don't
know what to think at all. Am I your child, Ma? Am I?'

'Oh Mouse!' she gasped, and was silent.

Eventually Isaac took hold of her work-worn hands.
'Tell him, Hanny. The boy's old enough to hear the
truth.'

'Tell me!' I said.

Ma took a big breath, and then her words scampered
out, like hares set running free. 'It was a wrong thing to
do,' she cried, 'but she told me to keep you safe.'

What on earth was Ma telling me now? Who said
what?

'You were so ill, you poor tiny Mouse! There was no

way she could take you on-board. The ship was char-
tered, the crew hired and the whole expedition planned.
She had to go, she did. She was going to send word for
us to follow when it was safe, but . . . oh dear! . . . it
took so long and it wasn't safe . . .'

'She? Who is she, Ma?' My heart thumped like a
drum.

Ma's hands twisted against each other, over and over.
'She? Why, Adeline, of course. Your mother. And your
father Albert too, for he was just as worried.'

Isaac handed us sweet strong tea. My hands held the
mug, but I hardly felt the heat. So I had a mother called
Adeline, and a father called Albert, and I hadn't known
about either of them.

'At Roseberry Farm I called you Ma, but you
weren't,' I whispered, so confused. 'You weren't my
mother. That was a kind of lie.'

Ma gave a deep resigned sigh. 'I know, Mouse, but
truly I never said I was your mother, did I?' Her voice
was less than a whisper. 'Though I loved you – loved
you as if you were my own. It broke my heart when
they took you away, child.'

My head was in my hands. Maybe I would just run
from all this. It had all become too difficult.

'Now listen, boy.' Isaac planted himself before me.
'I'm not one for words, so don't let me waste them. Are
you listening?'

'Yes.'

'Here's the truth, Mouse. Hanny was your nursemaid, and your mama asked her to keep you safe.
Hanny loved you above all the other babbies, and you

were always her best and dearest child. I was there, Mouse, wasn't I? So I know. Now, if that wasn't a mother's love, it was the nearest that I've seen, and that's something to be thankful for, boy. That's what I think.'

'But who am I then?' I groaned.

'Hanny,' said Isaac, 'tell the boy exactly why you brought him to Roseberry Farm.'

So my story went on, becoming more and more like one of Adnam's melodramas: an aged grandfather, whose heart hardened when his eldest son sailed off across the seven seas; an uncle – and here Ma sounded angry – who inherited everything if I, the little lad, met a sudden end . . . Ma must have been worried, because she – young Ma – had risked everything by bringing me to Isaac at Roseberry Farm.

'Afterwards, I heard that the ship was lost at sea,' Ma said. 'You did have a real Ma and Pa, Mouse, if that's what you wanted to hear.'

Too late for me to know them, it seemed. This news should have made me sad, but it was hard to grieve for parents I hadn't even known about before. Besides, I didn't recognise this other, grander child who was both me and not me.

Kitty was enraptured by the tale. To her, I'd been only the ragamuffin she'd rescued from the streets.

''Tis a long history, boy,' Isaac added, 'but seems to me that you were happier at Roseberry Farm than you'd have been anywhere else, including Epton Towers. You were safer too, and maybe that's what mattered most.'

'Epton Towers?' Kitty was starry-eyed, like whenever the stage was transformed into a palace. 'That place was in one of Tildy's magazines, Mousey. It has towers and windows and gardens and all. How very wonderful!'

'No, Kitty,' said Ma. 'It was not wonderful, not where it mattered. Then, even at Roseberry Farm, they found you, and that man took you off to school.'

'That man was Mr Button,' I said. His polished face glinted like a poisoned ruby in my memory.

'That was that, or so it seemed. You never wrote to us, Mouse, and so we thought you were busy being a grand gentleman. We thought you had forgotten us.' Hanny dabbed at her eyes.

How could I explain that Bulloughby never gave us anything to write on? That any scrap of a note or message was screwed up and thrown into the fire? That by the time Jarvey arrived, there had been so long a silence that I had lost heart in letters?

I answered one word at a time, to be sure Hanny understood. Each word was a weight on my tongue.

'I . . . never . . . ever . . . forgot . . . you!'

I closed my eyes and that awful time flooded through me, like water swirling round a dank drain. 'Ma? Isaac? Don't you know that school nearly killed me?'

For what should be a joyful reunion, there was a remarkable lot of sighing and sobbing and quite a few loud curses, but slowly, as our tales mingled, a kind of balance came back to my mind. I knew that Ma was true and loving, and that was what counted most of all. As for the fairy-tale palace that so delighted Kitty, if shiny Mr Button was involved, I did not want to hear anything about it, not yet. Maybe never.

My question had been answered. The old, old grand-father was probably dead and gone, and those who were my mother and father were no more. I would live my life as it was now.

So I turned to Isaac. 'What happened to your big horses?' I asked.

He scratched his head wearily. 'We brought them with us, but couldn't afford their fodder, Mouse, not here in the city. Had to sell the pair of them on.'

'Fair broke his heart,' said Ma, and she took hold of his hand and squeezed it tight. 'Never mind, Isaac.'

'But me and Ma get by, boy,' he said. 'That showy Mr Spangle employs me whenever he wants ponies or suchlike looked after, and when he don't, Ma and I get what we can from selling milk and donkey rides on the heath. It's enough of a life for us now, Mouse.'

I glanced around this pitiful half-stable, half-shack that was their home. There was little enough space for Ma and Isaac, and there could be no real room for me there, no matter what they offered. I could never return to the life that had been mine so long ago. I was not that little child of Roseberry Farm any more.

I smiled at this woman called Hanny, supping tea from a blue patterned cup. My mother she wasn't, but my dear Ma she was. One day my story would make sense, one day I might find out more, but not this time. Just for now, things were good enough.

Ma and I had met at last, and we would meet again. I was happy living at Nick Tick's shop, at least for a while longer, and being among friends with Kit and her family. And there was the excitement of the flying machine.

Kitty shifted and nudged me. 'Mouse, we've got to leave. Work to do.'

Ma and I parted with smiles and a hug. Yes, I was taller than Ma, and still growing.

'Look after yourself, dear Mouse,' she said.

'I'll come back soon, Ma,' I told her as I climbed back into the cart beside Kitty. 'I promise. I promise.'

Whatever happened from that minute on, I knew that I had not imagined Ma's motherly care. In all the muddle of my life, that was a crystal-clear fact.

Back towards the city we went, over the hill and down the highway towards the theatre. I could not utter another word. I felt as twisted and worn as a used dishrag.

Isaac's cart dropped us off at the theatre steps. And life continued.

PAUSE FOR THOUGHT

'Sorry, Mr Button, sir. Nuffink at all,' said the man, tipping his filthy top hat to the back of his head. His skin, rimed with soot, marked him as a master chimney sweep. Only around his eyes showed the piggy-pinkness of his un-sooted skin.

Button fixed his most forceful gaze on the man, but he stuck his thumbs into his belt and shook his head insistently.

'Nope. I've asked around, Mr Button, and there ain't no boys among my several acquaintances that fits your runaway. Believe me, if we found a champion scrambler, the word would get around quick. Nowadays we has to set fires in the grates to help the lads up the chimbleys. Not much nimbleness in the lazy creatures these days.'

As the master sweep extended a filthy palm for

payment, Button flung a coin so hard that it bounced across the floor.

'You ain't got no pity for my poor old back,' the sweep groaned, picking up the money. He hauled a grimy bag up on to his shoulder and examined the coin. As he left he called out, 'You ain't gifted with a generous spirit neither, that's for sure, Mr Button.'

Button gritted his teeth. He had been sure the boy would soon be in his clutches. Button did not like being made a fool of, not at all. He would get the wretched creature!

His one bright thought was that Bulloughby was no longer around to disturb his searches. His smile reappeared. His feet sprang from the pavement as he walked along, elaborating his plans in his head.

Yes! Oh yes! He would seize that child soon, for sure. When he did get the boy, the stupid Scrope would have to pay well to get what he wanted, whether he desired to have the child found or wished him to be permanently lost.

Button strode along, puffing short, quick breaths. The mistakes still nagged at his heels. If only the trail had not gone cold! That Punch and Judy man gave them no information at all, the stupid fellow, though when they threatened to smash his pathetic wooden puppets, he cried out as if they were his own children. The man seemed to believe that his bundle of sticks and canvas was a proper theatre, though it was wrecked and broken easily enough. Theatre? Silly wretch! Theatre?

Theatre! That idea made Button whistle out loud.

That was an entirely different area to consider, a world where a nimble boy might be needed, and might be hidden. Button must find out what was taking place in the playhouses of this city.

CHAPTER 55

A STEP INTO THE DREAM

My new history felt like a suit of clothes where no piece fitted comfortably. I had to get used to wearing this new self, so I only tried on the ideas one or two at a time. I needed to tread as carefully as if I was walking along a high ledge.

I had not told Ma everything about Murkstone Hall, or Punchman's last words to me, or my fear that Button and Bulloughby were after me. I wanted to keep the strands of my life far apart as long as I could. I was not completely sure I knew who I was any more and, far worse, I did not know if I was bringing danger with me.

'Kitty, please don't tell the Aunts or Nick or anyone at the theatre about the meeting,' I said.

'But, Mouse –' Her eyes gleamed with excitement.

'Not now. Not yet!'

She sighed and agreed.

*

These twists and turns in my life were easily hidden, because everyone's mind was on the hurrying days and rushing weeks and the manic fire in Adnam's eyes.

The Aunts were working all hours. More helpers arrived, like a flock of cheerful hens. Mrs Orpheus had brought an elderly sister along to assist with the ironing. Two tiny squint-eyed women sat stitching hems and making cloth buttons and embroidering rows of button-holes. They toiled away, supping tea, muttering fortunes and stringing out gossip between them.

Costumes were cut, sewn, finished, pressed and sent daily by carriage to the Albion. The theatre's rooms were crammed with freshly trimmed cloaks and gowns, the boot room was stuffed with neatly labelled slippers and shoes, and everyone was waiting for the rehearsals to end.

Voices shrilled behind closed doors, and shouts rang crisply along the corridors. Each day brought the open-ing night closer.

What was Adnam's new play, Adnam's new dream? It was a famous play by that man Shakespeare. It was about a king and his queen, and an ancient palace, and lots of people getting lost among the trees of a nearby forest – and magic.

'Magical is best of all,' Kitty said longingly. 'He'll have romantic scenery and distant shimmering lakes and beams of moonlight. The audience will love it.'

A Midsummer Night's Dream it was called. Adnam and La Bellina would appear in it, as both the royal king and queen and the fairy king and queen. This meant that the orchestra had to have enough music to cover the costume changes.

On the day when the famous pair rehearsed their lines onstage for the first time, we crowded in the wings, even though they stood there in their day clothes, with the dust of the street upon them, with Adnam ordering ham sandwiches for a late breakfast.

Adnam hardly needed to practise at all. He was already Oberon, the dark king of the Fairy Court, the very king of shadows. In magnificent anger, Oberon had made Titania, the proud Queen of the Fairies – La Bellina herself, in fact – fall in love with a clumsy fool in a donkey's head. His name was Bottom, but I learned that Shakespeare chose that name, not Adnam.

The Fairy Queen was to be marvellously enchanting and a star of the show, but she was also tragic because she was wronged. They had quarrelled about her love for a little orphan boy she wouldn't give to Oberon.

La Bellina would need her best acting skills for this, because most of us knew how she treated children. She raged when the fairy dancers were behaving perfectly, and would happily tread on any tiny toes that didn't skip out of her path fast enough.

'That besom would think nothing of tearing the wings off a butterfly!' fretted Miss Tildy, as she daubed the children's bruises with vinegar and wiped away their tears.

Nor was Vanya happy about Miss Lander and the four ponies. La Bellina had added in a new Titania scene, though Aunt Violet declared it was not true to the play, or to anything that Shakespeare had written.

'I will be shown riding the fairy chariot! It will be a remarkable moment for the audience, Hugo,' she insisted as she swept back to her dressing room. 'You must make sure the lighting is fixed upon me.'

So, a painted landscape sliding behind them, the fairy ponies pulled her gilded chariot along a rolling surface. The audience saw Titania travelling along in all her floating finery. We saw how it tired the ponies.

'Not good!' Vanya complained, as he calmed the ponies after rehearsals. 'That Bellina gives the poor creatures fidgets. Now I hear she asks for fairies bearing fire-torches in the scene too. I hope that wicked vixen gets a good pony kick right where it hurts very much,' he grumbled, 'and when the audience can see it too!'

There were other actors, of course. In the magical forest were four sweethearts, always arguing and crying, and comical workmen practising a play for the king, and one of these was Bottom who got a donkey's head instead of his own.

Arthur Boddy enjoyed being Bottom, with and without the donkey's head. He stalked about the front of the stage, trying to work his favourite jokes into Shakespeare's words and practising a song that Adnam did not know about, not yet.

'Arthur often acts like an ass anyway, Mouse,' Kitty added.

She explained that Oberon's impish servant squeezes magic juice from a purple flower into one of the sweethearts' eyes, just as Oberon told him to, but that the servant mistakes which lover is which. The play was all about the mixed-up troubles that followed – with a happy ending, of course.

I learned all this about Mr Shakespeare's play from Vanya and Kitty, and through my own eyes when I watched snatches of rehearsals. However, I had not seen what I should have seen all along. Adnam had plans for me.

Adnam called me into his room.

'Boy, how is the flying machine proceeding?'

'The machine works well, Mr Adnam.'

'So Vanya tells me. He also tells me that you work well with it too. So it is probably time to sort out your words.'

'What?' I gasped. I had been trying the thing out. I had been an experiment, not an actor.

'Your words, your lines,' Adnam said, handing me a playscript. 'Your voice is young and strong, and you are not afraid of heights. So, with a bit of extra help, you will make us an excellent Puck. Go on. Read.'

Puck was Oberon's mischievous servant! We went through the play, and Adnam told me exactly what I had to say.

I found that I liked Puck's words because they sounded magical, like the poems Jarvey had read to us. There were times when Puck was flying and times when Puck was speaking, and Adnam explained my lines and how to speak them aloud.

'Please, what do I have to wear?' All I had seen so far were bouquets of sequined fairy dancer skirts.

Adnam laughed. 'Boy, don't worry. You'll be covered in leaves and painted green all over, even your face and hands. You won't be Mouse any longer. You will be a mischievous spirit of the trees and wild places. Nobody will recognise you as the likely lad who sweeps the stalls and carries the boots – nobody at all. Now go, all is settled. Learn your words.'

Not quite. My heart was jumping at the pleasure of playing Puck. But then I had another thought.

'What about Kitty? She could play this part as easily as anything, couldn't she, no matter what Miss Lander thinks. Mr Adnam, sir, I'm new here, and Kitty would be wonderful –'

'Enough, boy!' Adnam raised his hand. His handsome face became a weary grey, and he sighed deeply. 'What can't be cured must be endured, Mouse. Quarrels have consequences, and Miss Lander, in spite of everything, is just as important to this *Dream* as good Vanya's flying machine.'

'But Kitty would be just right –'

He groaned. 'No more, child.' And then he gave me a strange look. 'If there was a way round Kitty's problem, I wish it could be found. Study the script. Study each and every one of Puck's entrances and exits. Ask Kitty for help, if you think she will give it. Use your brains, Mouse, and do what you can. It will be exciting.'

It would.

Peter bustled in then. He scribbled down Adnam's description of my costume for the Aunts and thrust it into my hand. I left, feeling very anxious. How would I tell Kitty?

CHAPTER 56

SHOUTING OUT

The boy on the corner pitch shouted into the raucous traffic and stamped his badly fitting boots against the cold.

'Albion! Excelsior! Lyceum! Empire! Read all about it! Best playhouses in the city! Read all about them here!'

He was sandwiched between wooden boards. Two hung from his shoulders, and above his head he balanced another. He was like a walking newspaper. Every surface was plastered with advertisements for new plays or shows.

'One for you, mister! Here you are, miss!' His pockets sprouted cheaply printed playbills, which he thrust at passing pedestrians. People whirled past him, stepped around him, ignoring his plaintive cries.

A red-cheeked fellow in a tight black suit stepped out

from the passing trade. He studied the boards on the boy's front and walked around to read those behind. The fellow had not seen what he wanted. He held out a bright coin, and the boy grinned.

'What ya want to know, mister?'

'A good show.'

'Scenery? Music? Girls with legs all upsy-tupsy?'

'Acrobats, boy. Trapezes. Wire acts. Clambering, climbing? That sort of thing?'

'Ain't no circuses 'cept at the old pleasure gardens, mister, and they ain't the place for gentlefolk no more.'

'Nothing else?' The coin glinted.

'Dunno. Wait! How long are you in town, mister? That Ugo Adnam's got a new play jest about to start. Transformations. Dancing fairies. Very spectacular and grand. If anyone's going to have high acrobaticals, it will be 'im.'

'And where might this feast of delights be seen?'

'Mate, don't you know nuffing? Adnam's the Albion, of course. Here y'are!' The boy smoothed out a crumpled playbill and offered it to his enquirer.

The fellow took the bill, slipped the bright coin straight back into his own pocket and walked off.

'Swizz!' shouted the boy. 'Rotten cheat!'

The man did not turn round.

A fresh flock of pedestrians crossed the road, coming his way. The boy's spirits rose and he began barking again.

'Albion! Excelsior! Empire! Amazing sights!'

CHAPTER 57

DOUBLED TROUBLE

November's cold had crept through the city. The days were brief patches of greyness between the long nights. Smoke poured from every kind of chimney, wreathing itself through the creeping fog, and making familiar journeys into strange adventures.

Travelling back from the theatre, Dora and Flora clung at our sides, seeing imaginary monsters and ghosts. They arrived home with faces blotched with tears.

'No more walking,' Aunt Indigo ordered, poking about in a big china jar. 'An omnibus from now on.' She placed some shining pennies on the table. Kitty hesitated.

'Kitty, it will be no good if the girls are on their sickbed and cannot dance when the theatre needs them,' Aunt Violet advised. 'The new costumes have brought us in more money, and it's only wise for you to take good care of yourselves. And that means all of you, my dears, even Mouse. Understand? Kitty, I will not be disobeyed in this matter. Put these coins in your purse.'

I didn't give Peter's costume notes to the Aunts at once. I wanted to wait until I'd told Kitty about the part I was to play in Adnam's *Dream*.

My sleep was uneasy. I was haunted by the nightmare of a building with towers so gigantic that I could not see the sky or stars above. As I knocked at the tower, the huge door creaked open. Someone was there, but the light was glimmering and shimmering so wildly that I could not make out who the figure was. I stood waiting, clothed in nothing but pauper's rags. I tried to speak my name, but with a terrible rushing and roaring of wind, the door slammed shut against my face and I was left outside, alone.

I woke up shivering, and welcomed the sound of Nick's ticking clocks. Dog Toby snuggled closer, wuffling away my fear, anxious to be my friend. All of a sudden – and nothing to do with my nightmare – I saw exactly what Adnam was intending me to do.

With breakfast over, I dragged Kitty into the scullery. I told her about my lines and about playing Puck. Immediately her eyes darkened, and she almost looked as if she was going to strike me.

'Wait, wait, there's something else. Look here, Kit . . .' I showed her the script. As we followed it line by line, I told her my thoughts. 'Is it possible, Kit?'

She studied me for a moment, our eyes level, our faces close together. Then she laughed and took the script from my fingers. 'Let me read it again, Mouse. I need to think this through.'

And then I gave the Aunts Peter's note.

'Stand still,' said Aunt Indigo, scribbling down the measurements for my costume. 'Don't fidget, Mouse. So this flying harness wears away the cloth?' she remarked. 'Well, if two tunics is what his lordship asks for, that's what he'll get.'

'Yes, certainly,' I murmured.

It was time to block in Puck's moves. Not all the scenery was in place, so we used chairs and stools and brooms.

'We'll rehearse the lines later.' Adnam gave a dismissive Oberon-like wave of his hand. 'We need to work out the pattern of your flight.'

Adnam described the arcs that I must swing in order to fly from one perching place to another. As Puck, I had to swoop above the fairy dancers and descend to gather the purple flower from a misty grotto and to put juice in the wrong lover's eyes. I also had to be scolded a lot by Oberon, and I had to lead Arthur Boddy around, about and out of sight, so that Bottom could have the donkey's head dropped on him.

I had to spy on Titania as she fell in love with this ass. I hoped that good old Arthur would take much delight in teasing the proud Bellina. Finally, I had to speak Puck's farewell speech, before the cast came on for the finale and lots of cheers and applause.

'Do you understand what I am telling you?' said Adnam, his eyes sparkling with the joy of his play. I hoped I did.

From that afternoon, I was no longer playing about on Nick and Vanya's machine, helping with their invention. I was flying for Adnam. I was Puck, the magical sprite, acting out my great master's scheme.

Strangely, maybe it was that thought which unnerved me. Once the stagehand had checked my straps, and I faced the long view down, that faraway floor brought childish memories back into my mind. I was Mouse, doing what others ordered. Sweat gathered in beads across my forehead, and my stomach lurched.

Kitty waved up at me. Adnam stood there, waiting, but neither knew how small they seemed or how very far away. I hesitated. Then I leaped.

This time my flight turned into a mix of ugly swoopings and landings as awkward as an overgrown goose. I tried again, and the second jump was even worse.

Kitty ran across the boards to me. 'Mouse, don't worry. Everyone gets scared at times, honestly. Try again. Become Puck in your mind, and only think about what fun the play will be!'

Up the rungs I went, telling myself I was not ordinary Mouse, tricked out in straps and lines. This time I was going to be Puck, because so much depended on this flight. This time the magic spell was going to work.

I took my position. Then, for a third time, I let go. Suddenly all was well. I swung and soared once more.

Down I went, slowly gaining control, until my landing was no louder than a soft footfall.

'Well done, lad. You will be even better tomorrow,' said Adnam, shaking my hand. He glanced towards Kitty, but she had gone.

For hours the happiness wouldn't leave my face. I was longing to fly in Adnam's *Dream*, to soar before any audience the Albion offered. I was longing to be in that bright lightness, to become part of the magic land, to be that impish green trickster, that merry, mischievous Puck.

The weeks before the first night passed like a busy dream, and even when I was not flying, I felt as if my feet barely touched the ground. Isaac helped by bringing comforting messages from Ma whenever he came to tend the ponies. I told nobody what she wrote, or what I wrote back. I put all her notes safe in a small box by my pillow. Soon, very soon, we would meet again. Of course, if I asked, the Aunts would invite Ma to tea, but they were caught in their frantic web of stitchery, so I did not.

This was not the only reason I kept Ma to myself. I was afraid that if I started to bring these different parts of my life together, I would have started something that I could not stop. Kitty, caught between the life she wanted and the life she had, understood.

Adnam's *Dream* appeared everywhere, not only on the cheap leaflets that young barkers handed out. Advertisements were all over the city – stuck on gas lamps, pasted on walls and hoardings, stuck on the panels of omnibuses – all announcing Adnam's new production.

Newspapermen in crumpled tweed jackets visited the Albion. Supping ale and oysters, they scribbled down Adnam's descriptions of the forthcoming play. The ladies' magazines published illustrations of Bellina Lander as Titania, trailing the iridescent cloak of peacock feathers she would wear onstage, a garment that had cost more than a thousand guineas, even without its silken lining. Just seeing that cloak, in all its coloured glory, would be well worth the price of a good seat. The opening night had sold out already.

Aunt Indigo smoothed out the printed pages. 'Hmm. "Proud queen" – that's Bellina Lander all right. Can you imagine how that cape will bring the grand dames and their daughters into the Albion?'

'All I can say is that I'm glad *we* didn't have to stitch all those feathers together,' Aunt Violet commented, rubbing her sore fingers. The Aunts' gang of helpers and seamstresses chortled and giggled and celebrated their clever stitchery with dainty glasses of sherry.

News of the *Dream* was definitely out and about in the streets of the city. It was buzzed around the drawing rooms. The other theatres had tried their best: the Excelsior was putting on a pantomime, the Empire had a comedy and the Lyceum a moral historical, but all these shows were nothing compared to the magnificent spectacle the Albion had promised. Each ticket booked brought extra energy to Adnam's stride and more confidence to the theatre's backers.

*

News of my new role soon spread. Everyone had some advice for me.

Miss Tildy, a little astonished, wished me well. Arthur Boddy grinned while others whispered gruesome tales of past disasters in my ears. Smudge complained about the lack of theatre sweepers and folk who got too far above themselves. I could ignore all those. It was the attention of my friends that made me anxious.

Nick kept reminding me how important it was to check every strap, clasp and fastening. 'Above all else, be sure of your own balance. Choose your own moment to fly, no matter how urgently Adnam needs you onstage,' he lectured. 'Any good actor can cover an unexpected pause, Mouse, but no actor can conceal a body crashing down on to the stage.'

At every meal, the Aunts recited my lines to me. Aunt Violet sang Puck's songs until Kitty told her I knew the notes as perfectly as I ever would. Even Flora and Dora instructed me in the art of bowing for the grand finale.

Kitty smiled at me and I smiled back at her, but nobody who saw us – not even Flora or Dora – could guess what plans we had, or how quickly we would have to work.

Puck's green clothes – tattered flags of gauzy fabric and dangling sprays of artificial leaves – hung in the theatre. I needed to get to know this new self, this flying Mouse, this woodland sprite.

First on was the harness, with its belts and straps. By now I could fasten that securely myself. Over that came the leaf-scattered tunic, and the trails of ivy that wound around my waist and shoulders.

'Ready, Kit?'

She nodded, nervously this time. I climbed up, trailing my false greenery. Kitty climbed too, all the way up the ladder and out on to the walkway.

We examined the lines that would hold the harness, and the thinner wires that steered the flight, and I showed her how they were all fastened together.

I showed her where I had to stand for the leap, and how I'd hold on till the last moment, and which of the marks on the stage below indicated my earthly landing.

Kitty tested the clasps several times, just in case. 'Watch out for those dangling leaves when you're landing, Mouse. Don't want to spoil things by tripping when you land, do you?'

'Then I'll take extra care, won't I?'

Kitty laughed. 'On the other hand, Puck's such an odd, impish creature that nobody will be surprised by anything that happens.'

We sat, the pair of us, on the darkened walkway high above the theatre, and imagined the magical forest growing beneath our feet.

So the days ticked past. The *Dream* was rehearsed during the day, before the evening show started, which meant that Adnam brought in model stages for us to study. Everyone, actors and stage crew, must know how the *Dream*'s scenery was designed to work, as long as they kept it secret.

Then it arrived, the day when every single plan and

scheme and wish had to come together. The transformation of the Albion was like nothing else.

All the old scenery was lowered and packed away. Then the changeover began. The crew set to work, raising freshly painted scenery into place, hauling backdrops and banner canvases into positions high above the stage.

The flat wings of each scene were hung so they could drop each side of the acting area. Small pieces like tree trunks and bushes and palace furniture were fixed with trolley wheels so they could be easily moved onstage or off. Prop tables and fire buckets were set out behind the cover of the great proscenium arch. Even the velvet house curtains had their heavy gold fringes dusted.

Up above, the lamps were cleaned and their new stock of coloured glass filters checked. Below, in the pit, the newly polished instruments caught the light, as reeds and strings and felt pads were replaced across the whole orchestra. One by one, all the costumes were labelled and set out in orderly fashion in the various dressing rooms. High and low, all was being prepared.

At last the final dress rehearsal came. Adnam was deadly serious. Every word and action must be observed meticulously. Vanya waited in the wings, his steady gaze checking every cue, every entrance and exit, and everything else in between. Even Bellina Lander acted graciously to the rest of the cast as she paraded around in her peacock cape, ready to steal the show.

Kitty caught me backstage. 'Good luck. Break a leg!'

*

Everything worked well: the costumes, the lighting, the words and the music, the scenery changes, the watery fountains, the actors and dancers, the fairy ponies, even Puck's longest flight, where it seemed as if I was looping right over the almost empty seats.

Nick Tick, with Toby on a tight lead, observed the machine's glorious action. All too quickly the magic hour was over. I felt happy, very happy, until I spied Vanya's face furrowed in gloom.

'Things are meant to go wrong on such a day, Mouse. The bad luck is still out there in the wings, waiting for its entrance. Not good, Mouse, not good.'

His face was dark with doom.

CHAPTER 58

THE PRODIGAL'S RETURN

The moon shone through the huge windows and outlined the classical sculptures in the entrance hall with silver.

Scrope crept across the entrance hall, trying not to disturb anyone, especially Epsilon. He wanted to be alone so he could think. Sorry for everything? Perhaps. Sorry for himself? Certainly.

Scrope had not found Mouse at Murkstone Hall, but he had found boys in worn clothes running and racing more happily than he, as a boy, had ever run in the grounds of his father's house. Scrope had found someone called Jarvey who had made that dismal school come alive, unlike the proud mausoleum to which he had returned.

Moreover, Scrope had seen another sight in his

searches. The sooty bones of that burnt-out farm were smeared across his vision, almost as if his bitter command to Button had only just been spoken.

It seemed the child had disappeared, and Scrope's quest had become cold as a grave. What was also odd, thought Scrope, was that Mr Button seemed to have disappeared too. He had not visited Scrope's city rooms, hinting about payments. He had stopped sending strangely threatening letters. Surely this absence was not some game on Button's part? Or some flickering of generosity? A faint hope lit in Scrope's soul, then faded. He knew that Button had never been amused by a kind act.

Scrope passed silently along the corridor, past the swags of velvet curtains, past the portraits on the wall. No doubt about it, he was in greater distress than usual. What would Epsilon say when Scrope did not bring the boy to him? What would he do?

Scrope entered the quiet of the midnight library. He had always found it a good place to think, to work out what he should do next. He took one step, then another, and then he heard a voice speak his name.

'Scrope? Is that you?'

Scrope was caught in the beam of a suddenly uncovered lamp. Someone who looked like Albert was there, shotgun in hand. Scrope gasped. A ghost, come to haunt him? As Albert advanced, gun pointing forward, Scrope saw that this presence was all too real.

'Where is the boy? Father says you took care of him.'

'What boy?' stuttered Scrope stupidly. Was this genuinely his brother? Albert was never so fierce a fellow before. And if it was him, how long had he been here? How did he get here? And why the gun?

Had a telegram told Scrope? Oh no! He'd ordered all telegrams turned away, in case they'd come from Button or his creditors.

'Where is my son?' shouted Albert. 'Where is Mouse?'

'I don't know. I mean I did, but he's run away.'

'How long has he been gone?' Albert's words breathed cold hatred. 'Where to?'

Scrope blanched. 'I don't know those either, Albert. It's all a terrible mistake.'

Albert raised the gun to his shoulder, making Scrope scream in terror. 'Don't, brother!'

Slowly, uncertainly, Albert lowered the gun.

'I did wrong, I know it,' whined Scrope. 'I've been trying to find the child, but I have got nowhere.'

'You creeping worm!' said Albert. 'You gave up! If you were not my brother, you'd be dead as the rug you stand on.'

Scrope bowed down under the battering of accusations, but he had to ask – he had to. 'Adeline? Did she come back too?'

'Yes,' answered another voice, and there she was. 'How could you, Scrope – when we trusted you so much?'

FLYING HIGH

All through the busy rehearsals, I kept thinking of Ma. If it were not for the quartet of fairy horses chomping in their pen, and the notes Isaac gave me, I sometimes found it hard to believe we'd really met. But now I felt nervous, uncertain about what had been said or promised, unsure what to do next.

Isaac had come to my rescue, most simply. 'Want to see Ma?'

The answer was simple too. Yes. We'd been given one last day's rest before the opening night.

The cart trundled out towards the heath. I rode beside Isaac. This visit felt stranger than the time before. I'd questioned Ma so quickly, so greedily last time. It had not been how I'd wanted it to be. I wanted to ask about everything all over again, but I felt ashamed.

So I sat there, in their little home, awkward and silent, stroking Dog Toby's ears.

'Don't worry, Mouse,' Ma said gently. 'We can still be the friends we were. We can get to know each other again, child.' Slowly, that afternoon, it began to happen. We only talked about good times; it was as if we knew the rest could wait.

Ma made it easy, talking of Isaac and joking about the donkey and the cows and the four ponies and other animals that had found sanctuary with them here on the heath. She handed me cheese and cake. When I had eaten, she beamed and laughed the great chuckling laugh I once knew.

'Now, Mouse, tell me about that great theatre of yours.'

So I told her about the flying machine and about being Puck all in green, suspended high over the audience. Ma chuckled even more, and reminded me how I was forever in trouble for climbing in the big barn.

'I was at my wits' end with you, you rascally clamberer,' she told me. 'You haven't changed a bit.'

'Will you come to see me in the *Dream*, Ma?' I asked. 'You and Isaac?'

Ma regarded her simple grey dress. 'Don't I need finery to visit such a place?'

'No! I will ask Vanya to find you both a quiet seat where you can wear what you like, but you must come.'

'If it matters to you, Mouse, I will be there,' she answered, 'though I'll probably keep my eyes shut the whole time you're up in the air, child.'

Maybe that will be best, I thought. At least, it will be for Kitty and me.

*

The first public performance of Adnam's *Dream*! It made me glad to know that Ma and Isaac would be there, hidden alongside the jostling crowds, watching me, their long-lost Mouse.

The Albion itself was crowded, tier upon tier. The stalls, the circle, the gallery, even the topmost level – the gods – were crammed with people. A heady scent – greasepaint and gas lights, cigars and perfumes, sweat and anticipation – filled the auditorium and surged up to the stage. Adnam's reputation had brought in a full house.

He addressed us in the green room, gesturing as if he was already King Theseus.

'Friends, actors, stagehands, I come to wish you well tonight, but also to warn you to be on your guard. Beware! Any error tonight may mar the entire season. Any mistake might plunge our noble Albion into a desperate crisis.' Then Adnam, with the crown on his head, dropped to one knee and declared, 'If ever you have any love for me, my kindest hearts, my dear ones, do your best tonight!'

I was now trembling so much I could hardly move an inch, let alone climb the ladder.

'Eh, young lad,' muttered Arthur Boddy in my ear, 'don't worry about him, the silly beggar. Adnam always says stuff like that, and we're still here, aren't we?'

The *Dream* began.

Backstage, the crew were busy with their own work, making sure that the scenery fell and rose and the changes of the lamps worked when they should. The actors fussed over their scenes in their dressing rooms, or paced about in the green room, chattering nervously.

As the great velvet drapes swept open across the stage, there was one still moment of surprise. The audience gave a long single gasp as the sun rose behind the columns of the royal palace. Dressed in white tunics, the little girls circled about, showering rose petals until King Theseus and his bride Hippolyta entered to thunderous applause, followed by the young lovers.

I was poised in the wings, with green leaves already concealing the harness. Kitty shimmered with excitement.

'Ready? Going up?'

'Yes,' she said, and with a determined intake of breath seized the rungs of the ladder.

We clambered up to the fly floor and padded along the walkway as quietly as we could, while the play unfolded beneath our feet.

Another burst of clapping, and the stagehands hauled at the ropes, flying the second set of painted scenery into place. The lighting men adjusted the shutters on their lanterns and lowered the flames.

Kitty checked my straps.

'All right?'

'Yes!'

By now the lovers were onstage, pacing, protesting and squabbling among the gauzy trees. The men on the fly floor nodded across, ready to set the marvellous machine to work. The man far below who would haul me back nodded too. Far, far below I saw the heads of the actors as they passed across the boards, and Nick

Tick in the wings, swaying as if he was a pendulum in one of his clocks.

My toes, in soft green leather, curled around the hard metal edge. I had practised this drop so often that everything seemed familiar, though tonight the ivy leaves around my neck and the heavy green greasepaint on my skin seemed to itch more than before.

As a single violin rippled and soared, a glittering lake appeared amid a wash of ferny light. One of the fairy dancers pranced about there, picking careless flowers. I felt the lines tighten, and Nick Tick grinned, delight in his eyes.

'Good luck!' whispered Kitty.

I heard my cue, and leaned forward. Somewhere, with the faintest of squeaks, a wheel trundled forward and I plunged into space. Down I dropped, down, down.

Suddenly another gear turned, and I reeled out, almost over the audience, and they gasped. I was flying, flying, flying. As a spindle swivelled, I swept across to the edge of the theatre circle, alighting for the blink of an eye, then fell into my flight again. Among the threads of darkness and light, I appeared to be flying freely, light as air.

But part of my brain was busy, counting the beats, timing each arc so that the machinery worked as it should. The straps dug in, the lines hauled me round, but tonight I flew, I swooped, I swam – free of my past unhappy clamberings, free of the hated Grindle, free to live my own life.

As I swirled down towards the boards, I thought of

Punchman, who taught me to speak aloud, and I cried my first lines out in thanks for him as I landed on my own firm feet.

'How now, spirit! Whither wander you?'

The play was a success. Adnam as Oberon was darkly magical, cruel in jealousy, kingly in victory. The fairy ponies did not disgrace themselves onstage. The water tumbled from the tank in a glorious waterfall. Even the moment when Arthur Boddy in his donkey head tripped was seen as part of the delight.

Kitty and I gazed down, waiting for the last scene. She was ready. We had had time to get the harness changed over, and this was a simple descent. Puck's last lines were only to the audience, not to another actor, his last flight a simple landing.

King Theseus's revels were over. A flute sang plaintively in the empty spaces of the palace, and hardly anyone in the audience coughed as the lighting deepened into a night scene. The lantern of the moon shone between clouds of drifting veils, and tiny candles made starry pinpricks in the dark painted sky.

A stagehand approached. 'Anything wrong?'

'Bit dizzy!' I mouthed, waving him back. 'Shh!'

I checked the straps, but not on myself. This time it was Kitty waiting on the ledge. Her hands were shaking on the railing, but she looked entirely full of joy.

There was a flurry of delicate tiptoe fairy dancing, weaving in and out and around. Sophie de Salle's last song flowed out from a box beside the stage, and she appeared, like a goddess herself, singing a hymn to the moon. All was calm tranquillity.

Backstage, at our feet, was a flurry of activity. Adnam and Lander were being rushed into their fairy robes as fast as could be. The dressers' arms were looped with crowns and jewels, and their hands full of brushes and paints. The rest of the cast were quietly shuffling into their positions in the wings, ready for the final curtain. Nobody would be looking. Kitty would not be missed backstage, and this was just an easy descent.

'Go well,' I breathed.

The ropes swung, and Kitty was off, falling and flying. She landed, light as thistledown. We had practised speaking the lines together so often that we were one Puck. I mouthed the words myself, a silent echo.

'Now the hungry lion roars,' she began. 'And the wolf be-howls the moon . . .'

Adnam and Bellina entered for their final speeches. The peacock cloak swirled out under the lights, and Adnam's deep and wondrous tones resounded magnificently. Only once they departed, to huge applause, did Kitty start on the final speech. The house erupted with applause and cheers. The Albion had its triumph.

Ma was almost weeping when we met, briefly, afterwards. 'Who would have thought it? My little Mouse!'

Isaac beamed with pride, though this might have been as much for the fairy ponies' gallop as for the magic of Puck's flight.

The cab set us down close to Spinsters' Yard. Flora and Dora skipped the last yards happily, watching the frost sparkling on railings and walls.

'It was just wonderful,' said Kitty, rather carefully. 'Wasn't it?'

'So what about tomorrow? Same as tonight?'

What could I say? I hadn't thought any further than getting through that first night. 'Maybe . . .'

Aunt Violet was searching for a scrap of silk to repair a torn skirt, and Aunt Indigo was making a pan of cocoa.

'Well done, you good girls!' Kitty leaned over to hug her sisters.

Dora screwed up her face. 'Nasty!'

'What's wrong, poppet?'

'Don't like that green stuff you've put in your hair, Kitty,' she sulked.

Flora joined in. 'Ugh, Kitty! I can see green behind your ears too.'

They refused to kiss their big sister. Kitty and I glanced at each other. Maybe our secret was not as easy to hide as we'd imagined.

I entered the shop. Nick was sitting there grinning, with a glass in his hand, while Toby munched broken biscuits on the floor.

Nick could not possibly sleep yet. He had seen too much − his great machinery in action! 'Just a little celebration. Most excellent work, Mouse. I was proud of you.'

I grinned, glad to please him.

'Tell Kitty she did well too.'

My heart missed a beat. What was this? Was it so obvious?

'Boy, do you think I can't tell? That the machine can lie to me? The girl was a dancer. She can't help landing more lightly than you. I felt it in the tension on the lines.'

'Nick, don't tell anyone. It's really, really important that nobody knows.'

'Course not, Mouse. Only an inventor would have noticed,' he said, then added a gentle warning. 'Though it will have to come out some day.'

In the tall mahogany clock case, I saw the proud sailing ship bob to and fro to the rhythm of time. Ahead of the vessel, from among the painted waves, rose jagged peaks of rock, but there was no turning back for anyone.

WORDS INDEED

Scrope was the first to see the envelope lying on the tray. The neat black handwriting was horribly familiar. When had the thing arrived? His hands trembled as he tore the paper apart.

Friend Scrope,

Did you think I had forgotten you? Or our arrangements?

I can now tell you that I know the whereabouts of the item that so interests you. I am writing to offer you a choice. I can return it to you, or send it very securely elsewhere.

However, for settling this dangerous matter one way or the other, I will require suitable recompense. I suggest you gather goodly funds quite promptly. The time for action is now. I await your reply.

Your most faithful servant.

Scrope groaned helplessly as he hunched over his desk scribbling long columns of figures, trying to work out how he could satisfy such demands. Each piece of paper was criss-crossed with scratchings, and a stack of bills was spread untidily at his elbow.

He looked up, hearing a swish of skirts. Adeline had entered the room. She saw the pale waxiness of his skin and the sweat glistening on his upper lip.

'This is a surprise. I wasn't expecting you to speak to me any more,' he said hollowly.

'Albert and I may be furious with you, but it doesn't mean that we won't speak to you. We *have* to speak to you so we can find Mouse.' She sighed. 'It won't make it any easier if you hide yourself away, Scrope.'

Cautiously he glanced up at her. That beauty was faded now, bleached by the years in the sun, but she still touched his heart.

For a second Adeline's bold stance crumpled. 'Albert and I have seen terrible things, you know. None of them makes it easier to know that . . .' she hesitated, trembling '. . . to know that our dear Mouse is lost. Once I believed that the world was a fair place, brother Scrope. I'm not sure that I do now.'

She turned away, straightened her back again and lifted her head. Then she stared at him like an angel on the Day of Judgement. 'So, no matter how hard this is, we need to do what needs to be done.'

He nodded numbly, clutching at Button's letter.

'Is there something you need to tell us, Scrope?' asked Adeline.

'No,' he lied.

CHAPTER 61

PAINTED FACES

As a pair of twin merry sprites, we had devised a careful pattern to our act. Kitty spoke the long speeches, and I made the big, spectacular flights.

We slipped into our roles behind canvas trees and scenery flats, and as one performance followed another we grew clever at acting as one, but the greenest of greasepaint would not have disguised us if we had forgetten to remember to mirror each other. If the one Adnam played both Theseus and Oberon, we were just doing the opposite.

It went well, or so we thought, and we were already five nights into the run. I was sure the only clue was Kitty's wearily pale face, as we struggled to keep up with the work of boots and shoes. Still, I thought smugly, we had planned well. Only Nick knew, and all his concern was for the flying machine.

On the sixth night, as Kitty ran forward for the final speech, I concealed myself in the darkness of the wings as usual.

'Mouse, you do know that Adnam will be in big trouble when La Bellina finds out, don't you?' Vanya muttered over my shoulder. 'It will not be pretty.'

'Adnam? What do you mean? He doesn't know,' I whispered, alarmed.

'Doesn't he?' Vanya's eyes twinkled. 'Do you mean the man who keeps his eye on every movement in a play, the man who listens for every line spoken within his own theatre?' Vanya chuckled softly. 'When one of you plays Puck, and hides beneath Oberon's vast cloak, believe me, young Mousekin, Adnam knows which one of you is which.'

My stomach gave a turn. 'What do I do, Vanya? What is supposed to happen?'

'I don't know, Mouse. Adnam has his own reasons for keeping quiet. One useful fact is that La Bellina thinks only of herself, so she will notice nothing as long as you are very, very careful. And as long as young Kitty remembers not to act very, very good.'

'What do you mean?'

'Mouse, how do you think Kitty got to be best fairy, if she cannot act better than almost anyone? If she was not hiding herself, pretending to be you, Kitty could draw the eyes of hundreds. But not this time, eh? You tell her, Mouse.'

Kitty was so happy to be onstage again that I kept Vanya's worries to myself. Nevertheless, at the next performance, I would not let Kitty take over every line. When I piped up from under the arc of Oberon's cloak, Adnam started, but recovered in an instant.

'How now, mad spirit!' he declared.

I told him that the Queen of the Fairies was in love with a donkey, and then the confused lovers entered, and my moment was at an end.

'I go, I go; look how I go, swifter than arrow from Tartar's bow!' I cried. Running and swooping, I flew back up to the walkway, landing awkwardly and out of breath.

'I could have done that scene better, Mouse,' Kitty said as I landed.

'Yes, but I'm supposed to be doing it. We have to take care, Kit.' She rolled her eyes with dramatic exasperation. 'We must, Kit,' I insisted.

Kitty had her own home with the Aunts, but if things went wrong I could be thrown out of the theatre. I could not stay at Mr Nick's, so close to Kitty, if I had brought worse trouble to her. My Ma and Isaac would find it almost impossible to give me a home, and every other part of my strange story was sounding as unlikely as a distant fairy tale.

CHAPTER 62

EXIT STAGE LEFT

Button stood outside the stage door, waiting as the actors and stagehands arrived. He winked confidentially to Smudge as the doorman opened up.

Smudge paused. Then, slowly, he winked back. Men often asked his help when they were interested in actresses like Miss de Salle or Miss Marianne Day. Smudge made quite a profitable trade in supplying admirers with mislaid gloves and scented ribbons.

Miss Tildy bustled towards the entrance, greeting Smudge lightly and briskly. He held the door open a little longer afterwards, inviting Button to move closer.

'What ya want?' Smudge grunted.

'A word.'

'What about?'

'That flying scene. Saw it from the back of the gallery yesterday.'

Smudge was puzzled. 'Eh? Aren't you asking about our lovely young artistes?'

'Not one bit. I want to know who plays Puck.'

Smudge spat on the pavement. 'Puck? That one? A right pushy new cove, and he ain't one bit afraid of heights. Adnam sent him up the ladder, let him flap about a bit. Been doing well for a week or more, but can't say as I likes 'im. Got a right funny name too. Not Harry or Charlie. Nothing reg'lar.'

'How about this?' Button whispered in Smudge's ear.

The doorman looked startled. 'How d'you know?'

Button's eyes twinkled more brightly than ever. 'Call it luck,' he answered, offering Smudge a guinea. 'Yours if you let me watch backstage. What do you say?'

'Well, I guess it won't do no harm, seeing as you're a generous sort,' Smudge said, and told Button when to return.

'So goodnight unto you all . . .'

Lightly Puck bowed, turned a running somersault and made his exit. The entire audience stood and applauded the end of Adnam's *Dream*.

The crew stood watching as the cast came on to the stage for the finale, entering in twos and threes. First came the walk-on parts, and then all the comic workmen, with Arthur Boddy loudly saluting his fans in the gallery.

Into this roar came the pairs of lovers, moving to the side to make way for La Bellina, who swirled forward in her peacock train, strewing flowers out into the rows of seats, though twice as many flowers were being thrown to her. All around her, the troupe of fairies fluttered prettily, all curtsying and blowing kisses.

Then came a long pause in which the applause grew. At last Adnam entered, bowing magnificently to the crowd. The cast bowed again, as if they were still waiting. And waiting.

Suddenly Puck sprinted on last of all, leaping and dancing and turning head over heels to make up for the hint of lateness in arrival. From the gods came whistles and cheers, and the Albion filled with the sound of another night's success.

Button, glad of the finale's uproar, had waited in the shadows of the scenery until he saw his chance. He seized hold of the green-painted child that waited to go onstage and clamped a wad of cloth across the astonished mouth. The green fingers struggled against his grip, and fell loose. In one easy movement, Button slung the limp figure over his shoulder and slipped quickly out of the theatre.

Smudge lolled back in his chair, mouth open and eyes shut, stunned by Button's bottle of doctored gin. As the small man hoisted his sleeping Puck into a waiting carriage, one green foot slipped from the sacking.

CHAPTER 63

DISAPPEARING ACT

An evening of celebration! A few of the Albion's most important supporters – bankers, merchants, press barons and their wives – were escorted through the narrow corridors and stairways towards the banquet spread in Adnam's own suite of rooms above the theatre.

Still costumed in Oberon's magical robes, Adnam stood at the door, greeting gentlemen in evening dress and whispering compliments to ladies shining in furs and jewels.

The ever-faithful Peter took them through to the tables, where champagne corks popped and La Bellina's tinkling laugh dominated the excited murmur.

Elsewhere in the theatre, other members of the cast celebrated too. Fairies scampered along, squeaking and giggling, greedy for Miss Tildy's sweet cocoa and biscuits. Arthur Boddy cheerily gathered up his gang of boozy friends and staggered off to the nearest tavern.

Vanya and Nick clapped each other on the back, and little Dog Toby danced around them. Adnam's *Dream* seemed greater than ever.

I could not find Kitty anywhere. I climbed the ladder to the walkway. I checked with all the lighting men and stagehands. I asked as the flymen swung the scenery back into position. No one had seen her. Nor was she tucked away in the boot room.

At first I wondered if she was hiding away from Bellina Lander, but she wouldn't do that, not on a night like this, not when she was in disguise. My bad feeling grew. Why hadn't she taken the final bow as planned? Why had I had to run onstage myself? It was a mystery.

Had she gone to the stage door to breathe some cool air? I didn't find her, but I found Smudge snoring groggily on his chair, a bottle hugged to his chest.

'Smudge?' I tapped his arm.

His eyes opened and goggled at me. I didn't know what I'd done to make him stare so.

'Have you seen Kitty?'

Smudge was like a fish lifted from water. His mouth opened and closed. No sound came out other than a terrified gasping. All his blustering manner had gone.

'Mouse? What are you doing here?'

'Looking for Kitty. What's wrong? Have you seen her?'

Smudge groaned again, and his stupefied eyes closed.

'Vanya!' I yelled, racing back through the corridors. 'Help!'

Vanya lurched towards me. 'Stop that noise! You'll alarm Adnam's guests.'

I jumped at him. 'Kitty's disappeared, and something's wrong with Smudge. You must come now!'

Vanya thundered towards the stage door. He grabbed Smudge by his lapels and shook him awake. 'What's wrong with you? Have you seen Kitty go past? Tell me, quick.'

Smudge's bleary eyes blinked. 'A man came. Didn't want Kitty. Wanted 'im!' He pointed at me sulkily.

'What man?'

'Little man wiv hard round eyes.' The gin bottle smashed on the floor, and Smudge's lips curled into an angry curse. 'Devil's spawn!' He glared at me. 'It's your fault, Mouse. Coming here and getting in the way, spoiling poor young Kitty's chances. I thought he was after you, didn't I? Oh Gawd! He's taken Kitty, hasn't he?' Smudge slumped down in his wooden seat. 'I feel ill.'

'Good,' said Vanya. 'Just feel ill and be quiet, you stupid fool. Let me think.'

A little man? I knew this little man, and his name was Button. An awful chill ran right through me.

Along the corridor trotted Flora and Dora, grizzling with alarm. Nick Tick, with Dog Toby, was in their wake.

'Where's Kitty?' Flora whimpered. 'She didn't come for us. Did we make her angry with our dancing?'

'Shh! Shh! No, my pets. Don't worry,' Vanya murmured. 'Mouse and I will find her.' He hugged them briskly, beaming. 'Now, you are two lucky girls. Mr

356

Nick – he will take you home. Is that how it will be, Mr Nick?'

'Delighted, my dears,' agreed the clockmaker hastily. 'An absolute enchantment.'

Dog Toby tipped his head to one side and looked at me. Then he looked up at Nick, wagged his tail and pattered to my side.

'Good boy!' said Nick. 'Stay where you'll be of use. Now, girls, we must go. Come, come!' Flora and Dora trotted off obediently, holding Nick's hands very tightly.

We both knew Nick had to tell the Aunts about Kitty. There was someone else who had to be told too.

ADNAM'S LAIR

Adnam's suite of rooms was high in the green copper dome above the theatre. It was not where the cast went uninvited, especially when Adnam was trying to impress his backers with a private feast.

'Sit, Toby,' I said, and he squatted on his haunches. Vanya and I entered Adnam's rooms unannounced.

Heads turned as we made our rough and sudden appearance. Peter, startled, nearly spilled wine over one of the fine guests.

Adnam rose to his feet with a lion's lazy ease, laughing at a guest's joke, but his eyes were not amused. Vanya would never have interrupted him unless there was a very serious problem, but Adnam needed to be sure this moment was shown as fun.

'Aha! My little Puck has flown here for your delight!' Adnam cried, tugging playfully at my strands of ivy.

'Bow before my guests, my wild green boy!' he ordered, so I made my deepest theatrical bow as if this was a finale all over again. 'Apologies, my friends. I must leave you to attend to a small theatrical concern. Enjoy yourselves well until I return.'

He bowed most energetically himself, then steered us quickly through to his private study, from where the street lamps below looked like gems laid out on the vast darkness of the city.

'What's wrong? Tell me!' He grabbed Vanya's arm.

'Hugo, it is Kitty.'

'My Kitty? She landed safely, didn't she? There's not been any accident?'

Discovering that Adnam did know of our deception hardly made things happier now.

'A man takes her away from backstage. He waits till we are all busy, then he snatches away Kitty.'

'What did you see, Mouse?'

'Nothing. I was still up on the walkway. I raced down when Kit didn't come on for the final curtain.'

'Yes, you were late.' The frown deepened across his face. 'But why Kitty? What will Indigo and Violet say? It is senseless!'

A fear wormed into my mind. I am Puck, and Kitty is Puck. 'I think . . . I'm sure . . .' I stammered, holding out my green-stained arms, 'that . . . that . . . person actually wanted me.' How could I have brought this on Kitty?

There was not enough time for long explanations. 'Well, where will the man be, Mouse? Where will he have taken her?'

'I don't know.' Button was someone I'd always wanted to get away from, not go towards.

Adnam whirled around. 'Vanya? How can I get Kitty back? Do you have any thoughts about what we can do?'

Vanya shook his mighty head. 'I have no answer.'

I shuddered as I said it. 'Sir, I believe the man's name is Mr Button.'

Adnam grabbed at this horrid name as if it was an evil but necessary talisman. 'Go find this Button, Vanya. Something must be done. Someone must know where he is − and where she is!'

Suddenly he clasped his hand to his forehead. 'Oh blessed Shakespeare! My guests! I must go back.' He glanced around at his fine room as if it was a cage. 'How can I carry on? The Albion is killing me,' he said in anguish. 'Vanya, do something, my friend. I'll get rid of the guests as soon as I can.' Despair lurked behind his smile as he strode back to his merry supporters.

'Vanya?' I asked.

'Yes?' The tall man gave a big sigh as if he knew what was coming next.

'Why did Adnam call her *my* Kitty?'

'That question is not for now, Mouse. Now is for action.'

Dog Toby growled under his breath and pattered purposefully along the corridor.

CHAPTER 65

POST HASTE

The hired cab moved through the silent streets. The driver flicked the reins, immersed in his own thoughts. At this time of night, he had seen many odd incidents and strange people. He had learnt to listen carefully to directions and ask very few questions, especially about any large bags and sacks.

Button packed away the acrid wad of cloth that had brought Puck, that naughty sprite, down to earth. The creature lolled limply, wrapped inside the bundle of sacking. Did the child know his value? Probably not. Did he know how much he had annoyed Button? He would, before long.

As the horses cantered on, Button mused over his plans. He knew that Scrope would already be in a fit of anxiety. However, now he had seized the wretched boy, he could play his trump card.

His spies had told him – joy of joys, news of news – that the older brother had returned home. Though Scrope might find it hard to get money from his father, big brother Albert would have no such difficulty.

Button twirled his stubby thumbs and chuckled to himself. He patted the letter tucked into his waistcoat.

As they passed the post office, Button knocked on the door of the cab. The horses were reined to a halt, while Button leaned out and thrust the ominous envelope into the post box.

'Hurry!' Button snarled.

As the cab turned a corner, the bundled sack rolled across the cab floor and stirred uncomfortably. Button moved his boot in case he needed to give the child a kick.

What would he do when the brat woke up? A sly smile slipped across Button's smooth cheeks, as he felt the cab slow for its destination. He'd do nothing for a while. He'd stow the brat in the back cellar until he had a better idea of the boy's worth. It had better be plenty.

And if not? Well, the river's turbulent brown flood could always be relied upon to welcome any guests who had overstayed their usefulness. All was going his way.

CHAPTER 66

ON THE SCENT

'What's wrong with this Toby dog, young Mouse?'
Vanya asked. 'Why he is fuss, fuss, fuss?'

The little dog was growling over something he'd
found. He wagged his tail frantically and placed the
object before me. It was a soft Puck-green shoe. Kitty's!

Immediately I remembered what a clever creature
Toby was. 'Vanya, listen!'

We left a message for Adnam.

In all the side streets around the theatre stood rows of
cabs, ready to get any night folk home. Many had
already taken one fare and returned. The weary nags,
long noses hidden in hay bags, occasionally scraped
their hoofs on the cobbles, while the drivers, wrapped in
waterproofs and mufflers, dozed within their cabs.

Toby, nose twitching, pattered along the rows,

searching for Kitty's scent. He whined, unable to find any answer.

'Are you sure the dog can do this?' Vanya grumbled, unimpressed.

There were only three cabs ahead, waiting by a street lamp. The last had just returned to its stand, its horses sweating and tossing their manes.

Toby ran towards it and stopped. He yelped three times and scratched insistently on the pavement.

'I speak to this gentleman. All right?' Vanya rapped on the cab door until a whiskery face appeared, wrapped in a muffler.

Vanya thrust his bearded face towards the driver. 'Mister, where was your last call?'

The man refused to meet his eyes. 'No need to tell you. Is there?'

'Maybe there is, sir,' Vanya said emphatically. 'Because soon you may be meeting the good men from Scotland Yard, and it will be a happy chance if you have someone like me to speak about your helpfulness.'

Whether Vanya's size or Vanya's words made the cabby speak up, I was not sure.

'Well, I did think there was something odd,' said the cabby slowly. 'Besides, he left green stains smeared all over me upholstery. Can't trust no one these days.'

'How about you take us right there this minute, mister?' Vanya growled, as we clambered inside the cab, Toby jumping up on to the seat beside me.

The horses clip-clopped off down the lonely streets, snorting and rattling their reins.

'Hey, cabman,' called Vanya. 'Not too close to the

place. We must make a surprise.'

After a while, the cab slowed down.

'Over there.' The driver pointed to the end of the terrace. 'Down in that basement.'

'You wait for us, mister. You better be here when we come out, or worse for you!' hissed Vanya.

We approached the place as quietly as cats. When we reached the top of the basement steps, Toby paused. He whimpered, softly, and Vanya got ready to act. I felt scared at the thought of facing Mr Button.

MISTAKEN IDENTITY

Kitty woke, feeling strangely groggy. Rough sacking was dragged tight across her face. Her body ached and her knees were scraped and raw. Moments passed before she remembered what had happened when she had stepped back behind the scenery.

Then she heard a voice, quite close. 'Stay still, stupid boy! You're not Master Puck this time. There'll be no flying away from me now, Mouse.'

Fear filled Kitty, turning her limbs to lead. She dared not move. Her mind began racing and her ears started listening, listening for any clue. Kitty almost shouted out that all this was a mistake, but she locked her jaws tight. Think! Was she safer just now as Mouse or as herself? Play for time, play for time. She counted, as she did when overcoming stage fright. One, two, three . . .

Kitty tried to pretend she had drifted off to sleep, but

she kept listening. Where was she? Each tiny sound echoed. Stone walls? The air stank with damp and with cheap tallow candles. Underground somewhere?

Her unknown captor drank in gulps. He scraped a knife on a plate, and munched. What? She could smell it. Raw onions and cold fatty mutton.

The man suddenly spoke, and Kitty almost moved, almost shrieked aloud.

'Could give you some grub if you were awake, Mouse, but lucky for me, you aren't. Now, I wonder which one of them relations will pay for you first, my wretched little bundle of money? Will it be your naughty uncle Scrope, or those parents in their fine, fine house?'

Kitty opened her eyes in the darkness within the sack. Blackmail! Though it couldn't be against Mouse's Ma, because she certainly didn't live in a fine house. Nor could it be the parents Ma spoke about, for surely they were drowned and dead.

Her capturer was roaming round the room now, or so his tip-tapping boots told her. Kitty curled herself up, as if sleepily. She wrapped the sack into a tighter bundle around her body and gave a gentle snore, acting harder than she had ever acted before. She had to stay hidden as long as possible.

If the man pulled away the sack, how soon would it be before he saw through the green paint and realised his mistake? If all he wanted was Mouse, what use was she to him, alive or dead? Kitty waited, and waited, hearing the man clear his throat and move around this room.

Before long, time had lost its pattern. She might have been there five minutes or five hours. Certainly she had been there long enough to want a chamber-pot, and the pain in her gut was tightening.

Kitty made herself think very hard about other matters. She thought about being onstage as she once was, dancing with her sisters. Silently she counted through the steps of one of their dances, but what would she do when the curtsy came? She changed her thoughts, concentrating instead on Adnam's *Dream*. She recalled the words as they stood in the playscript, marked with notes and stage directions, until she felt she could touch the words on the printed pages. Even so, the ugly sacking scratched harshly at her mouth and eyes, and fear was picking away at her courage.

Not far away, Kitty heard the pattering of paws, too eager to be any rat. Something scraped against a door. Somewhere near.

A fat clammy hand grabbed at her wrist, and she couldn't help gasping.

'Don't you dare move, Vermin,' the man ordered, pinching hard. 'Don't say a word, rat-boy.'

Wood crashed and splintered close by.

MORNING TEA

The cosy had not been lifted from the teapot. The toast was untouched. On the breakfast tablecloth a letter lay open. Button's unmistakable script delivered its precise message to Epton Towers.

'What sort of a person can do this?' Adeline paced about the morning room. 'Isn't it enough that our child is lost, without strangers making threats? Who knows if this child is our boy anyway?'

Albert stared bleakly out of the window. 'We must do what this man asks for now, my dear, just in case it's true.'

'And say nothing to anyone? How can that be right, Albert?' Adeline trembled with anxiety as she stopped by the window. Outside, the morning sun sparkled on the frosted lawn and the sky was a bright clear blue. 'How can the day dawn so beautifully? Cruel, very cruel!'

'You don't suppose Scrope is behind this?' Albert enquired.

On the floor above, in his own study, Scrope pushed his fingers through his hair again and again. He stared at Button's last letter, turning it over and over in his fingers. How could he deal with this request for money? What would happen if another letter arrived? Maybe he should tell Adeline.

For so long he had wanted the boy gone, but had he truly wanted such a situation as this? The boy in such real danger? Maybe once . . . ? But now? Button's invisible fingers dug at his heart. What could he do now? What could he say to his brother, and to Adeline? Scrope squirmed. It was all his fault!

'Brother,' Albert said, bursting into Scrope's room and into his thoughts, 'we have some terrible news.'

Scrope, transfixed, jumped at Albert's voice, sending Button's letter skidding across the desk. He slapped his hand down across the sheet, but not before Albert saw that awful writing. He snatched the sheet up and read it. Then Albert held up the message that he and Adeline had just received.

'Snap!' Albert said, and he was not amused.

Albert walked Scrope from his study. He took him along the carpeted corridor, down the marble stairs and into the library, where they found old Epsilon, blinking like a wrinkled tortoise, and the fair Adeline.

'Tell us, Scrope,' said Albert. 'Tell us exactly what happened to Mouse!'

Scrope's whole frame shrank. Unable to explain, he mouthed silent half-shaped words. Then he raised one finger towards his father at the head of the table.

'No. You tell them first, Father!' he howled. 'You begin. Tell them you ignored the boy. Let them know you never spoke to him as if he was your grandchild, just as you have never spoken to me except as a servant.'

The old man looked up from his porridge and gaped. His bony hands rose feebly and tears dribbled down his hollow cheeks.

'Father?' Adeline gasped. 'How did you treat my boy?'

The old man gathered his energy together. When he turned towards her, his gaze was venomous.

'How dare you ask! It was you, girl, who took my own boy away,' he hissed, and turned to glare at his firstborn son. 'And you, Albert, agreed to go. You left me, and everything I'd built for you. You chose her and a glasshouse of plants, rather than doing your duty by your own father. Why should I have treated the boy as a dear little darling?'

'Because he was your grandson,' Adeline spoke, hardly comprehending. 'We thought you would care for him.'

'Like you expected me to look after everything at Epton Towers for you?' said Scrope, his voice cracking. 'Who, out of all of us, failed most?'

Aghast, Adeline stared at Scrope, her eyes brimming. *True and trusted friend*, he remembered. That was what she had called him long ago. The silence went on for a long time.

Eventually, Albert spoke decisively. 'Whatever we have done in the past must be left for another day.' He rang the bell to summon the servants and arrange a carriage into town. 'First we need to work out how to find the boy. So, brother Scrope, explain this Mr Button to us. Why exactly do we find this person meddling so harshly in our lives?'

A Trick of the Light

There were splinters of wood on the floor.

'Stay!' Vanya ordered, as he blocked the narrow doorway.

Toby obeyed. So did I. For a breath's space, the little child I once was cringed away from the face I was about to see, the man who took me to Murkstone Hall, who tightened such webs round my life. I was glad to be protected by Vanya's mighty bulk.

Then Dog Toby barked sharply, reminding me of Punchman's bravery, and my fear shrank back to its cave.

Through the gap between Vanya's arm and side, I could see the smiling mask of Mr Button. Against the wall, concealed in a sack, was Kitty. Button had grasped one of her wrists, but Kitty barely responded, though whether from harm or terror or choice I could not tell.

Vanya stayed calm and steady. 'I have come to take the child away.'

Button regarded Vanya dismissively. He ignored the little dog too. 'You think I will give this wretched boy up now when he is about to bring me good fortune? You are mistaken.'

Charlie Punchman's instructions came into my mind. *Don't forget, Mouse, timing is everything. Always wait for your entrance, Mouse. And then, when that moment comes, make the most of it!* I stayed lurking behind Vanya's huge bulk.

'Huh! I can see no way out for you. That is surely a pity!' Vanya mocked, stretching out his arms so that he blocked the doorway entirely.

Button wrenched Kitty upright. She muffled a shriek. 'There certainly is a way out, you great idiot. I assume you're after this piece of vermin?' A pistol gleamed in his hand.

Toby growled.

'Which creature do I go for first, do you think, boy or dog?' Button gloated.

'Is no matter,' Vanya retorted. 'The dog? Then I will get you. Me? I am well prepared for fellows like you.' Vanya was playing for his moment in time too. 'The poor child? What harm has he done you, eh?' He moved half a pace forward. 'Or is it some harm that you did to the boy that makes you so angry?'

'Harm young Mouse?' Button chuckled. 'Mouse? No, Mouse has been what you might call my long-term investment. There are people who are aching to see his silly face, you see. People who long to see this!'

Scornfully, Button tugged off the sacking and glanced

down to mock the face he thought he'd see. Instead, with Puck's cap askew, and her hair tumbling down, there was Kitty.

'What the hell's this?' He put the pistol to Kitty's throat.

Out from the shadows I sprang, out from behind Vanya. 'Did you want me, Button?' I shouted, darting forward. 'Was it me, me? Did you want little Mouse?'

Button turned from Kitty, his eyes widening as another green-faced child danced in front of him. He could not mistake this one. This was the true Mouse.

'You!' he gasped, and suddenly Vanya sprang forward, wrestling Button to the ground. The pistol slipped from his grasp, and Toby's teeth dug into his arm.

I rushed across, grabbed the pistol and pulled Kitty to her feet and away from Button. We looked like two bruised green beans dropped in a muddy gutter.

Vanya was not calm or steady any longer. Like a bear, he hauled Button back to his feet. He dragged him up the steps, skinning the man's hands and shins, and across to the waiting cab.

'Get in, you cockroach, you black beetle!' he roared, squashing Button tightly against the corner of the cab. Kitty and I jumped in, with Dog Toby at my heels, and I handed the pistol over to Vanya.

'Now we visit the respected constables at their station, I think,' announced Vanya. 'They will welcome you so well!'

Vanya returned us to the theatre. The gas lamp was still flickering above the stage door.

'It is us. We are back,' called Vanya as we entered. 'All is well with the children.'

Adnam came rushing forward, his face hollow with worry. We stood there onstage, still daubed in green.

'Kitty? Are you all right, dearest child?'

Kitty stepped back from Adnam's outstretched arms. 'Yes, I am,' she said, 'but that awful man's not, and good riddance to him.'

'And Mouse?' said Adnam. 'What happened?'

Vanya started to tell Adnam our tale.

'Please,' said Kitty, 'I am so very tired . . .'

That night we were taken up to Adnam's very own rooms at the top of the theatre. Peter brought us sweet cake and settled us down to sleep, wrapped in several thick cloaks that smelled of greasepaint.

I woke only once. Adnam was sitting there, staring down at Kitty. I drifted off again, but I wished it was not Button's face that I saw in my dreams.

'Toby, where are you?' I murmured, reaching out. I was glad to find the little dog's body snuggling beside me again.

CHAPTER 70

A KETTLE ON THE BOIL

'Righto!' shouted the sergeant to the constable on desk duty. 'That nasty red-faced fellow is banged up for the night, and I'm away round the corner for my supper. The shop's yours to watch for a while, lad.'

When Vanya had first brought Button to the police station, Button was wary of the sergeant with the fierce handlebar moustache. However, he still had enough wits to gather several facts about the establishment where he was – not too wisely – being deposited.

Though the station had a well-polished desk, that piece of furniture was almost its only efficiency. As Button was dragged through the station towards his solitary cell, he assessed the situation watchfully. By the time his prison door clanged shut, he had a plan.

The pale-faced constable was a young lad, not quite used to the ways of the world. Desperately weary from too many night shifts, he had filed away twenty scrawled statements, put the kettle on to boil and settled himself by the fire.

Soon his sitting had turned into a snoozing, in which he imagined himself tackling the latest felon in the most heroic manner. This idle quarter-hour was just long enough.

Button's shouts roused the bemused constable, who woke amid a cloud of scalding steam from the boiling kettle. Quickly he took the kettle from the fire, then hurried to the cell. He peered through the peephole into the gloom beyond, and saw nobody.

Alarmed, he unlocked the door and stepped inside. To his horror, the new prisoner was missing. What would he tell his sergeant? What would happen to him now?

Then Button rolled out from under the low bunk, sank his teeth deep into the leg of the law and laid the lad low with a blow. The keys clattered to the floor.

All went just as Button intended. Free again, he crept past the empty desk without even admiring the expensive mahogany and disappeared into the icy mists of the dawn.

ADNAM THE GREAT

Despite everything – the kidnapping, the distress, the recovery – the *Dream* itself had to continue. However, it continued, as we quickly discovered, with a certain difference.

Just before the next performance, Adnam called everyone together. He took his usual place, centre stage, while the costumed actors nudged each other, gossiped and muttered around him, until he signalled silence.

We all waited – cast, stagehands, lighting men, dressers, musicians and even the fairy dancers – to hear whatever Adnam had to tell us. He stood there in his royal robes, a wreath of golden leaves in his carefully arranged locks, and began.

'Ladies, gentlemen, dear friends and helpers, we all know that Shakespeare's *Dream* is a play about deceptions and errors, but there has been a deeper deception, which I now choose to reveal.'

Everyone crowded closer to catch Adnam's words. He sighed deeply, as if the Albion's future balanced on this revelation.

'I must admit I did not try to stop this deception. In a sense I encouraged it, though now I find it has almost cost a precious life. So, friends, no matter what it costs this struggling production, I will tell you the truth.'

The mutters of concern changed to curiosity as Adnam beckoned me forward.

'Who do we have here? We all know, don't we? It is Puck, our dazzling sprite, our young climber of heights, our fearless flyer, our blithe boy. And many thanks to him too!'

There were smiles and some applause. I bowed nervously, not sure of what was coming next.

Adnam's smiles turned grim. 'But is not Puck a shape-shifter, a creature of mystery, a creature who is not what he appears? Or what *she* appears?'

She? She? That word, passed on, hummed like a swarm of bees.

'Yes, she,' continued Adnam. 'As some of you have guessed, more than one cunning sprite has been deceiving us. Young Kitty?' He invited her to step forward too. Kitty hesitated, but Adnam took her hand and brought her centre stage too. 'Behold our other Puck!'

Bellina Lander's cheeks flushed with bright patches of rage. If she could have become a spitting cat and scratched Kitty's eyes out, I'm sure that's what she'd have done.

'That child?' she screeched. 'How could you let her

onstage, after all you promised me, Hugo?'

La Bellina rushed over to strike him, but he deflected her blow easily. Shamed, she swirled about in her long robes and stood with her back to him, panting with anger.

'Some of you know that Kitty was once the best fairy dancer we had onstage,' Adnam said, beaming generously at all. 'I, for one, welcome her somewhat disguised return to the boards.'

There was much applause, though not from La Bellina.

'In fact, Kitty will continue to share the role of Puck with our bold flyer, young Mouse, and both their names will appear on tonight's cast list. So now you know what I, Hugo Adnam, choose, come what may.'

'Well done, lad! Well done, lass!' There were many cheers, with the loudest from Vanya. Then Adnam silenced us with a raised hand.

'I have done many things for the sake of the Albion, for these rough boards that give you all your noble employment, even the proud Miss Lander. My dream was to make this theatre into something grand and fine, not a tawdry playhouse to amuse common sots and hussies. I believe we have had some success.'

Greater applause rang out. I saw that Adnam's speech was almost a play that he was performing right here under our noses.

'I tried, against my better judgement, to keep a proud lady in my company,' said Adnam. 'But now I say, go stamp your feet if you wish, Miss Lander. Leave my theatre if you want to. Go. Stay. I no longer care.'

The fight had gone out of La Bellina. Her beautiful face was like a blank mask.

Adnam's proud voice faltered. 'But in following my dream, there was a story that I pushed to the back of my mind. I do not want to do so any longer.'

He hung his head for a moment, then raised it towards Kitty and the girls. He was not being Hugo the great actor then. All at once, something was so, so clear to me that I didn't know why I had not seen it before.

'More than a dozen years ago, friends, I loved a dear, kind woman. Then the dark angel we will all one day meet took her away. Bitterly, I turned away from the little ones I should have loved and gave my heart entirely to the Albion.'

In one single movement, Adnam lifted Kitty up high.

'This Kitty is that dear woman's child and my own daughter, and her two little sisters are my own children too.' He stood the astonished Kitty gently down to the stage and declared, 'Forgive me, Kitty. You too, Flora and Dora. Yes, I am your father.'

By then, Miss Tildy and all the actresses were blubbing. Even Peter was dabbing softly at his eyes. Flora and Dora, never missing a cue, rushed forward into Adnam's embrace. Utterly exhausted, he crouched down and whispered in their ears.

'Blimey!' muttered Arthur Boddy. 'Knock me down with a feather!'

Eventually, Adnam rose, breathed deeply, and spoke. 'Ladies and gentlemen, thank you for your attention. Please remember we have a play to put on this evening. Go, break a leg! Good luck, all!'

As we hesitated, Adnam's voice rang out again. 'Are you still with my company, Miss Lander, or do I have to make other arrangements?'

La Bellina's sigh was so melodramatic that it was a wonder she did not faint with the effort. She gave the very slightest nod of agreement, and swept off the stage.

It seemed to me then that Adnam, being Adnam, could not have revealed his secret in any other way. An actor was what he was, playing out his own life both onstage and off.

Only one person did not move. Kitty. She had not returned to Adnam's fatherly embrace, as Flora and Dora had done. She looked across at me and half smiled, but I could not read her thoughts. So the great Hugo Adnam was her own father? How did it feel to learn that after so long?

But we had not time to ponder. Within a few minutes, the curtain would rise, and we would begin again. That night the Albion would stage a story like no other.

CHAPTER 72

DIFFERENT PLACES

The Chief Inspector listened respectfully to Albert and Adeline. Privately he thought that their explanations did not entirely make sense, and it was odd that the brother, Scrope, remained silent.

Besides, a report had just arrived on his desk. He read, with growing alarm, the account of a Mr Button's sudden escape. As he sucked thoughtfully on his pipe, the Chief Inspector arranged for several urgent telegraphs to be sent and tried to calm his audience.

'Madam, sirs, there will be news but not immediately,' he told them. 'Go back to your hotel. I will send a messenger if anything is discovered.'

They trudged out into the fog. Albert and Adeline held hands grimly. Scrope scuffed his boots in their wake.

A pitiful, grubby-faced boy appeared out of the mist.

His rectangular wooden suit advertised all manner of amusements. He tried to step aside, but the weight of the boards almost toppled him into the gentlefolk instead.

'Sorry, madam. Sorry, sirs,' he chirped.

'No matter,' Adeline murmured. Did anything at all matter just now?

Apologetically, as if they were flowers, the boy thrust a fistful of printed flyers into Adeline's hands.

Back at their hotel, the three sank into padded velvet chairs. They were too wrung out to face any meal. When a waiter appeared silently at their side, Albert ordered drinks.

Scrope stared hard at his glass, downed it in one, then wished he had another. What else could he do?

Albert took small melancholy sips.

Adeline gazed into space, not reaching out for her drink at all. Her fingers were still clutched tightly around the flyers.

'Let me take those, my dearest,' Albert said eventually, trying to prise them out of her hand.

Adeline shook her head, then let her eyes focus once more. She glanced listlessly at the smudged print gathered in her grasp. There, among the crumpled lists of plays and players, she read one name.

'Oh!' Adeline gasped, and, without another word, leaped up from her armchair, and ran out through the hotel doors.

'Quick!' said Albert, gathering up his wife's fur wraps. 'After her!'

*

The swirling fog transformed every gas lamp into a yellow orb. Cabs and omnibuses were hung with warning lanterns. Only the rattle of wheels on cobbles alerted pedestrians and crossing sweepers to approaching vehicles.

Horses appeared out of the thick gloom, tossing their blinkered heads nervously. Cab drivers struggled to find their familiar stopping places at the theatre steps.

The never-ending murk silenced the audience that flocked towards the Albion. They were heavily wrapped in furs and shawls, cloaks and capes, mufflers and overcoats, but they hurried forward determinedly. Tonight they would be the Albion's most welcome guests.

One single green carriage came to a steady halt. The driver leaped down, and helped his passengers descend to the pavement. The smaller woman, neat and trim, reached for her purse, but the cabbie shook his head and gave a friendly grin.

'No, madam, thank you. This is himself's carriage. Mr Adnam told me to take good care of you both.'

'Then take this for your trouble,' Aunt Violet insisted, dropping a coin into his gloved palm.

She took Aunt Indigo's arm, and the pair set off towards the theatre. They stepped very daintily because they were dressed in silks and furs, and on their feet were buckled shoes they had not worn for years. They stopped to chat to the apple-women and chestnut sellers and then made for the grand entrance.

'Goodness me, Violet, isn't this exciting?' said Aunt Indigo. 'Quite like the old days, eh?'

'Like seeing our dear Katherine again,' Violet answered. The girls' poor dear mother was in both their minds.

As they entered the brightly lit foyer, the General swooped forward, presenting programmes to their gloved hands.

'Make room, make room!' he bellowed, ushering the Aunts up the grand staircase and into a private box close to the stage itself.

'Mr Adnam hopes you have a wonderful evening,' he said, and left them admiring the gilded cherubs and hissing gas lamps.

No sooner had the Aunts laid their furs and gloves beside them on the plush seats than a young woman appeared with a silver tea service.

'To warm you both after your journey, gentle ladies. Mr Adnam has arranged further refreshment for the next interval.'

The Aunts extracted dainty mother-of-pearl lorgnettes from their handbags and clucked over all the names in the programme.

As they sipped their tea, the orchestra began to tune its instruments.

'Almost time, my dearest Indigo,' Aunt Violet said, as they smoothed their skirts and got ready for the raising of the Albion's magnificent fringed curtains.

A far less grandly dressed procession pressed through the Albion's cheaper entrances, shouting and calling. They clattered up flights of uncarpeted stairs and rushed to the best places. From here, the highest point in the auditorium, up close to the painted ceiling, the view tipped dizzily down towards Adnam's wide stage.

No apron-clad maids with tea trays welcomed the boisterous crowd gathered up in the gods. From the crest of the proscenium arch, the blind masks of comedy and tragedy regarded the rough and ready theatre-goers cramming excitedly on to the narrow wooden benches. Snatches of tunes drifted up from the orchestra far below.

A short man was almost carried along by the crowd's enthusiastic ascent. He was nudged and elbowed and shoved onwards.

Once he had arrived at the gods, he fought his way across to the far side and pushed himself into a particular spot by the brass railing. He had little trouble obtaining that spot. Who would choose a seat with such a poor view of the play?

By now, the man's glossy polish was smeared. His rosy cheeks were blotched from exhaustion, and his neat black clothes were creased and scuffed from his visit to the cells.

Tonight Mr Button did not smile. Desperate hate was fixed firmly on his face.

CHAPTER 73

A VIEW FROM THE STALLS

'Many apologies, madam, but the house is already full tonight,' the General politely informed the three late arrivals.

'I must get into the play, I must,' Adeline pleaded, wild as a lioness and hungry for a sight of her child.

Albert took the General aside and explained. 'A matter of great importance, sir, so if you can help . . .'

Thankfully, a family party had argued over some private matter and decided to leave. Before long all three were seated, just in time to hear the orchestra start to tune up.

Adeline could hardly keep quiet. 'His name is in the programme, Albert. Look! Mouse! The flying Mouse! It must be our boy, it must,' she muttered fretfully, starting to stand up. 'Shouldn't we go to him now? Go backstage this very minute?'

'It might be another child altogether.' Albert pulled her gently down into her place. 'Besides, nothing can happen to the boy while the performance takes place. If it might be him, we'll go backstage as soon as we can, I promise.'

Scrope, meanwhile, hunched awkwardly down in his theatre seat, peering at the crushed paper. Was it at all possible that the name in the programme could be his nephew, the child to whom he had wished such ill? How strange that would be!

It was so dreadfully hot. As Scrope stood to loosen his coat, he gazed around the theatre. He saw two amiable elderly women fussing about in one of the grand boxes, adjusting their shawls and trying out opera glasses. They were not the pretty young birds that usually nested in such expensive seats, but Scrope, despite his own troubles, found he was glad to see the two dears looking so happy.

A moment later, a charming little man in an antique coat joined the pair. There was much smiling and greeting. A small black and white dog popped up, peered over the box and then vanished, as if it had settled down at someone's feet.

There were gas lamps all the way around the stalls, the circle and right up to the gallery itself. It must be terribly hot up there, Scrope thought, as he idly studied the gilded cherubs that fluttered around the domed ceiling and mirrored globe. How full the Albion was with brightness, even up there where the lamps lit the faces overhanging from the gods.

Scrope started. He almost rushed from his seat, but

hesitated, unbelieving. He glanced up again. One face, round as a balloon, had appeared over the handrail before, but now it was gone.

As the orchestra struck up, the velvet curtains trembled and slowly started to rise. Scrope fidgeted uncertainly, screwing his eyes up as if to be sure what he had seen.

It was him, he was sure of it. He had seen the face of the man who had helped to wreck his life, the man who enjoyed other people's misery as much as their money. That face, here in the Albion Theatre tonight, but why?

CHAPTER 74

DREAMS IN MIDWINTER

It might be midwinter outside, but onstage a sweet midsummer bloomed.

Roses cascaded down the pillars of Theseus's painted palace. Hidden wooden rollers turned, setting the silken waves of an aquamarine sea billowing. Concealed ropes dragged an antique sailing ship across the glimmering bay. The glowing sunset changed into purple evening light, and a waning moon ascended, shaking a little, into the artificial sky.

Adnam, as Lord Theseus, led a subdued Queen Hippolyta to centre stage. La Bellina's make-up was heavy enough to conceal her puffy, reddened eyes.

Kitty and I waited in the wings, green-painted and green-clothed, almost identical. It no longer mattered who saw us. We were a pair. I knew Kitty's voice was better than mine, and she knew that I was by far the better flyer, but tonight, together, we would make our Puck the most triumphant one of all.

Miss Tildy was having trouble quietening the fairies. Flora and Dora were bubbling with joy about Kitty's part, and their excitement had infected the others. Eventually the troupe ran to their positions at the front of the stage, ready to dance enchantingly while the entire set was being transformed into a leafy Shakespearean grove behind the canvas drop.

I had to be ready for my cue, for my first long flight. Up I climbed, up and up, and edged out along the walkway. Tonight I felt so light-headed that I could almost fly without wings.

I waved to the stagehand and clipped the lines to my harness. The lighting man prepared his change of coloured filters in preparation for the flight scene.

The melody that carried my musical cue began. Slowly the gas flames were turned up, and the lantern flaps opened, washing the boards below with the green of a woodland glade and deepening the shadows between the trees.

For a moment, as I gazed down, the shades below seemed like the malicious faces of Grindle and his gang again. I saw the tiny figures of the actors, waiting in the wings. Suddenly the drop below looked as deep as poor Pyeberry's fall. My stomach swung over. I thought about Kitty, and how Button carried her away so easily, and I started to shake.

A hand gripped my shoulder. I whirled round, almost expecting to see some awful ghost from my past, but it was only one of the stagehands. And I had missed my cue.

'Mouse, are you all right?' he asked.

'Think so.' How could I be in a panic this time, tonight, when all was solved and secure?

The orchestra covered my fault with a run of merry notes that wound back into the woodland melody, bringing my cue to me a second time.

Would I make it? Could I do it? The low mumbles and calls from the gods made hidden voices rise in my head, and I heard echoes of Bulloughby's growls, and Shankbone's groans, and even the cold moans of that place where Punchman's life had ended.

The thick, greasepainted air seemed to breathe with pretended joy and hidden sorrow. I was not at all sure I could do this tonight, yet the melody was about to call me. I closed my eyes, totally unsure.

Then the very slightest sound rose from backstage: the whinny of the fairy horses as they waited in the wings. I caught the merest breath of grassy sweetness. I remembered Isaac's barn, and the little mouse crossing the vast wooden beam, and I remembered sunlight and delight, not fear. I remembered Ma smiling at me across the yard, the Ma I had now found.

I rose on my toes, ready to fly once more.

A PRIME POSITION

Button, way up in the gods, had his eyes fixed feverishly on the space above the stage, on the line of the flight.

A cold fury gripped his heart, a silent rage, an icy hatred. His plans were supposed to work. His plans were supposed to deliver what he wanted.

What Button wanted he was used to getting. He would show everybody he was the one who pulled the strings, the one who got his own way. Him and nobody else, especially not that wretched boy, that vermin who had outsmarted him.

The music rose again for the woodland scene, and Button reached inside his overcoat. At the edge of the gods he leaned over the brass railing. This time he would not make any mistake.

CHAPTER 76

A GIFT FROM THE GODS

The music summoned Puck forth. Right on cue this time, I leaped out from my high place. The straps tightened. The wheels and lines ran, and I soared forward, flying out over everyone as if I was free.

I, the most magical, mischievous Puck, circled around, with my garments and ivy trails fluttering. The music whirled and swirled. I spread my arms out widely, weaving out towards the stalls. The crowd might be gasping and gaping below, but all I heard was the precious sound of my mechanical flight. I was a blithe sprite on the wing, free of the power of the earth, free of all that held me down.

Within too short a time, the lines tautened on my harness, and I swung out into one last wide arc, ready to return.

As the music softened, a single voice called my name.

'Mouse, Mouse!' A woman in fine clothes was standing below me in the stalls, waving her arms wildly. 'Mouse! Mouse!'

Who was she? Why did she shout my name?

At that very moment, a star of fire exploded from the gods, and pain burst in my chest.

Like a shot bird, I swung away into darkness, broken-winged. I heard another pistol shot, and that woman screaming and screaming and screaming, and suddenly the musicians stopped playing.

CHAPTER 77

A FIRM HAND

Scrope, racing up the steep stairs, heard the first shot. Too late, too late! He pushed his way along the gods, thrusting through the crowd, struggling to reach the silhouette of the man leaning at the railing.

Into Scrope's mind flashed that day when Mouse stood by the sunlit window, trusting him, his uncle. The day when he first considered that perhaps . . . that time when Hanny tried to stop . . . that moment when his bitterness set it all in motion . . . the boy, the boy and that dreadful place . . . though she had called him her true and trusted friend . . . Adeline, dear Adeline . . .

He shoved, he trampled, he forced himself onwards. No good, too late, no time to think, not even whether he was doing this for Mouse or for himself.

'No! Not again!' he yelled.

Scrope grabbed Button's tight black-coated person,

lifting him, flinging him forward so swiftly there was no time to break his own grip. The pistol cracked again, the weight unbalanced him, and together they toppled over the railing, down, down, down . . .

Mercifully, they crashed on the carpeted gangway below, not on the horrified audience. There was a pause, then sudden uproar in the auditorium. What was happening, and where and why . . .

As the stage curtains swished down, Arthur Boddy strode on to the stage. His comforting, chuckling persona reassured the audience.

'Nothing to worry about, folks!' he called out in a cheerful chuckle. 'Take your seats, please. Only a pair of acrobats, trying to draw Adnam's attention to their act – and our poor little Puck must have fainted. No wonder, watching such a blooming bad act! Ho ho!'

As Arthur's corpulent form chased the fears of the audience away, Adnam's well-trained theatre staff surrounded the fallen figures. In the space of one of Boddy's old-fashioned jokes, the bodies were removed, leaving no instant for the audience to reflect on what they had witnessed. The General's runner was already summoning the nearest policeman.

Meanwhile, Adnam got ready to make a swift speech, full of confident charm, and the musicians in the orchestra pit riffled through their stack of Miss de Salle's specially selected songs, most useful for all theatrical emergencies. The show must go on.

CHAPTER 78

A SENSE OF DIRECTION

'Mouse! Come on, boy. Come on!'

My eyes opened so, so slowly. I was lying on the stage, with straps and ropes about me. One arm ached most painfully. The lighting men stared down at me from their roosts above, but their lanterns dazzled me.

'The child's waking,' Vanya said, patting my cheek. Kitty was kneeling by me, her face anxious.

The thick curtains enclosed the scene, so the audience could not witness the panic around my fall.

'Ladies and gentlemen, excuse this short intermission,' I heard Adnam telling the audience, his voice heroically strong. 'We beg your honoured patience. The *Dream* will resume shortly. Meanwhile, for your delight . . .'

I heard the orchestra strike up, and Miss Tildy's hiss as she hurried the fairies out on to the front of stage.

'No crying, lassies. Just dance your best, my darlings. Dance as you have never danced before.'

Miss de Salle was out front, singing with much spirit. Arthur Boddy's rumbling voice warned the cast to keep back.

Dimly I felt the pain reach over to stroke my chest, to squeeze my shoulder, but not quite as harshly as before.

Vanya leaned over me. 'Does it hurt, boy? Here? Or here?'

'The blood?' Kitty whispered. 'I heard two shots, but where's the blood?'

As Vanya started to unbutton my tunic, I gasped. I had been brought to the floor too swiftly. My joints ached. I clutched at my chest, where it hurt. Then I heard footsteps running rapidly across the boards, and the dim shapes above me parted.

A strange woman – a fine lady who smelled of lilies and whose clothes swished like silk – was also leaning over me, so close I could feel her anxious breath. She stared, her face almost against mine, and turned to the man at her side. I could not recognise either of them, but she was surely the lady who screamed as I flew.

'It is. It's him! I'm sure of it! Mouse? My little Mouse? Oh heavens, I can't have lost him already, can I, Albert?' She tried to touch me, but the man called Albert held her back.

'Lady, please be very silent,' Vanya insisted firmly. 'The boy's arm is not so good. He may have hit his skull too.'

As Vanya undid the last button, the tunic fell open.

He chuckled softly. 'Fortune must love this boy.'

He held up something that seemed a scrap of crushed silver paper. No! I was filled with desperation. How had this happened? This crumpled silver was all that remained of my mouse medal, my precious compass. I tried to seize my secret back from Vanya, hide it from all the staring eyes. I grabbed about wildly with my good hand.

'Mine,' I shouted unsteadily, though my voice did not feel like mine. 'Mine! Give it me.'

'Saved your life, did this small thing,' Vanya told me. 'Softened the shot. Is not much use any more, Mouseboy. Sorry.' He placed my damaged treasure in my palm.

However, as my fingers folded over the twisted disc, the fine lady swooped forward to take it. 'I must see that!' she said, her voice almost imperious.

'No!' I heard myself scream as I fought her away, clenching the twisted unfamiliar shape. 'No! Nobody can have it. It's mine. I mustn't give it to anyone. Get away, whoever you are!'

The lady sank down on her knees beside me. She put a cool hand tenderly on my forehead. She gazed into my eyes, calmly and sadly. 'Even if I was the one who gave it to you, Mouse?' she said at last. Her voice was almost a whisper.

'You're not Hanny! Hanny gave it to me!'

I tossed my head from side to side, trying to see someone who could help, someone who could make sense of this moment. Everyone, even the mighty Adnam, was standing there open-mouthed.

'No, no!' I yelled, breaking the gathering web of silence, 'Go away. It's mine.'

'I know. I know that Hanny gave it to you,' the lady told me, her soft hand resting on my clenched fist. 'Don't worry, Mouse, I won't try to take your treasure. I gave it to Hanny.' She took a deep breath. 'I gave you to Hanny too, Mouse.'

Aunt Violet and Aunt Indigo pattered across the stage. They, and everyone else, heard the lady speak, saying words so fine they could be part of a play. Did they find the lines as hard to take in as I did? What did she say?

'Mouse, I'm your mother.'

Mouse, I'm your mother? She is my mother?

Too much, much too much. I closed my eyes, clutched my mouse medal and welcomed the dark.

CHAPTER 79

AFTER THE FALL

Sergeant Trudgewell turned up the gas light, and wrote a detailed report of the case in his plainest, clearest handwriting.

INCIDENT REPORT

9.05 p.m. I was called to Albion Theatre. Arrived to find two persons apparently deceased and an intermission act onstage. Cause of death reported to be a fall from upper gallery. After a brief investigation, I arranged for the bodies to be conveyed to station mortuary. The play continued.

Person A. Male, aged about 40. Small, round-faced, red complexion. Wearing a black suit. Pockets contain pistol (fired), bullets and a life preserver. Also small notebook, pencil, skeleton keys, several coins and sundry items. Carried no identification or evidence of his abode.

NB. Body fits the description of a known felon, Mr Button, recently escaped from police cells to the east of the city.

Person B. Male, aged about 35. Tall, thin face. Gentleman? Wearing clothes of quality. Before I could undertake further investigation, the body was identified by Mr Albert Epton of Epton Towers as his younger brother.

Sergeant Trudgewell rubbed his weary eyes, and longed for a cup of strong tea. He had expected an easy night of it: perhaps a pair of drunken beggars, or a failed pickpocket or a stray dog. Instead, all that fuss at the theatre had ended up on his shift. He stuck his pen sullenly into the inkwell. How he hated writing reports!

On the other hand, as the incident had occurred in such a public place, the whole story would be in the papers. He would have to get his wife to look out for the article. Maybe he would stick it in his scrapbook, next to the report on the runaway donkey scam. Maybe, if there was a picture, he might even frame it, if the toffs in the tale turned out genuine.

Cheered slightly, Trudgewell turned back to his laboured writing.

Account of incident as follows:

Two members of the audience, Clegg and Smith, were seated in the upper gallery, known as the gods, close to the site of the altercation.

Smith reported that the man now known as Button darted to the rail at the start of the main flying display, causing annoyance to several persons, who shouted diverse unrecorded expressions.

Clegg shouted out that the man must be inebriated.

Smith kept silent, having observed a pistol in Button's hand and a most maniacal gleam in his eyes.

Both men heard one shot fired. Smith added that the assailant then cried, 'That will finish you, Vermin.'

There were screams below.

Clegg said that as Button raised his pistol once more, a tall man raced forward. He grabbed Button to restrain him, but then seemed to throw both himself and Button over the rail.

Clegg and Smith both peered over the railings but could not see exactly what was happening below.

As a Miss de Salle appeared onstage, Clegg and Smith decided to remain in their places, though they later came forward to give evidence. They were not unfamiliar to several officers at this Station.

As Trudgewell laid down his pen, a young constable rushed in, his face pale beneath his pimples.

'It's the mortuary!' he cried. 'You have to come, sarge.'

They descended the stairs.

At the foot stood a cleaner, bucket and mop in hand, shaking ceaselessly. 'In there. Never saw such a fing in my life before. Never.'

The two officers adjusted their uniforms, took a firm grip of their truncheons, and entered the mortuary with slow, deliberate steps.

On a slab at the back, beneath a stretch of cloth, lay the long form of Deceased Person B, name of Epton.

The chest was moving slightly, and a dimple appeared and disappeared in the linen sheet, just above where a mouth might be open.

'Heavens almighty, sarge!' the constable gasped. 'I think the geezer's breathing.'

'More blooming paperwork,' said Sergeant Trudgewell gloomily. 'And I don't fancy being the one who has to explain it to that family of his, neither. They were angry enough at him being brought here. Toffs, eh? Always survive.'

EGGS AND TEA

The thick weight of sleep that had been holding me down grew lighter. I woke, with relief, in my small bed at Nick's. It felt the very best place to be. Time ticked reassuringly, the chimes sang their orderly songs and Toby waited, head on paws, beside me.

Something was not right, I remembered. Something had happened. I tried to think, and the flashing of lights started up again, and the screams and the darkness and the drag of the flying lines. That most magical Puck had been torn from the air. He had tumbled to the ground, fallen and flung as surely as if he was caught in a gale.

Fragments from last night swirled in my mind like a scattered script torn and thrown to the winds. Scenes came and went . . .

*

For some reason – though it was not in Mr Shakespeare's playscript – I heard Miss de Salle begin singing, and the fairy dancers pattering to and fro. Mumbled words rumbled around me, questioning, wondering, whispering and fading away.

Then Vanya lifted me and carried me offstage to the green room. I lay heavy against his chest as if asleep – maybe I was – while strangers crowded around me.

I heard some kind of medical man talking, and checking me here and there, and murmuring again, but then he had gone. I heard the Aunts talking, making arrangements about nursing, and Nick's soft voice agreeing with every hushed suggestion.

Who were they talking about? Me? Kitty? Where was Kitty? Kitty? I wanted to see Kit and tried to sit up, but Vanya told me not to worry.

Kitty was already onstage, being the one and only universal Puck. She was the one playing tricks in the midsummer forest with a magic potion and an ass's head, not me.

Unknown voices buzzed around my head, the words strung out with an emotion I didn't recognise.

'We'll take the boy back with us,' said the lady. 'Won't we, Albert?'

'No, madam, I beg you,' Vanya growled, firmly as a bear guarding its own cub. The rumble of his comforting voice held me safe. 'Arrange all the help you can, sir, madam. That will be welcome.' Vanya's tone grew fierce. 'But I tell you now that it will not be good for the boy to wake in a strange new place. It may alarm his mind for ever. Do you want that? The doctor said he must be kept very, very peaceful. The boy is not as wounded as we feared, but he is still injured and shaken.'

Silken skirts rustled crisply, as if the lady had drawn herself up. She drew a sharp intake of breath, ready to refuse. 'But I have waited so very, very long,' she protested bleakly.

Then the man's voice, which was steady and kind, broke in. 'Adeline, this man Vanya is right. The child should be with people he knows when he first recovers. When his mind is rested, we can make proper plans.'

The lady sobbed quietly. Was this over me? The things she said worried my head, but they could not be true. She was not Ma, so why did she fuss so, making me tired and muddling my memories?

'Have no fear, lady. Mouse is among very good friends,' said Vanya. 'We will be most careful of this boy. You will see him soon.'

She sighed most grievously.

'Adeline, I have all the names and addresses we need. We will not lose the boy again,' the man said. 'And now we must go. We are wanted at Scotland Yard. Questions are being asked about the incident. And about you know who.'

I was not sure who it was they were talking about, or what had happened to me. All I recalled was the flash of fire and the pain just after the shot.

'Very well, Albert,' the lady breathed, resigned to Vanya's plans. 'However, I shall send our own doctor round to minister to the boy. You understand that?'

All at once, her hand gripped mine, though my eyes

stayed closed. 'Child, if you can hear me,' she insisted, 'remember that we will meet again. I will not leave you this time, my little Mouse. I will talk to Hugo Adnam when he comes offstage. I will make him promise me that.'

Their footsteps passed through the green-room door and were gone. As I started to wonder, everything, even Vanya's strong arms, dissolved into the welcome darkness.

Another and another and another dream passed. I was trying to catch the pages of a playscript, but the sheets flew away from me as I reached out. Even when I had caught hold of each single page, it was impossible to place them in order, one by one. The wretched plot was fluttering away from my grasp.

How would I ever understand what I was supposed to do, or be?

When I woke properly, Nick was nearby, attending to his clocks as ever. Dog Toby lay beside me, nuzzling my back.

'Well, well! Good day to you at last, young Mouse!' Nick pushed up his glasses and placed his watchmaker's tools neatly on the bench. I was so pleased to see him, so pleased to be here. 'You have slept more than four whole days through, and now you must break your fast,' he said calmly.

Nick seemed to return in a moment, bringing me a cup of soft egg and a dish of buttered bread. Then the doorbells jangled loudly and the shop shook. Vanya, forgetting to step gently, had arrived, but Nick said not a word of reprimand.

Vanya's big face peered down at me. 'So, flying boy, how is it with you now you are down on the ground?'

'Very achey.' I winced as I tried to change my position. 'Was Kitty all right? What about Adnam? Was he very upset? Is he angry with me?'

As Vanya sat, he tipped back his head and roared with laughter. 'Mouse, do you not understand this business? Adnam is sorry about your fall, most certainly, but –' he grinned widely – 'I have to tell you, Adnam is also most delighted. You have done him an excellently good turn.'

'Pardon? I don't understand.'

Vanya and Nick swapped glances, amused.

'Fame, my boy. Rumour! Gossip! Tickets for Adnam's *Dream* have become more valuable than gold dust.' Vanya opened out his expansive hands, enjoying his tale. 'The newspapers tell such stories about a poor child shot inside the Albion. *Bang!*' He clapped his hands together emphatically. 'Is boy dead? Killed, the poor young actor? Such things make the blood freeze, the heart tremble. That's so, yes?'

He leaned forward, eyes wide with amusement. 'But such scares also make people grow very, very interested. To go to a play, knowing it might be the scene of a murder, Mouse! To witness the dreadful danger of the flying machine! Huh! Even fools who never think of seeing the play are wanting tickets. The papers are full of news about the Albion, and the box office is very, very busy.' Vanya slapped his thighs and laughed contentedly. 'So you see, Mouse, Adnam's dream happens. Hurrah! This winter, his Albion is even bigger news than the great Lyceum! It is the most famous theatre of all!'

All this puzzled me. Slowly I spooned up a little of the soft egg, feeling I had forgotten something. Then it came to me.

'What about Kitty? Is she flying? Why hasn't she been to see me? Is she all right?'

'She is. She has. You were still asleep,' Nick told me.

'Kitty is most triumphant in *Dream*,' added Vanya. 'Don't worry, Mouse. She does not do the big wild flight like you, brave boy, not now her father watches over her. Kitty says she will come and see you again very soon, especially now you are awake. Enough words, Mouse. Eat, child. Finish your food. The Aunts have sent a fine jam sponge cake and a baked rice pudding, so there is plenty to tempt you to get better.'

While I ate, slowly feeling stronger, Nick pulled out some scraps of paper covered in tiny pencil sketches, and hesitated.

'Excuse me, friend Vanya,' he asked cautiously, 'does our Mr Adnam have any thoughts about his next season yet? Because if he still has to decide, you might like to look . . .'

Vanya slapped the small clockmaker on the back so hard that Nick burst into a coughing fit. 'Most definitely, my friend Nick! Especially after all this triumph! And if he has not, then I shall make him think on this matter. We have ideas, do we not?'

They whispered excitedly, scribbling and scratching

down their thoughts. Another hour chimed. I tried to get up, but Vanya stopped me.

'Do not worry, Mouse. Just you rest. You will need to be strong for all the meetings ahead of you.'

I lay there, not knowing what Vanya meant, though, when the first meeting came, I was glad I had been kept ignorant.

CHAPTER 81

ONE LAST LOOK

'It seems,' said Vanya,' that I am to take you, Mouse. We are both needed, so that the police can be sure of the evidence.'

Over this last week, I had been tapped and checked and my chest and shoulder strapped up by Dr Bliss, who had been sent by the fine people – the ones we will come to later – and who was a good fellow.

Once the medical man had taken samples of our water supply and observed the freshness of the sheets the Aunts sent over for my bed and discussed the importance of good plain food with Nick, he was content to give me a few days of grace.

By the end of the week I was up on my feet, and by the next I could walk across to the Aunts' and back again. That was when Vanya told me what had to happen next.

*

A carriage was now on hand to take me everywhere, though this outing was certainly not to a fine address. The gas flame flickered behind the dark blue glass above the imposing red brick entrance. Nobody would have mistaken the purpose of this building.

We arrived at the officer's desk. We waited, Vanya and I. We listened to the jangle of keys and the cries from the distant cells. We watched as police constables came in from the fog, coughing and grumbling, with their lanterns still alight. Faint foggy tendrils followed them into the station.

A grizzled, grey-faced doctor, complete with black bag, appeared from deep within the police station. His lips were still curled in distaste at whatever he had just attended to. He nodded to the sergeant and handed him a bill.

We waited while the medical man was escorted off the premises, then the sergeant turned to us.

'Walk this way, please.' His heavy boots rang on the stone steps. We followed.

The iron door clanged opened. The tiled room was cold as ice. It smelled strongly of carbolic and something unhealthy, and the floor had just been swilled with water. Beyond the long empty tables, a man was sweeping a broom across the wet floor towards a drain.

I glanced up at Vanya, and then grabbed tight hold of his strong arm. Vanya placed his hand firmly over mine, but it was not the place that scared me.

'Ready?' said the sergeant.

'Not quite,' I answered.

He paused, but not patiently.

Who was I going to see?

The one who fired the shots.

Did I know who he would be?

Yes. I did. I knew his face well.

Had I known him long?

Maybe my life long.

Did I know why he hated me so?

No. Sometimes I thought he hated everyone.

Sometimes I thought he just hated me.

'Ready, boy?' The sergeant was brisk. He had other work to do and wanted to get this over with.

I squeezed Vanya's arm even more tightly.

'Only one glance, Mouse,' Vanya said. 'Then all is over.'

'Yes.' I took a breath. 'I'm ready.'

The sergeant drew back the coarse cloth. I could identify at once what was there.

Laid out on the slab was Mr Button. His piggy eyes were closed. His shiny round cheeks were dull. His skin had a waxy look, and his hair lay wetly against his scalp.

Once I believed it was Bulloughby – that horrid headmaster, and his foul son Grindle – weaving the trouble around me; but then I thought of the times Button had appeared at that school. Did that rough, ignorant bully of a man fear Button as much as I did?

I stared at what was left of that vindictive, red-cheeked man. His round eyes were shut and sunken.

His everlasting smile had faded. The hands that had once sought my friend Punchman flopped out of a rough shroud.

This was all that was left of Button, the cunning one who had sat tugging at the threads of the web. Button, the great dark spider, always watching and waiting. Button, the rotten heart of it all.

But no more. Button was dead. Button was gone. It was a kind of ending.

Mirror, Mirror, on the Wall

'Stand still!' The Aunts insisted on making me both presentable and respectable.

Everyone except me had decided that my new story was wonderful. I had long-lost parents, and I was their long-lost child, and they wanted me to be back with them and part of their life. Adnam and Vanya had explained that this had to happen, that I must go into this new life that I knew nothing about. I had decided nothing.

Vanya and Nick and the Aunts had tried to hold the moment off as long as they could, but it was a bare pretence. These long-lost, new-found parents could insist on my presence. They would shape my very future. I would no longer be living as I had been doing. True, my arm was not fully recovered, so it was impossible for me to fly in Adnam's *Dream*.

All I could do was wait to see what happened. Now I was strong again, Adnam himself was taking me to meet the people who called themselves my parents.

We all put a brave face on it. The Aunts rummaged in their cupboards and hampers. They pulled out shirts and stiff collars, tweed jackets and breeches and caps for me to wear. They had so many garments that Aunt Indigo suggested packing a large leather bag for me, in case more things were needed.

Once upon a time, when I was much smaller and knew far less than now, my own dear Ma had done this for me. I could not help feeling angry. I had been found, but I was no longer free.

'Do stop fidgeting, Mouse,' said Aunt Violet. 'And, for heaven's sake, take that sulky look off your face when you meet these people.'

Why did I have to? 'If this lady really is my mother, she won't care how I look, will she?' I protested.

'Not really, Mouse, but I suspect that you will care,' Aunt Violet remarked wisely.

'And we care, child! We don't want your mother thinking we kept you like a ragamuffin,' snapped Aunt Indigo. 'Do you want to shame us, and Nick Tick? Do you want her to think we used you as a scullery boy? Put on these boots, and be quick about it.'

The well-polished boots pinched.

'Scullery clothes are more comfortable,' I muttered ungratefully, but the Aunts just laughed.

'Hands?' Aunt Indigo checked my fingernails. She checked behind my ears, which were sticking out through my tufty hair, as they had always done. She tried one last time to make my hair lie down, which it wouldn't.

'Where's Kitty?' I longed to see her. Since my accident, we had not met, though Flora and Dora had brought me little notes. Things had changed, everywhere. Was Kitty too busy with her own life and new-found father, or was I too busy with everything that was happening to me?

A swift glance passed between the two women. 'Kitty went to the theatre early,' said Aunt Violet. 'I think she was afraid to watch you leave.'

Afraid? What of? How, when we both had what we'd wanted, and we had people who were here to help us, could things feel so uncertain? Had not Adnam himself promised he would take me to the Grand Imperial Hotel and the meeting with my apparent parents?

'Life is often complicated, Mouse,' Vanya had said. 'Believe me, Hugo Adnam will be the best person to have by your side in such a place and at such a moment.'

I hoped he was right, but I so wished that Kit was here too.

Adnam, being Adnam, rapped at the Aunts' front door. I had never seen it used before.

'Typical of the man. Always loved making dramatic entrances,' grumbled Aunt Indigo, scraping the warped timber across the uneven floor. 'So here you are, Hugo.'

Adnam appeared imposingly respectable. He wore a solemnly dark suit and cravat. He carried a top hat and a cane. Nobody could have had better polished boots.

He gave a crooked smile, as if to tell me he was the same Hugo Adnam inside.

'Once more unto the breach then, young Mouse,' he declaimed. 'Our carriage awaits.'

'Goodbye, Mouse,' said the Aunts, waving. 'Goodbye!'

As I tried to shout that this was not goodbye, the carriage set off at a brisk pace, toppling me back on to the seat.

Adnam placed his hat and cane neatly on the seat and studied my face. 'So, Mouse. Another act begins for you. It starts with a very serious scene indeed. Now you must think – what do you want to happen? What are the scenes in your head? Believe me, a man in his time may play many parts, but it is always a good idea to think about them first.'

I didn't answer. With all that was happening around me I thought I had no choice in the matter.

He sighed. This was the true Adnam talking, with all his masks stripped away. 'Listen, Mouse, you are too old to be a babe in the wood. You can no longer be a little boy lost. You will have a magic carpet spread out before your very eyes, so consider. Who do you want to be? Who are you? You must think about that, dear boy, you really must, because decisions will be made.'

I was thinking as hard as I could, but I had no answer.

'Remember, all the world's a stage, and men and women merely players,' he murmured, 'so choose the role that makes you happy in your heart.'

The horses trotted on.

*

Huge gilded doors wreathed with brass foliage swished open as we entered the Grand Imperial Hotel.

This place was nothing like the straw-strewn taverns where I had whooped and squawked alongside Punchman, delighting the raucous crowds. This was not like the jostling, excited realm of the Albion. This was like entering an enchanted mirage of a palace, where all worldly sound was hushed.

Lamps and chandeliers glowed around us, even though it was midday. Vast porcelain vases full of roses poured out their perfumes, so the hotel smelled sweeter than the Fairy Queen's own bower. Beside every corner or column, a host of brass-buttoned attendants awaited our command.

Adnam strode to the hotel's reception desk. A bald man, glossy as a pork butcher at a wedding, was immediately attentive. He regarded me as if I was a scuttling rat, but he smiled expansively at the great actor. I had seen Arthur Boddy playing his comic butler role in just such an overblown manner.

'You are expected in the Marlborough Suite, Mr Adnam, sir. You will find it on the seventh floor.'

Several heads turned at the famous name, but Adnam ignored them.

'Have you been in a lift before, Mouse?' Adnam asked conversationally, as we strolled across the wide marble floor towards what seemed like a double gateway. 'Modern invention. They'll be everywhere soon.'

Warm gusts of oily air puffed out from the shaft. A metal crate hissed down an iron shaft and shuddered to a stop at our level. The lift-boy merrily rattled apart the ornate folding gates, and a flock of chattering ladies exited enthusiastically, trooping towards the tea room.

'Going up?' called the lift-boy, proudly in charge of this merry toy.

Behind the great ropes and chains holding this shining elevator, I heard echoes of the broken tray-hoist clattering down into the kitchen of Murkstone Hall. This lift was not for me.

Before Adnam could speak, I went racing up the imposing stairs two or three at a time, smearing the brass banister rail with my fingers. In my fear, I forgot I was speeding towards another life until I slid to a breathless halt outside the gilded doors of the Marlborough Suite.

Smiling and at ease, Adnam strolled from the clanking lift. He winked. 'Here we go, Mouse!'

On either side of a blazing fire sat a lady and a gentleman, dressed in expensive mourning garments. They were fine rich folk, although their skin was tanned like that of any field labourer.

My parents gazed at me, searching for the infant they had left. Repeated in every mirror around that room was an almost grown boy who gazed back at them. He was someone I knew very well and they did not.

The fine lady, with her bright brown eyes, was alert as a squirrel. Straight away she spoke.

'How are you yourself, child?'

'Better now, thank you, madam. My arm aches where I fell on it.'

'And your side?'

'Bruised, madam, but I hope to be well enough to return to the play soon.' I had planned these words.

She was surprised by my reply and hid it by picking at the thick lace of her cuffs.

'I am not sure that will be happening,' she remarked, her voice low but insistent. Then she raised her eyebrows at Adnam. 'What did you tell the boy about us?'

'I left it to you to tell him what you want him to know,' Adnam said most diplomatically, giving a half-bow.

'Then where do I begin?' the lady asked herself. Sighing deeply, she beckoned me closer. 'Mouse, I want to look at you properly. Come here.'

I walked over. As she studied me, I noticed the freckles under her brown skin and the small scars of toil on her ungloved hands. She was rather proud and awkward, but there was an interested look in her eyes that I could not help liking.

'Do you still have that medal that saved you, child?'

From the way she spoke, the medal must have been discussed before. I rummaged in my pocket and held out the little piece of silver that had kept me safe from that shot. I kept my fingers curled tightly over it.

'Do you know what this object is?' she asked.

'I did not until Mr Nick explained it to me. It is a compass.'

'Clever Mr Nick. And what is this creature on it?'

She asked me as if I was a little child, so my answer came somewhat sulkily. 'A mouse. That's easy to see.'

It was also easy to see that my silvery whiskery mouse

was twisted where the bullet had struck the metal. He seemed to be twirling around, awkwardly searching after his own tail.

'Do you see these letters?' she said, pointing. The man, Albert, stepped forward, as if he was uncertain what to do. What did this pair want from me?

'The letters say Mouse. That's my name. That's what people call me. That's why it belongs to me.'

'Not quite. Look again. There are five single letters: M.O.U.S.E.'

She glanced up at the man, who rested his hand on my shoulder before speaking to me softly.

'Boy, we did call you Mouse. When you were born, you were the very tiniest thing, with your round brown eyes and tufty hair and those little ears! But the letters are really the initials of your own name: *Marcus Octavius Ulysses Septimus Epton.*

'Do you think you could get used to being that boy, Mouse?'

Who? What? Marcus Octavius who? 'Pardon, sir?' I stuttered.

The man repeated the long list. 'Epton is your family name, Mouse. Do you understand?'

'No, I'm just Mouse, sir. All my life I've been Mouse.'

'It's not easy to become somebody else, but you are our son. You are our Marcus,' said the lady.

I glanced helplessly across at Adnam.

'I'm sure you'll find that this is all true, Mouse,' he told me.

I stepped back, away from them. 'Then where have you been all this time? What have you been doing?

Why have I never seen you?' I asked. 'They said you were drowned.'

'Not drowned. Lost!' the lady said, wistfully. 'Long years of it!'

'We were shipwrecked,' said the man, 'on a small tropical island. Lived there for years. Only found by chance. Son, we did not intend to be without you for so long.'

I remembered Nick's mechanical galleons plunging up and down on the painted billows, bound for the dreadful reef of rocks. 'A very long time?'

'Yes,' he said.

'We found many things: plants and seeds and trees and strange flowers and more . . .' The woman was trying to explain the time away.

'But we could not get back to you, Mouse,' the man told me. 'Not till now.'

'Oh!' For a while we said nothing. My heart was beating hard.

A knock, an uneven rattling sound, and a waiter pushed in a fully laden tea trolley almost higher than himself, before backing out again hurriedly. The trolley stood like a huge silver barrow on the flowery carpet, brimming over with cakes and sandwiches.

To live like this must be almost like being on a stage, even if this audience was a flurry of servants and maids, people like my Ma. I was wishing I could see her now, and wishing I could remember more of the things she told me.

I gazed around. Over on a grand piano was the

portrait of a long-faced man with an unhappy scowl. The frame was wreathed in black leaves.

'My brother,' said the gentleman in a troubled voice. 'Name of Scrope. I think he once knew you, young Mouse.'

Sadness shaded the man's pleasant face. My own confusion had blinkered me to all the fresh signs of mourning.

'I am sorry, sir.'

'Good lad,' he said, and patted my head with hesitant friendliness.

'Now –' he sat down purposefully – 'here is the matter, Mouse. We are your own parents. We have a home to offer you.'

Parents? Home? These words were unreal to me. I had had neither for so long, not as most people thought of them.

Parents? I had found my own sorts of parents. Wayland and Punchman. The Aunts and Vanya and Nick. Even Adnam, who now stood beside me. I had my own Isaac and Ma too. What did I need with this unknown mother and father? I had Kitty and Flora and Dora for sisters. I had little Dog Toby.

Home? I had lived in so many places, good, bad and wretched. What would I want with the grand home they were offering me?

'We will arrange the date as soon as possible,' said the man.

'Come as soon as you like, Mouse,' the woman said eagerly. 'We are ready to welcome you back. Now?'

'No,' I said quickly. 'Not today. Or tomorrow. I do

428

not know you as my father or my mother. I'm sorry.' I glanced about awkwardly, feeling an urge to run. 'Even if that is what you are.'

'I see,' said the man. The woman closed her eyes, and I saw tears glimmer there.

I was sure I would have to go with these people sometime soon. But what would my life be like with these strangers? I did not know what they wanted of me. I glanced across at Adnam, urging him to end this meeting.

'Odds bodkins!' he declared, eyeing the great gilt clock on the mantelpiece. 'The world of the Albion Theatre is calling!' He announced this as grandly as if he was King Theseus. 'Madam, sir, I must take the boy with me, though I promise I won't let him fly yet. It may be best to take things slowly. Mouse is happy where he is for now. Pray send word when you want to meet again.'

My parents smiled rather stiffly and sadly.

'Bow, Mouse,' suggested Adnam, so I bowed as respectfully as he did. 'Bid your good parents adieu!'

Parents? Such a strange word when I had lived without them for so long.

We made our exit. This time I hurried into the lift, too confused to be afraid. The boy whistled as he slammed the gate across and the cage descended the long lift shaft.

The great Hugo Adnam smiled at me mischievously. 'Mouse, we have escaped! These rich people! They always want you to fit in with their plans. If there is one thing I have learned in my life, it is that one must decide for oneself. Remember that, my boy.'

As we stepped on to the carpeted entrance hall, Adnam added, almost shyly, 'Now, will you help me by taking a message to the Aunts, Mouse?'

A distinguished person passed us, preparing to ascend in the lift. He chewed on his moustache and swayed in his boots, as if he had awkward news to reveal.

The staff at the reception desk began muttering and scurrying quietly about.

'Police again? Who's not dead?' I heard, as well as a tired sigh. 'Must we fold all the black crepe away again?'

CHAPTER 83

MAKING UP

The Aunts' parlour was full of baskets of flowers and hampers full of delicacies. Adnam had presented these gifts with an unusual modesty. The Aunts nodded graciously.

'Thank you for these gifts, Hugo, and the message Mouse brought,' said Aunt Indigo. 'It's about time you came to see us and the girls properly, you know.'

'Even if our darling Katherine was dead, you didn't have to stay away, Hugo,' added Aunt Violet.

'I did not mean to neglect you all,' Adnam said, 'but . . . but . . .'

'But you were in pain, like us?' suggested Aunt Violet, dabbing her eyes with a handkerchief. 'Silly boy, Hugo.'

Fumbling in his long coat, Adnam brought out two paper parcels. The ribbons revealed two pretty china dolls dressed in silk and satin. The twins cooed with delight.

'Is it really true,' said Flora 'that you are our Papa?'

'Really, really, really true?' enquired Dora.

'Yes,' whispered Adnam, almost inaudibly.

'Then we shall kiss you on the cheek,' said Flora, smiling very precisely.

'Because that is what you do to a long-lost Papa in a story,' Dora told him.

Then the two girls kissed their fairy-tale father just as if they were acting a scene in a play. They played it most perfectly.

Adnam knew their response for what it was – a make-believe greeting for an imaginary father. They had been well trained, these two young actresses.

He felt a lump in his throat. One day the girls would know him for who he was, but they did not yet. He had stayed out of their lives too long. He had stayed out of Kitty's life too. As Flora and Dora trotted off triumphantly with their pretty prizes, Adnam's eyes filled with real-life tears.

'I missed my Katherine so much I could not bear it. I was so angry when she died,' he told the Aunts.

'So were we, Hugo,' said Aunt Violet, with a hot spark of fury. 'Don't you forget that! Sometimes one just has to face the hard things in life, even if one doesn't like what one sees.'

'And think of that when you are offering that young boy advice, won't you?' added Aunt Indigo.

THE LAST ACT

I knew the day would come, changing my life. Each night I tossed and turned, waiting for the light.

'It is a most good chance, Mouse!' Vanya told me, beaming. 'A grand life and you can learn to be happy in it!'

Then Vanya and Nick whispered together, their minds already full of their next theatrical invention.

The Aunts, having heard about the Grand Imperial Hotel, muttered ancient proverbs about riches and eyes of needles. Flora and Dora were bursting with delight. They imagined me as Aladdin in a house of treasures. But Kitty, my dear friend? She was always busy. We had not yet met, not yet spoken.

I had to find a place of balance, a space where I could think things through, before the final summons arrived. Not for the first time, I paced the streets alone.

*

The stage was where I wanted to be, surrounded by painted canvas and gauze. Below me, the hollow space opened out, magical, dark and resonant. Above me, the scenery cloths hid, suspended in the fly tower. I felt as if I was in a nest, a maze where I could hide myself away. I was aching from lack of sleep.

The lights and lanterns, shut like blind eyes, asked me no questions and wanted no word in return. No lighting men, no flymen were busy around me, ready to change my world. No story was being told in that wooden world, that painted universe. I was safe in a deep, resonant place. Up here, the silence was like velvet.

I closed my eyes to quiet the chorus of names buzzing in my head. My injured shoulder ached from the climb, but I was here, up high on the walkway. Maybe here I could see the way I had to go.

In all good stories, when a child sees their long-lost parent, they know all is well. All happy ever after. All contentment and joy.

So my story was only half good, because I felt nothing for Albert and Adeline, though they were in distress for my sake. Strangers to me, they offered a life that it would be hard to refuse, and the law would uphold their claim. Despite what Adnam said, I had as little power as on that day at Roseberry Farm, when the beetle-black carriage rolled into the yard.

Adnam! He was someone who had learned how to fly, in his way. He was someone who could soar on an idea, who knew how to rush to greet whatever came next. He was always sure he would find a place to land. Hugo Adnam, whose desire above everything was to keep his Albion alive, and who carried his fears lightly alongside, like small friendly charms.

A nearby church bell tolled: an hour had gone by. Then the stage boards creaked. Someone was there, far below me. I shrank down on the walkway, making myself as small as I could. The rungs on the ladder thrummed. I held my breath. Who was climbing up? Who wanted me?

The walkway shook. Feet edged along, closer and closer.

'Mouse?' said Kitty at last, crouching down beside me. 'They said you'd run off.'

'Hello.' We sat in silence. 'Oh, Kit! What do I do now?'

'What can you do? You'll have to go to them.'

'But what about all this? What about my life at the Albion? What about you? You have been such a friend to me.'

'You to me too,' she said.

'What about Vanya, and Nick, and Adnam, and everyone at your house? What about Ma? I don't know that I want the kind of life they are offering.'

Kitty gave a hollow laugh. 'I don't know that I truly want Adnam as my father, Mouse,' she said.

'You don't?'

'I am very glad to be back onstage, and glad that he stood up for me,' she said slowly. 'The Aunts told me that he always sent money when he had some to spare. But I know and you know that his first love will always be his theatre. That above everything. Even above me and the girls.' Her voice trembled.

'It is so much easier to live in the *Dream*, isn't it?' I said. 'Easier to take flight in the magical forest.'

'Easier to believe in good fairies, you mean?' Kitty said. 'Easier to wish that happy world into being? Yes, Mouse, it is.'

We sat in a long, friendly silence. After a while, doors started banging, and brooms swished along the aisles. The theatre was being woken for another day and another performance.

'What if I can't bear where they take me? What if I hate that life?'

'Mouse,' Kitty said at last, 'what if you don't? You can try out being their Mouse for a while. Then you can make up your mind. It's only acting, isn't it?'

Acting? We grinned at each other. I could act. We both could act.

'I promise that if I run away this time, I'll know exactly where to run to, Kit.'

'And maybe who to run to, Mouse?' she said, smiling.

We stood, up on the walkway, and gazed down together to the place where dreams are created.

CHAPTER 85

THE LONG PATH

The last moments.

'Isaac?'

He looked up from where he was brushing the white chalk dust into the coats of the fairy ponies.

'You look tired, boy. You well enough?'

I nodded quickly and asked Isaac what I needed to ask him. 'Promise me that you will do it?'

'Don't know as how it is a good idea, boy, and it might not turn out as you think.'

'Isaac, please?'

'But if it is what you want, I'll ask her. You just let me know when.'

The day and time were fixed.

Nick Tick sighed, shook my hand most seriously and wished me many joyous times. Then, as the hour struck, he dug his elbow nimbly in my side.

'Mouse? If you notice any remarkable clocks or cabinets, you will sketch the pieces for me, won't you, dear boy? Especially the detail? Don't forget the detail.'

I promised I would, and he grinned with anticipation. 'We shall meet again, boy, somehow, somewhere. Have no fear about that!'

All the Aunts' laundry was folded away into tidy stacks, marking the importance of this occasion.

'Well, well, young Mouse,' Aunt Violet said. 'So you are on your way to your grandfather's house. Do remember, dear boy, that we will always welcome you here.'

'Exactly. You must bear up, dear lad, even among the courts of the mighty.' Aunt Indigo hugged me forcefully. 'Some good may come of it. Try to enjoy Epton Towers if you can, Mouse.'

Flora and Dora clapped their hands, hopping around with excitement, as if this moment was when good fortune arrived for everyone.

Kitty glanced at me and shrugged. Whatever will be, will be. We both knew that. We hugged, briefly.

So the time to leave had come at last.

All the changes in my life seemed to be marked out in coaches and carriages, taking me to places I did not know, places I did not want to go. This time it was not Adnam who took me. Albert and Adeline were there, sitting side by side. They spoke to me kindly but often I did not know how to answer.

The carriage took us up a long gravel drive, through parklands where herds of deer gathered round ancient trees. We passed a home farm surrounded by fields and orchards, and then approached a huge mansion of soft yellow stone. Its mellow grandeur was very different from Murkstone Hall's grim bulk.

Eventually the carriage halted, and we descended. Servants stood in line each side of the entrance, bowing to my parents. The women wore crisp white aprons and caps. The men were in spotless shirts and jackets.

They even bowed to me. They bowed and curtsied to a boy who had lived on crusts, washed greasy dishes, slept in hedges and lived as a vagrant on the streets. Did they know this?

'Come, my boy!' Albert said. 'You are most welcome.'

Every step echoed as we climbed a double flight of stairs, decorated with carved mythical creatures. Grand portraits sneered down at me from the walls.

Next came a long gallery. It seemed to be filled with more statues than there were in the glorious palace Adnam had created. I could not help staring about me.

'The house will be familiar to you in time,' said Albert gently. 'It was strange to us when we returned from our travels.'

The first thing I saw in the room was a vast tiger-skin rug, spread across the floor. The golden glass eyes burned with familiar melancholy fire. Despite the heat from the logs in the hearth, there was a chill in the heart of this chamber.

Beyond the rug was a huge chair. The arms and feet

had been carved into feathered talons. There, wrapped in a thick woven blanket, was an old, old man. I had been told who he was: my grandfather, Epsilon Epton. Feeble as he was now, there was a terrible pride in his manner.

Hah! I think. Then I will be as proud as Oberon in return. I put out my hand for him to shake it, as I had seen Adnam do in fine company.

'Good day, sir,' I said as loudly and clearly as if I was onstage. I would not be overcome by this setting, or by this man.

My grandfather looked a little astonished to have me there, facing him so boldly. He looked me up and down, as if surprised to find me higher than his knee. He extended a wrinkled brown-spotted hand in return, but I felt as if I was almost a mirage among his sea of conflicting memories.

'Albert, this is the boy called Mouse?' his ancient voice rasped.

'It is, Father,' Albert said. 'We had proof. He had Adeline's compass about him still.'

'Then it was a useful gift,' the old man sighed, 'for it helped the boy find his way home again.'

A strangely beatific smile spread across the ancient wrinkled face, and he slowly dropped off to sleep.

Then it was time for a meal. No toasted cheese here, no corners of cake while we huddled two to a chair or on cushions on the floor. The vast mahogany dining table bore glasses and cutlery and crystal vases and tureens, and more place settings than we would need.

Servants came to my chair, offering me servings of fine food on large silver spoons. They removed and replaced plates. Adeline and Albert sat, trying to talk pleasantly to me.

Before the second course was over, I longed to be back at the Aunts'. There we ate in peace, and in half the time. Such a fuss was made here of every action. How Adnam must resent the hours he spent dining with rich people when what he most wanted was to be working on his next play! At last the meal was over.

'There is someone else you must meet, Mouse,' said Albert.

Up we went, my parents and I, to the top of Epton Towers. Gradually the staircase changed from heavy marble to smooth stone. Underfoot, the rich patterned wool changed to rough pile. When we reached the plain wooden staircase, the floor was covered in coarse drugget.

'This,' said Adeline, 'is the nursery where you once slept.'

I was led into a blue-painted room with pretty white furniture. All was light and pleasant, and newly clean and dusted. A table was spread for tea, and a fire glowed in the hearth, but this room meant nothing to me.

'Am I to sleep here?' I asked. Did they think I could return to the life of an infant?

'No, your room is further down,' said Albert. 'This is where your uncle lives. For a while we thought we had lost him too.'

Then I spied, over by the window, in a bamboo and

leather bath chair, a crumpled man. He could not be any older than my father, but his hands lay limply in his lap.

'Scrope, here's Mouse,' Albert said. 'You wanted to see him.'

Slowly, the invalid raised his drooping head and peered weakly at me. 'I do,' he said. 'Once I didn't, but I do now. Isn't that so, Adeline?'

My mother smiled, and Scrope gave a strange twisted smile too. His one good eye fixed on me.

'So you are what Mouse grew into, boy. I am sorry to meet you when I am in this state, child.' He chewed at his lip, and then his face brightened for a moment. 'Came looking for you, boy, came to bring you back. But you were gone, weren't you? Man named Jarvey in charge. Did you know him? Boy called Niddle there too.'

Then the light faded and he blinked, keeping welling tears away. 'I am truly sorry that you have been gone so long,' he whispered. 'Sorry. So sorry.'

My father patted his brother's twisted shoulder. 'Now, now,' he told him. 'We must look to the future. We must look ahead.'

I paused and gazed at the man who had sent me away. With Button gone, how could I have any hate left for such a pitiful creature?

'Come,' said Adeline. 'Let us walk. You can learn what we have been discovering, Mouse.'

We were on our own now, my parents and I. They led me down a chilly corridor, lined with glass cases full

of tiny birds and stuffed reptiles with needle-sharp teeth.

At the far end stood a carved figure draped in a toga. His marble eyes were blind, just as my parents were blind to my life without them. I realised I had to tell them, must let them know.

'Albert! Adeline!' They whirled round.

'Do you truly want to know me?' I asked.

So this was when I told them, one word after another without stopping, anger and grief coming out all in one go.

I told them about my baby time with Hanny and Isaac. I told them about the coming of Button, and the horror of Bulloughby and Murkstone Hall, and the time in the kitchen, and the awful return to Roseberry Farm.

Then I described my days on the road – part thief, part beggar, part puppet man – and my arrival at the city. I told them all the terrible times, sparing nothing, so they knew just what kind of boy they were claiming as their own. I told them about the charity hospital, and the kidnap cellar and the mortuary slab. I told them the places I'd been and the things I'd seen. Did they want such a child in their lives, with or without a shining silver mouse for proof?

Their faces had turned pale. Some moments they turned and looked away. Adeline dabbed her eyes.

Now I had begun it was hard to stop. 'And who looked after me in all this time, all the years you were away? A voiceless cook, a suffering scholar, a wandering tramp, a Punch and Judy man, a pair of almost penniless costume makers, an absent-minded clockmaker, a backstage giant and a young dancer who polished other people's shoes. These people looked after me. These were my parents. These were the friends in my life.'

'But we . . .' My mother tried to explain, but words did not come.

'I know you did not choose to be away. I know that you could not help what happened. But this is how life was for me, and you should know. I have not stepped from my cradle directly to this moment. It is too soon to call you my parents. All I have in my head are Adeline and Albert, the names Hanny told me.'

'You can remember Hanny so well?' asked my mother, and she had a hopeful smile.

'As if it was just last week,' I said, watching her face. Then I asked, 'What did you want to show me, please?'

They pulled themselves together.

Albert led the way. Despite the sunshine, the air outside was cold enough to make us gasp. We followed a covered pathway across the wide lawns towards an enormous glass conservatory.

As we grew closer, they walked more eagerly.

'You go first, Mouse,' said Albert proudly when we arrived, and I could see that this was the place within Epton Towers that mattered most to him. The pair glanced at each other, almost excitedly. They were revealing their life's work.

I pushed open the first set of tall glass doors, and a second set beyond, and I was in what felt like a mighty jungle, though my boots stepped on a pavement of black and white tiles.

The wintry wind was calmed in here. The warmth soothed. Bright sunlight flashed through a canopy of gleaming leaves and flickered on creepers cascading from a high crystal sky. All manner of plants were gathered here in this vast private palace.

Brilliant parakeets screeched among exotic blooms, and emerald frogs splashed into mossy-edged pools. Golden fish appeared and disappeared in the smooth water, and the air was hot and heavy and scented with lilies. As I looked up, entranced, the hairs prickled on my neck.

I knew this magical place! I walked on along the patterned paths, past fluted columns, as if walking in some forgotten dream. There, among the abundance of foliage, rose a familiar iron ladder. Its white-painted rungs circled around the painted pillar, leading up and up.

I stepped off the path and pushed through the fronds of ferns glistening with drops of moisture. I looked up to where this ladder led. High above me, cogs and rods and spokes turned, letting in the cool breeze.

At that moment I knew that once I had longed to climb up there, longed to reach that imaginary heaven, and that I had certainly stood here before.

I turned to the people who were my mother and my father, and saw the care in their worn faces and their anguished hope that I would be happy here. My own heart suddenly eased, and the hurt grew less intense.

I reached out and touched that rung, grasped the damp, cold metal in my hand. These were fingers that were strong, not an infant's soft and pudgy hand. This was a hand that had learned to hold on tight when that was what was needed.

I climbed, and climbed, and climbed, until I could see out through the ceiling's glass panes. I could see across the gardens and the grass and the drive. And along that drive came a cart, a simple cart, drawn by an everyday slow-stepping horse.

Riding in that cart, wrapped warmly against the weather, were three people. I knew who they were, for I had asked them to come. Isaac was at the reins. My Ma Hanny, hand raised to shade her eyes, was watching as the great house came into view. Beside them was a girl who would be anxious to get back to the theatre for the night's performance. Kitty.

'Mother? Father?' Would this work? I called down to where they were waiting. 'There are some people arriving! I can see them from here – friends of mine!'

Yes, it was a test, and maybe not a kind one. If my parents were who I hoped they were, they would welcome my dear friends with open arms, and if not, then this would be a different story.

I took one last look across the waving fans of the palms. Then, as I descended, I saw, near the ground, clusters of grey-green rosettes. There, surrounded by spear-like leaves, grew crinkle-skinned golden-brown fruits, bulging with juicy ripeness. I had seen this fruit before.

'Mouse,' I said to myself, 'P is for pineapple. Pineapple. *This* is the place of my dream. *This* was once my home.'

Maybe it could be a home again. Just maybe.

CHAPTER 86

MOUSE, DREAMING

I sleep. I dream.

I am in darkness, but I hear voices call to me, and invisible hands pick at me. Heavy iron chains grate and rattle within some vast open shaft close by, and at that very moment the ground disappears.

I snatch frantically at the empty air around me, my hands outstretched and beating at nothing, like featherless wings.

I am falling, falling, falling . . .

All of a sudden, the terror is over. The fear is gone. Somehow I am safely held by unseen ropes and fastenings. I will not fall.

And now I am flying, high above the stage in the beam of a glowing golden light. Backwards and forwards I fly, weaving and soaring through the heavy scented air and the cloud of happy murmuring voices. All that had held me down is gone.

Far below me, where the lanterns play across the boards of the stage, stands a girl, and at once I see it is Kitty. Her arms are open, her face alive to an unseen audience.

I know she is speaking her lines, though I cannot hear her laughing words. I discover I am mouthing the words along with her, but what they are I cannot be sure.

Now Kitty is not alone. The little girls are there, circling and dancing around her, scattering flowers. Somewhere, I know, Adnam and all the other actors are standing in the shadows, about to enter. Even the ponies wait, with their breath like sweet hay, for this moment.

The music is calling, calling . . . and all are ready to step into their chosen places. They do not look up. They do not see me, do not need me, but I do not mind.

I soar, I fly above them, and I dream. I know that all is well with them, these dear friends, these happy shadows of delight, this sweet company.

All is well with the Dream.

And all is very well with me, very well indeed.

THE END

Author's Notes and Acknowledgements

This novel, *A Boy Called M.O.U.S.E.*, is a historical fairy tale peopled by fictional characters and almost fictional settings.

My theatre research took in a variety of books, including novels, biographies, autobiographies and books on theatrical history, not all about Victorian theatre – a patchwork of studies to costume my tale.

Three theatres helped, indirectly, with the writing of this novel. My thanks to the West Yorkshire Playhouse for their production of *Peter Pan*, complete with stunning flying sequences; to Harrogate Theatre for giving a home for a while to a play-writing group and new writing festival; and to York Theatre Royal for an almost individual backstage tour. None of these became Adnam's beloved Albion, though I may have borrowed some small shadows and dark corners.

Thanks also to the many people who have helped me with my writing, even if they have not always known it at the time: to Dennis Hamley, for the writing courses that started me back on my writing path, to many members of the Scattered Authors Society – especially the Charney Manor gang – for their friendship and support, and to the writers and tutors of the Harrogate Theatre play-writing group.

At a very practical level, my grateful thanks to Pat White, Claire Wilson and Catherine Pelegrino of Rogers

Coleridge & White Literary Agency, who encouraged my 'Mouse' project. Thanks also to my editor Emma Matthewson, and to Talya Baker, who between them spotted all the words I'd repeated, and to all at Bloomsbury Publishing.

Finally, thanks to all my family – Colin, Eleanor, Tom, Vicky, Daisy and Milo – and most especially to Jim.